1ST
ED.

J

$5

#34016

FIREION

THE CRIMSON GATE

THE CRIMSON GATE

HENRY GIBBS

WALKER AND COMPANY
NEW YORK

First published in the United States of America in 1963
by Walker and Company,
a division of Publications Development Corporation.
Printed by offset in Poland from type set in Great Britain.

One

Heat increased steadily on this first October morning. It seemed to coagulate in waves of noise surging around triumphal banners. Steven Kendal felt his latent headache pulse as a formation of jet bombers howled over heavily armoured tanks crawling like prehistoric pachyderms across T'ien-An Mên Square.

Peking was a scene of celebration.

Flags floated above ancient and new buildings in a blaze of scarlet bright as blood. Others shone gold and lilac and apple-green in breeze-rippled silk which furled lazily, untwined in eddies of air and streamed in sunlight brilliance flat on a hot blue sky stretching in every direction from the Mên, the crimson Gate, first erected by a long-dead Ming emperor to add dignity to the moat-enclosed Forbidden City.

Since the first armed detachments had come into sight a quarter of a million khaki-clad troops had paraded in review before the official party on a balcony under the curved imperial-yellow roofs of the Gate.

Steven glanced up from the press stand to which he and his companions were directed soon after eight o'clock. He saw the leaders on the Mên balcony clearly. Their faces were earnest. He speculated on thoughts going through their minds. Unquestionably the Chinese political leaders in their drab Yat-sen tunics, and their top service officers in smart uniforms, were jubilant at their success in staging this mammoth military show. They had justification. Certainly the rotund Russian in his baggy fawn tropical suit, bald head glistening, applauded vigorously. So did his entourage. A wintry smile flickered across the vulpine features of the Tibetan puppet Lama from Shigatse, a thin youth in a saffron robe.

'They seem jolly happy,' said Jane Crofton in an unhurried voice.

Steven saw she was looking past his head at the balcony.

'Don't they so,' he agreed. 'Dear old pals.'

He had observed no visible change in her since their first meeting five years ago, or was it six, in Cairo or Baghdad, somewhere there in those days. At thirtytwo or thereabouts she was tall and had clear features which blended in cool beauty; dark hair curled above her small ears; the chocolate-brown coat and skirt, a cotton blouse of the same hue, showed up her fine skin. She was not the only Englishwoman he had seen during his three years in China but she was by far the most wholesome. Even her perfume was a freshness which laid no claim on attention.

'You were right, Steven,' she said.

'Good. When?'

'Last night. I do find this overpowering.'

'Ah, this is an historic day,' he said. 'They intend to impress their friends and neighbours. "But, by God, they frighten me" as Wellington or somebody said.'

Another howl of jets stilled whatever she was about to say.

He took another look at the Mên balcony. His first impressions had not been wrong; the Panchen Lama was uneasy, watchful and nervous. The youth in the yellow robe revealed the propagandist gilt edge on the fraternal concord around him, a living personification of the growing conflict for domination of the Asian heartland.

Steven was sure that others were aware of antagonisms among friends up there on the balcony. The other guests were clustered below the crimson Mên. An official estimate put their number at ten thousand. It might well be accurate. Every hour in the past week the teletypewriter in his room had clattered reports of speeches delivered on arrival. Several times a day his telephone had been rung by English-speaking officials of the Foreign Ministry's Information Department who told him excitedly of important delegations or individuals due to disemplane shortly. Since Monday their first call had come soon after dawn, while sellers of noodles and sesame cakes cried their wares down cold streets, and their last had been after ten o'clock at night, normally an hour when everything was silent, restaurants and cinemas closed, *hutungs* and main streets quiet in starlight. Every aspect of this year's National Day celebrations had shown meticulous planning.

Two days ago he had joined a group of other newspapermen which was driven out on the half-hour run west past the new University City rising outside the grey mud walls of the old Imperial City, down a road lined with poplars and willows, farmland and new commune blocks, to watch a Russian TU-104 touch down at the airfield. It released a contingent of East Europeans who were greeted by tunic-clad officials, smiling girls in dark blue coats and skirts who presented each visitor with a bouquet of chrysanthemums, and hundreds of students released from their classrooms to act as a reception committee. It was a bloodless affair, despite its waving silken banners. Then the Europeans drove off in Russian and American cars, and the students went off to drink tea while they waited for another plane to unload political dignatories. He had also stayed on. While he was there a shower of soft grey rain slanted across the airfield. As he watched ground staff in yellow or scarlet oilskins inspect runways and loudspeakers three girl clerks darted towards him, bare heads protected by gay paper umbrellas, their light blurred voices chattering in *pai-hua*, the 'white' or simplified version of *Kuo-yu*, the national language, and one smiled up at him beneath her umbrella; a pretty child with a lean face, mischievous eyes, and small white teeth. Such incidents of human recognition were pleasant in China even if they were second-hand; she had probably mistaken him for a Russian.

Now the guests were assembled to watch the huge parade debouch from Chang-An Chieh, Perpetual Peace Street, and pass in front of the crimson Gate of Heavenly Peace.

They came from every quarter. He could see fierce-eyed Kazakhs, Indians with salad-crisp smiles, thoughtful Nepalis, whispering Japanese, exuberant CTs smuggled from hideouts in the Malay *ulu*, alert Indonesians who wore their black songkoks at a jaunty angle, droop-lidded Arabs, others from farther afield, excited Central and South Americans, smiling Africans in grey suits and white collars. Some men were identifiable only by the national costume worn by their women companions. In the last few days he had seen the short jackets and voluminous skirts of Korea, an emerald Ceylonese sarong draped on its diminutive owner like an early Grecian gown, a Black Thai with ornate silver buckles down the front of her long-sleeved black bodice, the divided-panel dress and loose white silk trousers of Vietnam, saris in pink, heliotrope, russet, and peach, two stout Tibetan women whose bamboo *patruk* headdresses were studded with coral and whose *pangden* aprons blazed like wild horizontal sunsets.

Near them a swarm of radio commentators talked in two hundred languages and dialects into lip-microphones, live on short bands beamed round the world or prerecording for edited weekly transmissions. Television and film cameramen spun their tape. One New China News Agency photographer crouched on his heels to get a picture of tanks against the guard of honour, thousands of uniformed men ranged along every side of the quarter-mile rectangle of the Square.

Steven made an entry in his notebook. As he looked up he caught hold of Jane's hand and directed her attention to a policeman slipping melon or sunflower seeds into his mouth, confident that everyone was too taken up with the parade to bother about him. He was older than most policemen near them, corpulent in white tunic and blue-black trousers. His face was broad under his green-banded military cap; for a moment it stayed motionless, then his fleshy jaw jerked in a single decisive movement and Steven could almost feel the heat of a crushed seed sting his own tongue. He smoothed a thumb along the belt supporting his oldfashioned revolver in its holster, turning on his heels to watch the NCNA photographer rejoin his companions. In this setting his action amounted to a defiance of its thunderous panoply of emergent might.

'It happens,' said Steven quietly.

She smiled without looking at him, but did not speak. Her hand clung to his. Her fingers were smooth and warm; there was a slight moisture in the hollow of her palm. Surprised, he tightened his clasp as if he had taken the incident as an excuse to hold her hand. There was a responsive pressure.

He did his best to forget it by watching a contingent of exuberant *hua chiao*, overseas Chinese. None was older than seventeen. From conversations with their type he knew them to be proud, ardent, sensitive, firily racialist. Every year more of them came to the ancestors' land to obtain specialist education. Many stayed on to assist in its big leap forward. Others, latent patriotism aflame, returned to their parents' homes in Singapore, Calcutta, Kowloon, Djakarta, Bangkok, Cholon, a hundred islands washed by Pacific tides.

Vengeful as eagles a flight of jet fighters shrieked over the clattering tanks. Like the bombers and tanks they were of Russian origin; Mig-17s. Echoes of their engines fell on the spectators like invisible glutinous ribbons which seemed to be absorbed into bodily heat. The noise rolled in subsiding fury across the burning blue desert of the sky.

'A few years can create quite a difference,' commented Roger Laurent.

He stood on the other side of Jane, mopping a handkerchief over the high forehead under his wiry silver hair. He lacked most physical characteristics of Frenchmen; a leaf of a man with sloping shoulders, narrow hips, and delicate hands. His long face was composed on contradictory features, a heavy jaw and thin lips, a big shapeless nose, sunken cheeks tinged yellow by recurrent bouts of fever, and straight black brows which intensified the pale blueness of his eyes. It was a face which could have belonged to a clown or a priest; a habitual expression of austerity tilted it towards the latter.

'Everything waited for it to happen,' said Steven, 'though most Old China Hands wouldn't believe it came to pass.'

Laurent put the handkerchief in a pocket of his travel-worn grey suit.

'Old China Hands were sublimely human,' he said. 'Their European prejudices told them to ignore what they did not want to see. They held their *status quo* of their childhood to be eternal. It was a natural fallacy when I first came to China thirty years ago. You were a schoolboy then, Steven, and Madame Crofton was not born.'

'I was four years old,' she told him.

A second flight of fighters screeched low overhead. Steven felt pressure from the fingers folded over his knuckles. Her face was averted as she watched tanks crawl forward. As more jets howled past, her hand lay limp in his; its moist pliant warmth frightened him.

When a partial quiet returned, Laurent said: 'I find that excessively difficult to believe, Madame.'

'I'm afraid it's true. Was China depressing then?'

'I would have refrained from recommending it to idealistic young people. Unfortunately I was young and idealistic. We are foolish to suffer both afflictions simultaneously. I found China insupportable. Corruption was the *leitmotiv* of life. The Government could not impose authority. A fantastic pre-occupation with each day prevented contemplation of the future. It was a land of placid anarchy. There was also Japanese aggression and opium.'

'And poverty.'

Laurent let another shriek dwindle from the sky.

'Every city was full of beggars. Men, women, infants. The first Chinese words a foreigner heard were their cries. *K'o-lien, k'o-lien, hsien-shêng, k'o-lien, ch'ing-kei chien, hsien-shêng, ch'ling-kei chien.* . . . have pity, sir, have pity, give money, sir, give money. Naturally, few Europeans learned such words. But we comprehend some words without learning them. Now . . . no beggars, no Old China Hands except the little severed fingers in Shanghai, no missionaries. Only officials, soldiers, *les fourmis bleues.*'

Artillery units rumbled into view behind the tanks.

On the other side of Steven, John Butler asked: 'Will the missionaries come back?'

He had kept silent for over half an hour while he wrote copious entries in his notebook.

Laurent did not volunteer an opinion.

'I doubt it,' said Steven.

'What happened to established Christian communities?'

'Some exist under official guidance.'

'Where?'

'In the old treaty ports.'

'Have they any influence?'

'No.'

Butler nodded absently. He was a dark fresh-complexioned man of a year or so under thirty. He went to some lengths to appear imperturbable. Steven had met him at a reception for a European delegation and heard that since publishing an account of a visit to Sicily he had pottered around London literary circles. His neat face never registered a positive emotion.

'Are they atheists by conviction?' he asked.

'I wouldn't say so,' commented Steven. 'Taoism strangled itself in mythology and magic. They associate Confucianism with the feudalism which kept China graft-ridden for centuries. They regard Christianity as a tool of European imperialism. They're anti-religious and appear to believe that proves atheism right.'

Planes swept overhead like leaves flung by a howling gale.

None of the men who manœuvred earthbound armament heeded its airborne shield. They were in excellent physical condition. Among them as among the infantry Steven saw characteristics from every corner of mainland China: plump-cheeked men from Kwangtung, the smoky skin of Yunnan, slanted Kansu eyes, long Mongol jaws, high Sinkiang cheekbones, the perky sparrow features of Fukien and Kiangsu. Every man bore himself pridefully. Each one regarded himself as an heir of those hunted refugees of less than thirty years ago who ended their Long March of six thousand miles at the loess caves of Yenan and became the nucleus of this colossal army of three million men.

As the combat forces finally retreated from sight, borne

impassively on their dark iron tide, Steven felt gentle pressure from the hand in his. She twisted her damp palm on his, a caress sharp with sensual tenderness, then disengaged her hand and drew away. He was relieved. For a while she had scared him.

In the distance a white water-tank damped down Gobi dust blown over Peking in recent days.

An industrial parade wound into view. Its drummers had awakened him in a pink-flecked silver dawn on their way to assembly-points. Models of blast furnaces mounted on floats trundled forward. Behind them came replicas of factories, generators, diesel engines, enormous cows whose udders were incredibly swollen, giant pigs, still more factories.

Under banners and placards a river of people surged forward. It was a joyless procession, self-consciously formal despite a hubbub of voices chanting slogans. All the same, it provided a welcome contrast to the iron-shod tramp in homage to destruction. These people had a right to take pride in their accomplishments. Their voices were those of a China resurgent after centuries of neglect by ineffectual rulers; voices of people whose ancestors had been toilers in *padi* fields, coolies, labourers, small shopkeepers, ricksha boys, and who were no better off themselves except that they had hope and more food and better housing. Their placards told of industrial output targets attained. Their banners exhorted, pledged, proclaimed, noisy with intention. Among them were fading prints of the 'big leap forward' posters depicting a pink-cheeked soldier astride a galloping black horse and holding a streaming red flag against a yellow sky; its caption read 'In 15 years or less we shall overtake Britain'. When he took up his post here it had been on every available wall among others which explained a need for education and publicized a rat extermination campaign.

More banners bobbed into sight, lilac, green, blue, yellow, tossing like paper boats. Many were of paper, scarlet strips from twenty to thirty feet long between bamboo end-poles. Their ideograph slogans were painted black or scarlet on a row of overlapping white diamonds conventional as those in a pack of playing-cards. A Western note on many was an exclamation-mark, an odd touch alongside symbols resembling gates, concertinas, flowerbeds, television aerials, bungalows, saplings in winter. They lent a brightness to this mechanical celebration.

Most marchers were dressed in drab blue. They were miners, stevedores, factory hands, labourers. A number of younger women did their hair in a plait over each ear, a style which gave them a schoolgirl appearance. It was often the only sign of their sex. Whatever their instincts or emotional impulses, contemporary women in mainland China were less visually female than those among overseas Chinese. That was a classic understatement, Steven told himself. It would be more accurate to say that a Chinese woman was a worker who could bear children when not wanted for manual labour. Her female nature did not count. She was a worker: period.

Steven glanced at Jane. She was staring steadily at the river of people whose dry chants beat upon their ears, but he knew that she was aware of his attention. Her lips held a quietness which was not calm. She did nothing to hold his speculation, nothing calculated to give it excitement, yet her stillness told him that she sought it.

Against his will, this change in her intrigued him. No, disturbed was the word, he told himself. In his recollection she had striven to ensure a neutral presence; not a damfool 'one of the chaps' manner worsened by lapses into charm or bitchery. It had given them an easy conversation which they did not jeopardize by digging into each other's past; neither of them had lapped eagerly at hot little confidences; they had heard sufficient of the other's background to avoid mention of it. He had not been conscious of a change when he met her off the plane a week ago. Now, eight days later, she had changed.

It surprised him. He sensed it last night when they dined together but told himself that he was mistaken because in those conditions a woman expected to contribute an atmosphere be it of wife or mistress or candidate for either role or of vocational companion. In this noisy scene her feminality was aggressive. It was more than an instinctive reaction to these thousands of clandestine women trudging past under their banners. She exuded it as an essence of mind and spirit. She intended him to be conscious of her.

He looked past her long straight back at Laurent.

'Sorry, I was wool-gathering. What did you say?'

'How far away is Hongkong?'

He was grateful for an interruption to their secret perception of each other. He did not want any woman to imagine herself interested in him.

'Keep going left past the moon,' he said.

Laurent smiled. 'Hongkong has too much poverty. Too many people crowded together. But it has also vivacity. British of course, afraid of losing face, ashamed of being spontaneous. Even so, vivacity.'

'If anyone hears you talk like that, you'll be put on the next train for it.'

Half a mile of people up to a hundred abreast chanted past the Mên balcony.

'This spectacle has a terrific impact but it's monotonous,' said Butler. 'Do you see . . . what did Monsieur Laurent call them, blue ants? . . . everywhere?'

'You may find Canton more colourful,' said Steven.

'Otherwise drab.'

'It depends how you interpret it.'

'Does it shock other people at first?'

'Most Europeans have a positive reaction. Then they remember the Chinese first used a cheap blue dye for nankeen cloth centuries ago. The Communists didn't invent this blue work garb. What they did was to turn it into a uniform of pride, the dirtier the better. Dirt is dignity. Compelled labour is true freedom. Obedience is honesty.'

'We need a special sort of mentality to be objective about it.'

'Oh, I don't know.'

Steven could sense the younger man trying to place him as a do-gooder or a fellow-traveller. Either assessment was natural. Less than fifty of the hundred-odd British citizens and Americans in China were free agents. The twenty Americans were defectees.

'You'll find it a fascinating assignment,' he added. 'China is the most exciting country in the world at present. There's always something new. Medicine for example. Ever since I came here there has been a running fight between Chinese traditional medicine and Western methods. It crops up in unexpected directions. For example, the Party line has undergone considerable fluctuations on whether to advocate birth-control or not. A couple of years ago when it was under discussion one institute of traditional medicine dug up an old theory that fresh tadpoles would prevent conception. So sixty women in Hangchow volunteered to swallow a couple of dozen live tadpoles on each of two or three days to test results. The Chinese take their experiments seriously. Twentythree women became pregnant within a month. Others followed suit. You probably remember it. The Party *Jen-min Jih-pao* . . . *People's Daily* . . . ran an article on it. Several people blamed the tadpoles. One professor told me that when he was a boy village women in parts of Yunnan swallowed live tadpoles in order to conceive. According to him, they regarded an occasional frog diet infallible for ensuring they bore sons.'

'Volunteers, you said.'

'Why not? There are always people ready to be guinea-pigs.'

Butler gave a noncommittal nod.

'Always the Chinese are preoccupied with their fecundity and virility,' said Laurent. 'They are national alarms. Their old overseas millionaires in Singapore still pay thousands of pounds for an ounce of supposed rhino horn to strengthen their resolution. Others say a spoonful of the brains of a living monkey is more efficacious.'

Butler gave no sign of comprehending the point; the proneness of the Chinese to suggestion. His neat face was blank as he glanced at Jane.

'Have you been here before, Mrs. Crofton?'

'No, this is my first visit.'

'Do you find it monotonous?'

'I'm unused to it. Until Steven explained about their clothes,

I thought it unnecessarily drab. I still do. As it is their National Day, I would have thought it an occasion for their workers to put on a livelier parade. Or whoever stages it for them.'

'To everything there is a propaganda season,' said Steven. 'At present their rulers want everyone from school age up to associate themselves with labour. In ten years' time, maybe less, they'll select a handful of workers only to parade in blue work clothes, national heroes like Stakhanov in Russia thirty years ago and those Spanish large family champions. Are there tadpoles in Spain?'

Laurent said: 'There are Barbary apes on Gibraltar.'

'A point. It could be an incentive.'

'Do they have national heroes?' asked Butler.

'Heroes and heroines. Eighteen months ago we had songs to honour a cotton-spinner who discovered a method of doing without knots in yarn. Then there was a national heroine who caught ten thousand weasels.'

Butler nodded.

Once again Steven thought the younger man a dull dog. Butler never really smiled; he shrugged on a social expression which did service for it and took it off quickly like a sports jacket which he thought too loud.

'What is the school-leaving age?' asked Jane.

'Nineteen, if they complete a full course. They took their educational time-table from the Nationalists. There's a movement to reduce it to sixteen.'

'To free them for work.'

'That's the main idea. There are others.'

'Are they significant?'

'Some. At present eleven million people reach their sixteenth birthday every year. Less than four percent could benefit from another three years in school even if there were educational facilities for them. There are less than a million new jobs a year which demand advanced education. The regime would face a host of new problems if it produced even one million well-educated young people every year who could not be given work up to their ability.'

'I'm beginning to see what you mean about excitement,' she said.

'I knew you would.'

She turned her head to look at him. He felt a little shiver jump along his nerves. She met his glance serenely. Her eyes were large and brilliant, green flecks in their pale grey irises, their lashes free from sticky boot-polish crumbs, her black brows unplucked. A half-smile shaped her lips. Even without the raw near-vermilion lipstick, they were too thick and wide for her oval face. It was the only discordance in her cool beauty. He wondered why she used the atrocious colour.

As they looked at each other, he regretted his decision to avoid adventures bound to end in dissatisfaction if not in emotional turmoil. Until then it could be a pleasant interlude. At the back of his mind hovered a tantalizing knowledge that by this hour tomorrow she would have left on the first stage of her tour.

'I'm sorry Clive is unwell,' she was saying.

'He'll be all right. He got these bouts in the Middle East. This is a mild attack.'

'He's having lunch with you.'

'A quick snack.'

'I thought he didn't look really fit.'

Her level voice provided a screen which cut them off from the others. Its quietness did not delude either of them. Both of them knew that she was talking in order to prolong a moment when curiosity about each other had taken control of their senses.

'He works too hard,' he said.

She gave no sign of recognizing his lie about Clive Dixon. He had left Clive sleeping off a hangover. For the past week Clive had been carefully drunk again.

'Will I see him before I go to Shenyang?' she asked.

'I expect he'll be at one of the official gatherings.'

'I'd like to have a talk with him,' she said and turned away.

Her manner was more confident than he remembered it. He felt apprehensive and goaded.

He scribbled a meaningless entry in his notebook. Well, they would see. He looked up.

Through the hot golden sunshine the procession continued to wind past them on steps whose light quick pace told of pride. Mechanics in oil-stained blue overalls pushed a float bearing a vast replica of a railway engine. Ten large groups of road-construction workers accompanied models of soil excavators, crushers, cement mixers, a row of asphalt layers. Behind them marched rows of young girl coal-miners from northern pits, trim in boiler suits and scarves, lights shining in their steel helmets.

There could have been only one European equivalent for this spectacle, Steven told himself, a parade of guildsmen in the Middle Ages carrying their emblems of craft or trade. The similarity ended there. This parade was of a vast continental land mass whose people were racing headlong from village handicrafts into twentieth-century industrialization on a basis of political theories whose long-term benefits had not been proved. He detected more arrogance among these workers than he had seen in those who took part in earlier marches. For them every doubt appeared to have been answered by initial successes and propaganda. A brighter note was struck by women textile workers who wore pink or mauve or yellow jacket blouses above their faded dark trousers. Many had brought their children, boys and girls from four to twelve years of age, sloe eyes bright with the mischievous glint which brightens the eyes of Asian children; they wore red scarves; one section carried toy automatic rifles. As they passed the Mên they added a piping treble to voices chanting *Wan Sui*—Long Life!

Another hour went by. Then groups of folk dancers came in sight. Steven knew what to expect of them. The troups chosen were changed from parade to parade but the ingredients were constant: dragon dancers, ballet performers from Mongolia or Yunnan, members of the Peking Opera, footballers, gymnasts doing handstands on a horizontal bar, tumblers, silk and veil clad girls performing a lotus dance, film stars, Young Pioneer and Youth League cultural groups. Above them thousands of doves rose into the sky like a storm of dissolving snowballs, plump bellies glancing whitely across the blue sky, and swept away over the golden roofs of the Forbidden City.

He leaned over to Jane. As her shoulder took the slight pressure of his weight, he saw the slight breathing rise of her breasts. Her skin was cool and firm. A shiver ran along his nerves.

'This is the moment to go if you want to send your piece off ahead of others,' he told her. 'From now on it'll be colourful, but familiar. You can study it better in theatres and halls of culture.'

Without turning, she asked: 'Where do I go?'

He smelled the warm scent of her hair. 'I'll show you.'

'Don't you want to stay?'

'I've seen it. Coming, Roger?'

Laurent was wiping his forehead. 'At my age every dancing girl must be suffered to the bitter end.'

'I'll stay too,' said Butler.

2

Others who had witnessed earlier cultural displays were also leaving. Steven knew them. They were permanent correspondents from East European countries, men and women in safe jobs unless they experienced a sudden rush of freedom to the spirit, given more facilities than those granted to himself and other occasional free Western agency men who walked a tightrope every moment of their working and private hours. Only two were unpopular. They were Yugoslavs, the Tanjug and *Borba* men.

Steven put his hand under Jane's elbow. 'It'll be quicker if we duck down through the side streets.'

'Mr. Kendal.'

They stopped and turned as a cheerful voice hailed them.

'Hello, Han,' said Steven.

'You will agree it is a magnificent achievement.'

'It certainly is.'

Han Tso-lin beamed at them. He was a tall, sturdy man with a chubbily handsome face, its features bold, the strong brows, high cheekbones, wide-nostrilled nose, and broad lips, giving him a resemblance to Chou En-lai. His boyish smile stripped off a good ten of his thirtysix years. He wore a dark business suit and white shirt, a red tie, and black shoes. His thick oiled hair rising in a stiff wave from his broad forehead was glossy as wet sealskin. In his exuberance he swallowed quickly, a mannerism which caused his thyroid cartilege to jump in his neck. It added to his air of youthfulness.

'I do not intend to delay you,' he said gaily. 'News of this great day must reach the outside world quickly. I wondered if we shall have the pleasure of seeing you this evening?'

'We'll be going round the receptions,' said Steven.

As they walked down a side street, Steven glanced round. No one was near. Small boys leapfrogged past a debris of buildings torn down to provide a site for an office block. A pig-tailed girl licked a chocolate *bingku'er*, iced lolly, while she watched them.

'Han is a Party economic liaison officer,' he told her. 'He travels a good deal on planning missions.'

'He speaks excellent English.'

'He also speaks German, French, and Hindi. He has a German wife. He's ambitious, too ambitious to be under *kwantchee* though he's certain to do that on the side. All of them do.'

'What is under *kwantchee*?'

'Being a compulsory informer for the secret police. All officials are either under *kwantchee* or minor *kanpous*, government agents. The Party says it has three hundred thousand secret agents, but you can add the seventeen million Party members to them. They regard it a good insurance policy to advertise a huge secret police. Walls have ears for Big Brother.'

'I'll remember,' she said and sighed. 'That parade exhausted me.'

3

Clive Dixon rubbed a thumb and finger along his closed eyelids. His other hand massaged his stomach gingerly.

He crouched on a chair in a quiet corner of the European restaurant on the ninth floor of the hotel, a long thin man in a baggy greenish herringbone suit, a brown and green check woollen shirt, a green tie, and brown brogue shoes. Wings of greying brown hair dipped over his long ears. His hollow cheeks thrust his aquiline nose into greater prominence; his skin had a grey bloom; his hands shook; an aftermath of sorghum vodka soured his mouth. He felt as battered as a Port Said whore. Nonetheless, he was shaven; hooray for him. He wanted to belch.

'And then?' he prompted.

His deep voice was invariably gentle, sinking to a whisper whenever he became angry.

'We were given an industrial parade to end all industrial parades,' said Steven and provided details from his notes.

Clive kept his eyes shut. At least his brain could work. He played his daily game of watching it, a habit like reading an obituary column to find out if he was dead yet. It lived a secret, attentive life of its own and now he could observe it busily noting developments, keen as a boy scout to let no vital point escape its vigilant attention. That helped; long might it continue. Already it astonished him. They said an ability to concentrate was the first faculty to start slipping. It was one of his fears. He had forgotten how many he had gathered in his fortyseven frightened years but there were a lot of them; a fear of going blind, of finishing up old and futile in a gutter, of being burned to death, of cancer, of cirrhosis, of paralysis, of having nothing left to give. One day he would have to do more about his fears than fondle them in his mind like an incapacitated lecher aghast at the awful desires blooming in his imagination.

He sighed inwardly. He was inept. Like his father, that poor lovable nervous old bastard who had got out of focus from being squinted at down the long lordly nose of youth. Now there was a man, his father, more spirit than a cloister of archbishops, more guts than all the imitators of Hemingway's angry old straw bulls; a man scared of life yet prepared to go on living. A fearful joy: to sniff a bouquet of terrors like a drug addict, to touch daily at least one malignant bloom, caress its flaunting charm with a lover's touch and see it respond. Last night he had got drunk while he thought about cancer.

'Yes, bless your heart, I've got it,' he said. 'One day I'll do it for you. Was that the lot?'

'We didn't stop for culture. You can have these notes. My report is filed.'

'We?'

'Jane Crofton was with me.'

'How did she react?'

'Stunned.'

'Unanimous verdict.'

'Yes. There's no doubt they've decided to put pressure on the Kremlin. We'd better get assigned to Moscow next year for their October show. They'll have to live it up with the Joneses.'

There was proof, Clive told himself. He hadn't even thought about it yet. They were right. Steven Kendal, damn him to hell nicely, was an embodiment of good clean healthy fast concentration.

'It's a point,' he said as if he doubted it, 'but they're bound to have small dialectical differences.'

'Dialectical differences phooey. You know what they're up to and so do all of us. Meantime, I'm hungry. How do you feel about food?'

'Generally speaking, antagonistic.'

'You'd better nibble something.'

Clive opened his eyes. To his surprise, no shimmering white neon glare caused him to lose sight of people above their waists. Full vision did not improve them but it did help his morale. He saw that the restaurant was filling up. Most people present were East Europeans, fleshy Roumanians and Bulgars, thin Poles, good Party members, relieved that Russia acted as a buffer between China and themselves. He detected a wrong note of excitement in their voices. There could be no mistake about their uneasiness. He tasted his mouth and longed for an authentic whisky and soda.

While he and Steven had a snack of fresh eggs he glanced at tables nearest to them to be sure their occupants were engaged in their own concerns. Then he said: 'I expect you gave Jane some tips.'

'She asked to be put right about their official procedure.'

'Bless your heart. I intended to have a talk with her.'

'You'll have it tonight. I told her you were having only a mild bout of fever.'

'Thanks.'

Clive paused unsurely. There was no method for him to find out if she had confided in Steven Kendal about the occasion in Beirut when she nursed him through the aftermath of a five-day jag. Steven said nothing or talked at length without saying anything. His face never betrayed him. Clive envied him. Jane and Steven belonged to the same breed. She did not talk. She was not one of those bitches whose tongues had to wag confidences.

Or did she confide in Steven? Her image rose uppermost in his mind. He remembered an evening in Ankara when she avoided his attempts to make love to her. That showed how drunk he had been. The last women a newspaperman got excited about were newspaperwomen; you never tried to pick daisies with them, but never.

'She's a sweet woman,' he said. 'Real. Genuine, God help her. Why is it always her sort who get a raw deal?'

'They never give up.'

'You're right. Strange, how we use the same words as our farthest ancestors to describe fundamentals.'

'Are there new ones?'

'Well, the damnedest things happen. One day they'll rewrite the Bible in newspeak. It can't be fun for her to troll all over.

23

I would have thought a natter-patter column much better.'

'For her?'

'She'd be on hand, son.'

'I expect she prefers to be absent. Besides, she earns more on this work.'

'It's a hell of a grind for a woman and she is a real woman.'

'Yes.'

'How old is her daughter now?'

'Eleven? Maybe twelve.'

As they finished lunch, Clive looked at his hands. They were shaking at a thought of being Jane Crofton, solely responsible for such a child. He knew he would have to have a drink before he went out. But it would not stop him from thinking about the kid.

4

Steven went down to his fifth floor room to find out what had happened in his absence. Foreigners in Peking who were classified as semi-permanent residents, those who stayed longer than the routine two-months period allotted to delegations, invariably referred to their living-quarters as their 'room' though it was a compact small unit comprising a living-room, a bedroom which had a bed somewhere between single and double width in size, and a bathroom. Some units, occupied by family men, contained a cupboard-sized kitchen.

It had taken Steven some weeks to realize that correspondents from foreign communist newspapers were treated identically to non-communist agency men like Clive and himself, who were tolerated until they filed a despatch which offended the Foreign Ministry and had their credentials withdrawn. Even quasi-permanent foreign residents owned no rights; they were fellow-travellers and defectees. A fellow-traveller might be anyone. The defectees were young American soldiers captured in Korea who now worked in Chinese factories. Some had married Chinese girls. If they ever wanted to return home, a Chinese law prevented their wives from accompanying them. No defectees lived in the Hsinshih Hotel.

Steven had arrived in Peking shortly after the Hsinshih opened.

At that time there were sixteen hotels permanently reserved for foreign delegations but even so rooms were in short supply. Among parties then in Peking were a Ceylonese Women's Goodwill Mission, a group from East Germany, a Brazilian Film Writers' delegation, an Italian Socialist Mission, a delegation of Japanese students, an agricultural group from Pakistan, a Goodwill Military Mission from Indonesia, a British Labour Party Group, a youth delegation from France, a trade union group from Czechoslovakia, an Albanian peace group, and an Egyptian Mutual Economic Help delegation. Another eight groups and some newspapermen from South America, Africa, and Europe, were on provincial tours. Pressure on hotel space increased steadily. He had spent three days at the Hsinchiao, built with money invested by overseas Chinese, and then moved to the Hsinshih—New World—Hotel. He was its second British Commonwealth resident. The first was a Eurasian girl correspondent from Calcutta: Sheila Grant. Clive had come to Peking five months ago.

Among hotels in Peking the Hsinshih occupied a unique position. Outwardly it possessed no memorable features. It was a large red brick building shaped as a hollow square, ten storeys high, built on what had been an area of houses in the eastern part of the city close to Hata Gate Street. Its front faced east towards the Chihua Mên and where Japanese troops in their final assault had crossed the railway and breached the outer wall; its rear windows overlooked a corner of the Forbidden City.

There were four restaurants at the Hsinshih. On the ground floor one served Chinese food amid a collection of sombre rooms used for official receptions. Immediately above it on the second floor a smaller restaurant offered a Russian menu and above that a third had an Indian bill of fare. The restaurant on the ninth floor served only allegedly European food.

On levels between them the residents lived in identical three-room flatlets slightly larger than the single rooms with bath in other hotels. People at the Hsinshih bought their own cigarettes; delegates were given a daily packet of dark, rather acrid cigarettes and a box of uncooperative matches. Radio sets at the Hsinshih worked normally but only received local stations; sets at other hotels were usually out of order and a delegate who brought his own transistor found it had broken down during his first absence from it. This situation and a total absence of foreign newspapers kept everyone dependent on Chinese sources for news. Items of world significance were delayed for days before a propagandized version was released. No mention was made of any meritorious act by the West.

One feature singled the Hsinshih out from other hotels. It was the only one which had Chinese residents living alongside foreigners. There were seventy of them living on the third floor over rooms reserved for Russians. All of them shared two similarities; they were government employees and married to non-Chinese. Among them was Han and his East German wife Ilse. Their non-Chinese partners, overwhelmingly wives, were allowed more freedom to fraternize with foreigners than was granted to other Chinese citizens.

Every member of the staff was a potential spy. Even waitresses upstairs spoke a form of mission-school English which suggested they might understand it much better; they were patient girls, thin or plump, with round flat moon faces or bird-sharp features, often weary, often in their eighth month of pregnancy, all of them capable of using their ears to collect scraps of conversation which could be passed on. The floor-boys had greater advantages. They were always about, a total of eight men to each floor, and all were middleaged. Their tasks were to clean the rooms every day and take clothes to be laundered. They knew each resident by his habits and saw who talked to whom. Lift-boys also had opportunities to collect information, Each one took care to be self-effacing, none more so than the one who deposited Steven on the fifth floor and took Clive down to the next level, a thin short man named Tang.

As Steven walked along the corridors to his rooms, he was thinking that he should have warned Jane to be guarded about what she said in front of members of the staff at her hotel. She was in the Sunrise, half a block farther down Hata Mên Chieh. Among foreigners in Peking it had a reputation as a training-ground for hotel staff spies.

He heard a snicky clatter of teletypewriters from behind closed doors. Beyond one a woman chattered in Spanish, brisk as a grind of peppercorns. At present fifteen flatlets on the fifth floor housed Central and South American families, the men voluble, their wives of fiery temperament and given to wearing nests of costume jewellery which looked as insecure as stork nests on Spanish churches.

At the bottom of the corridor he turned left down another lit by electric lights. Their glare did something to diminish the gloom of brown-painted walls and a darkened floor on whose uncarpeted surface European shoes sounded noisier than a parade-ground trot. Halfway along the right side a narrow staircase ascended and descended to other floors. Facing it was a glass door which led to a fire-escape. His rooms were straight ahead at the end and looked west.

He turned the white porcelain door-handle to let himself in. He never locked his room. Peking hotel staffs were unfailingly honest. Nothing ever vanished; whatever he left hanging about was put in a tidy stack on table or bed by his room-boy, Hu.

A yards-long spill of paper like wet-smudged bunting twitched limply from the excited teletypewriter. He tore it off and tossed it onto the table in the centre of the room. Every piece of furniture was bleak: table, hard chairs, easy chair, radio, cumbersome television set, sideboard and electric kettle, the long settee against the bedroom wall, and two overloaded bookcases.

He opened the window to let in whatever air from outside

could reduce the warm stuffiness. Traffic noises pulsed in nearby streets. He took off his jacket, slung it over a chair, and opened a bottle of mineral water to wash down an aspirin. He lit a cigarette. Apart from traffic noises drifting up like clusters of balloons, everything was quiet.

He collected the length of drab bunting and sat down to see if the information contained interest for him. It did not.

After a quick run through he laid it aside, got up and went to the window. It gave a view over the artificial Coal Hill and over trees beyond it to the White Dagoba, that sad lighthouse-on-a-pincushion religious shrine, a Tibetan chorten erected as a face-saver centuries ago by an emperor who reduced Tibet to vassalage. A recollection of Jane unsettled him. His share in their game of sensual appraisal left a nasty taste in his mouth. Evidently his link to the original Adam still existed though he had forgone the idiocy of personal emotions since he parted from Gillian nearly ten years ago. On that day he echoed the words of John Hall:

> 'Now sound I a retreat; now I'll no more
> Run all those devious paths I ran before.'

And since Gillian, no such weakness. Almost the only feature of contemporary China which suited him personally was its stern puritanism. He did not approve of it. It was primitive, morality sanctified by propaganda. It reduced women to a squalid subhumanity where they were less important than machines or animals. But it suited him by making chance entanglements virtually impossible. Rationally, therefore, this nonsense with Jane was due to the monastic life led by woman-less foreigners in China. After all, even the best trained human nature took delight in playing absurd pranks. That was all. It wasn't important.

He rubbed his forehead, remembering the expression in her eyes and how her hand twined on his.

Two

DARKNESS brought out the flying needles of a hundred searchlights to stitch milky webs among emergent stars. Whole families gathered at vantage points to await a spectacular fireworks display scheduled for later on. Every street was alive with a blue river of people. They chattered, seethed, exclaimed, murmured, lost contact in eddies of other people and met again to wander on. Under blazing triumphal arches in main thoroughfares weary country grandmothers hobbled along, bodies bent, trousers flapping above bound feet. Many clutched the hand of a small child in their dry old fingers.

Their voices were a soft thunder on every side of the car which took Clive Dixon to a reception at the Roumanian Embassy. Although he had not seen a previous National Day in Peking he could tell the mood of these people. They expected a *nao-jeh* evening, loud and hot, full of noisy excitement. They would get it. From what he had learned this first day of October afforded Communist leaders a twofold opportunity to commemorate military victories which gave them power in 1949 by forcing Kuomintang troops to seek refuge on Taiwan and to obliterate Kuomintang 'Double Tenth' memories of overthrowing a corrupt throne fifty Octobers ago. Tonight there were organized parties for people in their *hutungs* and streets. For officials there were grimly convivial diplomatic receptions. He would have preferred to go to a *hutung* celebration to share a bowl of rice and kettle of soup and watch diabolo performers.

He had never been an ardent admirer of diplomatic establishments and those in Peking lacked distinction even more than those in other capitals. Sixty years ago appointments to distant lands did still have a smatch of adventure but nowadays diplomatic staffs were as adventurous as hopeful near-relations at a significant funeral. But those in Peking did provide leads to real news quicker than could other sources.

29

He looked out as his car halted at a street intersection. A string of buses and red and yellow trams crossed in front. An overwhelming majority of pedestrian sightseers were in their teens. He listened to the ceaseless thunder of their voices. Was there anything more frightening than a crowd of people? He doubted it. The mob; the horde; the blind murderous rabble. Individually none of them was worse than other people, but in the mass, merciless, bestial, a terrible instability anywhere from Little Rock to Timbuqtu in either direction. Strings of lights looped over the streets illuminated passing faces. Some peered in at him. Their eyes showed more confidence than he had felt at their age.

That took his mind back. With the best will in the world, people like Steven Kendal did not have a perception equal to their job. Neither did the public-school-cum-stately-home diplomats nor the American multimillionaire ambassadors, the cool glad-hand brigades. He did. Yes, by God. There was precious little confidence in a Lancashire cotton town thirty-odd years ago. In a magazine article published then, Aldous Huxley said that people who got into a train in London and stepped out at Manchester walked straight into another world. True.

He gazed at passing trams and heard those which had whined along the cobbled streets of his youth. He could never forget those grey street corners populated from morning to night by unwanted men. They put no trust in bosses or politicians. Those of his own age had felt their early manhood debased. No one wanted them. They lacked pride in themselves; you weren't given a dollop of pride when you joined a queue at a labour exchange to draw your weekly shillings of 'unemployment benefit'. Benefit! Their girl friends didn't see a benefit in it; they tried to leave home for work in another town or hunted for a new chap in a job, any job, and others risked another type of gamble by persuading their steady chap to take them up 't'Hill' to get out of the smell of defeat, a bit closer to the stars, for five minute fumbles of escape until the night air caused them to get sick mornings and they married in haste, two more drawing 'benefit'. Love on the dole. What was the last line spoken by the unemployed father in Walter Greenwood's play of those days? 'Ah've done ma best, haven't Ah? Haven't Ah?' It could have been his own father.

He was scarcely conscious of the car moving on. No, he had not seen much confidence when he was a young reporter on the local sheet which led him to a Manchester evening paper and to Fleet Street. He saw families sell furniture and hock their trinkets at the pawnshop, slipping in to see 'Uncle' like criminals lest someone recognize them; it was a social disgrace to be poor in Christian England, a social syphilis. He saw hungry men idle their strength and skill away on a thousand grey corners in a hundred ugly industrial towns where the brightest things were film posters and new 'For Sale' boards outside grey chapels.

Here in Chinese towns he saw new factories going up. Would they remind Kendal and others of what they reminded him: a day when he went to a small village whose entire life depended on a single old-established family cotton mill and stood in afternoon sunshine surrounded by a numbed silence of Lancashire folk to watch its chimney blown up because the owners had gone bankrupt? Only the millowner died, burning his stomach out with acid. And a week later he went to a coal town off the East Lancs Road to Liverpool, dirtier, shabbier, longer queues of men idle on its corners, and he saw them break up a labour exchange because the luckless clerks there were the nearest state officials to hand and too many of them acted as if they grew wings behind the counter.

That was the climate of industrial merrie England when he escaped to the hectic exhilaration of Fleet Street. Since then he had been lucky, foot-loose, his occasional fancy free to enjoy itself, a man who carried a typewriter. But he would never forget those days. They put fear into a man. Fear of what could happen to his beliefs and illusions. Fear of what was bound to happen if he did not earn money. Fears about a woman if he regarded one as his. Fear of health, old age, incapacity, the quirks and pranks of outrageous fortune which jumped up and kicked you in the teeth. Back in those days it was a commonplace story, but a man needed to carry it in his mental luggage to understand the present frame of mind of these Asians. Even so, unemployed Britons of thirty years ago had a proud life compared with Asians among whom poverty was an heirloom, and from his observations the average British trade unionist of this year had a standard of living about seven hundred times greater than that of Chinese in comparable jobs. And the Chinese envied the Briton his comfortable life. They probably envied the Briton's right to strike.

He glanced up frowning.

'What?'

'Is this the Embassy you want, Mr. Dixon?' repeated Nieh, his driver.

2

The large room beyond the receptive glad hands was full. Clive collected a glass of *amalfi*, a rust-hued drink concocted from vermouth and *tuica*, Roumanian plum schnapps. He had last drunk *amalfi* in the Journalists' Club in Bucharest, once the Millionaires' Club, a good pull-in for drink and tasty dishes like *ciorba*, shrimp pilaf, and a hash of rams' testicles. Two days later the Roumanians kicked him out of the country for trying to learn if they had already handed Imre Nagy back to the Hungarians for execution. Dear democracy.

He glanced at the crush and babble to see where he could circulate. The place was a sardine tin of embassy staffs wearing routine expressions of carefree diplomacy. Their vocal gaiety deafened him. He saw Jane Crofton talking to Han and two stunned-looked European women. He circled two pale-faced Roumanians smelling of toilet water and sweet arabi, threading through the charade to Jane.

The sight of Jane freed his attention from this excited wag of hypocrisy. She appeared elegant even while just standing. Once again it struck him that she was too coolly handsome for her own well-being. But girls who gasped and flushed did not work on newspapers. He regretted that she had given him the brush-off.

Her grey eyes did not remind him of it as he slid past a thicket of elbows to join the group.

'Hello, Clive,' she said. 'You look cheerful.'

She sounded pleased to see him, despite a familiar restraint in her contralto voice. Perhaps she had changed her mind about him.

'I've just written a magnificent article,' he said. 'In my head. Unanswerable logic enriched by Churchillian prose. Of course, no living person or editor would dare print it. How are you?'

'Still dazed by what we saw this morning. This is Mrs. Cihak and Miss Kounadis. Clive Dixon is a countryman of mine.'

He bowed. The Czech woman was an applecheeked farm-wife with a Mona Lisa smile and the body of Tweedledum. There was no mistaking the Greek girl for Tweedledee. She had a long face, a willowy body, legs like a miler, and a mop of wiry black hair. Her obviously boundless energy made him quail. Both women spoke good English.

'Did you enjoy our parade this morning, Mr. Dixon?' asked Han.

'Most impressive.'

'I did not see you.'

'Weren't there a lot of people?'

'Were you with Mr. Kendal?'

'Nearer the back.'

They smiled at each other. Everyone at these receptions was amiable; it was all very bourgeois. A burst of fraternal delight provided a distraction. They saw humanity congeal near the doors. Clive stretched his neck above a copse of heads. He caught sight of a thin man in a Yat-sen tunic, his white hair shining. When he turned to Jane the two women had joined another group and Han was swopping pleasantries with an Indian.

'It may be Liu Shao-chi',' he said, 'but I'm not sure.'

'Who's he?'

'Chairman of the Republic.'

She heeded the warning in his eyes.

'Are you better?'

'Bless your heart, I'm as good as old.'

'You don't look too good.'

'These attacks take a couple of days to work off.'

'It amazes me that we don't get ill more often,' she said. 'We lead a desperately unhealthy life. Pills and planes don't improve it. They only help us get from one extreme of climate to another. Our nerves never have a chance to grow cushions.'

It was generous of her to give his little weakness a carte blanche and lie about it like a real woman.

'You're right,' he agreed.

'Why do we keep on? I can't think of a good reason. The work never gives us genuine satisfaction. Who can get satisfaction from being a human airline time-table and a name in a wrapper for tea-leaves and potato peelings? We've even forgotten what it's like to be people. The only people in us are those we may meet tomorrow. We've forgotten those we met yesterday. Our deepest emotion is a string of sentences we hope a sub-editor will leave alone to be read by somebody in a dirty railway carriage smelling of sweaty feet and grime and worried about his overdraft and indigestion.'

Her voice became lighter as she chattered on in a rare bout of sweet Fanny Adams. He had not believed her capable of abandoning her usual impersonal form of conversation. Her fluency reminded him of Steven Kendal scampering through a dictionary if he did not intend to commit himself. They were both cagey, two of a kind.

He finished his drink while he listened to her. There could be more to her switch of mood than mere acceptance of his hint of it being dangerous to speak freely. She gave an appearance of welcoming a chance to talk inconsequentially, her manner almost experimentally feminine. He gained an impression that she was watching herself and trying to gauge his response to her in this guise. It beat him. Twenty years ago he had decided that he only understood women in bed. He was not alone in that. They didn't understand themselves, not even when they remembered beds they had lain in.

'It's a bit harsh to call our life unnatural,' he commented. 'It's a trudge, an exasperation, and more, but would we fit into a ten till five tedium thinking about places we hadn't even smelled? Could we stick office intrigues, squalid bits of business connivery, get cross with the tea-trolley girl for forgetting we always like a sugary bun on Monday, watch the same brick walls and televisor and wallpaint grow older every year? God bless those who like a safe job. What do they get from it? Colds in the head and income-tax demands. Don't blame our job. It's our excuse for not staying in our own parish. We wanted out. We got it.'

He thought she might be depressed over loss of the life which ended when her husband was killed eight years ago, some private event causing her to contrast now and then, perhaps an anniversary, and he wanted to blunt the more hurtful comparisons. His words had the opposite effect. A frown drew her brows together.

'Must it be one extreme or the other?' she asked in a flat voice.

'What else for us? Few of us has a second line.'

'Don't you think there can be a workable compromise?'

He put down his empty glass and rescued two in healthier shape from a passing tray.

'It may be different for you, it should be, but have you watched us when we sit down, fidgeting for an excuse to get up again? Our feet get miserable from neglect. They pester us to get going somewhere. Anywhere.'

Her eyes searched his. She disliked what he said. The corners of her lips flickered down in a grimace which thrust their scarleted thickness into prominence. It ought to have made her plain.

'I expect you're right,' she said in her usual voice.

'Eeh, lass, it's nobbut a reet daft world wheer ever tha goes,' he said in an attempt at humour, and held out one of the glasses. 'For the journey?'

'No, I still leave it alone.'

So she had not forgotten their episode.

'Clever of you.' He tasted one, then the other. 'They had the same parents. Did you come with Steven?'

She nodded towards a group of people on their left.

'He's over there talking to Mrs. Han and some East Germans.'

'He said you were going to the Forbidden City this afternoon.'

'Yes. Mr. Han took me.'

'Did you find it interesting?'

'I would have liked to see it in the time of Matteo Ricci.'

He nodded. Two of a kind. He had never heard of the Jesuit's arrival in Peking nearly four hundred years ago until Steven mentioned it. He hoped it did them good. History held no interest for him. Why fuss about centuries as dead as yesterday? Enough was enough.

'Wanderlust has strange forms,' he said. 'It reminds me of a chap I met down in Valparaiso one time.'

Steven said: 'I saw the Olympic Games in Berlin in the nineteen-thirties. I was a schoolboy, but my parents let my brothers and me go over. We were terribly excited.'

He was speaking in German. Members of the official party had shifted on to another group.

'What did you like most in Berlin?' asked Ilse Han.

Her voice was husky. She was younger than most women present, attractive in a cold Teutonic fashion, her sharply blue eyes and sleek blonde hair, bright as sunlight on daffodils, giving the skin of her heart-shaped face a chilled whiteness. At first glance most people took her for thirty; her features were devoid of animation. He doubted if she was more than twenty-three, a young Brünnhilde with full breasts and rounded hips. She wore a dark green woollen dress whose skirt hung low over her strong legs. Her unfaltering restraint in public might mean that she restricted spontaneity to her home. It might go deeper.

'I only remember Unter den Linden and Wansee and a street which became or was a nightclub centre,' he said.

'Kurfürstendamm?'

'Yes, Kurfürstendamm.'

'I did not like it. There were many homosexuals and drug addicts. I preferred Tingel Tangel and the old woman Hitler liked. She sang *So wie ich hier stehe, so bin ich geleiben*. Did you go there?'

He shook his head.

'Did you bomb Berlin?' she asked. 'Tso-lin told me you were in the RAF.'

'I was a fighter pilot.'

'Were you one of—"the few"? *Ist der Name, ja?*'

'I joined too late to be one of "the few".'

For some moments they talked about the war. Her flat voice revealed curiosity. Perhaps she considered it strange for them to meet here years later.

He became conscious of being watched and raised his eyes. A Chinese girl was studying him. She stood alone near a cluster of European backs. There was something familiar about her. Tall and slender, a fair skin, black hair curled over her forehead like small pointed leaves, a delicately triangular face with compact lips and a clear chin: where had he seen her? Her eyes implied independence. Although she wore the black coat and skirt in favour among women officials, he was sure he had not met her in a Ministry building. More likely she was a guide he had encountered near the lakes or at the Temple of Heaven. He imagined a gleam of recognition in her eyes and risked a cautious smile. A brief response touched her lips.

'Did you not want to fly after the war?' Ilse Han was asking.

'No. I had become interested in more complex machinery. People.'

A faint humour came into her gaze. 'Do you expect to understand them?'

From across the room Han watched his woman talking to the Englishman Kendal. Ilse was enjoying herself. The signs were too subtle to be apparent to others but three years of marriage had taught him much about her. Her weaknesses were no secret from him. He searched them out.

'Our policy contributes to world peace,' the Indian was saying.

Automatically Han said: 'We sympathize with the desire of the Indian masses to shape their own destiny.'

A jealousy like sickness twisted in his stomach. It was a principle of right thinking for him to hate *hoong mo kwai*, red-haired devils as his ancestors called Europeans long ago, but his hatred of Kendal was personal and bitter. He had no real cause for it yet he enjoyed it. Ordinary Western reporters soon offended officials at the Foreign Ministry by crude anger because they were not allowed to go where they pleased or were challenged over their lying reports, actions which led to their expulsion. Kendal was crafty. He never quarrelled. He asked officials to check points on which he was unsure; if no one passed them he cut them out. Intensive searches of his rooms revealed no evidence of him being a spy; that proved he was one. One day they would expose him as an enemy sent to prepare a war plot. Han prayed to be the one to unmask him. He hated Kendal.

He saw Ilse raise her face. He swallowed quickly. It was one of her tricks to arouse lust in a man. He knew how it felt to see Ilse lift her face, expressionless as it was now, to goad a man to contrast her cold eyes with what his blood told him about her body. One night four years ago at her home in Leipzig she had sat on the floor in front of the fireplace and looked at him exactly as she was looking at the Englishman now. They were alone. Her parents were on a visit to relations in Dresden; her brother was speaking at a rally in Halle; they were good party members and he was ignorant of the extent of her wrong thinking. He had undressed her, his fingers clumsy until he felt his climax on him and tore her European underclothes to shreds on her body. Her total indifference gave him an unusual excitement. Nothing about her had reminded him of other European women. They were brainless creatures whom he despised even while they twitched at his touch. She remained still, let her strong arms lie slack, kept her eyes shut, did nothing to stimulate or aid him, yet her single deep shudder told him how fully she responded to his lovemaking. Then they went up to her bedroom. Neither of them slept that night but they did not speak a single word.

From then on he spent all his spare time with her. His language studies gave him plenty of leisure. Every night he went to her room. They never discussed their lovemaking or used words of endearment, but he did wring from her an admission of having had a lover, a scared and nerve-racked ex-soldier who seduced her during her last term at school. That experience meant nothing; intuition told him that his virility gave her satisfaction. What pleased him most was her intuition. She never allowed herself to show need of him or express pleasure in his demands on her. Instead her indifference became more pronounced. But she was conscious of her power over him. That had to stop. He had known it at the end of their first week as lovers and it was still his intention to force her to admit one day that he owned absolute power over her. For them his dominance over her meant far more than a normal, happy relationship between a man and the woman he selected.

He saw no indication of her thoughts on her face as she listened to the Englishman. Whatever schemes she might make were bound to fail. She could not deceive him. He saw every daily report on foreigners at the Hsinshih prior to it being taken to the special department at the Foreign Ministry which correlated dossiers on their activities. Moreover, Kendal had no interest in women: two who had been carefully chosen to test him reported complete failure. Only a foreigner would be curious about Ilse. Normal men would hate her because her fine body hair would remind them that she was one of the *hoong mo kwai*. He hated her too, though not on account of her hair, which gave him a secret incitement, but for her attempt to keep part of her mind hidden from him and particularly for the sacrifice he had made to own her. Ever since he was a boy he had wanted a family of fine strong children to follow him; in Germany he wanted only to be her owner. On the night of their marriage he told her of his decision that they would not have children. He said his career must come first. He did not tell her that he could not insult his ancestors or his own loins by breeding half-cast scum, *chup choong kwai*, much mixed-up devils. What man gained happiness from staring at a dirty mirror?

As if conscious of his attention, Ilse turned her eyes. Their glances met. No hint of recognition came into her face. He might have been a stranger. He could guess at the mockery in her mind, her silly delight in brazen behaviour which a good Chinese wife would regard as below her dignity.

He smiled. Her indifference stared at him like an ice mask, then she looked at the Englishman. He almost laughed. Her contempt here had no significance. Both of them knew him to be master where it mattered. There she was defenceless, dependent on his goodwill. He swallowed. She had forgotten humilities which it had been his duty to inflict on her because the woman of a man in his position dared not tell of her wrong-thinking at a public confession or it would ruin him. He watched her steadily, remembering how she behaved when he first disciplined her. As he was going to Chungking tomorrow for two weeks, she must be given another lesson tonight. The prospect excited him.

Steven wove a path across the room through a squash of people talking ever more loudly in their efforts to be heard. He skirted a large group and bumped into the Chinese girl he had noted earlier. She was talking to an angular man who might be a Hungarian. She glanced up as he caught hold of her arm to save her from falling. Recognition replaced startlement in her eyes.

'*Tui pu ch'i*,' he apologized and let go of her.

She smiled. It added to her youthfulness. On the left side of her face a scar ran from her temple to the angle of her jaw. Below it, partly hidden by her hair, he saw graft puckers on her neck. He smiled and went on.

He found Jane talking to a thick-set Egyptian. They chatted

about nothing for a while. Then the Egyptian took himself off.

'Hungry?' asked Steven.

'Ravenous. Those bits have given me an enormous appetite.'

'We'll attend to it now. I propose to feed us on Peking duck.'

'It sounds delicious.'

He put his hand under her elbow to guide her to the doors.

In a crowded corner John Butler stood bemused and silent. There was too much talk in too many languages for him to think coherently. The voices bore a distinct resemblance to a parliament of furious parakeets. People came to shake his hand and say things he did not understand. His answers in French and Spanish earned a sigh.

He shut his eyes against a sparkle of flash bulbs. He wished to God he had followed his other idea of going to South America. At least he had an ability to talk to people from Mexico City to Cape Horn. Why ever did he come here? It bore no relation to what he had foreseen when he weighed up pros and cons in his flat in Kensington and in talks to his friends in riverside pubs over in Chelsea. There he had seen solid arguments for a visit to China now. Everything told him that South America could wait a year or two. So here he was, bewildered and stunned by the terrific impact. Every day he saw fresh complexities, each one spawning more and more in frightening confusion. God, what a fool! He would have done better to go up the Amazon to reconstruct the disappearance of Fawcett. Where did you start to unpick this tangle?

He smiled ruefully. The din and heat in the Embassy had started his head throbbing in one of those aches which were not a headache so much as a consequence of what he had tried to stuff into it in this one day alone. He longed to sit down entirely alone somewhere to try to sift everything into order. It had already led him to cast aside his preconceived ideas. His careful plan, the theory he had intended to support by skilfully introduced argument and shrewdly observed scenes, his penetrating analyses, even his casual wit: they had all gone up the spout. Even his reading had been a waste of effort. None of it was

41

applicable. He needed a month in the country to become re-orientated. Better still, a month back in his small flat among beautifully forgettable things: the electric kettle which suffered from asthma on cold winter mornings, his wood-wormed work-table, books, gladioli or daffodils bought off a barrow-boy and plonked in milk bottles on his window ledge—a luxury when he was in funds after selling an article—and the girl through the wall practising Litolff's *Scherzo* or de Falla's *Nights in the Gardens of Spain* in a hope of getting a concert, poor wench, exercising her cold fingers before breakfast on a fog-bound November morning of drip and shiver: oh blessed peace and honey for tea. He even felt nostalgic about the Albert Memorial and draughty corridors in the Albert Hall.

'Do you feel ill?' asked an angry female voice.

He blinked his eyes open. She was Indian. No, half Indian though her crimson and gold sari and a lot of stuff on her eye-lids did their best to persuade people she was pure Indian. She had a dotty nose, large eyes which were glaring at him, and long tight lips. She might be quite pretty if she smiled.

'Good evening,' he said. 'Thank you. I am all right.'

Her eyes glowered at him.

'You don't look well. Are you here alone?'

'I came with a friend who has gone.'

'Well?' she snapped. 'Who is he?'

'Oh. Mr. Kendal.'

'He had no right to leave you here.'

'He had another engagement.'

'He ought to have cancelled it.'

'I did not expect him to cancel it.'

'Then he ought to have taken you back to the hotel. You live at the Hsinshih. Your name is Butler. I am Sheila Grant. I live there.'

Her gaze fidgeted over him as she spoke. Her voice was just too light to be called acid. She spoke rapidly, getting rid of every sentence as if she loathed each individual word.

'You are kind to have been concerned, Mrs. Grant.'

'Miss,' she hissed.

'I'm sorry.'

She wheeled quickly into the crush. He raised his brows. Quicksilver. One of those women who hungered for an occasion to show bad temper in a belief that it gave proof of individuality. Her voice could probably get as shrill as an old bus brake on a hill. Nonetheless, it was pretty decent of her to show concern. How did Luis de Gongora put it: Leave hardness to stones, heeding that occasionally, despite their strength, they obey the chisel—*Deja a las piedras lo firme* . . . The rest of it had slipped his memory.

'Have you got a car?' asked her irritable voice beside him.

'No, Miss Grant.'

'You can come to the hotel in mine. I'm going to the Egyptian Embassy.'

She set off across the room at a furious pace. He followed her in more confusion than ever. He had no clear idea why he was following her except for something to do.

When they were in the car, he said: 'I was just going to the Egyptian place myself. I'll come along with you.'

Clive Dixon took a couple of healthy young drinks over to where Ilse Han stood alone. Alone but not unheeded. Her husband was chatting nearby, content to admire her statuesque stillness from a distance, unable to prevent a gloat in his eyes. Clive had met men like Han in every country. They were pretty obvious. Her eyes gave as much heed of his approach as frozen pools gave of a passing cloud.

'*Guten abend, gnädige Frau.*'

'Good evening, Mr. Dixon.'

'Isn't this a merry scene of celebration?'

'Yes.'

'Has Steven Kendal gone?'

'Yes.'

He held out a glass. 'Do you want a drink?'

'I do not now drink alcohol.'

'Never?'

Ilse widened the corners of her eyes. It was a cute trick. Like one of those statues suddenly afflicted by life, taking an aghast first peek at what they'd got themselves into. Poor little statues. He felt friendly to her.

'I was afraid you wouldn't,' he said. 'Can you hold one for me? I don't want Comrade Whoever to catch on that I'm robbing his cellar. He might think it was anti-something or other. Besides, I would dearly like to drink a drink warmed by your lovely hand.'

A glint like winter sunlight drifted across her eyes as she took a glass from him.

'I think you are a little drunk.'

'Doesn't that sound repellent?' he asked. 'A big drunk or nothing. May I congratulate you on your beauty? Now, what shall we talk about? Something deeply human. Like Kirschwasser. There is a real drink. You know? One year I had a drinking holiday in the Black Forest. I put on my velvet knickers and those bright braces and scampered out to hunt bottles. A friend and I went to Freiburg for the May festival. We had a wonderful—*Feuertag*?'

'*Nein. Feiertag.*'

'Thank you. Holiday—*Feiertag*. I'll remember. We had Kirschwasser. Kummel too. Schnapps. Cognac for breakfast.'

'Did you like the Black Forest?' she asked. 'I went there once.'

After some moments she raised the glass in her hand and swallowed half of the drink at a gulp.

Three

CROWDS of people milled about outside when Jane Crofton and Steven Kendal left the Muslim restaurant. They swarmed along to admire decorations, glowing lanterns like huge *hsiang-shan*, red melons, and chains of electric lights strung among triumphal arches where scarlet flags framed enormous photographs of communist rulers. They talked cheerfully, laughed, joked, ignored a sharp Gobi air, took simple pride in what they saw. A fuss of searchlights fanned the stars. Peking had never seen such a spectacle as that whose excitements had filled every hour of this unforgettable day. The thoughts of these people were easy to discern: China was shaking the world on her march to victory, the coolies would inherit the earth. Steven heard pride din on a thousand passing tongues.

'Shall we walk to my hotel?' he asked. 'It isn't far.'

'Why, yes,' said Jane and heard nervousness in her voice. 'Are we going there? It's getting late.'

'I'd better put you in the picture or you'll go off unprepared for some things. You won't get a chance to sleep for hours while this hubbub is going on. As a special treat, I can give you a cup of English-style tea in my room, genuine Tunbridge Wells or Wapping, whichever you prefer.'

'Can you?'

'Certainly. A cup of maligned English tea was a luxury I missed. Oh for the careless rapture of being able to go into one of Uncle Joey's caffs and hear a voice breathe "H'yar, ducks, sorry I slopped it in yer saucer." Bliss! I used to go to one at the bottom of Farringdon Street, near Ludgate Circus. Very dark and nineteen hundred. I loved listening to slow trains to Holborn clanking over the railway bridge.'

She laughed uneasily. This is it, she told herself in panic. Her brain refused to think of how she could escape. Even her feet betrayed her, kept her close to him for fear of getting lost in these crowds, hurried her on to the moment she had foreseen as she looked at him on the sunlit stand. Whatever had possessed her? Why had she encouraged him to play a game of sensual appraisal, let him imagine it gave her pleasure?

He said something which helped her to laugh but she heard its falsity. Her thoughts were chaotic. As they walked, she wished she could tell what he would do. How could it matter? Yet she did not doubt his kindness. That was an odd word now. Was it? Since they completed his round of calls he seemed younger, aided by the ability men had for forgetting their daily selves and what they learned of the futility of life. They were lucky. Only one woman in a thousand shared their talent for becoming selfless, ageless, classless, shorn of anxiety, able to dabble their fingers in the fresh exhilarations of endless private dawns.

She looked round. On every side the chattering crowds streamed under the gaudy decorations. Against her will she felt her dread of these people bind her to him.

As he led her across an intersection in front of laden trams and Russian cars, she saw how street lights threw her shadow forward beside his until they dissolved together. He said something which gave her an excuse to glance sideways to smile at him. His face was quiet. Sure too. He had cause to be sure of her. What impulse prompted her to let him assume she felt involved with him? Did she? Had it been more than her horror at seeing those millions of marching women turned into ants to serve Almighty Slogans? Had she acted in response to an instinct stronger than reason? Was it even new for her to need to draw strength from a living man? Perhaps, once. Now she seldom felt anything clearly, never for long. Everything drifted past like those clouds which rolled around a plane. Herself in the centre, going somewhere. She wasn't sure where.

'How can you endure such ghastly isolation?' she asked. 'It must drive you absolutely frantic.'

She listened in horror to her voice clattering clichés like a talking doll.

'Most often we're too busy to notice it.'

'Thank goodness.'

She felt cold and awkward. Instinct told her that he was thinking about his former wife. Some men never forgot even bitches like Gillian. He ought to have forgotten her here. That was the difference between them. Whenever she saw a Chinese she remembered how Chinese soldiers tortured and killed Alan in Korea eight years ago. Alan Crofton. Captain. Another British soldier, close to middleage when they murdered him, his youth gone while he did his duty in Hitler's war. Fortunately

46

for Alan the Chinese murdered him three weeks and three days before a hit-and-run driver left his daughter Ann lying on a Gloucestershire road scented by honeysuckle and hay, her four-year-old body paralysed from the waist, her nervous system affected by complications which would remain. Alan had been spared that.

Jane shivered. Eight years ago. Other people in another age, ignorant of what was around the corner of their next year. Nothing of that age existed now, its shadows gone from the pageant of life. This was reality: her feet hastening her on beside a thoughtful man in another foreign city under a shine of retreated stars. These people around them, whose voices were like a beat of rooks' wings rising from trees at nightfall, drove her thoughts back. But this moment would go too, blown like a grain of sand.

In reply to a question asked by the section of her mind poised on the woman whose body was hers and this man who might seek it, she heard him say: 'Oh, read, listen to the radio, watch television. They show vintage Russian films. We had a real oldie not long ago. *Turksib*. We're expecting *Arsenal, Mother, The End of St. Petersburg*, and *Battleship Potemkin* directly they're disinterred.'

'How long are their programmes?'

'Three hours a day at present.'

'Do you meet Chinese people apart from work?'

'Fraternization? Here? My dear girl!'

They walked round people halted to crane their heads back to peer at photographs on a triumphal wall. She thought the younger children looked extremely tired. They squatted on the ground, their faces drained of animation. Their small eyes blinked at her. Another row of overhead lights threw her shadow alongside his. She felt this night fold down on her. She smelled its coldness, heard its babble of strange voices, saw its unfamiliarity. Reality now.

She was stricken by guilt. Poor Steven. How could it matter if he did make love to her? She had no right to pretend she was a nervous Victorian girl on the threshold of enchantment or calamity. It might do them good to use their bodies to break free from ordinary hours, like a dose of medicine.

They crossed a street where there was scarcely anyone in sight. In the distance a fountain of sparkling golden rain sprayed the sky. Blue and magenta lights brushed the darkness like a sway of peacock feathers.

'At the hotel.' Steven spoke in a quieter, quick tone. 'Talk casually. Don't say anything leading until I've put on the radio. Keep your voice at about its level. Every hotel has plenty of microphones at present.'

'Even in private rooms?'

'Especially the private ones. They reckon we may get careless while we have friends and vocational neighbours around us.'

Several people stood in the large bleak lobby as they went into the hotel. Most of them were Chinese. As he led her to the lift, she was conscious of their bright almond eyes appraising her. She talked fluently and readily. It gave her a sense of satisfaction to protect him from the Chinese. When the lift stopped he led them down a long corridor shaped like a reversed L.

'Here we are,' he said as he shut the outer door. 'Make yourself at home.'

'Do you always leave your door unlocked?'

'Always. Let me take your coat. Always. Hotel staffs here are the most trustworthy in the world.'

'That's unique.'

'Isn't it? If you want to freshen up, you'll find the bathroom beyond the bedroom over there. I'll put on the kettle.'

She laid her hand on his arm impulsively, smiled, and turned away into his bedroom. Her confidence increased. A day-long fear of having rushed them into a miserable predicament began to fade from her mind. It would be all right. She took a tissue from her handbag to wipe off her lipstick.

Noise from crowds walking about below reached Clive while he undressed. He hoped they would soon go home. They had no right to deprive a man of his sleep. Tonight he did feel tired. At present his mind was amiable, heedless of alarms which usually sent it jittering in pursuit of trouble like a pack of hounds in full cry, blissful as a film star being chased by her very newest husband over their half-acre second best bedroom and its six-inch deep carpet of oil shares, and may the best lawyer win next month. It would be just his luck if people kept him awake tonight. On other nights he did not get a wink because a terrifying stillness kept him awake like the solitary survivor on another planet which had given its all to progress and politicians. And the best of interstellar luck to him out there.

He took off his vest and scratched his chest. His ribs were even more noticeable this week. That was a sign of more than good health. There were few sadder sights than a man wrapped up in flesh and whose stomach was pendulous to his fat-encased knees. Such an apparition would Dixon never be. He was a fine physical embodiment of undernourishment, able to swing through the trees if his breath held out. He scratched his navel, poor innocent site of human chain reaction. He belched.

At one moment he had an urge for another drink. He decided to be brave. One glass of Chinese hilarity now might wake him up.

He sat down on his bed to inspect a pile of socks for holes. One thing he never let hotel servants do was to get someone to darn his socks. They always messed it up and gave him whopping blisters on his heels. It was dangerous to be face to face with a politician yattering on as if he was an archangel or God or Nogod, first in line for the job on His retirement, while a blistered heel prevented you from sustaining the archangel by the obsequiousness to which he believed he was accustomed. Besides, he had found it a solace to stitch, up and down, across and back. He had become a dab needle. Somehow he must have acquired the knack from his mother. She had been a misfit as a woman but her needlework was a miracle of beauty.

While he inspected his socks he thought it had been quite a good evening. Far better than he expected. It even contained a surprise. The German girl could be almost talkative. Those icy eyes weren't likely to cheer up a morning pillow, the fifteen minutes when every man and woman needed to look their best. He would not be surprised if Han wore snow boots at home. She probably led him a cold dance round the family kayak.

He yawned and scratched his head.

3

Hu heard the radio in the room of Kendal *hsien-sheng* as he walked up from the floor below. It was tuned to a programme of music. He could hear it clearly. Unusual. He did not recall hearing ordinary Chinese music from the room for several weeks. Most often the Englishman watched television.

At the head of the stairs Hu paused to get his breath. He was a small thin man in a dark blue hotel uniform, his narrow face hanging slightly on his neck, his withered left shoulder bent forward, his left hand held loosely against his stomach. Hardly anyone was in their rooms. Most people who lived in the Hsinshih were visiting embassies, having dinner, or had taken their wives to watch the fireworks. His quick ears could hear only one radio.

His soft-soled shoes were noiseless as he padded quickly to the end flat. Outside he stopped, his closed right hand raised above his shoulder in case a resident came into the corridor behind him and would think he was knocking to see if the flat was occupied. The Englishman was talking too quietly for his voice to rise above the *yin-yo*. Then a woman spoke.

Hu was astonished. At no time had he ever discovered

evidence of a woman having been there. He had told them the Englishman did not like women.

He glanced over his shoulder to be sure the corridor was empty and then leaned closer to the door. He kept his hand raised. She spoke too quietly for him to tell what sort of *man-tze* woman she was. She was certain to be a barbarian, but her voice did not remind him of those from South America who dwelt on this floor. They chattered like cuckoos in springtime, screeching louder at night than at daybreak. Her voice was too slow. It sounded like a light voice. He was not sure. Ai, when a woman got into a man's room she kept changing her voice, honey, stone, rippling water, sunshine, iron, earth, quicker than a cat flicked its tail, according to what her mood told her that she wanted from him. He could not hear a single word clearly.

He turned round, alarmed at being defeated. He would have to report her. What could he say? The police got angry if reports gave no details. They replaced men who did not supply full reports. Three moons ago Ma Teh-hai had been sent to Mongolia, and no one had heard what happened to Kung Shai-ch'i since he was dismissed. He did not want to leave Peking. He had lived here all his life except for those three years in Hongkong and now a woman threatened to disgrace him. A *man-tze* woman. He would have to invent details about her. He had done it before. Everyone invented stories to help the secret police.

He pattered along the corridor at a dog-trot to the lift. Only two voices reached him from beyond closed doors. Tang was alone in the lift when it rose in response to his code ring of urgency. He went into it at a run.

'Take me to the basement,' he ordered.

Tang shut the gate without a sign of having heard. People called him 'Tang the Mute' on account of his habit of going for days without uttering a word even in answer to questions, his eyes vacant as if he did not see people who spoke to him. He was a short stocky man in a shiny blue uniform which fitted tightly over his shoulders and belly and heavy buttocks. His wrinkleless moon face gave an appearance of being balanced on the collar of his tunic like a balloon still being blown up. His broad lips, wide-nostrilled short nose, and straight brows, cast hardly any shadows. His thick hair, sleek as sealskin, did not show a single white hair. He looked thirtyfive and was fiftyone. In contrast with his impassive bearing, the nails of his hand were bitten down to their quicks.

People said that Tang the Mute had never recovered from seeing his mother and two young sisters raped by Japanese soldiers at his home in Tsingtao. He was a young man then. He saw the Japanese kill his father, unbutton the flies of their trousers and fall on his screaming womenfolk, their naked bodies held down by Japanese eager to take their turn. That was when he lost his left arm. While he struggled to free himself a Japanese bayonet nearly severed it at the elbow. Men told how, despite loss of blood and pain, he had escaped that night while the Japanese ate. One of his friends hid him for days and an American doctor attended to his injuries. Tang the Mute evaded a search for him by the *kempei tai*, the Japanese secret military police, and was smuggled out of Tsingtao in a lorry laden with rice to relieve famine in Ichow. Those to whom he had talked in one of his rare moods of conversation related how he worked as a saboteur in Shanghai, Hangchow, Tsinkiang, Swatow, and Canton, and organized cells of resistance fighters, until he escaped to Chungking. Tang never told what happened to his womenfolk or to two small brothers who witnessed their pollution. At the revolution he was one of those released from the gaol at Whampoa where the Nationalists had imprisoned them. He never discussed his experiences there. He was womanless and sometimes for weeks his eyes were cloudy as a river gorge in a winter dawn.

Hu disliked Tang the Mute. Silent men upset his method of work. Hu liked to ferret into the minds of other men, learn their nature, pin their weaknesses in his memory in case he fell into disgrace, and needed to redeem himself by informing against them. Tang the Mute had paid no attention to his efforts to be friendly. His impassive silence infuriated Hu.

As the lift descended, he ignored Hu. His eyes stared blankly ahead. Hu fretted irritably. He did not want to speak to Tang yet he ought to find out what he knew about the woman in the Englishman's rooms. Why did this dumb fool have to anger a man?

He acted quickly.

'Did you see the Englishman Kendal come in?'

'He came in nearly an hour ago.'

'He brought a woman.'

'I saw her,' said Tang.

'A *man-tze* woman.'

'She was not one of the barbarian women who live here.'

Hu clenched his fists. Rage trembled in him. This lunatic intended to thwart him. He would drop hints that Tang was guilty of noncooperation in the national safety. They executed men for it.

'She is a woman from England,' said Tang. 'She talked in their language without him having to speak. The men from England like it if they are busy in their heads. She is tall, strong, big in the way they like, and her hair is dark. She is not young and is married. I think she is a reporter.'

'Is she his wife?'

'She wanted him to like her.'

'So. What did they talk about?'

Tang stopped the lift. 'The lands of the Arabs.'

'The Arabs?'

'No, their lands. I have given a report.'

Hu seethed. This man intended to ruin him. He felt a trickle of cold sweat run down his thin chest and was afraid of what they might do if he did not tell them more about the woman than Tang had done.

He sniffed. '*Hao. Tsai chien.*'

Tang stood in the lift doorway as Hu hurried off to the room of ears. For a moment his eyes lost blankness. The expression of knives came into them. Tang hated many people, none more than Hu, though for no reason except that Hu was an informer. What people here did not know about Tang was that, too late, he had realized what the Party intended to do, and had fought for the Nationalists, fought and dynamited for them, until it was hopeless and the Party was triumphant. Hu, the room-boy informer, under *kwantchee*, epitomized how the Party got power. He licked his lips. Then he used the stump of his arm to shove the lift gate shut, and pressed the button.

Hu opened the door of the room of ears. It was hot and airless. Four men were on duty. Two had single phone receivers clamped on their heads; a third was tape-recording a conversation in a private room: the fourth read an English edition of *Oliver Twist*. Their ages ranged from sixty to under thirty but they had two things in common. Each was conversant with at least one European language and each was handicapped. Chien had lost his right leg at Amoy; Wei and P'eng were without an arm; Li had been severely wounded during the Japanese War. None could undertake hard work.

They turned their heads from the large board on one wall which showed lights glowing in rooms where microphones were live. Hu wiped his eyes with a dirty finger.

'The Englishman Kendal has a woman,' he reported importantly.

'We have been trying to hear them,' said P'eng in a voice shrill with rage. 'You placed the microphone badly. We cannot hear.'

'I will change it tomorrow.'

'What good is that? What will they say when I confess we did not hear?'

Li giggled. 'The Eurasian scum is telling the Englishman Butler how cruelly the *kee king kwai* treat half-castes.'

They laughed at his description of Indians as 'clanking devils'. Hu tittered and waited for another angry outburst from P'eng.

4

On a floor overhead Han lay in bed watching Ilse undress. He relaxed in a sense of profound wellbeing. This hour invariably gave him satisfaction. Tonight it contained an unusual edge of pleasure. Her neglect of wifely duty amused him. Her refusal to humour him, her tricks to keep her back to him now, even a German nightclub tune she hummed to herself, pleased him. *Ai hao*, they were truly mated despite her skin. What other woman would deny her dependence on him?

'Did you enjoy your conversation with Mr. Kendal?' he asked.

'He is interesting,' she answered in German.

'We will speak English. You will practise it every day while I am in Chungking. It comes in damned handy. Is he fascinating to women?'

'No.'

'Would European women regard him as a goodlooking fellow?'

'No.'

He did not trust her denials. All women lied to save men they fancied as lovers. He had seen her and Kendal talk on other occasions, pretending they did so out of politeness though they seldom spoke to the South Americans and showed no interest in each other. They wanted people to laugh at him. It was a sport for those who wanted to be lovers. He did not think they were lovers already, but his absences gave them opportunities to intrigue against him. He was more skilful than they. He swallowed. A spurt of rage like electricity burned in his brain.

'You fill me with astonishment. I imagined he was a terrific hit with the weaker sex. Why has he no fascination?'

'No one can tell what he thinks.'

She knelt at the chest-of-drawers to search for a nightgown.

Han swallowed. You think you do, he told her silently. He looked at the yellow light shining on her shining yellow hair. It was like gold, a smooth cap on a statue in a shrine. He stared at her long back, curved forward from her hips. She was still wearing her slip, intending to take it off after she put on her nightgown, to prevent him from seeing her naked. He smiled.

'It must be annoying, old girl. Women like to think they are mysterious. Eh?'

'You have more experience of what they think than I have.'

Stupid woman. By now she should have learned how her taunts sharpened his anticipation of joy in teaching her that she belonged to him. European women were stupid. They expected to be treated as important individuals even in their homes. Here only those who were senior Party officials were more important than their husbands. Instinct ought to have warned her of his pride in her defiance. It quickened his desire for her.

She shut the drawer and stood up holding the nightdress she had chosen.

He nearly laughed aloud. It was one she put on to show her displeasure or to keep him at bay, a plain shapeless garment longer than a *p'ao* and covered her from neck to feet in bright pale blue silk which made her arms appear as cold as marble. On their return from Germany she had brought several of the same colour. This was the last one she had left. They did not do what she intended. It gave him satisfaction to have a *nei-jan* who owned many nightgowns. They were another proof of his rise to importance. Millions of Chinese women did not have one, slept naked or in their day clothes, smelling of honourable sweat and dirt. Only women who belonged to successful men wasted money on nightdresses.

She shook it out of its creases. Her arms were bigger than those of Chinese women whose ancestors had gone hungry for generations, kept alive by a daily bowl of rice except during seasonal floods by rivers which destroyed the *padis*. But they were shapely, once a man got used to seeing a woman whose limbs were big as those of a Chinese wrestler, and their white flesh was firm. Her legs had shape too but their flesh was soft. He swallowed. Ai, one day soon she must learn to be a good wife, a true *pao chuan*, precious wife, and other men would forget her skin.

He did not speak until she let down the straps of her slip, keeping it on her body by pressure of her upper arms on her sides.

'You will not put it on.'

She glanced over her shoulder at him.

'Tso-lin——'

'You heard my instruction, my dear.'

'I am tired.'

'From tomorrow you will be on your sweet ownsome for a couple of weeks to rest up, old girl.'

He spoke in a quiet voice, strong, masterful, impressing his authority on her.

She raised the straps resignedly. Then she threw the night-gown aside, casually, careful not to show dislike at having to obey him. She was magnificent, he thought as she started to brush her hair. It needed courage to risk his displeasure. His anger on one night had frightened him; successful men never permitted a woman to let them reveal anger.

After some moments she went to switch off the light. In a patient voice he told her to leave it on. She shrugged her shoulders and turned her back to take off her slip and sat down on the bed to provide another delay by massaging her toes slowly.

He smiled and reached out. She pretended not to feel his touch. Her flesh was warm beneath his fingers. He let his hand search over its smooth yielding wealth, part of the richness a man hungered to enjoy when not-knowing tormented the heaviest moons of his youth and only the farthest stars fenced in his turmoil of hope. In this light her skin had a golden tinge, deepest on her shoulders and the sweep of her hips. Her false meekness mocked him. Whatever she felt, repugnance, hatred, misery, self-condemnation for allowing sensuality to induce her to marry him, she was careful not to betray it now. Instinct counselled her to accept the truth of being a woman where she most depended on his sympathy. It infuriated him. He dragged her back alongside him, held her down as she tried to turn away, and flung himself along her. His voice was thick in his throat.

'Kendal will never be your lover. I own you.'

His taunts gained no response. He did not expect one; here only he gave orders. She lay resistless, eyes shut, her limp arms an acceptance of subjection. His hands raked over her white body to impress his right of possession on her.

In spite of her goads directly they left this home which millions of fine good loyal Chinese women would give half their lives to have, no matter how she behaved among Europeans, whatever she wanted from Kendal or he from her, even if they met beside a lake to talk as lovers unable to be alone, however his countrymen in Ministry offices criticized or pitied him for what they regarded as an unnatural lust, although she did not help his career: despite her enmity, he ruled here.

He hated her empty face which sought to deny his right to rule her mind. Its cold foreign pride did not do what she intended. It transformed them into symbols, her submission a proof of how her peoples must accept domination by his race in his lifetime. One day she would seek strength from being one of the first European women to heed the wind rising in the east. His hands revelled on her. He saw muscles in her neck swell as she stifled a moan.

He stared down at her blank face and straining neck. Even in aversion she was undermined by nature, a prey of impulse and memory. So was he. So was he. *Chung huang lien te huang lien*—sow a bitter plant, reap a bitter plant. It was truly said. He mastered weakness just in time. This was not the night to let her body triumph by humbling his strength or to believe she was able to conquer by mock surrender of her flesh to his manhood. He grasped her clenched fingers and spread them open. A cry scraped in her throat. He smiled; she understood. Her hand fought to free itself. It did not succeed. He compelled it to gather knowledge of his male power to deny her at his will however great her need.

'Never pretend it is him. It is me. It will always be me.'

In the silence his voice rang sharply. She cringed, squirmed under him, trembling as he palpated her.

'Do you hear? It is no use pretending it is him. It is me.'

5

Steven put his tea-cup down in his saucer. A recording of speeches on the radio covered his voice. He stretched his arms.

'That's about it,' he concluded. 'It's another case of prevention being better than cure. The absolutely essential point is not to drink water unless you've seen it boiled. It's like Middle East *ab*, fully of swimming things. Oh yes, and always get permission to take photographs and give your guide the spool to develop. If you keep a diary, leave your thoughts out of it. You may leave it around.'

Jane nodded. She sat on the settee, a cushion between her back and the wall, legs tucked under her. For the last half-hour no fireworks had dropped beyond the uncurtained window. She felt at ease, yet cheated and ridiculous.

It had not been what she expected. She had come here unsure of herself, expecting to temporize, enjoin, relent, indulge, finally to concede, seeing herself behave as she did in imagination during hours of loneliness until she took hold of her mind. His avoidance of a glance or gesture likely to lessen her confidence exasperated her though she was grateful for his consideration.

She often caught herself noting how the light planed angles of his face, his untidy grey hair, its greyness still a shock as it had been when she got off the plane, how he moved, how his eyes were younger here than under Arab suns. More than once she noted how he bent forward and let his hands hang loose between his thighs. Her symptoms were too pronounced to be mistaken. She wanted a love affair, however useless, just to feel herself fresh and quickened by a belief that a man needed her to crowd his hours, share endeavour, dispute, even at second-hand or for less than a month. Instead of being alone. In exchange for so much sex was a trivial payment.

'You make it sound worse than anything we've experienced.'

'It was bound to be worse,' he said. 'We shouldn't lose sight of the forest of Chinese history by examining its individual trees. The glory of China died centuries ago. The seven centuries which have passed since Marco Polo left his record are remembered for cultural accomplishments. They left no spiritual, social, parliamentary, scientific, or industrial accomplishments of value, only glazed pots and golden roofs. Chinese rulers were corrupt, tyrannical, and effete. Their courts were as useful as a funfair beside farmland falling into uselessness through neglect. Where the court had influence, China was a gentle anarchy. Outside it, the entire country was battered by warlords raging about, up and down, like waves in a winter sea. The people endured a big squeeze for centuries. We played no part in that.'

'Not a pleasant record.'

'No. It left them chaotic, outwardly servile. Yet they kept their fantastic racial pride. That is, it's fantastic to me. I can't whip up enough energy to be racial or proud.'

'Are they suspicious and secretive?'

'They have been for centuries. They are the most arrogant people in the world. Their early imperialism proved it. They showed no mercy then to the Tibetans, the Burmese, the Malays, or the Ceylonese. It didn't do their pride a bit of good when Western countries hove into sight bringing industrialism, a better life, an evolving social morality, impartial justice. And, unfortunately, opium. They hold our good points and our bad ones against us. There's a question they never answer directly.'

'What is it?'

'Why do they introduce industrialization by harsher restrictions on liberty than we used at the outset of the Industrial Revolution nearly two hundred years ago, instead of planning for a larger life of personal freedom? Their methods of organization are primitive.'

'Will I be able to talk to ordinary Chinese in their homes?'

'You'll talk to some in show-case communes through guides.'

'Unsatisfactory. What about their revolutions?'

'Well, you know empires always collapse from internal weakness, inability to maintain an organic society. China was stagnant for centuries. The Kuomintang Revolution got rid of the Manchus. The communist revolution was a coup staged when a weak government, with a quantity of corrupt men dissipating its authority, was too disorganized from fighting Japan for twenty years to produce strong economic policies.'

She folded her hands together. They were cold, the skin dry to her own touch. She wished they were smooth and soft, warm, instinct with the urgency of youth to be strong or weak or clinging.

'What we saw this morning frightened me, Steven. And soon they'll have nuclear weapons and rockets.'

He nodded. 'Yes, the Russians will have to capitulate. China is riding a tiger. The most stupid thing said about this China was its description as "the newest America" by a character in Han Suyin's novel *And the Rain My Drink*.'

As he talked, she averted her tell-tale eyes. This provided part of the companionship she craved for but only part. And it was transitory. Hours dissolving like fine ash. Fading quicker than leaden hours of loneliness. She heard no sound from anywhere outside their immediate surroundings. She was suddenly overwhelmingly conscious of being inadequate to her need to give him cause to want her to return.

She asked: 'What do you miss most here?'

'You've probably guessed. A glass of water straight from the tap.'

'And then?'

He stared at her. 'Oh, the sort of music I like if I'm in a mood for it. There's some lovely Czech-sort of symphonic music being composed in South America. I wonder if British orchestras have heard it. Does this make me sound like an intellectual townsman? I hope not. Such a sad description. Like a highly-strung goldfish wearing a bowler hat.'

'Nothing else?'

'Oh yes. Some peculiarly English-style, "footprints in the dew; and oaks; and brown horse-chestnuts, glossy-new; and new-peeled sticks; and shining pools on grass"—was that how Brooke put it? English-style.' He laughed. 'A couple of weeks ago I had a nostalgia for fish-and-chips wrapped in a tabloid. Why do they always wrap fish-and-chips in photos of chorus legs and Italian bosoms? Do they think vinegar and hot fat smears will prevent lecherous fancies?' He stopped. 'You're letting me talk too much.'

'I'm no good at conversation.'

'Nonsense, you listen beautifully. Much more difficult.'

Sometimes she caught him watching her. At others she sensed his gaze moving over her. His eyes did not tell her if he liked seeing her here. Yet once, only once, she did half imagine they held the speculation she had seen clearly hours ago. She might have been mistaken. It would not surprise her. Since the evening started she had been unable to act naturally. Now she was restlessly conscious of this silence enfolding them, unifying, the outer darkness palpitant in a thin moonglow. Lovers' meeting? She couldn't tell. Ah God, I'm just another dull randy woman unable to do anything about it, she condemned herself. In a few years I shall fidget too and pretend I'm disgusted by what younger women do and envy them like hell.

She felt her face twitch in a mechanical smile at something he said.

The time went too quickly. At length she could not ignore it any longer. She looked at her watch and saw it was nearly half-past twelve. She uncoiled her legs and stood up.

'I must go,' she said.

'The night is still in its cradle.'

'If I don't join it I'll miss that damned train in the morning.'

'You'll catch it.'

She shook her head.

'I must.'

'Well, if you're determined I'll walk you home,' he grumbled and got up. 'You'll have to wait a moment for me. I'm not used to drinking so much tea.'

She smiled, irritated by his ability to make it easy. The silence in the room after he left her held mockery. Its quietness jeered at her failure. She stood beside the table and looked round. Her lips tightened. She went swiftly across to the light-switch.

When he came back she had hung her overcoat from her shoulders and stood at the window. In the distance moonlight glistened on curved golden roofs of the Forbidden City. The bright ceiling light was off; she had left on a lamp on a ledge above his books. She was appalled by her clumsiness. It was worse; it was obvious prideless, quixotic, but she didn't mind. Her clasped hands were icy.

'Aren't they exquisite?' he said in a cheerful, unchanged voice. 'You'll be able to recognize them better through the glasses.'

He fetched them. As she trained the binoculars on the shining roofs, he identified them for her. She saw sprays of black leaves toss in a ground wind. Though starlight robbed space of its arid chill the scene was inscrutable, remote from herself.

'Is that Coal Hill?' she asked in a soft voice.

'Yes. Ugly name. It reminds me of slag heaps.'

'Has it a nicer name?'

'It has several. None fit. The most common is Prospect Hill. I prefer one Chinese name *Ta nei chih chen shen*, the Protective Hill of the Great Within. It protected the Emperor's household, the Great Within, from evil spirits blown by the north winds. Actually, it was soil cleared to make the lakes and dumped there to cut down winter winds which gave one emperor's family continuous chest complaints.'

She put down the binoculars and turned suddenly, coming against him as she intended. Her coat fell from her shoulders. She chattered frothy words to feign surprise. You damned hypocrite, she told herself. She scarcely heeded his answer, obsessed by their nearness, and suddenly, wearily, she leant against him, ashamed of hypocrisy, wanting to be held and delighted as his hands clasped her shoulders. He went on talking about Peking. That maintained her silly dignity.

She was happy and miserable. His touch seemed to brush layers of loneliness off her, to enrich the pores of her skin. She wanted much more, longed to be treated brutally, handled like a wanton, stripped of loneliness and nervousness, yet dreaded revealing her need. Her hands betrayed her, a heady intoxication in his male warmth and smell, bringing weakness into her loins. If only she wasn't an Englishwoman. She thought miserably that old age must be a blessing.

'How—are things?' he asked and she knew the question referred to Ann, motionless, vacant, while other children ran in swift pursuit of their urgent special fascinations. Healthy. Sure of their feet. Strong. Communicative. Intelligent. Was it wrong to think Ann far away from her?

'The same. They're hopeful. There's nothing I can do.'

'No. I wanted to hear.'

'You didn't do wrong by asking.'

'Good.'

She twisted her face hard on his shoulder.

'Steven, I've enjoyed this evening.'

'So have I,' he said and talked about other things.

At length she raised her head.

'It must be half an hour since I started to go.'

He prevented her half-hearted effort to free herself. 'You don't have to. As you saw, the bed's a bit narrow, but it can be fixed. I don't think we'd haggle over terms though you'd have to remind me about them. Do I sound bloodless? I'm backward in my propositions.'.

'Are you propositioning me?'

'Didn't you know I intended to?'

She had a stupid longing to cry and laughed instead. I'm being obvious, she told herself; like an old man who sniffles in public directly someone reminds him how fine he was fifty or sixty years ago and he feels lost suns warm on him; like that. She didn't care. There was pride in being able to arouse desire and gentleness. They put a flame in her, rid her of kinship to those millions of anonymous ordered women who marched through the morning.

She looked up at his face. Her hands drew him hard against her.

'Of course I did,' she said, 'but I never thought you would.'

'I'm slow. Have I offended you?'

'No. But why now?'

64

'Well, this evening has been unique for me, and you have been remarkably patient, and, well, it struck me as one of my better ideas. I'm conceited. Of course, there are other reasons, but you might not want to hear them.'

For a moment her eyes blurred his head into shadows behind t. Was she really overwhelmed by loneliness only hours ago? Incredible. She was enormously grateful to him for not taking her for granted or to relieve his own boredom. How could he understand what it meant to her to be given the right to decide?

'I don't think it conceited,' she said. 'Terms would be hell. I'd break every one. No, we'd have each other properly. We'd hate hair-shirts, wouldn't we?'

'Wrong place to wear 'em. So?'

'No.'

He hesitated. 'Now in simple words.'

She undid his jacket to spread her hands on his back. Her fingers did not detect an ounce of surplus flesh on him.

'I want to, more than anything. It doesn't surprise me, it feels too inevitable, so I must have wanted to for a long time, and I did send you a cable I was coming, didn't I? I've never sent one before. But I want us to wait a little longer.'

'Ah, I see, getting rid of rules.'

'It isn't a rule. We need time. I do, lots of it, not this handful of hours with that blasted train getting nearer every minute. I'd hate to feel we were filling in a whistle-stop halt.'

'A point.'

'It's only three weeks. Then we'll have four days. We'll lock the door and keep everything out. Planes, trains, schedules, rush, politicians, the lot. Unless we allow them to interrupt us.'

'You're wheedling me.'

She laughed on a drawn breath. 'Do you think I want to?'

He tilted her face up and his thumbs stroked down her cheeks.

'No. But maybe you're right.'

She scorned the affectation of keeping her lips closed under his. There was no need for deceit. She hung onto him fiercely. A long deep tremor shook her. She was achingly alive for the first time in years, long empty years.

When he let her go a shadow hid her eyes. She wished he could see them. She wished many things.

'Shall we do the cups?' she asked.

'Hu or I will do them in the morning.'

They met no one in the street. The only car to pass was a Pobeda. It weaved an erratic path over the empty road.

Four

DIRECTLY the celebrations ended Peking underwent a change. Almost every hour members of official delegatiors clustered round their leader like polite sparrows alert for crumbs while he tossed anticipated farewell sentences in predictable tones at a microphone, then followed him into plane or train and were whisked off. Visitors left on tours. The ceremonial *pai-lou*, triumphal arches, and large red lanterns began to disappear. Voices in the streets became predominantly Chinese, speaking in the blurred gentle Peking intonation.

When Steven awoke in the mornings fewer traffic noises rose to his window. He lay in his warmth and heard distant liltily plaintive cries from noodle-sellers, pedlars who carried sesame cakes and basket-loads of vegetables hung from bamboo poles balanced on their shoulders. Within minutes they were overlaid by a whine of trams and buses, vanishing like a skirl of Cape Town fish-sellers' horns. Soon afterwards a racket of twentieth-century building noises started to hammer at the sky; one story round Peking told of a man who met a country cousin unexpectedly and, hearing where he was staying, said: 'That is the hotel they built yesterday—come with me, I'm going to buy trousers in the department store they put up this morning.' It was not far-fetched. There were new buildings everywhere.

He regained enjoyment of his walks. By noon he could see

copper workers and contrivers of artificial flowers having their lunch bowl of *jow*, soft-cooked rice, and tiny meat dumplings, in their open-fronted shops, no longer hidden by sightseers. Everywhere he detected signs of *ch'iu*, the autumn of North China. Overnight the brightest colours inside the red and ochre city walls were stacks of chrysanthemums whose brilliant scarlet, yellow, bronze, crimson, a gorgeous russet brown, defied a new blueness in the light. Layers of Gobi dust accumulated along *hutungs* whose surfaces had not been macadamized. Old men roasted chestnuts in older streets. One ancient who still wore a queue round his balding head fried skeins of dough for pedicab drivers who had transported bevies of pink-cheeked children to school. At dusk clouds of vociferous crows settled in temple groves of the West City.

Those were sights he appreciated. They were China. He disliked the featureless new buildings being rushed up.

2

One evening Steven went to see Roger Laurent start his homeward journey on the Peking-Canton Express. People crowded the ornate station. They shoved, exclaimed, clutched babies, and stared at official instruction placards. Whoever had disinfected the trains was evidently engaged on a crusade for hygiene. Even the potted aspidistras in sleeping compartments appeared to wilt in so much healthy ozone.

'Come and stay with Annette and me for a holiday soon,' said Roger. 'She was saying it is two years now since you visited us.'

'What a memory!'

'She also forgets people she dislikes. When will you come?'

'If nothing happens, how about the spring?'

'Nothing will happen. We will creep on along the rim of the cauldron smelling the new ingredients.'

'The spring then.'

'If Madame Crofton is near, she also might come.'

'She'll probably be somewhere else.'

'Asia is perhaps too gentle for her. Outwardly, you comprehend. I do not think she seeks gentleness. It is too remote.'

'Yes?'

'She has not retired from being a woman. Men are strange creatures. They long to retire and potter about in boredom. Women are more logical. They never retreat from their personal drama.'

'Wise of them,' commented Steven.

3

Within a few days life resumed its familiar pattern. Steven attended abruptly summoned news conferences said to be called to hear important Government announcements. They usually produced another flurry of statistics of output which, according to his experience, were likely to be lowered later on. He took his journalistic ears to embassies. He wrote routine stories.

The only unexpected event was an instruction from London for him to supply profile stories on other cities. The cable named Shanghai, Canton, Chungking, and left others to his discretion.

He scratched his neck over it. London had evidently not heard that the blooming of 'the hundred flowers' of toleration was over. He foresaw endless complications, efforts to encourage him to concoct articles from NCNA material on spike. The officials had no chance of the latter: he was not a satellite newsman, content to get a high polish on his backside. Foreign Ministry officials were noticeably coy about aiding foreign newspapermen who wanted to visit distant cities for a second or third occasion, able to use their eyes and ears more purposefully. He had done two trips to Shanghai, three to Canton. London didn't care about complications. He guessed this idea had been dreamed up in the Press Club.

Early the next afternoon he walked past the khaki-clad

military guard outside the gloomy grey Foreign Ministry and went for an appointment with Mrs. Peng. She received him in a room which had a chandelier, rosewood tables, leather armchairs, and the inevitable cups of green tea dictated by etiquette.

Mrs. Peng was a small rotund woman of about forty. She was an official of the Information Department. Sometimes she wore a dark brown coat and skirt. This afternoon she preferred a blue boiler suit. She had taut lips, forgotten hair, and eyes which gleamed like wet coals behind steel-rimmed glasses. She spoke fluent English flavoured by Americanisms acquired from living in the United States for thirty years. She was flanked by two women secretaries, homely souls, interested in their hands. Before and after an interview Mrs. Peng bowed to a portrait of Mao Tse-tung, the leader, as if she saw an altar beneath it. A lot of people went in fear of her anger. No one had seen Mr. Peng. Rumour said he had got himself sent to Mongolia.

She sipped tea while Steven explained about the cable. He gave it to her to read and embarked on arguments to forestall a suggestion to read agency copy. She nodded patiently. He shunned charm; she would interpret it as a capitalist manœuvre. So would her secretaries. He was never sure if she trained them or they spied on her.

Finally she treated him to a gold-toothed smile. 'I'll surely do whatever I can, Squadron-Leader. I guess you've realized we've lots to do right now.'

'So much organization,' he said. He never understood why she addressed him by his wartime rank, whether to acknowledge that he had fought the Nazis or prove she kept abreast of things or to establish him as a trained military opponent. No one else had addressed him by the rank for at least fifteen years.

She nodded.

'I'll certainly attend to it rightaway though I figure it may take a whiles to get a go-head to finalize a schedule.'

'You are most kind.'

'We want the world to learn the truth about our country.'

Her sing-song voice lent formality a benedictial air. Then she started to talk.

Her interest focused. In a bright tone she told him of planned developments for the information services: they tied into rumour's he had heard of the bid by Peking to take over leadership of communist groups in uncommitted Africa and Asia. He gave no sign of surprise and limited his contribution to nods. His instinct started to work rapidly. Mrs. Peng was too cagey to drop broad hints unintentionally; therefore she had been primed; therefore all had not gone well according to the Peking view of talks held by its top men and those from Moscow while fraternal gladness sweetened the public air; therefore signs of dispute on specific points should appear in the not too distant future; and therefore Peking was out to run the bigger camp. It was a calculated leak. His troubles were to locate its expressions and devise means to inform London while safeguarding his position here in case Peking abandoned the plan.

'Will news releases give us details?' he asked.

'Shortly. African delegations will visit us soon.'

'I see.'

'Miss Yu will forward you particulars.'

The homelier girl bared her teeth at him.

'Thank you.' He stood up. 'You've been most kind.'

Mrs. Peng smiled, affability incarnate. 'You're welcome. I guess you'll go to the meeting of the Warsaw Treaty Powers in Moscow next February. I wish I could go along with our observers.'

He smiled. Here it was again. Someone high up was going to the meeting; therefore a statement was intended; therefore it was designed to represent a Chinese viewpoint on a fundamental issue; its open declaration in front of Russia's satellites could only be intended to unsettle them; from then on the camp would never, repeat never, be the same again. Moscow was going to run looking back over its shoulders.

'I'm not sure if my agency will be allowed to send a reporter,' he said. 'You deserve a holiday after all your work.'

'You never take a vacation.'

'I'm too lazy. Has there been a release of who will represent you at the meeting?'

Her gold-toothed smile flashed at him.

'It's slated for publication shortly,' she told him and rose from her chair to bow to Mao Tse-tung.

As he left the interview, he decided it had been a profitable afternoon. His nose felt longer, in good sniffing condition.

In the hall he passed Alfred Wilson and his Eurasian wife Rosemary on their daily call for instructions. Wilson was a short grey man whose angular face had a collapsed appearance. He corresponded for Left-wing periodicals in Britain and helped the NCNP in its English news service. His middleaged wife had an air of defiant nervousness. She read English news-bulletins from the Central People's Broadcasting Station; her voice went out on short-waves to the Middle East, Europe, India, the Pacific, and North America. Wilson avoided Britons. The British Government had accused him of brutality to British soldiers whom he interrogated when they were captured in Korea. His face now was a sunken hang-dog profile.

Outside the Ministry in flat apricot sunlight Steven paused. A good afternoon, yes. He felt a need to clear his mind in order to decide where to search for straws to support the hints given him.

On the spur of the moment he instructed his driver to take him to the park surrounding the Temple of Heaven. They drove south down Chien Mên Chieh through mid-afternoon traffic: Russian cars, Czech and East German diesel buses, trams, mules, bicycles. Every pavement had twining skeins of children.

As he mounted the steps to the wide grey stone causeway sloping up to the Temple, a partial solution to his problem came to him. A bid for leadership of the communist camp could not be concealed. The obvious source of disagreement, inherited rivalry for control of Central Asia, now extended to India, had become a carefully engineered stalemate; that left only a dialectical tussle roughly similar to disputes by sixteenth-century European Catholics and Protestants over interpretation of tenets of their common faith and cast Mao Tse-tung as a sort of Martin Luther. And therefore evidence must be some-

71

where in speeches and articles by theoreticians and writers; their line would urge return to the basic militant argument for ensuring world communist supremacy through revolution and war.

He began to feel confident. The theory gave him a line to follow. He smiled; he was in what Roger had once called his spiral ascent through deduction; it always gave him a working theory; he had no other method to obtain one. Yes, by golly, a good afternoon. He glanced round.

There was hardly anyone about. On his last visit he had seen companies of soldiers drilling for the parade. The crests of woods of imperial dragon cypresses were dark as the sea at nightfall. Ahead of him four young mothers in drab blue jackets and trousers, wide-peaked caps covering their hair, trolled stoically up the incline, persuading their lagging offspring to effort. Their voices knitted into the sunlight.

Beyond a *mên* in front of them soared the Temple. Its three circular porcelain-tiled pagoda roofs burned darkly blue against the cloudless sky. Sunshine glinted on its golden cap. Until fifty years ago the Manchu emperors had come here at the winter solstice, gone to fast in the Hall of Abstinence, and then walked a short distance south in the chill dawn to sacrifice a bullock and pray for a good harvest at the Altar of Heaven. The Temple was too exquisite to destroy or deface and had been left alone, one of the architectural splendours of the world. Steven supposed that Jane had come here. Everyone did. She might like to come again. He didn't have a clue what she liked or was like, only that she reported, carried her share of life, and was a pleasant companion.

As he went through the *mên* and down into the sunken marble bowl from which flights of steps led up to the temple, he had muddled recollections of their evening together. It still bewildered him. No, wrong; their extraordinary last half-hour bewildered him. Up till then she was another serene Western woman. Then she was clinging to him, fired by her own contrivance, hastily spinning a web, her mouth like despair in intensity, somewhere in her a collapse or cancellation, striving to see themselves as new realities. He'd bungled badly. By now his dullness had probably caused her to regret her admission of sensuality. And loneliness. Mainly loneliness.

On his climb to the Temple he passed a small girl who had decided to take a rest and sat gazing at the sky. Shrill orders from her mother higher up gained no response. The tot scratched her grubby knees and let her innocent eyes contemplate the big blue.

He smiled at her grave face. Long may you be able to, he told her silently.

His thoughts went back to Jane. That shrewd old beggar Roger was right; she needed to be plunged back into living. But Roger and he might be wrong for he had been wildly wrong about Gillian though she was unusual; it required great stamina to be a drunk and a nymphomaniac who delighted in hotel pageboys; his fights in the big blue had given no guidance on tactics to use with Gillian. He supposed he ought to have scratched up some persuasive arguments to induce Jane to have stayed, whistle-stop halt or not. Well, they'd learn about each other when she got back; if she saw him; after his failure to rise to the event she might prefer to avoid him.

At the top of the steps he paused to admire the Temple. As his eyes enjoyed its symmetry he wondered what he was doing in China. It was a question which often irked him. He couldn't find an answer. Come to that, he didn't know what those he met most frequently were doing here. They were as ineffectual as characters in a Chekov play; Clive, running from faces of life which terrified him but drinking in order to let his mind fondle each terror more sensitively; Jane, adrift without a haven; John Butler, one of a generation taught to barter its souls for the illusion of security; perhaps the icy Ilse Han, grown up in a stench of defeat. And himself, more useless than the rest, a would-be idealist without a positive ideal, full of ideas agile as half-dead flies, animate futility personified. Chekov had been wrong in one fundamental; his characters were too knowledgeably aimless; futile people usually hugged a conviction of their importance in the rat race. In this half-century events were in the saddle and the Europeans were being ridden hardest. The

West should be represented in China by those strengthened by a burning conviction of Western rightness. No newspaperman could be so singleminded. They were self-protective cynics, supping on the ambition and greed and folly of others.

The ardent sky-gazer interrupted his rambling thoughts. She appeared at his knees, bland sloe eyes peering up at his face; one day they were going to get her into mischief. She was too young to attend schools he had visited, grim places where education was a three-point programme: to prove communism right, instil fear and hatred of noncommunist countries, teach total submission of self in bringing about a communist world where China would be top dog. She regarded him solemnly. Then, regardless of giggled reproofs from her watchful mother, she took his hand to lead him to the Temple.

'*Hsieh hsieh,*' he thanked her.

'*Hsing shih mo?*' she asked.

'Steven.'

'Ste-ven?'

'Yes. *Shih mo ming tzu?*'

'Sao.'

'Sao is a pretty name.'

'*Hsien shen shih na li lai ti?*'

'I come from another country, Sao.'

They got on famously. She was a natural charmer and overlooked his efforts with her language, which was jolly decent of her.

A voice addressed him in the Indian restaurant that night.

'Are you alone, Mr. Kendal?'

He stood up. It was Ilse Han. A glitter in her eyes belied her smile. She had put colour on her cheeks and wore a red dress calculated to attract attention.

'Alone, Mrs. Han. Will you join me?'

'My husband has gone to Chungking on business.' She sat down. 'There are not many people here.'

'There's a reception at the Egyptian Embassy.'

She nodded uninterestedly. 'Can we please talk English?'

Tang the Mute frowned down at his bitten nails. He was conscious of uneasiness in Hu standing beside him. Across the table in a small office adjoining the room of ears Sun Teh and his two assistants sat upright on hard wooden chairs. Sun Teh was a security officer.

At length Tang raised his eyes.

'No, neither Kendal *hsien-shêng* nor the woman spoke critically of the Arabs. They did not speak of Suez. I am certain. I read our instructions of what to listen for while these foreigners are here. The woman told him about a holiday she spent in Iran last year. She said she met two of their friends in Tehran. One was called Ni-gel and I think the other was Rimmy. He asked if Tehran had changed. She did not stop talking.'

'Did she talk so much to stop him from speaking? Was he drunk?'

'He was not drunk. Her talk was to please him. I told Hu'.

'Yes yes,' agreed Hu.

'Was she drunk?'

'No.'

'Have you met a lot of Britons?'

'I worked for several when I was young.'

'This man and his woman were not different?'

'No.'

Sun grunted. He felt uncomfortable among these men. He was a large man who appeared larger on account of heavy rolls of fat covering his bones. They swelled in his tight blue Yat-sen tunic so that his breasts resembled those of a woman past her youth and soft from feeding many children, filled its sleeves so completely as to make them resemble an extra skin, and gave his narrow shoulders an illusion of being deformed. Fifty-seven years ago he had been the largest of eleven children at his home in Swatow, a healthy baby to compensate for those born dead because of famine in the previous two years, and had grown big and strong. But in middleage soft layers of fat had grown over hard muscles. Heavy bags under his square eyebrows almost hid his eyes as he watched a fly walk around a telephone on the table.

'Go,' he told Tang and kept his gaze on the fly until he heard the door close.

He looked up. Amid pouches of fat his eyes were protuberant, gleaming under their folds. From now on the interview did not worry him; every sentence fitted into a familiar pattern. He fixed a stern and disappointed stare on Hu. The man was terrified.

'You are a weak-brained fool,' he said. 'An old mule has more intelligence.'

Hu giggled.

'Why did you not go to find out if she was the woman in the lift?' asked Sun.

'I did not expect him to have a woman there.'

'Afterwards, you blind dog, after you reported here.'

'P'eng told me their voices were not clear.'

'You are a liar!' shouted Sun. 'He told you he could not hear them.'

Hu wrung his hands.

'Yes yes.'

'Why did you stay here? Did you believe P'eng was lying?'

'No no, P'eng does not lie.'

'Why are you sure he does not lie?'

Hu fidgeted on his feet, unable to think of a safe answer.

'I have never been able to prove he has told me lies.'

'Is it part of your duties to prove P'eng is a liar?'

'No no. Our committee tell us to be vigilant and watch for Nationalist spies.'

'Do you accuse P'eng of being a Nationalist spy?'

Hu trembled. A trickle of sweat ran coldly down his neck. This interview had taken a course he did not expect. He had thought that Sun would congratulate him on his prompt actions. The man twisted everything he said.

'No no, I am not accusing P'eng of being a Nationalist spy.'

'Are there Nationalists on the staff?'

'I have not discovered any.'

'Your vigilance tells you to search for them.'

'Yes yes.'

Sun widened his eyes in anger. 'Did your vigilance tell you to use the telephone in the staff room on the fifth floor to tell P'eng the Englishman had a woman in his rooms? No no. It told you to come down here. Did it tell you to go back to be sure you saw her? No no. It told you to stay here. Did it tell you to go to his rooms directly they went out to see if she had left him instructions from the British Government or the Americans or the Nationalists? No no. It told you to follow them to the hotel where she was staying. We do not know if she was the woman, the only other person, in the Englishman's rooms. There may have been more, people who walked down the stairs. Tang did not take anybody down in his lift after the Englishman went out with her. Tang is observant and resourceful. Your brain is less useful than a dog's belly. A dog's belly will vomit what is bad for it.'

Hu was furious, resentful, indignant, outraged by the scurrilous comparison with Tang. Sun affected high and mighty airs, his tongue more abusive than those of merchants and compradors in the old days. Only fear kept him silent until Sun finished. He was more terrified than ever before. He tried not to betray it.

'It was an emergency. P'eng and his comrades do not go to the rooms. I thought I might be able to hear what was said because my ears are at home in the rooms. *Ai*, I know them and those occupied by eighty other people. Better than my own room. Everything in them is familiar to me.'

'Why was the microphone in the wrong place?'

'He changed the position of the radio set.'

'When?'

'On the day he brought the woman,' lied Hu. He recalled having seen that it had been put in another place more than a week ago, but was too busy to change the microphone and kept putting it off.

77

'What part of the day?'

'After I left in the evening.'

Sun grunted. The man was lying. Until now Hu had shown alarm, hesitancy, indecision, an inability to give direct answers. He had tried to shift responsibility onto Tang, people who delayed him on his rounds, P'eng, fireworks; now it was the Englishman himself. Hu was too big a liar to trust. Sun decided to end this nonsense.

'Where is the microphone now?'

'In the ventilation shaft.'

'Above the window.'

'Yes yes.'

'Why did you stay down here?'

Hu tittered. 'I thought he intended to order her into his bed.'

'Is there a microphone in his bedroom?'

'No no.'

'Why not?'

'I was told the factory making them did not reach its target in the year that the hotel opened, and those which were available went into other hotels.'

'Is there one in his bathroom?'

'No.'

'Has he entertained other visitors since she left?'

'No no.'

Sun dismissed him curtly, sitting silent to watch the fly stand on the telephone and clean its front legs. He had always been fascinated by the miraculously delicate structure of flies. At length he ordered his assistants to go and question other men about Hu, find out whatever they could about him.

He raised his eyes as the door closed. No expression came on to his big face yet relief flooded through him. He did not like having educated men round him. He sensed them laughing at him, watching him for signs of ignorance.

After a moment he sighed. What would Yi-hai have advised him to do about this frog Hu? She had always seen exactly what to do. She had been educated too, her wits sharp as a knife, yet always laughing and merry, a tiny woman, fragile as almond blossom, proud of his strength. *T'ung i*, strong he was forty years ago, stronger than anyone in Swatow. He used to be able to carry three men simultaneously. As a wrestler he threw his opponents around like starved chickens. That was wrong. He saw it clearly now. You began life with great strength or an agile mind or money left by your ancestors and thought it solved every problem you would find in life. You were wrong. It was the point where your weaknesses began.

He looked at the fly again. But strength had given him fame as a wrestler. And Yi-hai who taught him to read and count. She was more than a teacher. Young people now sneered at romantic love as a bourgeois delusion but Yi-hai defied her family to run away with him. Although her family was wealthy, her father a clerk who met important people every month, she sacrificed comfort for him. And how he loved her. Within a month he stopped thinking of her as a wife; she was Yi-hai. Those years gave them much happiness though their only wealth was her courage and his strength. What other woman who enjoyed her advantages of beauty and intelligence would have accompanied him when the Red Army set out on the march which ended six thousand miles farther on in Shensi? Why was she captured by Nationalists near the Tatu River? Why did they execute her too, a gentle woman who only wanted to fight oppression and corruption?

Years ago. Closer than yesterday. Often he thought that she had been spared much unhappiness. There was no one to whom he could confide such wrong-thinking.

He gazed back through years drifted between them like clouds. Something in him ceased to live then. He never felt whole again and hated men who were whole. Perhaps he was lucky in being too busy killing Japanese for the next six years to heed how soon they passed. Then he took a wife. Two months later the Japanese killed her. Eight years later, after the Party took power, he married Ling out of pity. She too was educated. He felt sorry for her, the illegitimate daughter of a wealthy Hongkong merchant, a plain thin girl in rags, half out of her mind, kneeling beside her dead mother in the ruins of a house shelled by the Nationalists. He hid her until security officers no longer searched for her to blackmail her father. But Ling could not help him to be whole again, not Sun the Butcher, who had caused three thousand enemies of the people to be executed.

Ling did not object to him being called 'the Butcher'; it increased her safety. Their four sons were proud of him, this strange gross fat man who felt old and who trembled among educated people.

What shall I do about Hu and the Englishman, he asked Yi-hai in his heart. I do not hate Englishmen now. Not as I did years ago when you and I were in Shanghai and you took me for a walk and you wore that pretty dress of pink and looked so young and beautiful, the day we saw the park which Europeans kept for themselves and you read out the notice which said: 'No dogs or Chinese allowed'. *Ai*, for years I hated them. The past stays in a man's mind. Our past.

He clicked his tongue. A man who had sons and a loyal wife half his age had no right to brood on his youth like a miser counting coins spent long ago. Without education for high office, no longer young, he must do what they told him, like thousands of men from the old Red Army because they too were uneducated. Millions of men wanted to get rid of old heroes. So he wasted his life listening to 'Small Group' informers, and hotel staffs always imagined more spies than a dog digging out fleas.

Hu was incompetent. They needed a reliable man to report on the Englishman. It was useless to send a woman to Kendal; the dossier on him revealed no exploitable weakness. He would guess that any woman who went to his room intended to spy on him. The Englishwoman Crofton must not be given a chance to collect information on her travels. Why had Kendal's employers ordered him to visit other cities? Were they spies?

Sun stared at the immobile fly.

5

Every day convinced John Butler of ignominious failure ahead of him. The main fundamentals were too complex for him to grasp in the short time at his disposal.

Most people tried to help him. They explained, described, gave long accounts of dialectics or economics or history. Only Kendal got tired of questions. Kendal was a typical damned newspaperman who wanted to keep his information to himself. Ilse Han was much more helpful. She went out of her way to spend two whole evenings talking to him.

Each conversation increased his confusion. The Chinese were incomprehensible. However long he lived here he would never, never gain insight into these bland, volatile, callous, indifferent, proud, and eternally evasive people. They defeated him.

6

After dinner most evenings Steven Kendal went straight back to his room. He worked for several hours every night. None of the NCNA press releases supported the leads given him by Mrs. Peng, so he spent hours studying Chinese in order to increase his search through official journals. There was always a chance that he might find a sentence which would warrant him calling on someone to provide a full translation. His conviction of having been given a calculated leak never lessened. Mrs. Peng did not chatter gaily to European newspapermen out of a deep affection for them.

A week after National Day he escaped from Butler earlier than usual to gain an extra hour for study. He did not want to be inconsiderate but the younger man asked endless questions on points which he should reason out for himself.

He looked round as he went into the room. It had been

tidied in his absence. Thank heaven, Hu would not interrupt him. He went over and switched on the radio. On the set lay a mimeographed programme of the evening's telecast. He saw that the main items were a film on cooperative farming and an excerpt from a traditional opera. He took off his tie, hung it over a chair, and undid the top buttons of his shirt. As sounds of a Mozart sonata came from the radio, he went through to the bathroom. When he returned he took off his shoes, lit a cigarette, and sat down at the table.

Once during the next hour he looked up. He smiled wrily. This was precisely the scene which had most annoyed Gillian. She loathed to spend an evening at home unless it contained a crowd of people, sulked like a schoolgirl whenever he worked, communicating her boredom by long audible sighs punctuated by tossing aside whatever glossy magazine failed to hold her attention. She had the entertainment world too deeply embedded in her to regard home as more than a place to sleep and dress in. He lit a fresh cigarette and renewed his search.

When he was halfway through a translation of a speech by a professor on Russian cold-war tactics, a knock on the door interrupted him. He glanced at his watch. It was almost nine o'clock.

He smiled over-cheerfully as he opened the door. A Chinese girl looked at him. He saw her eyes widen in startlement. She stood compactly, poised, alert as a fawn. Behind her the corridor was a yellow-lit emptiness. There was a glisten of raindrops on her hair and a bunch of huge gold-bronze chrysanthemums in her long hands. She had gathered the collar of her black over-coat close around her neck against a chilly air outside which had stung colour into her cheeks. Under her pointed chin frothed a wispy magenta scarf. He recognized her even before he caught sight of the long scar far back on the left side of her face, and regretted her being sent to entice information out of him. At the embassy reception he had not imagined her cast in this shabby role. Her flowers added novelty.

He plunged into commonplace courtesy. *'Kung hsi.'*

'Hsien-shêng, kung hsi. Shao hsiao chieh tsai chia ma?'

This was a new line. He had no recollection of a Miss Shao who regarded these rooms as her home. The girl spoke in a quiet voice which lacked the more lilty Chinese inflexions. Her smile was unsure, in no degree ingratiating or brazen.

'You are mistaken,' he said in English. 'Miss Shao does not live here. This is my apartment.'

Only a necessity to face each other saved her appraisal from being a stare. It was obvious that she recognized him. Then she grew aware of impoliteness unbecoming to a Chinese woman and diverted her glance to her flowers.

'Oh dear,' she said. 'I'm lost. She is going to let me see the opera on her father's television. Do you know which floor they live on?'

It did not surprise him to hear her speak English. Even her faint American accent was predictable.

'I've no idea. Did you inquire at the desk?'

'No. I was sure I remembered her directions accurately.'

The next move appeared to be up to him, the temporary owner of the ever open door.

'Would you like to see it on my set?' he suggested in a tone loaded with charm. 'It's due to start soon. If you want to see the beginning, there's scarcely time for you to get downstairs and then to your friend's apartment. After all, we do know each other, more or less, Miss——'

'Chen Mei-ling.'

'My name is Kendal. I owe you more than an apology for nearly knocking you down. Please come in, Miss Chen.'

She hesitated for so long that he began to think she intended to decline. One part of his mind, the persistent sentimentalist forever hopeful of being stunned, willed her to go. Another, the cynic, clambered lethargically to its usual perch on the fence, rubbed cold shrivelled fingers, and sat down to wait. At length he saw an infinitesimal tension in her lips; they were child-smooth, their fullness magnified by the inward slant of her cheeks. She nodded.

'Thank you,' she said and stepped forward. She had a longer, freer stride than most Chinese women, casually confident.

It did not go according to formula. She let him put her flowers in water and consented to take off her coat, but displayed no interest in conversation. She sat too tidily to be comfortable, a bland profile, clasped hands motionless on her lap, entranced by scenes of the bustling little king of the monkeys fighting venomous crabs and squid around the Dragon King's sea-girt palace, a contest accompanied by wailing flutes, crashing cymbals and joss-gongs, a scrape of string instruments. It was typical Chinese opera: ballet, fairy-tale, acrobatics, allegory, and heroic folklore, a whiff of the *Odyssey*, a touch of the Capeks' *Insect Play*. His European ear longed for less noise; his eyes wanted to see the superb dancers in their magnificent costumes.

When the performance ended, courtesy forced her to accept a cup of tea. His attempts at conversation fell flat. Belatedly she showed interest in his books and crouched down to inspect their titles. Neither of the other girls had come to this point; their instructors had evidently not heard of spies having a book where pinpricks above words or letters supplied a code. He saw how her hair was arranged to conceal the scar on her neck, and speculated on what caused the injury. The turn of her hips was more feminine than that of most young Chinese women.

'Borrow any you would like to read,' he invited.

'May I?'

'Please do. They're only collecting dust at present.'

She chose the memoirs of a Russian ballet dancer of pre-revolutionary days and stood up saying she must go. As he helped her put on her coat, he told her not to hurry over the book. At the door she thanked him for his kindness. They said goodbye, and he watched her walk away. At the turn of the corridor she glanced back and smiled. He raised his hand, and shut the door, saw her flowers blazing, and stared at them. After a moment he settled down to work and forgot her.

Five

INTOURIST travel brochures announced China as a country of ancient arts and modern industrial skills, traditional medical practices allied to contemporary therapeutic methods, ruled by a people devoted to peace. Some statements were as true as those put out by other countries, but foreigners were unable to prove to what extent the claims about intangibles were true. The physical immensity of the country, more than twice the size of Europe and containing half as many more people, provided one set of obstacles. Another arose from the fear which forced visitors to talk to selected people through officials. How on earth could you be sure you were listening to the truth when a government employee stuck to you like a plaster? In a dogged attempt not to be beaten, John Butler waded through a history of recent years given him by an Information Department official.

His bewilderment increased. Modern Chinese history was basically simple. It began when Dr. Sun Yat-sen and the Kuomintang overthrew the decadent Manchu dynasty in 1911, the start of twenty years of intrigue and inertia. When, after years of pouring armies into the North, Japan did attack China, the Chinese were divided into two camps, Kuomintang Nationalists and Communists. They effected a rapprochement when Japan entered World War Two, but after the defeat of Japan it ended by a communist refusal to participate in multi-party government. In 1949 the communists launched a civil war which put them in sole control, and immediately inaugurated a campaign of terror whose victims, according to their own spokesmen, numbered over two million people in three years. They also invaded Korea and occupied Tibet.

Often he read a single sentence: 'Thousands of patriotic young men, their faces radiant and proud, volunteered to give their courage, their strength, the splendid white blossom of their early manhood, to drive the evil imperialist aggressors from Korea.' He could almost read the unprinted line: and all the maimed dead men cried out in pride: 'Our war was unlike others; inspect our wounds.'

He wondered if it was cynical jingoism, China-style; Mao, bless our battles. Or was it true?

2

Two evenings after Steven Kendal escaped from questions, John Butler went to attend a small cocktail party given by Sheila Grant. The foreign community in Peking threw parties on every available pretext to relieve their monumental boredom. She had not even bothered to tell him her excuse.

At six o'clock he wandered downstairs to her flat. He put on a clean white shirt and wore his better flannel suit. His dark blue silk tie was done in a precise Windsor knot. Above his breast pocket rose a rim of white handkerchief. He felt irritable. He wished to heaven that he had not accepted her invitation.

He dawdled to avoid people whose footsteps echoed along the lower corridor. His mood of sullen self-criticism increased. It was damned daft to set out here for one of those dates he avoided like the plague everywhere else, a session of tooth-flashing and wee-waffle. What use were such parties? You never had a decent conversation and success among the grin-twitched faces came from swiping contemporary clichés about nothing.

As he neared the third floor, he halted to keep out of sight of a Chinese room-boy whose feet pattered softly along the corridor. His watch said it was five-past six. If his luck was in, Sheila should have at least two guests by now.

Several seconds passed before he heard her answer his knock by asking who it was.

'John Butler,' he said and listened to a key turn in the lock. She locked the door again directly he entered.

'You're early, John Butler.'

She resembled an exotic parrot in a short robe of rough towelling which enveloped her from neck to knees in huge blinding sworls of scarlet and yellow and green. An old stocking secured it round her waist. Her stained violet silk mules had an air of nostalgic sins. She must have come straight from the bathroom; sweat glistened on her forehead and chin. Her hair perched in an insecure twist on top of her head. He bent to retrieve a fallen hairpin.

'Didn't you say six o'clock?'

'Seven.'

She jabbed the pin into her topknot, shedding two more as she did so.

He picked them up and gave them to her.

'Sorry,' he said and turned to the door.

'You can stay and talk to me, John Butler.'

'Must you always call me John Butler?'

'It isn't easy to call you John.'

'I regret your inability to feel at ease with me.'

'Oh, don't be such a stuff-shirt,' she said impatiently. 'Why don't you try to get people to like you?'

He saw derision in her eyes. Her lips quivered in fluttery coming-and-going smiles as if only a strict upbringing in lady-like conduct prevented her from laughing aloud at him. He wondered how long it had taken her to perfect it. He raised his brows.

'Why should I?'

Sheila ignored his question.

'I don't want to get a sore throat from shouting so you'll have to come into the bedroom.'

As he followed her, he saw bottles of Chinese wine hedged on a table pushed back against the wall. From some source, an embassy contact he supposed, she had obtained a bottle of brandy and another of some mysterious Balkan fire-juice. Alongside them were plates of bits to nibble.

He obeyed her instruction to sit down on the bed while she began to dress behind him and chattered about her guests.

From what he could judge, there should be about fifteen Central and South Americans and Asians, a hell of a squash in a small room. Out of the corners of his eyes he saw she had given the room a feminine aspect by using brightly coloured fabrics, a couple of stone jars of good shape for flower vases, and some brassware, a circular bowl, candlesticks, an oblong salver, on her dressingtable. An incongruous note was an atrocious folding screen, dark, floridly ornamented, carved dragons writhing in square panels. She moaned worriedly about her dilemma over getting fully fashioned nylons.

'Do you find it peculiar to be in a bedroom with a woman, John Butler?'

'I've got three sisters.'

'Have you got a mistress?'

'No.'

'Why not?'

'Do I have to have one?'

She could not restrain her curiosity. 'Was she nice?'

'I was twenty.'

'She was older than you.'

'She had teeth, hands, eyes, and walked on feet. Anything else you want to be told?'

'You're being rude.'

'We can't all be as polite as you.'

'Englishmen are always coarse, vulgar, bad-mannered, and brutal.'

'Jolly good.'

'I met an Englishman in Calcutta who beats his wife every Sunday.'

'She probably screams nicely.'

For some moments she flounced about muttering angrily to herself. Then in a curt tone she announced her belief that Ilse Han wanted an affaire with him. Her voice paused interrogatively.

'Do you imagine I'm quite so daft?' he asked.

'Something has happened to her since her husband got a new position. They say he'll soon be in the Foreign Ministry. She used to be friendly. Now her eyes go glassy directly she sees people. I wonder she doesn't hiss. She may be in love with you. You look clean and silent. Why don't you find out? You might enjoy it.'

She prattled on like a mixture of Daisy Ashford and a lesser Nöel Coward character until he could bear it no longer.

'Must you talk drivel?'

'Doesn't she attract you?'

'She's probably madly fascinating to Kendal. They're cold fish.'

'Oh, you and he are very alike.'

That riled him but he refused to get angry with her. He bent forward, staring at the carpet. It was green, several shades darker than her furnishings. Sometimes on late spring mornings there were similar greens in woods rolling like soft tides over the wide gentle hills of Kent. He had spent happy days, alone, walking along footpaths remote from a petrol stench of main roads and their wasp colonies of motor bikes, putting up overnight at small white-washed pubs smelling of beer and floor polish among untidy orchards and mathematical hop-gardens. His feet eighteen years old, his head ablaze with ideas. Good days for God's gift to English literature, up to his knees in hope.

Her hand rested on his shoulder. 'What's wrong, John Butler?'

He reached up to pat her hand. 'Nothing of consequence.'

'Is it a secret? Have you fallen in love?'

'Oh, for God's sake!'

After a pause she said: 'I'm sorry.'

His eyes searched the room. It frightened him to contemplate defeat, hear his own mouth shovel away his dreams because he knew he was beaten. But it would be worse if he disregarded the danger signals. Who was that fellow who wrote a best-seller and finished up on a park bench in Glasgow, alone with an attaché-case of short stories and lavatory cleanser chewing his guts? Even he had forgotten the man's name.

'No, it's not a secret,' he said. 'I've decided to be realistic. I'm doing no good here so I'm going home.'

He felt her hand tighten on his shoulder. There was nothing more to say. He had heard himself admit his deficiencies, his lack of depth or breadth of reasoning, certainly of clarity. What astounded him was his calmness.

'I don't understand,' Sheila prompted.

'It's simple. I don't understand these people. They're—they're . . . look, you and the others are here for another purpose. News. News isn't ideas. News isn't people. News is events which may involve people. I'm not saying what I wanted to write was more important, only, well, another angle. I can't do it.'

She was immediately practical.

'Will you lose money?'

He laid his hand horizontally under his jaw. 'I'm into debt up to there.'

'What will you do?'

'Work in a factory. Go on strike.'

For a moment she was silent, her fingers drumming lightly on his shoulder.

'Would you rather not come to my party, John Butler?'

'It'll do me good to grin at people.'

There was a pause and then she said that she must dress. Her hand left his shoulder.

He hunched forward uncomfortably, staring at his thoughts. Sheila did not talk, proof of kindness and commonsense when put to the test. Extraordinary girl, he thought and tried to evolve a plan of action. There were urgent issues to consider. It would be advantageous to stop somewhere cheap for a while; there was no sense in rushing back emptyhanded and his creditors didn't expect him yet. Why alarm them? He looked up.

'Mmmm?'

'I said you must help me.'

Her haughty tone failed to conceal exasperation. For some absurd reason she had chosen to wear a new black woollen dress of the variety referred to by his sisters as a simple little thing but had stepped into it instead of lowering it over her head.

Although the side zip held it snug over her hips, the top half sagged from her waist, the sleeves flapping round her ankles. Loops of rose coral necklace dangled near her thighs; more coral swung from her ears. She had on a white silk brassiere of the strapless type and enough junky bangles to open a shop. Her hair was a precise shining coil on the nape of her neck.

'You'll have to take it off,' he said. 'They don't go upward.'

'But I've done my hair!' she wailed.

'Too bad. Turn round.'

She complied, nearly tripping over a sleeve.

'Have you enough money to get to England?' she asked.

'A return ticket from Hongkong. By air. Hold still.'

Her foot tapped the floor impatiently while he undid the side zip and eased the dress down. Her silk-clad hips were compact and taut. The dress fell round her ankles.

'Step out.' As she did so, he picked it up. 'Take off your bangles. They'll tear the sleeves.'

A hail of trinkets spread round him.

'Why not cancel your ticket?' she suggested. 'You'd get some money back. You can get easy work on a ship to London. You'd have free food. They give you a uniform. That will save your clothes. Your laundry is done free. You may meet a rich old Australian widow. A friend of mine did. But he was handsome and healthy. He said the food was very nourishing. Every ship has a doctor and a nurse.'

'It's an idea. I tell you I was not ill when we first met.'

She ignored the interruption.

'One of my friends in Calcutta wanted to write poetry. He's very wealthy now. He owns a guava jam factory.'

'Good for him.'

He shook out her dress, blew face powder off one shoulder, gave its back zip a trial run, and laid it aside. He looked up. For once her face showed no irritating play of emotion. It had a blank childish innocence. Unthinkingly he reached up. She stooped for him to kiss her lips. He undid her bra and it fell to the floor. She straightened to let him lay his face against her body; her breasts moved firmly, ripe as those of a Hindu goddess.

After a moment she sank down and coiled an arm round his shoulders.

With each instant his sense of incredulity increased. They had never exchanged a glance of curiosity yet now she lay against him, allowed his hands to rove over her willowy body. When he raised her head on his arm her lips were firmly closed. She patted his shoulder consolingly. Some moments later he raised his face. He felt foolish.

Sheila watched him from her fear of poverty, not that of writers and poets she used to meet in Calcutta, but from an abasement of human life that she had seen in *bustee* hovels, Bombay *chawls*, a hundred Ganges villages, poverty worse than Englishmen experienced. She felt very sorry for him. He did not have enough ruthlessness to be successful. It must be awkward to be a man from a country which no longer ruled, trying to be friendly to everyone now. Its men and women had never been friendly to her English father after he married a Hindu woman, a worse sin to them than if he had lived with her and let their two daughters be born bastards. John Butler would never sacrifice himself as her father had done. He was weak. She smiled radiantly, trying to cheer him up.

He cleared his throat. 'You have lovely breasts.'

'One of my friends in Calcutta said so too. He is a millionaire. I was a model for him. He took up painting when Sir Winston made artists respectable. My legs are nicer. Go on, look at them.'

He thought them too thinly shapeless to excite admiration.

'My sort of Eurasian is very nice,' she said.

'Physically? Yes. Xanthomelanous.'

'What does that horrible word mean?'

'Someone with black hair and your sort of brown skin. Is your friend the jam manufacturer?'

'No. His sons are millionaires too, but they're too busy making money and hating each other to paint.'

'Poor them. Sheila, I wasn't shooting a line. It's true.'

'I know,' she said. 'Do you want to kiss me any more? I'm getting cramp in my neck.' When he had done so, she said:

'You haven't asked why I'm going to wear a dress instead of a sari.'

'Why?'

'It will stop my guests from being embarrassed. They are all mixed up. I am the only genuine half-caste.'

'And jolly nice too,' he commented. 'Well, it's getting on. I'd better tart you up to meet them.

She stood up at once. They managed to get her dress on without mishap despite her squeals of alarm. While she completed her toilette he cut her necklace to a third of its length. His hardest task was to persuade her to wear only one bracelet. Finally she came for his approval. Her eyes darkened.

'We'll talk about your trouble later. I'll think for you. Some of my ideas are very good. We must decide how you can get money. Money is more important than anything in the world. Eat a lot, John Butler. It'll give you energy.'

'I'm not hungry.'

She frowned. 'Do as I say. Where did I put my bloody lipstick?'

Her choice of adjective was not wrong.

3

There was warmth in the sun as Jane set off from the hotel in Harbin on Sunday afternoon for a walk in an endeavour to sort out her thoughts. Since she left Peking nine days ago she had been given no chance to consider her own affairs, her days a rush from early morning until late at night. On her three day-time train journeys she had written notes or looked at the northeast countryside, gleaming rice *padis* like sheets of molten silver under high grey skies, labourers beneath bamboo yokes trudging along raw dirt roads, mule waggons and pedicarts. It was sheer bliss to have what travel agency brochures would call 'day at leisure in Harbin'.

She smiled. Harbin: that dated her. To those who learned

geography when she was a schoolgirl the recent Chinese name of Pinkiang for this town spawned by Holy Russia on leased Chinese territory to serve a railroad pushing imperialism east, hub of a hundred thousand of the Czar's subjects in Manchuria, then home of forty thousand White Russian refugees fled from Bolshevik revolution, and later a centre for Japanese imperialism pushing west, would always require mental adjustment. They would always think of its Russian name.

Crossing the station square, she encountered a large contingent of those for whom it would always be Pinkiang, a name blown on victorious trumpets. They were Chinese colonizers arrived from overpopulated southern cities to extend agricultural areas and establish new industrial projects inside the northern frontier.

Their shrill dry voices filled the air as they poured out of the station. She saw excitement brightening their young sloe eyes. Their clothes were old and ragged. Each one carried his or her personal belongings in a bundle or string bag slung on their backs. They were greeted by a small drum and cymbal band, brought by a red bannered party whose shouts and handclaps were tumultuously returned. Armed policemen and herself were the only spectators. They watched the colonizers clamber up into old open lorries to be taken to hostels.

She walked on at a leisurely stride. The people abroad were too preoccupied to heed a blank-faced woman, her skin pale as soap, eyes rimmed by fatigue, hair uncovered, the strap of her old handbag slung over her shoulder. Cosmopolitan since its origin, Harbin was too accustomed to visitors to heed them since it became the farthest northern point of the Peking tourist milk-run. Guides had told her of a weekly appearance of emigrants, scientists who came to search for minerals, office workers who arrived to share the dignity of manual labour for some months. They estimated that half a million colonizers had been drafted to Manchuria in the last three years. As Steven said, China resembled Soviet Russia in the period of NEP, the New Economic Policy, thirty years ago.

She quickened her pace past an Orthodox Church and across

a wide boulevard. Out of direct sunlight she felt a stab of chill air and was grateful for her thick overcoat. She thrust her ungloved hands deeper into her pockets.

To her eyes Harbin had a sinister louring brutality. She had disliked it at sight two days ago. Steven said she would. Its planned magnificence was incomplete, clotted in ornate indigestible lumps, its recent additions starkly utilitarian, their combined effect like a monstrous stage set for a dramatization of a novel by Gogol or Dostievski. It reduced people to ants. Most of those who passed her were Chinese. She was no longer afraid of them; only hating and suspicious. There were two distinct Russian groups. The younger was loud-voiced, aggressive, well-dressed, and drove in cars. The White Russian refugees were pitiful to behold, shabby old people, brown-papery leaves clinging to the tree of life. She had no sentimental regard for Czarist aristocrats, overwhelmingly effete and tyrannical and superstitious, their own executioners, yet a large number were harmless, their only crime to have been born into the wrong class in its death throes. She noted Japanese characteristics in some faces. They were probably children born to the twenty thousand whores imported by Tokyo years ago to act as spies.

She walked round the town for an hour before turning down to the river.

On the embankment she paused. Flowing like cold molten steel went the great grey Sungari on its course to the Sea of Okhotsk. Around her legs fumbled a cold air rising from its burden of snows. Overhead the illimitable sky flamed in barbaric golden brilliance, flushing scarlet on swirls of high vapour, elemental arson on a gigantic scale. She gazed at the river, her mind renewing its incoherent struggle to decide what to do about herself and Steven.

Her hands clenched miserably. No, not about him. About herself. She could not decide what to do for the best. No, that was a hypocritical lie. 'For the best' did not influence her. She wanted a fulfilment of her womanhood. Why disguise it as a moral issue merely because her upbringing told her to be ashamed of the truths of her body and nature? No race was more

95

hypocritical about the effect of sex than the British, proud of preserving the emotional immaturity of their children and letting them grow up confusing sex with dirt. Yes yes yes yes, she had desired him; on the night when her ridiculous vanity led her to leave him she had lain sleepless, tormented and distraught.

She heard herself promise them four days together, laying down rules like a conceited girl. Afterwards. What then?

Beset by doubts, she stared at the river. What would he do if those days prompted her to bind them together? What could he do? Ancient jokes about possessive women were vilely true; they had no scruples. Was her unsought excitement only a passing phase, due to emptiness behind and ahead? A protest against the plight of these women? What if she bound them closer together and then regretted losing her independence? She knew women who turned every day sour by craving what they lacked, accumulating years useless as rotted twigs.

Complexities filled her mind. She might regain forgotten instincts and comprehensions yet be unable to express her happiness. Few women could show their deepest emotions; those who tried usually became lost in meaningless wrong words. If that happened, could she refuse men as she had refused poor Clive and others? Would Steven remain loyal if she ruined their companionship by being afraid to give herself fully lest she lose again? Were there other risks?

Her head throbbed. She stared at the river until her chilled body demanded heed, then turned wearily into the gardens.

With inexpressible longing she wished Steven was here to share this placid autumn day.

It was warmer among the trees. The Chinese strolling over the lawns appeared to be administrative workers. Ahead of her a plump mother, sprigged white blouse loose over hips, trousers flapping, pushed a dilapidated wicker bassinet which had screechy wheels. There were others in sight, all typical of the conformist women she saw everywhere, prisoners of the communes even though they might not realize it yet, disciplined into blind obedience to the Establishment here, ignorant that their vaunted 'liberation' from domesticity was a propaganda catchword and that they were enrolled in industry and agriculture to achieve the Party's economic aims quicker; accidental women doomed to the communes from cradle to grave.

She saw groups of unmistakable White Russians. They were old. Worse, they were beaten. They sat on the benches huddled in their threadbare rags like old old dolls, rheumy-eyed men, women who managed to keep erect like polite little girls at a party despite white hair strained back from their blue-veined temples. Beside a bed of geraniums an old man supported by sticks talked to a gaunt Orthodox priest in fluttering black vestments. The white-bearded face of the priest reminded her of holy men painted on mediaeval peasant triptychs. She wondered if these people dreamed of their youth in Holy Russia, primitive opulence hedged in by snows and superstition. Did they believe they lived in an age of atonement? Did their faith teach acceptance of suffering, as priests had once taught resignation to disease and still taught that poverty was God's will?

It was a day when her mind conjured unanswerable questions.

The old priest gave her a stricken smile and raised his hand in benediction. She bent her head to acknowledge his blessing, hastening past lest he came across and learned his error.

In the distance a freight train racketed across the skeletal iron bridge over the Sungari.

She joined a queue paying its dues to pass through the elaborate gateway into the vast wooden pleasure pavilion. There were only Chinese in its rooms. They drank beer, stared at Chinese and Russian magazines, frowned over games of chess and mahjong, studied large anti-British and anti-American propaganda cut-outs of John Bull shooting Arabs and a vast fat woman clad in the Stars and Stripes whipping Negro children. She went into a hall where people were dancing decorously, Chinese fashion, men with men, women with women, to a laborious rendition of *The Blue Danube* played by a six-piece orchestra. None appeared to be enjoying themselves.

Back in the gardens she sat down on an empty bench.

Before long a White Russian limped up on a heavy malacca cane and seated himself. She studied him covertly. He was a bird-faced man in his late sixties, clad in a long shabby fur coat, a shapeless grey trilby squashed down over his narrow skull. His swollen arthritic fingers trembled from darned black woollen mittens and his heavy boots were caked in dirt. Pince-nez glasses hung lopsidedly on his high-bridged nose. His skin was like dirty wax. He said something in Russian. She responded in French. There was a silence before he spoke in the same language. Their conversation was awkward. He talked about the weather, the cost of food. She longed to question him properly but here every confidence had to be spontaneous. He lost interest in her, sunk in his chewed-looking coat, vacant. He did not answer her farewell.

The sunlight lost warmth on her return walk. She saw no shining solution to her problem, no brave answers. If only she had taken her opportunity; by now they would be impatient for each other or content to part. That she should drift without clear purpose! She heard herself moan, wanting him here beside her. If only she could expect to go back to the hotel to lie in his arms, feel his strength and smell his warmth, obliterate herself in them. Only lonely? Randy? No more? She wandered on.

4

While Steven prepared a pot of tea late on Sunday evening there was a hasty knock on the door. He told his caller to enter and when he turned Miss Chen stood inside the closed door, her face thinned by cold, hair dishevelled by the strong wind that had blown through Peking since dawn. One woollen gloved hand held the book she had borrowed.

He returned her smile. 'Sit down. Just in time for tea.'

'I cannot stay long.'

'It's ready now if you can take it English fashion.'

'I got used to it when my father and I were in Britain.'

She drew off her gloves. He noticed her beautifully formed hands, slender and pale, their nails shaped in narrow ovals. He collected another cup and saucer, hunting round until he found a spoon.

'When were you there?' he asked as he poured out tea.

'Years ago. I was young.'

'And now you are old. Help yourself to sugar.'

She smiled. 'I am thirty.'

'Tell me about England.' He reached over to switch off the radio.

'Please leave it on,' she said. 'I like this music.'

According to her story, her father had taught philosophy in California and had been invited to lecture in Britain. They spent the last year of the war in London and Scotland.

'The doodlebug and V-2 period,' he commented.

'That was where I got these scars. We were having dinner in Soho when a doodlebug dropped near the restaurant. The windows blew in. I was lucky. The families of other people were unlucky.'

She spoke familiarly of English towns and her references to the soft green countryside contained the usual Chinese envy. She refused a second cup of tea, saying she had to meet a friend from Tientsin who was sharing her room. At his invitation she borrowed another book, Somerset Maugham's *Summing Up*. She held it out to him.

'There are pencil marks on some pages. Do you want to rub them out?'

He shook his head.

At the turn of the corridor she glanced back. He raised his hand.

Six

LATE the following Saturday afternoon Steven returned to his room in a mood of exasperated despondency. It had been an irksome week. There had been no news, only publicity. His daily search for official confirmation of hints given by Mrs. Peng had proved fruitless. Embassy calls had failed to give him a single reliable lead.

In his absence the room had become stuffy. He opened the window, took off his overcoat and tie, hung them over a chair, and glanced round, unable to decide what to do. Nothing demanded his attention. Impatiently he turned on the radio. There was a knock on the door as he stood at the table studying the scheduled evening telecast.

'*Chin lai*,' he said.

His recollection of a similar knock proved correct. Chen Mei-ling hurried into the room. There was something furtive in the way she shut the door by pressing her back to it. Her dark eyes gazed at him nervously. She carried a large woven rush shopping basket full of groceries; out of it hung one of the gauze masks which many northern city Chinese wore in winter to prevent them from inhaling germs. Judged from her scarlet duffel-type jacket and grey slacks, she had not been on duty. Small embroidered flowers decorated a white silk scarf concealing her scarred neck. Her smile hinted at relief.

'You were out when I called earlier,' she said.

'I've only just got in. Can you stay for *ch'a*?'

She nodded pleasantly. 'I brought sweet cakes.'

Over tea she developed vivacity. She looked remarkably young sitting curled up on the settee, her red pullover tucked into the waist of her slacks, yellow woollen slippers which she had carried in her basket, Tibetan house *lhams*, emphasizing the smallness of her feet. She kept on her scarf, its ends tucked into her pullover. Although she liked to have the radio on, her

100

voice never developed stridor. It had a wide range of inflexions.

He did not have to prompt her to talk about her childhood in California. She seemed grateful to do so, telling him it was her home for nearly twenty years, pleasant years, sheltered from extremes. Her father's career had kept them among people without racial prejudice, unafflicted by great wealth or poverty. For some moments she was silent, looking down, a smile on her lips. When she resumed, her voice had a dry flat quality. Shortly after she and her father returned from Britain her mother died from a heart ailment. That marked a turning-point. Surrounded by memories, her father decided to return to China. Less than a year later the civil war recommenced; he was one of a crowd of trapped non-participants killed during a street clash in Shanghai. Somewhere in America were her sisters Yulan and Feng-shu and Elder Brother Hsi-lan. They had not written to her for over ten years.

He watched her expressionless face. It would have been wholly false for her to display emotion; in private at least individual Chinese did not embarrass strangers by shows of grief.

'I expect their letters went astray,' he commented.

'The American authorities are probably suspicious of Chinese who try to trace anyone here. Does your wife still go to America?'

Her switch of conversation caught him unprepared.

'I'm a bit behind-hand.'

'My father and I saw her in a revue in London. I forget its name. In one scene she wore a dress of blue sequins. She sang beautifully. We went on to a supper club and saw both of you there. The next day we saw your photograph in a newspaper. You had been to Buckingham Palace to be decorated. You looked very cross.'

He supposed that could explain the recognition in her eyes at the embassy reception. On the other hand, it might be part of an elaborate plan to put him off his guard. They certainly had information about him.

'Photographers upset me.'

'Did you shoot down more German planes?'

'I'd already been grounded. You saw Gillian in America?'

'Once, on television. Does she like you being here?'

'I doubt if she heard about it. She got involved in her career. We've been out of touch since the divorce.'

She made no comment, asking if he wanted more tea.

'Thank you.'

'Why did you come here?'

'It's easier to tell you how. After the war ended I hadn't a clue what to do. I met a man in Fleet Street who gave me a drink. Here I am.'

'Do you like the Chinese?'

He had anticipated that question. He took his cup from her and tasted the tea. 'Mmmm, good. I haven't got around as much as I'd like, but officials have been most considerate.'

The glint of amusement in her eyes could have several causes.

She settled back against the cushions. 'Did you go anywhere before you came here?'

'The Middle East.'

Her questions revealed either a well-informed or well-prepared mind. She asked about people, their life and customs, especially about nomad tribes, avoiding references to Anglo-French action over Suez. If her intention was to persuade him to slacken his vigilance, it did not succeed. He played it casual. She seemed interested. She certainly had an agile mind; it followed him into details for which no preparation could have been given her. He watched her hands. They were indeed beautiful.

A ring on the telephone interrupted his description of Baghdad.

When he answered it a staccato female voice brisk as a flurry of castanets announced its owner to be Miss Yu of the Information Department speaking for Mrs. Peng who wished to interview him at once on a matter of great urgency. She rang off without giving him a chance to ask why Mrs. Peng wanted to see him. He laid down the receiver, stared at the darkened window-pane for a moment, then turned on his heels.

'I must go out,' he said, more sharply than he intended. 'They want me at your Foreign Ministry. I've no idea how long it'll take. You stay for the telecast. Hu, my room-boy, will be along in half an hour. Don't bother about him.'

He shrugged into his overcoat while he spoke.

'Wait.' She got off the settee swiftly, picking his tie off the table as she went to him. 'You forgot this.'

'So I did.'

'Do you wear a hat?'

'No.' He knotted his tie hastily. 'Am I decent?'

She tugged the tie straight.

'Better.'

Her raised face held a slight smile, demure, tractable, the smile of a young woman, scarcely more than a blandness, quietness in her calm eyes and the lovely shape of her lips in repose more than justification of her name of 'Beautiful Mood'. Suddenly, entirely without warning, he was violently angry at what the rulers of this country were doing to its youth to ensure conformity and loyalty to themselves, forcing it to grow stunted and warped, clipped like the dwarf trees cultivated by the Japanese, forcing it to find enemies to hate. He saw her eyes darken.

'Why do you look at me like that?' she asked flatly.

He did not answer at once. A radio newscast overlaid their silence. Then he cleared his dry mouth.

'How am I looking at you?'

'As if you suspected me to rob you.'

He forced a smile. 'Sorry. People have decided to rob me of your company. Make yourself at home. The place is yours.'

He walked out still angry. No doubt Mrs. Peng would delay him long enough for a more expert search of his rooms than Hu ever gave them and by more practised hands, and they were very beautiful hands.

Mrs. Peng was already waiting. In addition to her two assistants, Steven saw John Butler, a thin-faced spectacled young Chinese whose black hair resembled an old bird's-nest, and a bullet-headed older man in a drab indigo Yat-sen tunic and trousers whose vast body sagged on a thin-legged gilt couch. His moon face was vacant.

'This is Mr. Sun,' said Mrs. Peng. 'Mr. Wen is his interpreter.'

Steven said: 'Good evening.'

The younger man stared at him blankly.

Sun said: '*Hsien shêng, kung hsi.*' His voice creaked rustily. The effect of speech spread over his huge face liked wind ripples across a pool.

'Please sit down, Mr. Kendal,' invited Mrs. Peng. 'This is just an off-the-cuff chat. I'm happy to say we will accommodate you. We want the world to learn the truth about our country. Mr. Sun is one of our new officials in Shanghai. You and Mr. Butler will accompany Mr. Sun when he entrains tomorrow afternoon. Your reservations are arranged.'

'Tomorrow?'

'Mr. Sun was delighted to cooperate. You will stay in Shanghai for ten days. Mr. Sun has gotten out an itinerary to provide a picture of our city reconstructions and ancillary urban projects. One day is viable for your convenience. Photos are subject to regulations.'

Steven returned her brilliant smile. His mind raced. Never in his experience had a request been granted so effortlessly. Did it presage a more liberal attitude to foreign correspondents? He would have to leave Jane a note to arrange a meeting on her return from Chungking. There was nothing else he could do.

'You are most thoughtful,' he said and tasted the cup of tea an assistant had placed on a small table beside him.

'You're welcome, you're surely welcome. I figured you'd be happy to take Mr. Butler along.'

Butler looked anxious, his face paler than usual. 'I hope you don't object, Kendal.'

'I'll enjoy your company.'

Sun said something. His fat-pouched eyes blinked repeatedly. The unkind years had shaped him into a malicious caricature of the Buddha, gone to seed; pendent breasts ridged his tunic like bicycle tyres, the thick pillow of his belly squatted on his thighs. He reminded Steven of Japanese wrestlers in old age.

In a piping tone, the interpreter said: 'Mr. Sun wishes to learn if you require to see particular projects.'

'We are happy to see whatever he decides we can see.'

'Mr. Sun asks if you want to take photographs.'

'A souvenir picture.'

'Do you want to tour the port?'

'We would like to see whatever is not covered by security.'

'Mr. Sun asks if you would like to meet friends in Shanghai.'

'I have no friends there, only acquaintances.'

'I don't know anyone there,' said John Butler.

'When were you last there, Mr. Kendal?'

'Fourteen months ago.'

Sun said: '*Hsieh hsieh.*'

Mrs. Peng beamed and raced them through the proposed itinerary. Sun sat silent, gazing in front of him. When the interview ended he stood up to shake their hands and bowed, a smile dissolving across his face. Mrs. Peng curtsied to the picture of Mao Tse-tung.

As they left the Ministry, Steven thought it curious, very curious. He glanced at his watch. The interview had taken exactly twenty minutes. On the steps he halted to look at the falling rain.

'Can I give you a lift back to the hotel?' he asked.

'Thanks,' said John Butler and then blurted, 'Kendal, I'd like your opinion on a private matter.'

'Save it until we get there. These drivers have long ears.'

Butler drew a long breath. 'We'll have a drink.'

'Fine.'

Butler shut the door. 'You handled them—what is it?'

'Have you got a radio?'

'Over there.'

Steven gave a diffident laugh. 'Do you object if we have it on? There's a regular programme that I never miss.'

'Of course,' said Butler in an offended tone and switched it on.

Steven hesitated, uncertain if he should warn Butler. He did not expect this babe in the wood to provide secret information; on the other hand, he did not want to scare him into peering continually over his shoulder. He decided to keep his own counsel.

'Well now, what is it?' he asked. 'You don't look too good.'

'I'm all right. Can you drink Tonghua? I've nothing else in at present.'

Steven overcame his dislike of the sweet syrupy taste of grape wine to sip appreciatively at the glass given him. 'Good. Now.'

Butler showed reluctance to discuss whatever was on his mind.

'Won't you take off your coat and sit down?'

'I'd like to, but I've got a date.'

'Oh.' Butler frowned. 'Well, um, look, Kendal, this is rather tricky, you know, confidential. You won't let it—um, no, sorry, you wouldn't. Look, what do you know about Sheila? Miss Grant?'

'Nothing.'

'Oh.'

'Do you want my opinion?'

Butler stared worriedly, discomfited. 'Um, yes.'

'Highly intelligent. I imagine she's been kicked around too much for her own good. In consequence, she may be a bit hard.'

Butler started to wander the room. 'Is she one of them?'

'A Commie? I've no idea.'

The younger man gestured meaninglessly, staring at the floor, his brows drawn. He sighed. 'Look, I'd better tell you. The other day she invited me to a um party in her rooms and I um told her I'd have to go home because well I've bitten off more than I can chew here and well um anyway I'll be broke when I get back. I don't expect you to understand.'

'Let's keep to you.'

Butler glared indignantly, his cheeks flushing.

'I was trying to explain why I'm not like you. You've had plenty of experience. Look, this is what happened. Three days later a man named Fou rang me up. Fou Ting-kai. Have you met him?'

'No.'

'He's an editor. He asked me to write an anonymous article on my first impressions of Peking for one of their Spanish magazines. You know, new eyes stuff. I wrote it. Why not? It gave me something to do. I stuck to architecture and industry, the new university. Fou liked it and paid me twentyfive pounds. He asked if I'd do um other pieces for a glossy Spanish magazine for South America they're bringing out next year. Same sort of thing, no by-line, fifty pounds an article. He said he'd heard I lived in Spain for a while and wanted a piece for the first issue giving my opinion of the Falange. I hate Fascists. How can you stomach people who yell *Muera la inteligencia!*—"Death to intelligence" and "Long live Death!" like their General Millan Astray? The Spanish Fascists stink to heaven. This afternoon Fou rang up to invite me to accompany you to Shanghai. Expenses covered. And they're going to extend my stay. He's fixed it.'

Steven tasted his wine. 'Did you write a book on Spain?'

'No, only articles for those small magazines.'

'Why not? How long ago?'

'Four or five years.'

'You were up at university?'

'Yes.'

'Did you tell Sheila you'd written them?'

Butler frowned. 'I see what you're getting at. I can't remember if I did. I may have done. Look, Kendal, I had to write those articles. I've nothing against religion in Spain, but the Falange allows people to live in dirt and squalor like um well I had to write them.'

'If it's not a rude question, how do you feel about Fou's offer?'

Butler nodded. 'That's it. So long as they don't ask me to write politics, why not? They can get scores of people to write new-eye pieces. Why should I refuse? It won't corrupt me. Fou has offered me a chance to express some opinions. I could starve to death at home because people won't bother unless you conform to Establishment or Antiestablishment. You don't have to write well, no, you need influence, back scratchers, chums upstairs. They manufacture reputations for those prepared to write to rule. So, there are bad things in China and good things at home. All right. There are good things here and bad things at home. Show me one Establishment or Antiestablishment Prime Minister who can persuade bosses and strikers to work together as these people work. You'll say I'm mad, but I want to write independently, not drink my way into a reputation among darling chums who'd drop me directly I disagreed with them. I won't lick boots just because their owner has sold a book for a film and I spoke to him last week.'

The words poured out of him and sweat shone on his forehead.

'I see,' said Steven.

Butler snorted sarcastically. 'I don't suppose you want to see, Kendal. I envy you for being my age in the last war. Your generation believed it was fighting to bring about a solid sane world. Look what you got. Look at the older people. Listen to them, just listen to them. They've lost faith in everything except money, influence, the golden handshake, the platinum belch. Their conversation is maggot-eaten by money. They can't talk for ten minutes without pricing everything. Let's not fool ourselves about the teenagers. They get more sense from a broken-down juke-box than from most of their parents. Parents! My God! They're not parents. They're people able to breed. They don't give their kids anything to believe in. Except to get money somehow. They go down on their knees to it and cross themselves only when they send off their football coupons. True?'

'Carry on.'

'So why the hell shouldn't I write for the Chinese on my terms? That's practical, that's hardheaded business. At home they'd call me a success of sorts. Fifty quid an article. Money for jam. The Almighty Lolly. Success success success! The parrot cry of the creamier radio interviewers. And what do radio comedians say? "Money won't bring you happiness but it'll help you to be unhappy in more comfort" and all the in-free audiences snigger hee hee hee. You can get away with anything in the West so long as you're successful. Then your friends and typists sell the dirt about you while you cool off in your coffin and they get ten thousand quid or more for entertaining the good clean upright decent public on Sunday. Then they scarper out of the country for six months and a day in order not to pay income-tax on the ten thousand. These Chinese don't allow that. They're ruthless, but they work. There's a golden rot going on in the West. Is that what your generation fought for, Kendal? Is that what your friends died for? Is that what you wanted?'

It was not the first time Steven had heard a newcomer indulge his native freedom to criticize what he had left behind by comparing it with what he found in China.

'No,' he said. 'Have you talked to Sheila about Fou's offer?'

Butler gestured again. 'No, only to you, I don't know why, yes I do. I think you see through the hypocrisy and corruption going on there, the quick rot. And you never act the war hero. The truth is, Kendal, your war is only names to my generation. We see you now, not as you were, tricked out in uniform.'

'You think Sheila prompted their offer?'

'She's the only one I've told about my being in debt. There's another point, Kendal. With a dozen articles I can pay off what I borrowed to get out here. Will my debtors care a damn that I got the cash by writing non-propaganda articles in Spanish for the Commies? Is it flaming likely?'

'Will you feel under an obligation to her if you accept?'

Butler got a handkerchief from a pocket and wiped his forehead.

'No, I don't think so.'

Steven nodded absently. 'Well, it's civil of you to take me into your confidence. I can't give you advice, only an opinion. It's your problem. And I can't give it now. This is new to me.'

Steven went back to his rooms in a thoughtful mood. Butler had done such a good job of answering most obvious objections to Fou's offer that his qualms over accepting it were not immediately obvious. He wished the younger man had confided in someone else. People always held your opinions on their affairs against you.

Nearing his rooms, he looked at his watch. Less than an hour had passed since he left them. He let himself into darkness. The sudden light gave no sign of Miss Chen. Every trace of her vanished. Their tea-things had been washed up and put in the cupboard. He lit a cigarette. Barring accidental encounters, that was their last meeting. He had a vivid recollection of her face in their last moments together. For some inexplicable reason, it hurt him.

As he wrote a note to Jane, Hu bobbed in offering affable apologies for being late. He finished his letter, stubbed out his cigarette, and walked down the cold rain-swept street to give it to a reception clerk at the Sunrise Hotel.

A car pulled up outside the Hsinshih as he returned and Clive got out. His ancient brown hat was tilted back on his head, the storm collar of his equally ancient fawn raincoat turned up, its strap hanging loose. He ran across the pavement. There was a gleam in his eyes.

'Wait a minute, old boy old boy,' he said. 'I want to see you outside this place. It's too much like home. Everybody listens. How are you, old boy?'

'Getting damp.'

'You have no need to trot about indecently exposing your venerable head, my gallant friend.'

'Tell me.'

Clive laid a finger along his nose. 'See? Long. Yards of it. Have you read their press releases recently, Father William?'

'Faithfully.'

'Have you seen mention of the Panchen Lama beetling back home?'

'I saw him at a reception two days ago.'

'Bless his heart,' said Clive. 'It must have been him. They can't dig out anybody who looks like that on purpose.' He glanced round. 'There are Tibetans here. With my world-famous flair for being first with the news, every dramatic item guaranteed to make my beloved readers belch, rattle, and burp at breakfast, I, the man on the spot with the office telephone, am soon to meet Khambas. Kendal! thou shoulds't witnesseth

that hour! Khambas, "men of the east" of Tibet, proud, un-
quelled. Now dig for yourself son.'

'Well well.'

'Bless your heart too.'

'Are they fighting again?'

'My lips are sealed.' Clive cocked his head on one side. 'See
the mud on me ear? It comes from listening to the ground.
You chaps don't realize the hardships borne by genuine newspapermen. You're a soft lot. Let's go and eat.'

'You are gay.'

Clive nodded. 'Yes. But yes. It's nice for me.'

2

Three nights later in his room, Clive read through notes copied
onto rice-paper from those taken down while two Khambas
talked to him through an interpreter at their secret rendezvous
that afternoon outside Peking. He had burned his original
notes and washed away their ashes earlier that evening.

The night was still after a cold windy day. While he studied
his notes he heard only an occasional footstep in the corridor.
He believed what the young Khambas had told him. Even
allowing for word-of-mouth exaggeration, they spoke with
authenticity. They told of thousands of Tibetans killed in recent
months, active men shot down in combat, older men, women,
and children, machine-gunned by execution parties. Several of
the executed men were named, leaders of resistance groups in
the three Tibetan towns of Lhasa, Shigatse, and Gyangse. The
heaviest casualties had been along the Bhutan frontier where
weather conditions kept the Himalayan *las* impassable except for
a few short weeks in spring; refugees who hoped to winter there
and escape through Bhutan to India directly the *las* were
passable had been trapped when reconnaissance planes guided
military units to their encampments.

Clive read each item twice to memorize it. As he did so, he

fitted its significance into the general pattern. There could be no doubt that the Peking men were committed to a policy to incorporate every area claimed by previous Chinese emperors. Tibet and Korea were only two. They were nibbling at Burma, Outer Mongolia, Kashmir, parts of India. They intrigued in every south Asian shore country. Imperialism is dead; long live imperialism. What puzzled Clive was why Peking should antagonize Moscow by implementing a plan which camped their troops and airplanes on the borders of the Soviet Union. Tibet had no significance to Peking, none except as a springboard against India and Nepal. He reasoned that they must have other cards up their sleeve, pretexts for conduct which Moscow would instantly denounce as imperialism if undertaken by another country. It beat him.

He picked up his glass and revolved it in his hands. These notes were not sufficiently documented. Not for a Peking dateline. Not to risk sticking out his neck. His thoughts followed his experience. The main Tibet story had ended months ago when the Dalai Lama reached India to take refuge from the Chinese. These notes gave a follow-up piece which sub-editors would slash to ribbons to give space to spicier, shivery stories of the body among the milk bottles on the next doorstep to their readers. He needed more details to outwit officials certain to yell blue murder when he filed a story.

'Coming,' he responded to the voice which called him. He finished his drink, folded his notes into a hiding-place that never failed him, went to switch off the light, and carried his shoes into the bedroom. As he entered, Ilse opened her eyes. Lying on his bed, hands under her head, shining hair loose, she looked magnificent. The warmth of her smile still surprised him. He put his shoes beside the wardrobe and said: 'You didn't take long.'

'You did. Have you locked the outer door?'

'Uh-huh.'

They talked casually while he undressed. As usual they spoke in her language. Neither of them mentioned her husband; earlier she had said he would be at home for two weeks when he returned from Hankow the day after tomorrow. That mention constituted their sole references to Han, and suited Clive. He detested the bumptious idiot. Tonight her voice sounded lazy. To his relief she had quietened considerably since she first came here for a drink, left him to attend to her makeup, and called him in to find her like this and talked in an anxious, rapid voice for hours, mostly about her home, as if powerless to control her memories.

He sat down beside her. It was good to observe her new composure. He had spared her questions calculated to cause evasions or revelations, preferring to wait until she felt a need to confide in him.

A flurry of rain scratched on the window. With a contented sigh she stretched luxuriously, smiling at him. No excitement or impatience fogged his appreciation of her like this. People who yattered about a man having to experience lust directly he saw a naked woman only revealed their own plight. Nature had intended her to be seen nude. That was the word: nude. He found the sight of her a delight complete in itself, like a statue by Bernini, the grace of her shoulders and arms, the contours of her breasts, her white skin, the sweep of her hips and legs, so individually and wholly perfect that he saw lines, symmetry, exquisite proportion, without consciousness of her humanity. Another spatter of rain interrupted her thoughts. She reached out to him.

'You are very patient,' she said. 'I am natural with you.'

'Bless your heart, I'm young with you.'

She pulled him down beside her. Following on his thought, it was a shock to feel the warmth of her body and its lithe stir as she moved closer for his caresses. For an instant her hands held his face above hers, then she drew his head down to her breasts.

And gradually a feeling of peace invaded her. She listened to a silence free from whispered defilements trying to force her to abase herself. There were no debasements here. Under these hands her bitter flesh was restored to freshness, given pride, her unhappiness soothed by a gentleness which searched her, acknowledged, laid claim, but never demanded total subjection. They saved her.

Once she opened her eyes, narrowing them against the blazing light. Momentarily she thought it strange to lie here conscious of quickening responses to a man two years older than her father, to hold his thin body in her arms and see his greying hair on her breasts, but no, not strange, for he had the power to comfort her and she eased his own fears. She resolved to tell him they would do without the light on her next visit; she had no fear in his arms. She shut her eyes, let her senses drift, misery and loneliness forgotten, and relinquished herself to the rage in their flesh.

3

Two days later Hu carried to the window a letter he had found on the table in Kendal's room. The afternoon light helped him to read the big words scrawled over the notepaper. He picked his nose while he whispered what the British woman had written:

'Steven dear, I'm sorry to have missed you. No one told me you were away. The receptionist here cannot say when you will return. The one at my place could not find a message from you. I tried to get Clive on the telephone, but each time the switchboard people said he was out. I had a frantically busy trip and did so want to discuss points with you. I got back absolutely exhausted. Now they've put forward my journey to Chungking by two days to allow for extra visits. Poor you, I shall have ever more questions to ask. In ten days. *Salaam alaikum, Allah yafazeq.* Jane.'

An idea came to Hu. Nowadays a man must take care of himself: he might need to get money from Kendal. He collected a pencil and sheet of paper and carefully copied out the message and put it into his pocket. Then he folded the letter back into the envelope and licked the gum carefully so that it stuck without anyone thinking he had read the letter.

Scratching his backside, he set off to give the letter to a man downstairs in the room of ears.

Seven

BUTLER began to ask questions directly they set out on their long train journey down to Shanghai. His insatiable curiosity sprang at everything they saw; peasants spreading buckets of human manure on flat Hopei fields, an arrowhead of wild duck speeding south under an early azure sky, factories rising alongside brown marshy wastes, frail country grandmothers in black trousers hobbling on bound feet, harvesters at work in effulgent coppery afternoon light, gaunt new concrete commune housing estates five storeys high, the decaying squalor of inhabited mud huts, a hundred evening suns drifting like phosphorescent onions across patchwork *padis* in Anhwei. On every side were immemorial Chinese scenes from ages lost in legend but he was temporarily unable to distinguish them from sights brought by this era of violent transition. Commonplace mechanical feats took him by surprise. One was Chinese ability to divide their train into four sections to ferry it across the Yangtzekiang, recouple them, and send it on to Nanking in twenty minutes. Yet it meant nothing to him that they were held up for two hours outside Shanghai to let through freight trains smelling of wet coal and iron, crates of vegetables and noisy chickens swaying precariously on each truck.

Steven felt sorry for Butler. First, garrulous rage at apathy and hypocrisy left behind; now, swamped by strangeness. He had gone through similar phases; in silence. Sun also showed sympathy; answers passed through his interpreter were unduly long. His massive bulk sagged opposite Steven every day, his heavy breathing like a private torture while he gazed longingly at the passing countryside. Steven gained an impression that Sun understood English.

What they saw in the insectivized parts of Shanghai reduced Butler to monosyllables. They toured through the pulsing roar of factories turning out textiles and electrical equipment, went over pharmaceutical plants producing antibiotics from imported ingredients and aspirin from coal tar derivatives, clambered about new buildings going up to house equipment for producing heavy machinery.

One day they toured wharves and warehouses, never far from the gentle suck and slap of lapping water. Activity surrounded them. Hundreds of men and women unloaded cargoes of rice, flour, and vegetables, and loaded exports of cotton and woollen fabrics, shiny mass-produced bicycles in bamboo frames lashed by rush thongs, sewing machines of remarkable simplicity, hand-embroidered silk goods, toys, kitchen utensils, all to be sold at between a quarter and a tenth of similar goods produced in the West, and tons of free propaganda literature. The ships being loaded were bound for South America, a thousand islands scattered across the Pacific, hot teeming cities in Southwest Asia, the Islamic states, great areas of Africa rising from the narrow mists of tribalism to the status of nations. Some ships in the Hwangpu came straight out of poems by Masefield, smokestacks crusted by salt, decks in need of swabbing, paintwork flaking and plates rusting.

Steven watched chattering women load sewing-machines into sampans to be hauled onto a grimy old tramp bound for Indonesia. The women were sweaty, dirty, and harassed, as women in wartime Britain, in pioneer America and Australia, had been sweaty, dirty, and harassed. On the next wharf the shrill voices of another bustling gang of women stevedores singing *wei-ho wei-ho*, the ancient cry of coolies, rose above a blare of nearby klaxons and the apologetic putt-putt of a donkey engine. He looked across the dimpled oily water at rivetters clinging to a scaffolding.

'Such lies!' exclaimed Butler furiously. 'At home they say Shanghai is a dead port.'

'It was. Picking up, isn't it?'

Sun took them to a show-piece commune outside the city. They were accompanied by a woman guide, Miss Hau, slight, pretty, and precisely vague. The commune was based on an electrical goods factory. According to Miss Hau, its bugles blew at six every morning for fitness development, breakfast was served at six-fifteen, work began at six-thirty and went on until a half-hour break at midday, and finished at seven-thirty. Miss Hau smiled gravely. This schedule had been suggested by the workers, who hoped to exceed their fixed production target. They attended four instruction classes and one discussion meeting every week and had one day off in eight. At an interruption from Sun, she explained that it was a pilot project and its seven hundred workers were highly skilled.

Steven studied intent figures along one assembly line.

'Are there special work schedules for expectant mothers?'

'Oh yes, and they receive extra food. Meat and sugar are still rationed, but their allowance is increased. In most cases babies are cared for in the commune crèche after a few days. The Women's Committee decided to free mothers from the responsibility.'

Her answers were amplified by an assistant manager. He was stocky, jowly, and middleaged. His name was Tsong. He was the son of a Shanghai millionaire; he had opted for the Party and acted as a technical adviser in exchange for life and three percent of dividends earned by extensive foreign holdings which would have gone to his overseas relations if the Party tried to obtain them. Mr. Tsong smiled athletically.

'We have had thirtyeight lovely little babies born in the last eleven moons,' he said in a pensive penny-whistle voice. 'Cute little beggars. Their mothers went back to work within days.'

'Ah,' said Steven. 'What wages are paid here?'

Mr. Tsong beamed. 'They vary according to work.'

'Are there deductions for communal expenses?'

'We held several meetings to discuss such issues. They voted unanimously for a scheme which relieved them of avoidable worry. We were delighted to accept their orders. Most keen, they are.'

'Do living expenses swallow up a large part of their earnings?'

'It depends what they earn.'

'Do higher paid workers contribute more? Or the same amount as lower-paid workers plus an additional levy?'

'All agreements were reached by unanimous decisions of the Social Committee on recommendations by various sub-committees. Everything works a fair treat.'

Steven saw no valid reason to be fobbed off by committees or half-forgotten English colloquialisms.

'Can individual workers opt out of paying for one or other facility?'

Mr. Tsong threw up his plump hands in horror. They were beautifully manicured. 'None has ever wanted to weaken our common struggle. The committees report gorgeous unity in our humble role in the big leap forward. Frightfully encouraging, what?'

'Indeed. Can we be told what wages are paid?'

'Yes yes,' said Mr. Tsong. 'The chairman of the General Management Committee will send them to your hotel.'

Steven doubted if they would ever appear.

'Jolly good.'

Mr. Tsong took him affectionately by the arm. 'Press on we must,' he said smilingly.

Next day Steven went in search of colour stories on available civic officials.

He also took advantage of an open invitation to visit the Club started by the RAF Association. There were less than forty members now, Britons, Danes, Frenchmen, Swedes, lonely representatives of firms which did manage to maintain hazardous trading relations, sole survivors of thirty thousand Europeans once based on Shanghai. Their clubrooms were sparsely furnished, a fifth-floor bar and diningroom, containing large photographs of the Queen and her father, and the RAF wings.

They listened to his description of the National Day parade. He had great admiration for them, treated like pariahs by supercilious Chinese officials, their work on import-export plans and to conclude disputes over appropriated business subjected to endless obstructions, yet he had never heard them grouse or despair. None criticized China. Most of them had spent their entire adult lives working in it. They were vastly unlike those Europeans who swarmed into Shanghai to pick at China like vultures and who flew off directly their rule ended.

'Why do they spend so much on arms and industry?' asked Randal, one of the older members. 'They need to concentrate on agriculture for five years, maybe ten. You can't feed seven hundred million people on guns or industry. What's the feeling in Peking?'

Steven smiled ruefully. 'We don't even get decent rumours.'

'Try to remember some,' encouraged George Wragg in his strong Yorkshire accent. 'Your beauty isn't enough to pay for your chow.'

'I'd much sooner you talked.'

'Nothing ever happens to us.'

They raised their glasses to the Queen and sat down to lunch.

Sun had arranged for Steven and Butler to attend various evening amusements. They were hustled around Palaces of Sport and Culture where ludo was rated as intellectual. One night they attended a performance of *Hamlet* in Chinese, and the next evening went to a workers' club cinema. When they went dancing, Miss Hau brought along her friend Miss Liang. Miss Liang came from Kwangsi. She was older than Miss Hau, frail, hipless, snub of nose, her pale thick lips given to sharp smirks of politeness. Clad in white blouses, drab blue coats and skirts, both girls embarked on the entertainment like nice girls committed to dull chores. One glance at Butler told Steven that neither of them was in danger of joining the seven foreign sailors currently in Shanghai gaols for attempts to 'demoralize members of the female sex'.

Miss Hau danced extremely well, gliding lightly on her feet. Her confidence aided Steven. Occasionally, in wayward moments, her attentive body yielded as if she was tempted to abandon her excessive decorum. The orchestra merited good dancers. He supposed its members were trained by the highly paid Filipino musicians who departed during the civil war. Around Miss Hau and himself trudged earnest couples, too busy learning culture to show verve or enthusiasm. He glanced down at his partner. Her eyes were shut. The ghost of a smile wavered on her lips.

'You dance beautifully,' he commented.

She opened her eyes, startled, her cheeks flushing.

'It is due to your skill, Mr. Kendal,' she said as if offended.

'Oh, I'm pretty hopeless unless I get a partner like you.'

For a long doubtful moment she gazed at him, and then seemed to decide that he did not intend to get fresh. But her face remained solemn. Casually, she glanced round, speechless until they came to an empty corner of the floor. She moistened her lips.

'Have you seen your new dance, the rock-'n'-roll?' she whispered.

'Only in films.'

'What happens?'

'People fling each other about, turn cartwheels, fall on their knees, leap around, and collapse.'

She shuddered.

'It must be very decadent,' she murmured interestedly.

Did he detect perplexity in her voice? It was a thought. Her ancestors had condemned the waltz as symbolic of White decadence; now it was cultural relaxation. He took heart. However strenuously one generation laid down positive rules of right and wrong etiquette, the next challenged the ruling.

'I wonder that two pretty girls like you and your friend don't get married,' he said.

Miss Hau was scandalized. 'I am a happily settled career girl. Marriage is a worthy occupation, but we have to fulfil our greater duty to the People's Republic.'

'I see.'

Then, for no apparent reason, she said: 'Miss Liang is over-joyed by her duties. They give her great happiness. She has invented a new method of typing to prevent errors.'

'She must teach me.'

'She has been promoted to a government position in Peking.'

'Then I may see her there.'

Miss Hau smiled at a stiffly passing couple. 'Not yet. She is to accompany Comrade K'ang Sheng to the Warsaw Treaty Powers meeting.'

Her soft voice implied urbane indifference.

'Ah yes,' said Steven. He wondered how Miss Hau could supply offhandedly an item of information denied him for weeks. K'ang Sheng was an alternate member of the Politbureau. Why did she tell him? The Chinese were marvellously skilful in leaking information when they deemed it necessary.

'They say rock-'n'-roll is noisy,' Miss Hau whispered furtively and in a momentary feminine weakness added: 'I would like to see it.' And she trembled delicately in lingering alarm while they drank glasses of blueberry juice to freshen themselves for an-other waltz.

They spent an afternoon at the Pengpu Machinery Plant, an afternoon at the No. 1 Iron and Steel Works at Wusoong, and toured the Farm Equipment Plant.

Their evenings. passed in tours of reformed churches, Buddhist temples, and mosques; they saw a play performed by workers of the Meat Processing Plant, shook hands at the Music Conservatory, listened to poems written by workers at the Wire and Cable Factory, saw amateur ballet dancers at the No. 19 Cotton Mill, admired an exhibition of woodcuts by artist-workers of the Machinery Plant, and went to a rehearsal of the dockers' band. One night they finished up at the Seamen's Club on the Bund.

Once upon a time it had been the most exclusive British club in Shanghai. In its marble lobby they were welcomed by a huge plaster cast of Mao Tse-tung. There were showcases of

Ming and T'ang pottery, vases to spittoons, to entertain sailors in search of culture.

Sun led them heavily into the bar. Its fame came from having the longest alcohol counter in Asia, a relentless hundred and fifty feet of dark mahogany to accommodate the thirst of vanished millionaires and those who had bought drinks for them. Sun insisted on buying vodka for Steven and Butler. He and their interpreter, Kwan, drank orange-juice. Two distant figures talked happily of putting out for Saigon on the morning tide.

Sun spoke wheezily to Kwan.

'Do you wish to see anything in particular during your last days here?' asked Kwan.

Steven let them see him consider the question.

'I don't think so. We're obliged to Mr. Sun for being so helpful.'

Sun nodded his massive head. The action was like the soft roll of a balloon in a draught. '*Pu kan tang.*'

'I hope Mr. Tsong will let me have the commune wages I asked for. They would be helpful.'

'*K'o hsi, k'o hsi,*' apologized Sun. '*Wo ie kei nie ta-t'ing.*'

'*Lao chia, lao chia,*' Steven thanked him.

Sun smiled politely. Steven wondered what the man thought about during the courteous exchanges. He maintained a bland vigilance, a wheezy Buddha whose expressions were unfalteringly formal.

Butler set down his glass.

'I wish I'd been here in the old days,' he said gloomily.

Steven lit a cigarette. 'Mr. Sun will supply you with historical information. I can give you a rough notion of it prior to the recommencement of the civil war. My paper then sent me to Japan. I spent a month here. There were three sections. The International Settlement, the French Concession, and the Chinese city. The Allies had relinquished extraterritoriality during the war.'

'Fascinating?' queried Butler.

'It depended on how you interpreted fascination. Corruption and graft were commonplace gimmicks. Mr. Sun will tell you there are no prostitutes here now. In those days there were ten thousand blossoms of the street, blooming here on the Bund, along Kiangsi Street, Foo-chow Road, everywhere, riddled with syphilis. Every morning beggars lay dead in the streets. Old people, women, children, boys hunting jobs. On winter nights they froze to death. Mr. Sun, was it in nineteen-thirtyseven that twentynine thousand people died of starvation?'

Sun nodded wordlessly.

'And in this club you could pay ninety pounds for dinner? Yes, so I heard. And there were sweat-shop conditions in the factories. Round about thirty years ago a British official outraged non-Chinese feeling by inviting the Chinese mayor to see a polo match.'

'God!' exclaimed Butler.

'And directly the Japanese were beaten it grew even worse,' said Steven. 'That was when I saw it. Unfortunately for us, many Chinese believed that the truth of Shanghai in those days was true of Western conduct everywhere. That's why they read Dickens and believe what he wrote to be true today.'

'It's a point,' said Butler.

Steven glanced at him. 'Other things should be remembered too. Europeans built Shanghai on marshes. No one else thought of it. And Europeans introduced machinery. But then—"the evil that men do lives after them".'

Sun ordered another round of drinks.

Butler scratched his forehead perplexedly. 'Shanghai seems moral now.'

'Oh, very moralistic, yes,' said Steven.

As they walked back to their hotel, electric light spread pale white blankets across the darkness. High on one scaffolding a shift of workers sang *wei-ho wei-ho*.

Steven was up early the next morning to see the demolition of mud-hut slums in the northern suburb of Fan K'ua-lan.

It was too early for the rush of conducted foreign parties. Steven took the lift up to the sun-lounge breakfast-room to see if Butler was waiting for him. They were at the Ching Chiang, once the Cathay Mansions, its oldfashioned furniture and appointments giving it a dusty Edwardian atmosphere. Its cuisine lacked inspiration, its breakfast of sardines and pickles a sad monotony. He saw no sign of Butler.

Down on the Bund the early bustle was in full swing. Thinking about the well-informed Miss Hau, he watched the crowds clot and dissolve in their '*jijimangmang*' rush. Opposite the old Hongkong-Shanghai Bank building files of pigtailed girls hefted sacks thrown ashore from blackened tugs. One girl reminded him vaguely of Chen Mei-ling. He frowned. She kept returning to his thoughts. First anger over, he had a growing conviction that he had belittled her by thinking she was a spy; calmer reflection indicated that all the evidence exonerated her. The trouble was that Chinese obsession in having *kwantchee* spies everywhere led a foreigner to suspect everyone automatically.

The scene below differed considerably from his first sight of it. There were few cyclists, fewer pedicabs. He did not see a single pith helmet, once displayed as a badge of office by the trusted clerks of compradors. A squad of workers performed callisthenics near a large poster of armed sailors storming into battle under a cloud of red flags; it was captioned 'Taiwan is ours!' Farther on were the inevitable nests of rifles stacked for militia practice. Towards him came factory workers, men and women in dungarees marching behind a cymbal-and-drum band and banners announcing an increased output at their factory.

Watching two brown-sailed junks drift down river, he wondered if Jane intended to come here. She had mentioned only journeys to Harbin and Chungking. Her silence since they parted was capable of several interpretations; she probably regretted her unexpected weakness. Everyone had them; everyone regretted them. Life.

'There you are,' said Butler. 'Oh, did I startle you?'

'I was mulling things over.'

While they had breakfast, Steven said: 'Two days to go.'

Butler added sugar to his tea.

'I'm not coming yet,' he said in a defensive voice. 'Sun has laid it on for me to visit Nanking.'

'Good. It'll break your journey.'

Butler frowned, and went off on another tack.

'Have you considered what I discussed with you in Peking?'

'Uh-huh.'

'What should I do?'

'You must decide for yourself.'

'Well, give me an opinion.'

'No one except you can honestly assess the pros and cons.'

'What would you do in my position?'

'How can anyone answer that truthfully?'

Butler lapsed into glowering silence. It did not last long.

'You surprised me last night by speaking candidly about Shanghai in the old days,' he said approvingly. 'Men of your generation usually cover up in front of foreigners.'

'Oh?'

'It's sensible of you to admit times have changed. Yesterday's heroes usually live in their brave past and forget time doesn't stand still.'

That was the last straw.

'I suppose it's because no one taught you manners,' said Steven thoughtfully. 'There must be a reason for you being so bloody rude.'

Butler flushed scarlet. 'Look here, Kendal.'

'No, you look here, as you call it. You ask questions like a dripping tap. You never listen to answers. You want someone to decide your private problems. Hell, you got yourself out here, so presumably you can work out your own problems. And so far as my generation is concerned, remember you're like the new Chinese.'

'And what does that crack mean?' asked Butler offendedly.

'You can do better. As you remind me, times have changed.'

Butler shoved back his chair, stood up, and stalked out of the restaurant, disdainful and sullen.

Steven shook his head. Naughty of him to deflate the pup,

but really there was a limit. And in fact he was vaguely alarmed for Butler, who had several points in his favour.

They did not speak to each other on their tour of the old Chinese city. The slums presented a horrible spectacle, tumble-down, decrepit warrens of stinking hovels which reminded Steven of *bustees* in Calcutta and shanty-towns on the high veld outside Johannesburg. On average, each hut was about eight feet square and seven feet high. They had to stoop to get into them and found bare concrete floors, windowless mud walls discoloured by rains which had seeped through, under the luxury of corrugated iron roofs. Every one stank of humanity, tin sanitation buckets and stale fumes from vegetable oil lamps.

'Two or three families lived in each house,' announced Miss Hau. 'Now there is only one. There were frequent epidemics of cholera and smallpox. Many people died of tuberculosis. The water supply was uncovered. The cess-pits were not attended to by the municipal authorities.'

'Now it has changed?'

'It is changing,' she corrected punctiliously.

They went on to new apartment blocks where each single room had a family, but provided electric light, a charcoal cook-ing stove, and a landing lavatory and bathroom. Their occupants were obviously proud of their new quarters though furniture was almost non-existent. On a wooden bench outside one dwell-ing three bearded old pensioners sunned their recollections.

Steven did not see Butler again. He was reported to be in bed suffering from a feverish cold. Sun and the clear-eyed Miss Hau saw Steven off from the airfield She waved to him most engagingly .

2

It was late afternoon when Steven let himself into his room. Everything looked excessively tidy. Coming in shrammed by a chill north wind blowing like molten ice through the streets the hotel heating had a feather-bed morning warmth against his skin. He carried his suitcase straight into the bedroom and unpacked.

Back in the other room, waiting for the kettle to boil, he glanced through information accumulated in his absence. An unfamiliar urge for neatness had prompted Hu to undertake semi-secretarial duties instead of behaving like a thoughtless chambermaid. Daily communications on the teletypewriter had been snipped to manageable lengths, assembled in sequence. Beside them were English translations of leading articles in *Jen-min Jih-pao* and *Hung Ch'i*, government documents, pamphlets, another volume of Mao's speeches translated into English. His letters included weekly lists of official events, invitations to two skating rinks, a presentation copy of a book describing the Long March. There was no letter from Jane.

He rang the Sunrise Hotel. The switchboard operator put him through to a soft-spoken male receptionist.

'Mrs. Crofton left for Chungking several days ago, sir.'

'When is she coming back?'

'Sir, kindly allow me to enquire.'

Steven glanced at some woodcut reproductions while he hung on. They were admirable. Then the soft voice caressed him into attention.

'Sir, I am informed Mrs. Crofton has decided not to return to Peking. Please, who is speaking?'

'Steven Kendal. Did she leave a message for me?'

'Hold on, if you please . . . sir, I am sorry there is no letter.'

He rubbed his forehead. 'Did Mrs. Crofton leave a forwarding address?'

'Sir, no no, I am sorry.'

'I thought Intourist notified travellers of hotel reservations in advance.'

'The usual procedure has had to be suspended this year due to many many tourists, sir. Intourist may be able to give you more information than I can, sir.'

At Intourist a woman official announced that her file

showed that Mrs. Crofton has chosen to go to Hongkong by another route. She offered to contact their Chungking office for details: it would take a few days. It occurred to him that Jane might have given a message to Clive, a more satisfactory method in this land.

'No, it doesn't matter,' he said, and rang off. Then he put through a call to Clive, and learned that Clive had not seen her.

As he brewed a pot of tea there was a knock on the door and an unknown Chinese in hotel uniform came in, bowing politely.

'Kendal *hsien shêng*?'

'Yes?' queried Steven.

'I am Shuen Nien, your room-boy.'

Shuen smiled ingratiatingly. He resembled an angry mouse, a short middleaged man, black hair swept back from short forehead in a wave which broke over his small pointed ears, slim body swaying gently on his narrow hips. His thin face was sharp, its leanness enhanced by flat cheeks, a thin nose, a girlish neck, his long teeth bared in a smile. The fingers of his left hand ended at their second knuckles, the skin drawn tight over stumps left stiff by amputation.

Steven put down the tea-pot. 'Is Hu ill?'

'He has retired and left Peking,' said Shuen. He gentle voice had a pronounced lisp and marked r-trouble. 'He was in bad health for several months. He has gone to a nursing-home somewhere and has been given a big pension. Most unworthily, my poor services will be at your instant disposal. Did I arrange your documents correctly?'

'Fine, thank you.' said Steven, and supposed that Jane would write to him from Hongkong.

3

Sun heard the Public Security official in Peking say: 'He told Intourist it did not matter about the woman. He was offhand.'

Out in mid-stream opposite the Bund a tug hooted in the rain-swept darkness.

'How did he say it?' asked Sun. Tonight he was more breathless than usual, weary from going on long tours and eating heavy meals every day. He massaged his belly tenderly.

'He said "it doesn't matter" and "forget it".'

'Did he mean he wanted her to forget speaking to him?'

'It is possible.'

'He must be aware that such communications are properly handled.'

'He may have been trying to influence her. I will try to find out if he knew which woman he was speaking to. He could have recognized her voice.'

Sun straightened on his buttocks to let out a long belch. 'Did Crofton have a chance to tell him where she was going?'

'She will not be told until tomorrow that she is not coming back to Peking.'

'Has she behaved suspiciously?'

'As if she suspected she will not return here?'

'Yes yes.'

'No.'

The man in Peking gave his answers crisply, offering no information unless asked for it. Sun stared round his room.

'Did you search his rooms thoroughly after we obtained the letter she left for him?' he asked.

'Yes. There was no other letter.'

'What were the foreign words she wrote him?'

'They were an Arab blessing.'

'Love words?'

'Her use of them gave them an appearance of being love words,' said the man in Peking cautiously.

'What was their meaning?'

' "Peace be on you" and "May God preserve you".'

' "May God preserve you" could be a warning.'

'The possibility is being investigated,' said the man in Peking. 'She may know that he is in touch with Kuomintang or American agents. She sat beside Prince Sergei Oubletski, a White

Russian, on a park bench in Pinkiang. We have him under close observation.'

'Has Kendal met Shuen Nien?'

'This afternoon. Shuen reported that Kendal put his own clothes away.'

'Unusual for a foreigner.'

'We shall test his underclothes and shirts for secret inks.'

The conversation ended, Sun sat staring in front of him. There was nothing he could do except wait for Kendal to unmask himself. Sooner or later every spy gave himself away. At length Sun struggled to his feet.

As he walked out of the hotel, the rain streamed down his dry old-feeling face. It got into his mouth, tasting of salty dirt and coal fumes sidling along the river. He glanced round furtively, saw nobody, and committed a crime by spitting into the river. He trudged on, feeling tremendously old and weary, a hundred thousand moons remote from the man who first saw Shanghai when the future seemed to be a ripening harvest of sunlit dawns, and Yi-hai was a rainbow on the green mountain of his youth.

Eight

TANG THE MUTE lived in terror of exposure as a Nationalist soldier. It had happened without warning. An attack of influenza had kept him in bed for some days. Within an hour of his going back to work Shuen Nien had come into his lift.

Since then he had forgotten what it meant to be at peace. Shuen was the most venomous of the interrogators who questioned him after he had been found injured in his communist uniform following an abortive raid to blow up a Red arms-dump near Hankow during the civil war. The other interrogators believed he had lost his memory. Shuen did not, his wily suspicious mind never satisfied by answers given him. Shuen had questioned him day and night for three weeks.

Every day Tang felt fear tighten in him. It gave him no relief to learn that Shuen had taken the place of Hu in order to spy on the Englishman Kendal. Nor did it help to tell himself that they had not seen each other for ten years. Shuen had cause to remember him; he was one of Shuen's failures. Ten years ago Shuen was famous for the quantity of people killed by his accusations. Tang was conscious of Shuen watching him intently whenever they met.

Tang was glad he had no woman to pry on him. Women were quicker than men at sensing a man's fear and nowadays a woman shared a man's home only to satisfy her physical needs; in the old days a woman might hate the husband chosen by her parents but she gave him her loyalty. At least no woman was able to betray him to Shuen.

2

Steven obtained no figures of wages paid in Shanghai. Hard and fast information on the condition of workers as economic units was never willingly supplied by Chinese officials. The details given in speeches could never be verified. Steven had tried to obtain reliable information directly he took up his appointment, but he had never succeeded; the figures most frequently given placed the annual average wage of a commune worker at about £7 plus what was received in kind: housing, electric, food, and medical services. It set a major problem for foreign newspapermen. Steven had evolved his own methods for avoiding censure. 'Shanghai officials explained how wages are under frequent revision,' he wrote in his profile article; 'due to adjustments in the national economy, brought about by the "big leap forward" campaign, and to gradations of a works' points-system in various categories of skilled labour. This conforms to the latest pronouncement of the Ministry of Finance . . .' and he added a short quotation of no importance.

It was not always simple or adventuresome to be a foreign correspondent.

He filed the story. At the same time he sent off a news-item: 'It is rumoured that K'ang Sheng, alternate member of the Politbureau, is expected to head deputation to Warsaw Treaty powers meeting in new year, and may contribute important policy statement on Peking attitude to world situation.' He kept his fingers crossed.

The Foreign Ministry did not issue an immediate denial.

Three days later Steven was summoned to appear before Mrs. Peng. She welcomed him happily.

'I've just gotten details of your visit to Tientsin, Wing-Commander,' she announced delightedly. 'I guessed you'd only want three days there.'

He had not asked to go to Tientsin.

'Excellent,' he assured her warmly.

'You're surely welcome. My guess is you'd be glad to get going, so I asked you here to meet Mr. Ku, and he's ready to take you off this evening. He's a friend of Mr. Sun. You'll get along fine.'

3

No occupation reveals a futile expenditure of energy more rapidly than journalism. You do not have to set off on an assignment to have a lively appreciation of whether it will be worthwhile or a dead loss. Steven foresaw that Tientsin and he had nothing to give each other. But he went. There were perils in avoiding an assignment. A classic example was provided in the 'thirties by a North American newspaperman who left friends in the bar of his favourite pub to telephone in a report of the safe arrival of an airship from a trans-Atlantic crossing; he dictated a routine item, unaware that a radio reporter at the airfield was even then on the air giving a live and horrifying description of the blazing airship disintegrating in front of his eyes.

Steven strolled around Tientsin for two days. He visited an

Automobile College where students were taught to drive and service *Tung Fang Hung* tractors and KT-3 combine harvesters. He went over factories. He played strenuous table-tennis at the Palace of Sport. At Mr. Ku's suggestion they went out to Taku, a short distance away, where the excursion yielded an hour of tranquillity as they saw the sun rise out of the Yellow Sea into a grey-glass sky, scattering a golden rain among wide reedy swamps and splintered marshes. Steven felt the early knife-like chill scrape his face, numb his fingers to their reddened knuckles. Ku talked enthusiastically about the migratory habits of wild duck and waders.

Steven went back to Peking in a resentful, irritated frame of mind, sick of listening to people yatter their gobbledygook ideological double-talk, authentic Orwellian newspeak.

He dreaded to contemplate where all this right-thinking and right-talk was leading the younger people. They were being conditioned more ruthlessly than Pavlov's dogs to ensure their blind conformity and total obedience to the Establishment.

4

The evening that Steven returned from Tientsin he went to an embassy reception to celebrate someone who had tossed off right-thinking speeches and bombs.

Sheila Grant was there. He detected changes in her. There was no visible tension and she did not indulge in her usual gesticulations; she hardly needed the latter for her companions were four Cuban *pistoleros*, their beards curling like wirewool, come to establish relations of comradely honesty, as NCNA put it, and, judged from their appearance in tropical-weight camouflage uniform, likely to sample China-style pneumonia; their gestures were frequent. She wore only a thin gold chain round her neck.

During a gefuffle of excitement over political newcomers she joined him near the bar.

'Are you alone, Mr. Kendal?'

'I am, Miss Grant.'

They talked about nothing in particular. She was bored; it was her ninth embassy function in eleven days.

'How is Butler since he got back from Shanghai?' asked Steven. 'I haven't seen him.'

'I hardly see him. His new friends keep him busy.'

'Oh?'

'Alfred and Rosemary Wilson.'

'I caught sight of them at the Foreign Ministry some weeks ago.'

'Burke Hauser. Elmer Krantz. Lana Kobler. Dorothy Wang. Jack Pick.'

He nodded as her toneless voice added to the list. Butler was being given the treatment. Everything laid on to impress him of hardy independent souls, pioneers working for the brave new world. The same bunch had collared him when he arrived, to explain their viewpoint; he had never heard of them until they came to introduce themselves.

'He gets around,' he commented.

'Yes. You look tired.'

'Jaded.'

They talked until one of her Latin American friends took her off to meet someone. Steven had another drink on the embassy and then, fairly sure that nothing spectacular or news-worthy was likely to happen, took himself home to work.

His endeavours to concentrate on the Tientsin piece were useless. He hunched at his typewriter unable to invent a lead peg on which to hang a mere three thousand words. No single idea beckoned to him to set words tramping across the flimsy in the roller.

No one responded to his invitation in reply to their knock on the door. At the second knock he called out irritably. The door swung open to reveal Sheila Grant standing selfconsciously on the threshold, an expression of astonished meekness in her eyes and a heavy black woollen coat belted over her emerald

134

green sari. She grasped a bottle in one gloved hand. As he got to her, she held it out to him.

'For you. It's very good brandy.'

'That's a nice gesture. What do I owe you?'

'Nothing. My friend believed it was for me. Good night.'

'Wait a bit.' He studied the label. 'Why for me?'

'You looked bad-tempered and miserable. Good night.'

'Don't be in such an infernal rush,' he said irritably. 'I can't crack this alone. You'll have to help me.'

She turned back. Her eyes searched his.

'Ah, come on,' he said.

'Do you want to make love when you drink?'

All in all, a fair question. He hunched his shoulders and said: 'It's so long ago, I haven't the vaguest idea. It's up to you to find out for yourself.'

She followed him into the room. 'Just two then, Kendal.'

'You'll find music on the radio.'

'I'd sooner talk.'

She discussed words. She had collected a ragbag of English oddities like nithered, ducify, quodlibertarian, fantique, prolegomenical, numinosity, and expected him to explain each one precisely. He had scarcely ever heard of them. He poured out more drinks.

'Who dug them up? Butler?'

'Yes. Another was edentulous.'

'I know it! Toothless.'

She watched him carefully. 'He said I was a slummocky besom fustulated with trinkelments. What does it mean?'

'I've no idea,' he said, furious at the supercilious bastard for insulting the girl by trying to take the mickey out of her in a sniggery-schoolboy fashion.

'Kendal, you're lying.'

'No no.'

She finished her drink, shoved the glass towards him, and held out her hand. 'Give me a cigarette. And we'll have another drink. You're still lying. He meant I was an overdressed whore.'

After that things grew hazy while they drank and talked

about poetry. His brandy-fired zest rediscovered other men's flowers in forgotten corners. She was a good listener. She sat still on the settee, her thin face like carved wood, the folds of the sari slack over her breasts, her hands folded.

In the midst of one verse he stopped, suddenly conscious of China pressing in from every side. Its leaders paid lip-service to peace and did everything possible to push Russia into war with the West because Big Brother, 'a living Buddha' according to the NCNA in October '59, wanted the lot. Big Brother, the world's foremost exponent of the cult of the personality. Don't talk so loudly, she warned. I named no names, he said, but he is, a military genius, a scientific genius, a political genius, an artistic genius. His propagandists say so though they leave out his genius for killing people. He's also a genius at whipping up fear and hatred of everyone who disagrees with him. It shines through his propaganda. Why, if not to create war? Have you heard Big Brother call for peaceful coexistence, not ruddy likely, he said violently, and picked up his cup and saucer and flung them at the wall. They shattered and fell in pieces.

'How does the poem by Yates about the pilot end?' she asked. 'You'd got to "this tumult in the clouds".'

He rubbed his forehead. 'Oh yes,' he said.

> 'I balanced all, brought all to mind,
>   The years to come seemed waste of breath,
>   A waste of breath the years behind
>   In balance with this life, this death.'

He persuaded her to have a last drink. They laughed at something idiotically funny that he didn't understand. She said, I must go. Shall I take you home? No, I can just manage it. You know, you're a prettier girl when you let yourself relax.

'Good brandy,' she said.

'Excellent. I'm glad you acted on the impulse to bring it.'

'I nearly ran off. You're a grim man, Kendal.'

Oh dear, oh dear. Her head shook a denial. You've explained yourself now. Jolly good; let's do it again. She smiled up at him, the skin of her face a peachy smoothness, enormous eyes shining like jet, and shook hands politely, and went away.

He slept badly. His dreaming mind relived a confused chaotic dawn scramble, pushing his patched old Spit upstairs after a Junkers 88, getting in two bursts just as the Hun vanished in cloud, then he came out of cumulus into a primrose-yellow sky full of the bastards, tiers of Messerschmitts rising one above another, spaced out like a geometrical pattern, dog-fights going on around them. His R/T went dead. He saw a 109 going down, pillaring black smoke, then shining yellow tracers streamed ahead of his starboard wing, and he twisted his head round to see one of the bastards tight on his tail, and oil sprayed from his tank, dripping over the cowlings, fogging the bloody windscreen. His muscles ached from throwing the Spit about in evasive action, sweating, and then flames came from his engine and he fought to jettison his hood, release his strap, the lead, ready to bale out, falling, falling, walking into the private bathroom in the Liverpool hotel that Sunday afternoon, every detail clear, Gillian naked and dead drunk in the bath, her blue eyes meaningless as the sky, the first of her hot-pants pageboys drunk on the floor, mumbling into his vomit, gilt buttony uniform slung over a chair, and then the blower went, and he and George and Kiwi and Johnny belted out and climbed into the cockpits, and he cleared the trees by inches, feeling tired, so goddam bloody tired tired.

He opened his eyes. Long ridges of cloud stretched across the pale sky. He felt exhausted. At his first bid to get up everything dissolved and blew across his eyes in a malevolent glittering dust of silver confetti.

He waited. He kept his eyes shut. A residue of fright from the war crusted over his conscious mind. He couldn't remember the last time he dreamed about it. Years ago. He lay rigid, sweating.

An hour later, fear absorbed, he went into the bathroom. For some reason he hated it. It smelled dirty, like that place in Liverpool.

He envied Clive Dixon's control of his liver.

5

Han listened attentively to the recording of what Kendal and the half-caste cow had said to each other. At first he believed they had called him down to hear it because the woman was Ilse. He had expected to be given proof of her unfaithfulness, expected it for months. But the light voice prompting Kendal to quote poetry belonged to Sheila Grant. Her gentle tone amazed him.

Shuen switched off the recording. 'Was it poetry?'

The other men watched Han intently.

'It was poetry,' agreed Han.

'There is no record of them being friendly until now. Both of them have been here longer than others. Europeans are clever at inventing codes. Was he talking to her in a code?'

Han smiled superciliously. 'Europeans behave strangely about women. My observations in various European countries showed they do not act like normal men. They become friendly after ignoring a woman for years.'

Shuen grunted.

Han frowned importantly. 'I do not think they were talking to each other in code.'

'Why not?'

'I think they would have given each other written messages rather than talk,' replied Han, and forestalled Shuen. 'They could have written messages while they talked, yes yes. It would have been simpler for them to write such messages without talking.'

Shuen considered each point thoughtfully, his lips pursed, his dark gaze switching about the room of ears. At length he said: 'We must take every precaution to protect our People's Republic from imperialist spies.' He began to lecture the other men.

Han lapsed into boredom. Without exception these credulous fools were visibly impressed by Shuen's erudition. Peasants were always easily swayed by men who spoke fluently. He studied them curiously. Their faces were intent, their eyes shone. They forgot everything; their ailments, their bellies, their women. It did not really surprise him. None of their enjoyments or illnesses were of sufficient excitement or intensity to help them forget themselves or become interested in life. No day brought them adventure, satisfaction or novelty; they added nothing of importance to life; they were meaningless and useless. Three hundred millions of them could well die today without their dying being a loss. But it would be advisable to have them killed by an enemy. They might as well have propaganda value.

As the meeting ended, Shuen motioned to Han. 'I want to speak to you on another matter.'

'I am happy to assist,' said Han.

Shuen remained silent until the others resumed their duties, rubbing his maimed fingers along his forehead. Then he motioned Han to accompany him into the smaller office. He shut the door.

'I want to talk to you about the liftman Tang,' he said. 'Where does he come from? I have met him, but I cannot remember where.'

An hour after Han returned to his flat Ilse came in carrying two bags loaded with groceries. The raw afternoon air had whipped colour into her cheeks. She wore a red scarf over her fair hair. As she sorted out her purchases, the sight of her twisted in him like a broken knife. Suddenly she glanced at him and merely by seeing her eyes he could sense a man who gave her happiness. But not Kendal, he admitted.

Crazed by jealousy, he smashed his fist across her lips. The blow caught her off-balance. As she fell he struck her again, and again. Blood spurted from her lips and chin. For a moment she lay still, and then crawled away on her stomach as he kicked her in the ribs and on her naked thigh. She collapsed, moaning.

Abruptly a measure of sanity returned to him. Blinded by tears of shame, he rushed wildly from the room.

Nine

Almost every third day now evidence of a developing ideological wrangle between Moscow and Peking came through in translations of speeches given by Party mandarins. Quite often Steven had no need to go out in search of news. It clattered at him on teletypewriter and in radio voices whose solemnity was in marked contrast to restless tongues yelling trigger-happy threats against Taiwan. He saw how swiftly this new campaign developed its particular tone, sure proof in these monolithic countries of having been carefully planned well in advance. The first speeches set the atmosphere, an indication of injured faith and indignation at methods by which old and trusted comrades were allowing themselves to introduce new interpretations of doctrine which defied the strict orthodox Marxist faith taught and practised in China. Then came conferences of workers and students which passed unanimous resolutions. These stated that the Peking mandarins based their interpretation solely on the theories of Karl Marx and intended to establish its everyday reality by accepting the theories on organization and development formulated by Lenin, father of the coup in revolutionary Russia which won power for the Bolshevik group. Significantly, the speakers insinuated that the present rulers of Russia were forsaking the pure doctrine of Marxism and Leninism, defying the creed, by their expressed intention to try to win control of Europe and America through peaceful propaganda or political rebellions rather than by war. Repugnance dripped from virtuous lips. Innuendoes were rampant. Student speakers, always more virulent and outspoken than Party leaders, declared that Lenin had foreseen world warfare as a necessary phase of preparation for the final success of world communism.

All this was equal to accusing the Kremlin of deviationism,

its own favourite condemnation of those in the camp who disobeyed it.

Steven was astonished by the arrogance of Chinese leaders in allowing no newspaper or radio mention of Russian rebuttals to their charges. Their silence was retaliatory: no mention of the communes had been made in Russia. Future historians would name this the most significant period in the schism of communist states. China, conscious of her power, ablaze with her future, was preparing to claim leadership, and Russia, technically superior, felt squeezed by China and economically predominant America. No wonder the Kremlin wanted lengthy peace talks with Washington, to gain a breathing spell; no wonder China wanted war, to crush both America and Russia. And Russia would have to pull technological successes out of the hat to retain dominance over China.

The Politbureau mandarins, drunk on their own publicity, were bungling their challenge. The men in the Kremlin did not give in or forget easily. The mandarins had only population strength at present. They had telegraphed their intentions too early.

One evening Steven finished his notes and shook his head.

'It's a great life if you can take it,' he said aloud. 'Mad, utterly mad. Those in agreement? Thank you. Those against? None. The representative of Euthanasia abstains. Motion carried.'

The next morning he went over some of the nineteen factories in the Peihsinchiao commune in the northeast of the city. One factory was turning out record quantities of children's shoes, starting a competition for children's shoe-factories throughout the country. He was given a lunch of rice and steamed bread, fried beans, and turnip soup in the canteen. At the next table a serious woman read one volume of Mao Tse-tung's collected speeches. Later his car drove him across to the western sector to the Chingshi coalmine, where miners were chasing mines with record outputs in other regions.

He shivered in the icy air. The black turtles of winter crawled over the land. And more than turtles. He had a strong sensation of being followed wherever he went.

On the following Saturday the sun rose in a cloudless sky. Steven took himself up to the European restaurant for a solid breakfast. Fortified by a China-style kedgeree of rice, fish, eggs, pork, and shrimps, he decided to give himself a holiday from paper work, and set off on a roundabout walk to the Forbidden City. He encountered no foreign sightseers.

He developed a liking for the morning. There was a tonic freshness in the cold air, all the more welcome after being mewed up in the hotel for several days. Although it was still early the city thrummed with activity. Blue-clad cyclists spun across busy intersections. Every pavement had its chains of almond-eyed children toddling along hand-in-hand or halted to gaze wonderingly at poster campaigns on hoardings screening new building sites. An aged turnip-seller loped down a side-street, chanting in the dry muted voice of his ancestors. On one busy stretch of road two agitated bus-drivers chattered like frenzied castanets beside a bus whose tank boiled ominously.

When Steven reached the vast man-created desert of T'ien-An Mên Square, companies of militia were engaged on rifle drill. In the far distance, beyond the monument to heroes of the revolution, several hundred school-children were doing physical jerks. He skirted round a squad of workers, mostly young girls from shops and offices, gaining instruction on how to carry and use their rifles. They provided an unusual sight, silk ribbons tied in their glossy pigtails, grey dust on their flushed faces, ears reddened by the wind, eyes intent as they stood, knelt, and sprawled full-length cuddling their rifles. His attention was caught by the farthest girl, a strong hefty wench, solid of blue-trousered buttocks, massive of bosom, and whose single plait, thick as a cable and tied by two frivolous pink bows, reached her waist. She was down on one large knee, in some difficulty of lying comfortably on her front to use her Czech rifle. Her transparent health and vigour had equipped her for more productive lists than these and she evidently realized it. As he approached she was blowing out her cheeks in exasperation, nearly dropping her weapon in efforts to discover a comfortable method of falling. She wiped a large grimy hand over her small wide-nostrilled nose. She saw him watching her, grinned hugely, yelled something which set other soldiers giggling, flopped down on her big soft belly, and trained her sights on him.

He spent the morning looking at treasures accumulated inside the crimson-walled, imperial yellow-roofed palaces of the Forbidden City. They ranged from the delicate and exotic, exquisite fans and carved ivory war chops, to the cumbersome idiotic, the inevitable chiming clocks presented by European kings long since come to dust. He wandered round the empresses' rooms. Their courtyards, scented by jasmine and shaded by pines on his last visit, were cheerless and forlorn now, but the rooms shone, a blaze of gold ornaments, chains, chased foot-bowls, fruit dishes, drinking cups, pagodas, and necklaces, set amid petrified rainbows of beautiful hand-embroidered silks and brocades. Here the empresses had played their roles in dynastic fortunes, borne their children, intrigued to outwit ambitious concubines, schemed to defeat tyrannical mothers-in-law, and sustained weak husbands; the Party mandarins were obviously proud of them. And in other rooms he studied the jade, an aqueous forest of urns, figurines, daggers, and boulders carved to depict sylvan scenes of amiable aristo-crats and monks strolling through grottoes, temples, woods, and up mountainsides under clouds wrinkled like morning sheets.

When he left the Forbidden City at noon the militiawomen had vanished. A crowd of out-of-town sightseers in padded blue jackets was clotted round the base of the frosty white monu-ment. His sensation of being under close scrutiny continued. You developed an intuition about such things.

As Steven sat in his silent room in the middle of the after-noon, reading teletype bulletins, the door opened behind him. Before he was fully conscious of it a hand folded over his lips.

Its light pressure conveyed a warning, not malice. He twisted his head round to look up and saw Mei-ling gazing down at him. Her dark eyes entreated his cooperation. Unsurely her hand left his face.

Without speaking she went over to the radio and switched it on. She kept her back to him, waiting for the volume to come up. He drew a breath; something had told him that she would come. She wore the same jacket and slacks, carried the same shopping basket. When the radio came on she switched to a wavelength airing recorded music, and turned to face him. Motioning her to silence, he stood up. To be sure, he opened the door. The corridor was empty. He locked the door, pocketed the key, went across the room and took her basket, putting it alongside his typewriter. Her eyes were nervous.

'How are you?' he asked conversationally.

'I have been in Canton.' She tried to take quietness from his quietness. 'There's a microphone in the air vent.'

'Is there?'

Her eyes widened at his tone. 'Golly, you knew,' she said and her shoulders slackened.

'How did you know?'

She smiled cynically. 'I knew there was bound to be one and discovered it after you went out that evening. I had to tell you, but I didn't get back until two days ago. If I'd left a note your boy would have seen it. I took British trade unionists to Canton the day before you left Shanghai otherwise I would have come sooner.'

'You don't have to explain.'

'I must.'

'Not really.'

They searched each other's eyes while they spoke. Hers were worried, hiding no shade of expression from him. Inconsequentially, he noted that she wore a brighter scarf, a frivolous conceit of baby carp fleeing in golden profusion through emerald reeds over a blossom of crisp white silk. He looked at her eyes again. They met his steadily, nervousness flown, waiting. Her lips were impassive.

144

He took hold of her naked hand.

'I could not ask about your friend.'

'She lives on the——'

'Tell me later,' he interrupted. 'I need tea. Did you bring cakes? I've got an appetite like a rhino these days.'

Her hand lay claspless in his.

'I may not have brought enough.'

'Unkind.'

'I thought you would tell me to go.'

'No.'

Her eyes sharpened. 'What about the microphone?'

'They've shifted it. It's near the door, in the wall under that chair, to catch voices as people come and go.'

'When did you find it?'

He smiled. 'Foreign correspondents who aren't prepared for these gadgets don't remain foreign correspondents for long.'

'It's terrible.'

He released her hand. 'Put your things in the bedroom.'

He watched her go into the other room. He was glad she had come, relieved, and more than relieved. And that was wrong, he told himself. So was the way they had looked at each other, their words insignificant compared with what they learned in each other's eyes. Wrong.

She reappeared tucking the blouse into the waist of her slacks. Her hair was an unruly cloud over her ears. She paused to glance out of the window, her body silhouetted against the apricot sky, then came across in response to his instructions. Her eyes grew fearful as he loosened her scarf, ignoring her whispered pleas, and tossed it onto the table, a bright foam among his books. 'Forget it,' he told her.

Gradually her voice gained confidence. They talked of nothing at any length, dipping into a score of topics like bargain-hunters. She was unfeignedly hungry for conversation free from caution and propaganda. Her contribution had a penetrative observation, the silken probe of detail absent from male speculation. He asked no questions about her life; she told him that she shared a room with two other women guides in one of the new blocks for government employees near the University. Until two months ago she was a guide in Chungking, a position she had held for six years.

They kept their voices under a sprightly tinkle of radio music and an intermittent hailstorm patter of teletype messages.

'I don't see why they haven't given you a job to bite on,' he said. 'Heavens above, they've got a flock of women who speak English.'

She sat silent, her eyes cast down, her lips smiling slightly, her quietness unarmoured. Then she raised her eyes.

'I am a Catholic,' she said. 'You have seen what it means to be a Catholic in this China. My mother was a Catholic. Her faith gave her strength and comfort. Our father could not bind himself to one belief. He let our mother decide our religious upbringing and he went into any church or temple if he thought it necessary to talk formally to God.'

So that was it.

'He and I appear to share the same attitude,' observed Steven.

'Of course,' she agreed as if surprised at his saying what was obvious. 'So I am doubly suspect, because I'm a Catholic and will not attend their so-called catholic services. Catholic priests here are state-licensed civil servants. My countrymen imagine they can kill the Catholic Church here. At first I was too naive to realize why they imprisoned European missionaries instead of deporting them. Now I understand that they wanted to debase both Christianity and Europeans in front of my people. They revealed their hatred of white men by persecuting the most defenceless. We Chinese have always been the most xenophobic of races. I have felt its acid in my own pride, telling me I am superior to other women because I am Chinese.'

'Recently?'

'Oh no,' she said. 'When we were in America.'

'All of us grow up fearful of the strangeness of foreigners. We Britons have colossal face. There is much in common between the British and the Chinese. Your people have a long proud history.'

'It is not as proud as I expected,' she admitted bitterly.

146

'When we were children our mother told us stories about our relations, even about Fourth Aunt and her husband in Canton. We never saw them. She knew everything about our family for several generations and taught us to respect their memory. We believed her. Chinese carry the dust of their motherland in their blood. But truth is alive or it does not exist. Since I came here I have learned that Chinese family unity was an elaborately dressed corpse. It died long ago. Now the communists have buried it in the new tribalism of their communes. There would be no communes if family unity had been true.'

Her lack of emotion distressed him more than what she said. He caught a glimpse of her youthful illusions dying torturously in the bitter desert of this China.

'Did we Europeans contribute to its death? I suppose so. We misused our strength badly when accidents of history gave us advantages.'

'Europeans took no part in it.'

'You're more generous than I can be.'

'How could they? Our xenophobia should have protected our family life from alien influences. Yet within ten years of Europeans giving up the treaty ports here the communists were able to reduce it to a mockery.'

'We ought to have strengthened it.'

'Our ancestors, yours and mine, met in strangeness. How can we be blamed? My people were wrong to allow foreign businessmen to exploit other Chinese.'

'That's an over-simplification. We weren't blameless.'

'It happened elsewhere. I prefer your description of accidents of history. I want to believe in an essential goodness in people. We are all casualties of our own age. Must we be crippled by those which have gone? These men fashion hate-propaganda from the faces of dead men. That is evil.'

Before she left he took her hand and said: 'You ran a risk to come here, but I'm glad you thought it worthwhile.' She smiled and said: 'I did not want you to go on thinking I came to spy on you.' He adjusted her scarf round her neck. Her eyes were calm.

.   .   .   .   .

147

She came on several shorter visits and one evening came in unexpectedly while he was finishing off a piece to file in the morning. Looking at her face, he saw its pointed weariness and heard fatigue in her voice. At his suggestion she sat down on the settee, resting against the wall. At first she spoke tiredly, then his attempts to amuse her by recounting personal anecdotes started her giggling until at last she was laughing behind her hand. Soon afterwards she went away, quickly, her footsteps a hasty whisper fading down the staircase. Uneasily he wondered why he did not have the strength to end it, why she wanted to come, when both of them knew it could not give her more than a string of talks. He began to question himself, and lacked the courage to continue.

As he walked down the corridor he came face to face with his new room-boy, who asked politely if there were special instructions for him.

3

After that evening the thought of her was seldom far from his thoughts. And twice in that week she came to see him. Late one evening she hurried in breathless from running up four flights of stairs, borrowed a book, and ran to catch a bus. On Christmas Eve he returned from a quasi-festive drink in Clive's room to find an unfamiliar yellow box on his table. It contained white handkerchiefs.

And shortly after Shuen had gone the following Saturday afternoon she came into the room, standing still to let him turn up the radio. There was an aura of excitement about her. At his signal she locked the door and gave him the key.

'Cakes full of seeds,' she whispered.

'Jolly good for the teeth.'

Smiling, she took the basket into the bedroom.

He switched on the kettle. Some prescience had warned him of her intention to come here. He frowned, aghast at what he was beginning to realize about her and himself.

He walked to the window. Over the Forbidden City bright copper flags of sunshine advanced through a greyly clouded sky. Away on his right men swarmed like ants over piles of rubble, extracting whole bricks, scraps of iron, anything capable of second use. Northward he saw rivetters climbing over another skeletal scaffolding. His thoughts were chaotic. It was useless, he told himself, dead wrong.

This afternoon she was in no hurry and did not return until he was squatting on the floor to brew their tea. He glanced over his shoulder to speak, and said nothing. The transformation took him by surprise. Her too, he guessed. Since leaving him she had changed into a turquoise-hued cheongsam and the beauty of her filled the room like an exultant shout. He longed to turn away but her eyes pleaded for attention. Everything about her told of youth, gave him need of forgotten words; the poise of her head, the clasp of the high stiff collar round her neck, the curve of small hand-embroidered gold bows from the base of her throat to the right side of her waist emphasizing her willowy body, the deep hemline of the skirt whose slits rose to her knees, the slender arms whose honey-pale smoothness he had not seen till now, even those alarmed eyes hoping for approval in this land where it was an unwritten crime to expect admiration simply as a woman. She was terribly nervous of herself in this guise. He looked at her eyes, and saw her beauty, poised and unsure, absurdly eager for reassurance. He sensed it in his veins, the fact of her raw and personal to him. It brought no comfort to remind himself that there were young and beautiful women everywhere, millions of them. The immediacy of this recognition was unexpected, threatening to rush them headlong towards unhappiness. In this land. And for her worse, far worse, than unhappiness. He hardened himself.

'You ought to carry a loud-hailer to warn people,' he commented.

'Is it terrible?'

'Actually, no, it's gorgeous. Have they allowed cheongsams to reappear?'

'They are trying. This was a present from my father in

Honolulu on our voyage here. I haven't worn it for years. I was fatter then. Have I taken it in too much?'

'I don't think so. How does it feel?'

She spread her hands on her stomach and giggled. 'I'm breathless.'

'You look pretty good,' he said casually.

She was right about the cakes. They were made from regional recipes, Szechwan and Kwantung, Yunnan and Kwangsi, cakes which had small hot seeds, slivers of ginger, chopped nuts, and a sugary filling like marzipan. She bought them from an old baker who was permitted to conduct his business in order to serve satellite embassy staffs; he gave her a special discount for those left over from regular orders which she purchased. She laughed. At first her old confectioner had mistaken her for a *kanpou*, government agent. All nice people treated her cautiously lest she was under *kwantchee*, she told him without acrimony.

He set himself to share her gaiety. She enjoyed seeing herself in one of the lesser roles she had expected as part of life, the woman in a feminine dress entertaining a friend by her conversation at tea. Her stories came from her girlhood, a stuff like dreams in her mind. The intensity with which she recalled them hurt him unbearably; she sounded like an old old woman remembering her life.

After one smiling pause her attention reverted to a question she had asked him much earlier.

'You've never told me what you think of China, Steven.'

'The opinions of newspapermen are unimportant. We trade in news, rumours, ideas. We like to assume ourselves astute. We watch, we listen. The rest is guesswork.'

'I wasn't asking newspapermen,' she chided. 'You said ideas.'

He crossed his legs and put his hands behind his head.

'Oh, plenty of them. Combustible material anywhere. Some do relate to the situation here. But not because it is China. That's too narrowing.'

'Tell me one.'

'Well, I'm opposed to regimes that reduce human beings to

decomposing clay devoid of spirit. They waste time. There will never be an ideal state because people are too human to carry the appalling burden of perfection. The waste of time in materialism arises from the history of man being based on a single social division. Not between the haves and have-nots. That could be solved easily by legislation. It hasn't been solved because, as you said, we drag our feet in previous centuries. No, the basic division is between leaders and led. The overwhelming majority has travelled at a pace fixed by leaders, be they saints or sinners. The world is a graveyard of political theories based on leaders and led. But we'll never have a stable human society until a majority of people in every country are educated, economically content, and individually responsible. Even then there will still be human cupidity. It isn't a political problem. It's moral.'

'It is an appalling problem,' she said. 'And Utopia now would be insufferable, worse than the state in David Karp's *One*. The rulers would disregard human feeling to ensure that people conform to their rule. That is happening in China now.'

'That's another problem. Emotionalism has no intrinsic part in government, yet in this dreadful century politics everywhere are muddled with emotion, real or simulated. Successful politicians are not good rulers but men who use emotion to whip up popular support. Hitler was only one who held his audiences spellbound by raving emotionalism. Every political gutter is awash with floods of deliberately created emotionalism which only creates new problems. And now they're dirtying television with it.'

For a moment she was silent, her head lowered, watching her hands smooth her dress as if it felt strange to wear a gown. Then she said: 'I'm frightened by the deliberate distortion of intelligence to serve temporary expedients. My people are being trained to hatred and violence to serve Party slogans. They have no political experience to guide them, so they accept every distortion at face value. They cannot reason impersonally. Their xenophobia and fear are being conditioned into hatred of other men, whoever the Party selects as its enemies.'

'Large worms nestle at the heart of every communist rose,' said Steven. 'Communists will claim to be wiser than other politicians. That's impossible. They are men. They claim to be bringing perpetual social justice, which will ensure "From each according to his ability, to according to his needs". What an idiotic slogan! It means nothing. In single party states the Party decides who are able men. If a man turns against the Party, it says he is not able and kills or imprisons him. And will the Party say that the needs of a member of the Politbureau who has six children are equal to those of a peasant who has ten children? No no, his position, power, prestige, guarantee him preferential treatment. The slogan is a childish lie. Communism is only another division of people into leaders and led.'

She nodded assent. 'When my father was a boy the old fishermen had a saying *Yan to peng ping*—many men, life cheap. We Chinese have always held life cheap. We have many people. How can other countries respect us when these rulers say they will sacrifice four hundred million people to bring about world communism? And their own domination over all people. Can they force Russia into war on the West?'

'They're having a darned good try. They've made it impossible for Russia to disarm. If every American dropped dead tomorrow Russia wouldn't disarm. Her nuclear weapons and rockets are her only security against China. I suppose the mandarins will justify their war by saying capitalists want to enslave workers and say "We will grind your revolutionists under our heel and we will walk upon your faces; the world is ours, we are its lords, and ours it shall remain. As for labour, it has been in the dirt since history began, and in the dirt it shall remain . . ." '

'Jack London is still read by our University students.'

'They must be the only ones who do.'

She twined her fingers together. 'It will not be simple for the rest of the world to wear our yoke of bamboo. It would be better for humanity if our mandarins asked themselves "O human stupidity, do you not perceive that though you have been with yourself all your life, you are not yet aware of the thing you possess most of, that is, your folly"?'

'You're right again. Da Vinci is one who should be in China now. We newspapermen are no use. We look through people, including ourselves, and see the furniture behind them.'

Her interest reverted to the first point. 'Do you think the government here can permanently improve living conditions?'

'It has every good chance to do so,' said Steven. 'It can avoid all the technological problems we in the West had to solve by trial and error. There is no reason why China should not be the wealthiest country in the world. That doesn't mean it will succeed because of communism. It could have been powerful, wealthy, assured, rid of beggars and discontent, long ago, but the advantages were never accepted by those who led. The Party is going the wrong way about it. We British have made innumerable mistakes, so have the Americans, the French, and the Germans, and others, but we've increased the importance of the individual, particularly in Britain. The mandarins have reduced the individual Chinese to nothing.'

After some minutes she sighed and asked: 'Why do we talk of politics?'

'Wasn't it Thomas Mann who said: "In our time the destiny of man presents its meaning in political terms?" '

They went on to discuss topics which gave more comfort.

While they talked the advancing banners of night overwhelmed the last torn bronze pennants of sunlight flying among the pillowy clouds. At times a brusque wind lapped at the window-panes. On its tide a stealthy silence of snow laid possessive fingers over gold and azure pagoda roofs, left sticky thumb-prints on dull crimson walls, crept down grey slates above narrow *hutungs*.

He knew how greatly she enjoyed the illusion of ordinariness they conjured. She radiated contentment. For her this scene represented both an achievement and her defiance of political edicts. He did his utmost to abet her mood. Her own resolution made it easy. From where he sat near the window he watched the multiplying shadows dim her lovely hands, rise over the small breasts to circle her slender shoulders, until only her exquisitely poised head was visible in the smoky bronze glow, dusk smudging her slanted eyes, the lovely deep curve of her lips and then her carefully modulated voice alone betrayed her presence.

Darkness loosed his imagination. He experienced the assault of forgotten impulses. They were too acute for him to overcome them promptly, mocking his affectation of bland indifference. After this length of time their unfamiliarity provided their true danger. She sat close, not more than ten feet from him, her voice the least link, her defiance, her audacity and fearlessness, her candid enjoyment of being with him, forging stronger bonds. His thoughts were madness. Here. Anywhere else they would be two ordinary people owning a right to follow instinct and see where it led them. But here they were irreconcilables, a Chinese girl and an Englishman in China, a woman of independent views and a newspaperman from another camp, certain to be branded criminals if their companionship became public knowledge. Was he mad—or the mandarins? It must be them. They left him no escape in redeeming laughter. China was too serious, too grimly resolute in all its volatile moods, to laugh at itself.

At length she said reluctantly: 'I must go. Send me away, Steven.'

He weakened. 'If you haven't got an appointment I can rustle up cold chicken legs, pineapple in toffee, and rice wine. And coffee.'

'Golly, here?'

'Uh-huh. Yes?'

'Oh yes, Steven!'

They picnicked on the settee. She sat nearest the bedroom in order to hide if anyone disturbed them. Misty light from the television screen provided illumination. They used their fingers, balancing their plates on their knees. He had bought chickens cooked Szechwan-style in red peppers, ginger, and *hua chiao* spice, another delicacy restricted by price to foreigners and higher-paid government officials. She amused him by describing Chinese food sold to tourists in San Francisco.

'You must go there to see the New Year festivities on Grant Avenue,' she decided. 'They are very colourful. Lots of noise and firecrackers and dragons. People laughing, being happy. So noisy, Steven. I love it. Of course, there was the district called Chinatown in the side-streets but we never went there. I wonder what it is like now.'

'You will see it again.'

'No' she contradicted gently. 'I shall never see the land of my childhood again. It is better so. None of us ever walks those miles again.' Her hand touched his. 'Stay there. Let me make the coffee.'

Directly they finished she took their plates into the bathroom to rinse clean, and on her return went to the cupboard, crouching down to put them away so that no one should see he had entertained a guest.

He watched her moodily. It was insane. Because she defied the Party ukase on private association with a foreigner, she risked being branded a heretic. And he, because he enjoyed her company, liked her, admired her spirit and her intelligence, risked being condemned as a *man-tze* of the worst character, a corrupting lecher. They were criminals. Forced to speak cautiously lest an eavesdropper assume they were hatching some heinous plot. Always listening for an intruder. Their every word hunted by a microphone. It made the asylums seem like retreats inhabited by the abundantly sane.

It could not go on, he told himself. Sooner or later she would crack under the strains imposed on them. Women had extraordinary powers of resilience, but there was a limit to their endurance. He had to do it. Their pipe dream of ordinariness was bound to be ended by others in malice if not by their own wish. At least they could share the dignity of denial.

She walked back lazily, wraithlike in television owl-light. Settling down beside him, she sighed contentedly. That stung him. Her attitude could so easily persuade him to become smug. He finished his wine and put the glass on the table. It wasn't going to be easy. He did not possess the cool ingenuity which might have lent it charity.

From some source he plucked up the nerve to rest his hand on hers. They were soft and warm. Then he said: 'Be patient with me, my dear. I have to say this.'

Her stillness took on an atmosphere of rigidity. As if in relation to something remote from themselves, she asked quietly: 'So soon?'

'I think so. You know what's happening. To us.'

'Oh yes.'

Her serene voice whipped him past half-formed cautious preliminaries. 'We have no alternative. This situation will drive us up the wall. They say there's a moment when what is happening to us can be stopped by people in ordinary circumstances. This is it.'

Her hands smoothed slowly down his, pressing it in her palms.

'You have such long fingers. Bony. Why are you so sure?'

'We've got to be coldblooded.'

'How terrible. This is the first time I haven't felt coldblooded and lifeless for years. Why now?'

'Everything except ourselves denies us the right to behave normally. We have a score of tolerances in good faith pulling us together. You wouldn't be here now if race troubled either of us. It doesn't alarm you that I have a tenuous belief instead of a religion. I'm glad you're a Catholic. I'm always glad if an intelligent individual has a faith. It's proof that they seek more than ephemeral values. We have another bridge, delicate and rare. Ideas. Oh, so dangerous! And I would willingly build dams or factories for your people. They've had a wretched life for centuries. They deserve a better, fuller, healthier life. But I won't help this government. It's tyrannical. It's a warlord racket with slogans.'

She drew his other hand into hers. 'How strange to be accursed by our own goodwill. We should have met in a civilized age. And where we could have faith in mankind.'

'Yes. This is a century of know-how, scientific barbarians, stuffed with gadgets empty of spirit, a hole in its heart.'

He relaxed. It had gone better than he had a right to expect.

Her quiet voice interrupted his thoughts. 'What you say is not the whole truth. It cannot be. There is ourselves. You are always in my thoughts. I could have shut you out of my mind. I have never tried to do so. It is natural to take you with me when we're apart. It would have happened wherever we met.'

'And I think of you in the same way.'

'I know,' she said gently. 'Steven . . . the good memory, however brief, gives more courage and pride than compromise. I have never compromised. I will never compromise. Never.'

He shook his head at what she was telling him.

'No. No, it'd be hell to endure, my dearest.'

'You're wrong,' she said, and her calm voice faltered, stumbling miserably. 'This is worse . . . darling, what else can I say?'

Her unhappiness defeated him. It was unbearable. He released his hands to put them on her shoulders, turned her gently, and drew her to him. They were both unsure. Her lips were cold against his, nervous, as if she was frightened. He raised his head, saw her eyes were closed, and pushed back hair tangled over her forehead. A tremor went through her. After a moment she raised her face and as he kissed her again she put her arms round him, and they clung together.

When they drew apart he knew his fine resolutions were smashed and useless. Whatever happened, there was no going back. She laid her forehead against his shoulder, her hands tight on him.

Cold air threw snowflakes on the curtainless window, tinily glinting multiflora which stuck to the panes till heat in the room caused them to melt like dissolving glass ferns.

He felt a terrible unreal tranquillity in the silence of their seclusion. Once a spurt of disquiet forced him to resume their conversation but instantly her hand covered his lips. Her placidity hid an iron-clad resolution. Held in his arm, she rested against his shoulder. He had forgotten the passage of time when she turned her head to kiss his neck, and said: 'Don't leave me alone too long. It will be best not to talk in there.'

For a moment he kept her beside him, to say: 'You'll have to be patient, my dear. I've been abstemious.'

She put her lips to his forehead and said: 'I bring no memories to burden you.'

Alone, he paced restlessly round the room. There was no means to guess why they met here or what lay ahead. Life, whatever it was, brought perplexing mysteries. There must be sense in it somewhere. The thought stayed in his mind as he did his routine round to close down on another day and went to join her, led by habit through the darkness to where she waited.

His fears were proven true. Neither of them lost their sense of oppression by circumstance. Long abstinence denied him the assurance to guide her to fulfilment in this aspect of love. The culmination which overtook him was solitary and joyless, leaving an aftermath of defeat. Wordlessly she turned onto her stomach and feigned sleep, holding his hand.

Later his senses emerged from an uneasy stupor in answer to a light whispering breath and he saw her lying close, moonlight in the cleared sky showing the shape of her head on the pillows, and faultlessly they took possession of each other, following instinct until together they endured the small death in life. And when their bodies divided she went to sleep with her head on his chest.

The next time he awoke a grey dawn fingered the sky. Keeping still, he watched it squeezing out the darkness. He felt hurried and vaguely excited. New sensibilities conflicted in his waking mind.

He turned and saw she was still sound asleep. In the night she had drawn away, one arm reaching out of the bedclothes. Her thick hair was in a fine old tangle. The youthfulness of her sleeping face came as a shock to him. And suddenly the sight of her defencelessness awoke compassion in him; she was infinitely more vulnerable than she realized. He was reluctant to end her rest. He had no idea where this drab sunrise would lead them, only that those ahead must be unlike those behind, weighted by new needs. They had created the other's passion, shared mouths and loins, coupled, and thereby they had become conspirators, their clasp a criminal act, its consummation a treason. *It was a blow struck against the Party. It was a political act.* He frowned, his morning brain unable to fathom why the words assumed an atmosphere of memory. The thought died as he stroked her body and bent over to lay his lips on hers. The sun put a weak gold sheen among the heavy clouds.

Ten

CLIVE DIXON was busy. He preferred to be so. It meant going out to collect material. That suited him. He had never taken satisfaction from rewrite pieces, least of all from those concocted here out of repetitious NCNA reports clattering out hourly on his teletypewriter. By his reckoning, agency men or stringers in lookouts amid the feverish vitality of Hongkong and Saigon, closeted in *avenida* offices in the torpid degeneracy of Macao, were fully capable of forwarding précises of official data, the task which Peking firmly believed to be the sole function of newspapermen. He did not share their attitude. In his view spot men expected to justify their presence in China by filing authentic first-eye material. And it was precisely this attitude which Peking officials sought to prevent.

The Tibet story awoke his crusading instincts. To obtain it required continuous subterfuge and planning. Day by day it grew bigger, occupying more and more of his attention. It differed in particular from cream-and-honey stories put about by the Information Department.

The Department handling of what was going on inside 'the Tibet region of China', as it miscalled the country, was a grim object lesson in how history could be deliberately manufactured. Every propaganda journal sent from Peking spoke of 'the peaceful liberation of Tibet' in nineteen-fifty. None of them

mentioned that it had been an armed invasion resisted by tribesmen armed only with rifles. They stated that nine years after
the liberation the landowners had sought to reimpose their
rule but 'the Tibetan masses rose against the rebellion of the
serf-owners and against slavery'. They did not mention the
shelling of the Potala in Lhasa, battles fought by Chinese troops
armed with automatic submachineguns, tanks, armoured cars,
and airplanes, against the same tribesmen armed only with the
same rifles. They talked of a land of boundless joy, of corn
growing where none had grown hitherto, of friendly commis-
sars, led by Peking's man in Lhasa, Tan Kuan-san, filling simple
peasants with wonder by growing apples, peppers, potatoes,
maize, pumpkins, and spring onions, of roads being laid, of
telegraph poles going up, schools and hospitals being founded,
and they quoted statistics and printed photographs to prove it.
They added deft touches of poetry to the record by claiming
that these accomplishments were due to 'the heroic spirit' of
'Let high mountains bow their heads and rivers make way.'
Clive soon found the largest fly in the ointment. Although Tibet
was claimed to be a show-piece of Chinese progress, not one
foreign newspaperman, not even those from satellite countries,
was allowed to enter it.

The story that Clive unearthed at considerable risk to himself was vastly unlike the glowing propaganda accounts. His
investigations were hampered by the winter weather. Weeks of
intense cold, days of snow or icy north-westerly winds laden
with Gobi dust, forced him to abandon the Temple of Heaven,
Coal Hill, and other open-air rendezvous points where Europeans and those seen talking to them were certain to attract
attention. His contacts arranged meetings at places where
brief conversations passed unnoticed. Late in December he met
two Tibetans at an exhibition of posters at Zhongshan Park.
The next week he talked to others during a concert given by
the Central Philharmonic Symphony Orchestra at the Wu Dao
Kou Club, then in intervals of a performance of La Traviata in
Chinese at the Tiangiao Theatre, after the screening of an East
German anti-fascist film at the Workers' Club, and during a

morning session at the Beihai skating rink. There were risks attached to each meeting, even in a city of five million people, but they were greater for his informants. Some were young Tibetan students from Lhasa or Shigatse or Gyantse, but wherever possible he avoided those enrolled at the Institute of National Minorities; most of them had been brain-washed. Four of his informants, men whom he met more than once, were members of the secret nationalist underground movement *Mimeng*. There was no mistaking their sincerity. And there was no mistaking what they told him. The masters of China were committed to a ruthless policy of genocide in Tibet.

That underlined every statement. He heard it in descriptions of the slaughter of Khamba tribesmen and of how their women were being acquired by womanless Chinese colonial settlers imported into eastern Tibet in their thousands. It echoed through accounts of aristocrats being summarily executed in Lhasa, of lamas being burned alive in their *gompas*. It was starkly emphasized by two personal narratives describing the total extermination of villages which had sheltered refugee families fleeing down the Chumbi Valley to cross eastern *las* of Himalaya to seek sanctuary with the Dalai Lama in India. The exodus of Tibetans was one of the classic Asian stories, old before the days of Genghis Khan and the Golden Horde; a flight of people, poor, rich, young, old, influential or insignificant in their community, from conquerors who denied them freedom. It was not the first occasion on which Chinese communists had persecuted a small people. Less than ten years ago they had nearly annihilated sixteen thousand Kazakhs from Sinkiang who tried to cross Tibet to safety in Kashmir.

Within weeks Clive had obtained a mass of information. Much of it was horrifying. Tibet was one vast concentration camp. Once wealthy households and nomad polyandrous families in black yak-skin yurts were alike living in conditions of slavery. On the surface many Chinese claims were true. Roads were being constructed; the labourers were pressganged Tibetans and Chinese political prisoners, men and women, working sixteen hours a day to build military roads from China to Nepal and India. Schools were being set up; their staffs were Chinese, teaching the Peking lines of hatred and economics. Hospitals had appeared; they gave preferential treatment to Chinese colonial settlers and were all close to Chinese military barracks. Telegraph poles were going up; they were used by the occupying power. Tibetan women were marrying Chinese settlers: they did so to avoid road-gang work, and the Peking policy of sending unmarried men as settlers was to breed out Tibetan racial strains and national consciousness within a generation. And lamas, the superstitious and conspiratorial monks who had frustrated every attempt to introduce new ways of life into Tibet for fear of losing their power, were paying for their folly, existing under duress, given the choice of being labourers or servile nonentities under the Panchen Lama, the creature of Peking.

Clive saw no reason to doubt his informants. The standard of Peking conduct had been set by what it did to the Chinese themselves.

Although fearful of being followed, he went to every rendez-vous. As the days passed without sudden flurries of officials he began to take heart. Why should his outings be questioned? Every foreign correspondent city-bound on account of winter and restrictions on travel undertook entertainment assignments to avoid boredom and develop a closer understanding of people than he obtained from official sources. But the strain made him edgy. Only his old newspaperman's habit of following a story to the bitter end gave him the courage to keep digging at it.

2

One snowy evening Clive drove from a rendezvous at the 'Theatre of Heavens', the large planetarium with its fascinating combination of astronomy and mythological architectural decorations, to an embassy reception to welcome a delegation of Latin American lawyers.

His driver, Nieh, was in a talkative mood, anxious over the seventh pregnancy of his wife Yen-tze.

Nieh had talked of nothing else for weeks. He was a small thin man in his late thirties. His face had a long jaw and thick lips whose drooping corners gave him a permanently lugubrious expression entirely alien to his active sparrow liveliness. When worried he ran his fingers through his untidy hair and let the car take care of itself. As they had driven round in recent weeks, the confinements of Yen-tze had taken on the dimensions of an epic. He gave them the drama of world championship fights, every detail scrupulously described. Clive had never seen Yen-tze, but his knowledge of her was husbandly. Their discussions about her had an 'our wife' complexion.

As they reached the embassy, Clive said: 'It may not be too bad.'

Nieh thumped his forehead distractedly. 'We have an awkward time ahead of us, Mr. Dixon.'

'Cheer up,' said Clive and left him to read *Oliver Twist*.

Conviviality droned through the embassy reception rooms. Threequarters of the foreign press colony had assembled to kill a couple of hours on free liquor. Their collective tongue swirled like a tidal wave. Everyone was earnest, was frank, was cautious. Their glances sprang about like trained grasshoppers. They were in the wrong capital for parenthetical diplomacy, thought Clive. Moscow was the stage for unpredictable waggishness.

He collected a couple of brandies to steady himself. It required phenomenal stamina to withstand the physical wear and tear of diplomatic gossip. He tasted one drink while he took his bearings.

At the far end of the room hovered a cluster of swarthy men, shivery looking in biscuit-coloured suits. They had slumbrous eyes, draped black moustaches, cosseted paunches, the rapid vacant smiles of guests of honour poised for recognition. Around them pale blue Yat-sen tunics floated like crisp butterflies.

Clive sampled his other drink. It was bathtub-raw, guaranteed to yank every eyelash rigid. He lost it on the nearest available furniture and began to mingle. It did not take long to discover that conversation was down to par. No one had an original thought or topic, their chat as listless as anaemic sardines battling through heavy water.

While Clive leant on the weather to commiserate with two homesick Egyptians he caught sight of John Butler surrounded by ex-Americans, erstwhile Britons, unchanged East Europeans. Butler was giving his liveliest performance of local boy making good. Clive did not know why he disliked Butler. They seldom spoke and Butler kept at a distance. But he did dislike him. One member of the group appeared to relish him hugely, an East European woman in a mauve coat and skirt, a recent assistant press attaché replacement. Her protuberant dark eyes ate Butler as if he was manna. She bore resemblance to the sort of portraits painted by Modigliani: incredibly red hair, sooty black eyebrows, an oval head whose tiny pink lips appeared to have been borrowed from a doll, drain-pipe neck, oval breasts, oval hips, minute feet. As he speculated on her and Butler a Yat-sen tunic came alongside.

'Mr. Dixon, will you meet members of the delegation? Señor Parana is eager to talk to you. He speaks English.'

Clive limbered up his facial muscles for the strain of etiquette.

He cut it short. Then, formalities completed, he decided to go home. The reception was due to churn on for another hour, but he saw no reason to stay. Besides, Ilse might come to see him. The prospect worried him.

As he crossed the entrance hall to collect his overcoat, Sheila Grant came in. She wore a heavy black coat over her green sari. The chilly air had thinned her face. She came across to him frowning.

'Do you want half a pound of coffee?'

'Can you spare it?'

'Here.' She gave him a small paper package. 'One of my Brazilian friends gave me two pounds. What is it like in there?'

He put the coffee into his pocket. 'They're all praising the

Americans for their sense of moral duty, and drawing up plans
to send their sons to Eton or Harrow.'

'Like hell they are.' She sighed. 'Another same evening.'

'Your friend Butler is there.'

'He isn't my friend. Did he bring Ilona?'

'Red hair?'

'And exophthalmic eyes, so he says.'

'Wouldn't he? Yes, she's there.'

'Is Steven there?'

'No, he went to Hankow yesterday,' said Clive. 'He won't be
back for a week.'

3

Sun saw the half-caste girl Grant leave the Englishman Dixon
and walk to the reception rooms. Her attitude gave no sign of
furtiveness. But he had seen her give the Englishman a small
package.

Sun reacted instantly. At his instruction one of his companions set off to follow Dixon. His other assistant went to ask
permission to telephone the Ministry on a forgotten matter.
Sun spoke quickly to his office, giving instructions for Dixon's
rooms to be searched in the morning. Then, smiling politely,
he followed the half-caste girl to arrange for the delegation of
lawyers to tour Shanghai.

4

Clive walked down the corridor to his room, experiencing an
odd sensation of suspense. Odd for him. He might well be the
young Dixon who had gone to meet the girl who first set his
imagination at work on life, feeling hope at the prospect of
seeing her and anxiety lest she did not keep their appointment.
Twentyfive, thirty years ago? God, so long? He had forgotten
her name except on occasions when it blew across his mind like

a leaf, and the colour of her eyes, her face, much else, once more vital than food or cold rainy nights, or copy banged out on that ancient typewriter for the local rag, but not her spring-tide freshness, her quick laugh, her patience while he talked at her for hours, poor girl. And these years later it had happened again.

Imagination, the quicksilver of the human condition. That was the explanation. It freed the individual from himself, made him weightless in time, unbowed by his years, and, between two people, let them ignore whatever other considerations divided them. You daft fool, he warned himself.

As he neared the door he slowed down to brace himself. He almost wished that she would not be waiting. The mornings were hell. Then the gods howled laughter at him for the light showed her shining hair close to his thinning pepper-and-salt tangle, her firm smoothness and his bony ridges, her unblemished legs entwined in his old newspaperman's trophies of varicose veins, one of the best collections in the business, much more, and, above all, her reluctance to wake up and his impatience to rush into another day: the gleam of spring, the sourness of early autumn. Thank God, he had his own teeth. Most days he could whistle one verse of *Land of Hope and Glory* around noon and still have some wind left. Every little helped.

He shook his head. He was getting sentimental. He could not risk it. Sentiment was all right, whatever the eggheads said, but he did not want it clawing at his vitals.

Outside the door he paused, reluctant to go in lest it meant disappointment. Then he hardened himself and went into the darkness, switched on the light and turned the key in the lock. The bedroom door stood half open.

'Me,' he said and took off his overcoat.

At the sound of his voice she came into the other doorway. She had slung her overcoat round her shoulders. He sensed tension in her, knife-sharp in her smile, smouldering in her eyes, poised ready in case Han burst in on them. His resolve wavered. He almost wished that Han would storm in to enforce decisions.

He turned from putting his coat on a hanger behind the door. She had crossed the room and stood beside him. She wore his old dressing-gown under her overcoat. For an instant her eyes questioned his, then she was hard against him, an impress to renew memory and anticipation. He could smell brandy on her breath. As he kissed her neck she shivered at the coldness of his face on her warm flesh. She had a fresh-smelling perfume on her hair. He let go of her and whispered: 'Something tells me I have it bad about you.'

She smiled. '*Danke Gott*,' she murmured. 'Did you get it?'

He nodded and pointed warningly at the radio. 'Does my breath smell?'

'I do not mind if you smell of drink.'

'I do, at present.'

They knelt side by side at the radio. She took off his tie, throwing it onto a chair. She hissed concern at the coldness of his hands. Her jujitsulike manœuvres to warm them caused him to overbalance and they fell. His efforts to get up were prevented by his feet becoming entangled in the coat fallen from her shoulders. His pantomimed struggles to rise were rewarded by her amusement. She lay on the carpet laughing helplessly while he floundered around. At length he tuned the radio, then stood up and helped her. She hung onto him, fighting for breath. Her hands shook his shoulders.

'Ah, Clive, Clive! Even our silliness is good, yes?'

'Why not?'

Her eyes glistened.

'I do not care what happens!' she exclaimed. 'You will never understand what these hours mean to me.'

He started to pat her shoulder and stopped, realizing it was an ageing man's action.

'Let's have coffee,' he said.

The notes given to him in the planetarium cinema provided a record of Chinese actions against Tibetan families in Gartok, the far western town being transformed into the main military base north of India. He read them to her while they had coffee. The incidents were written down in a careful school textbook English on thin paper. They were fully documented, more carefully detailed than most of the statements passed to him. The record covered four months of the previous summer. It described forced labour, disappearances following visits by Chinese troops, accusations of disloyalty to Peking, the flight of three families into Nepal. The final incident concerned the unexplained murder of one old Tibetan in his house.

She listened in silence, sitting on a cushion on the floor, her back resting against his legs.

'How much more do you need?' she asked at length.

'Whatever I can get. Not much.'

'And then?'

'A careful article. No names. Facts.'

'What will they do?'

'It isn't written yet.'

'The writing will make a difference?'

'Inevitably.'

'You will do it better than anyone else.'

'Oh no.'

'Why do you want to write about Tibet?'

'What is happening there shouldn't be forgotten or glossed over,' he said. It was on the tip of his tongue to add that a similar pattern of aggression occurred in Europe twenty years ago when Nazi Germany overran her weaker neighbours, but he checked himself in deference to her possible sense of loyalty to other Germans of that era. 'If it is forgotten, it will happen to another country, then another, and another. To be honest, Steven would write this much better. He has a flair for it.'

She laughed cynically. 'He does not run risks.'

'That shows ability.'

'He is concerned with his own affairs, a cold man.'

'Oh, he's basically sound, just off-hand like most war pilots yanked out of school into the cockpits. That's not his fault. The West told his generation what to fight against when they were boys. It hasn't shown them what to believe in since then. The West has lost direction and vision and faith. The whole of Europe is an apathetic society. Its politicians are effete, lost in petty wrangles and clichés which fool no one, and apparently incapable of giving a lead. Consequently, the people are listless. The Western leaders haven't given men of Steven's generation a charter for living.'

She did not mention Steven again, neither there nor later in the other room, sensitive to the sort of loyalty which united men isolated among their self-appointed opponents.

He let well alone. He had his own troubles. Some demanded attention now. Bathed and lazy, he lay in bed while she prepared to join him. Tonight she was taking longer than usual, wandering round thoughtful and naked, her inventive delays assuming another form of defiance. He gathered a clear impression that she longed for her husband to burst in on them, and would accept him into this setting as a welcome guest. As he watched her seat herself at the mirror his previous alarms were suddenly trampling through him again. Some perverted desire to flagellate himself mentally forced him to go on looking at her. She sat relaxed, her body lithe, her hips compact, too engrossed in the task of brushing her hair to heed him.

That was fortunate. For him it amounted to a moment of truth. After years of transit gratification from propinquitous and unmemorable *bints*, this relationship was digging far deeper. He could not see himself becoming indifferent to her, not since they did actually get lost together without subsequent revulsion or speculation on what was for breakfast. As he looked Ilse turned to give her long legs more room, her hair shifting like sunlight, her incredibly white skin gleaming.

Anger filled him. It would be absurdly simple to become insanely possessive of her. He had seen men of his age create tiresome spectacles of themselves over much younger women. And what was the use? Even in other circumstances, he did not expect to live more than five or six years. You noted the symptoms and developed an instinct, like a man hurrying in a crowd who waited for a hand to grasp his shoulder and direct him off in another direction. His vocational hazards might bring it sooner. The plane, the fearful terrifying mob, the stray bullet, the rendezvous with death when spring came back with rustling shade, or at midnight in some flaming town. Amen: he would not be in a condition to mope or fidget. But what if some venomous trick left him half-dead, hanging onto existence by his shoelaces?

With unconscious malice she pointed his thoughts by raising her arms to push back hair fallen over her face. The movement lifted her breasts, taut on her ribs. There was a connexion between their calm stir and the truths stamping in his mind: fifteen years from tonight her magnificent body would be at the fullness of its need to take and give carnal satisfaction.

He shut his eyes. It made him feel dusty just to look at her. Fortyseven and twentythree plus fifteen. Sixtytwo and thirty-eight. If he was still in existence then, by God, he'd be a sorry specimen; no one would take him for a day under ninety. He cringed. It was no use. For once cynicism, the anodyne which usually soothed him, gave no relief. He lacked the heart to be flippant. What was he going to do? What was he going to do?

When he opened his eyes she had finished brushing her hair and leant forward, staring intently at her reflection in the mirror. She studied it closely, giving the skin under her eyes a meticulous examination as if she expected to see it cobwebbed from age. He smiled to himself: she had no cause to worry. Then she stood up, wandering lazily across to the light-switch. She stopped, turning to him. '*Bitte*?' she said.

'I said you need to be paid danger money just to live.'

She smiled, completed her journey, coming to him through the stinging darkness. Wordlessly she sank down between the sheets, sliding into the place warmed by his body. They were silent for a while. Her preparatory caresses did not fool him; tonight he was beyond bland disregard of differences which would strike at him in the morning. He cleared his throat. 'Do you realize I am old enough to be your father?' he asked. 'I find that terribly interesting.'

'You will always be young.'

'Careful how you hand out curses.'

'I never think of it.'

Her voice implied boredom. He touched her neck, ran his

hand down to her loins and hips, and cheated. 'In ten years,' he said, 'this woman will still be young.'

'Why do you tell me this now?' she whispered unhappily.

'Unless I get things settled while they're in my mind I'm too weak to face up to them,' he said wearily. 'I'm constitutionally incapable of long-suffering heroics. Child, I'm agreeing with one thought that's worrying you. You're right. They may kick me out if I file this article here.'

'Yes,' she muttered.

'They may not, but it'd be idiotic to assume they'll do nothing. Now, you wouldn't bother about me if you were content. This country stifles you. There is better outside. If you're willing to take the risks and they do kick me out, come with me. Directly you want to leave me say so. You can go.'

'How can you belittle me?' A desperate bewilderment ached in her voice. 'Why should I think of other men?'

'At this moment I should hope not.'

'You use cynicism like an insurance policy,' she said savagely, then her fury died into hopelessness. 'Naturally, I would come The longing torments me. But it is impossible. Ah, dear God, it. is my own fault.'

He interrupted her unhappy voice. 'You don't have to tell me.'

'One day I will tell you everything. Yes, it is true, when I first came into this room I was insane with want of a man to make love to me as if I was more than an animal. Now I am here because it is you. Trust me, believe me.'

He said: 'Remember this. If you want to come, you can.'

He had not finished speaking before she wound her arms round him. She kissed his mouth, his chest and stomach, pressed her face into his side. Against his will, her warmth, her smell, her moans of happiness, lessened his anxieties. Her whispered endearments were new between them. On other nights she had followed his guidance. Now she revelled in giving full expression to a desire equalling his own. It was hard to doubt her as she stretched up along him to seek his mouth again, her body marvellously soft and supple, her warm hand stealing over his belly. Everything that divided, left them. She took the husk of his staleness on her, gathered and sheltered him in her youth, and while their flesh possessed them she spoke of love for the first time, and his response wrenched a cry from her.

When he fell beside her, she continued to hold him in her strong young arms and wept unsteadily. He wanted to say something particularly nice to comfort her. 'Bless your heart,' he said gently.

She wiped her nose on his shoulder. 'You shall never regret being kind to me. If again you must drink we will be drunkards together,' she told him in a thick voice.

5

At noon next day Sun sat in his office reading reports. He felt ill. He had been awake in pain all night. Twice Ling, good patient woman, had got up from her *kang* to prepare herbal drinks. They gave no relief. He became convinced that his treacherously thundering heart was about to burst. Ling blamed it onto their food, her voice a whisper in order not to be overheard, telling him they were selling putrid food since the shortages began again and how she walked miles from market to market rather than buy rotten turnips and bad rice. Unable to sleep, he got up before dawn.

He was too tired to concentrate on this work which insulted a man who should be training other men to grow strong. His temper was short. This morning one man in particular awoke his fury: Fong Yun, a building construction worker, who never let a week go by without accusing a workmate of deliberately preventing the big leap forward by inattention to work or wrong-thinking. None of Fong's accusations ever repaid investigation. He and his wife Pao-lan were always in active pursuit of traitors. Sun had met Pao-lan one afternoon last summer, a thin childless woman who spent her days knitting furiously while she carried her ears along her *hutung* to catch traitors, a typical 'Small Group' informer, one of millions.

It enraged Sun to waste energy on such fools. There were too many of them seeking praise. Did they imagine human nature changed? Women loved to gossip, men to grumble, children to tell tales. They were not traitors. Only twenty percent of the people were officially estimated to be hostile to the Republic: he would put it higher, but not on account of people grumbling. There was that ridiculous investigation which followed the remark by the riveter Mo Hsi-jo that the new railway station was ugly. So it was, so it was. Big and impressive, and his old legs enjoyed the flying stairs, but ugly in his eyes. He too must be a traitor because he disliked it.

He raised his stinging eyes and looked round at the large photographs of Shanghai which gave his office an illusion of being a tourist office. Some were old. He must have them changed.

His secretary crept into the office. She shut the door stealthily, using both hands as if she were sealing them in a tomb chamber to evade pursuers. Whatever Soong Shu-lan did had an air of excessive secrecy. She was a small middleaged woman and had round plump cheeks but the body of a child. Her hair was dragged back in the style of peasant women. He had chosen Soong Shu-lan carefully. She never pretended to be more intelligent than himself though a British mission-school education had taught her to speak, read, and write fluent English. Also she obeyed him unhesitatingly. It was incredible to think of her tiny hands holding the automatic rifle with which she had killed a Japanese patrol near Hankow station one night. No doubt that was why she still respected men who fought on the Long March.

She came across to him. Her regretful face hung forward, her heavy Kansu chin dipping over her neck.

'What is it?' he asked, irritated by her slowness.

'Mr. Shuen is here for his interview.'

Sun had forgotten Shuen. 'Let him wait for two minutes.'

As she went out he put away the reports and glanced round.

173

His filing cabinets were neat, his reference books in order. He rubbed his aching eyes. His heart was beating furiously again for no reason. No reason? He lifted his jowls in his fingers and let them fall over his collar.

He belched sourly. He expected Shuen to be obsequious, grovel like a beggar of the old days. Every report on Shuen spoke of his frenzied determination to climb back to importance in the Party, accusing, intriguing, hounding, betraying, driven on by his relentless ambition. Shuen had much in common with Fong Yun; their methods were identical. But Shuen would not rehabilitate himself. He had many enemies and his name meant nothing to younger men.

Shuen came in bowing politely. He carried his cap and wore an overcoat. His gaze flickered hungrily round the office, lingering on the three telephones, his envy unmistakable. That showed how they differed; Sun would willingly have given up the office and this worthless existence for the cheerless Yenan cave he had lived in after the Long March, in those years when every man could name his enemies and his friends. Soong Shu-lan crept in behind Shuen, notebook in hand, going to her usual place near the desk.

Sun indicated a chair. '*Ch'ing tso, ch'ing tso,*' he said and glanced at his secretary. '*P'ao ch'a.*' She reached forward to press the bell-push on the desk. He gave Shuen no chance to take the initiative. 'Your reports have provided no evidence against the Englishman Kendal,' he said and pressed his hands to the ache in his belly.

Shuen started to talk. Words rushed from his mouth like China's Sorrow in flood, a torrent intended to prevent Sun from asking questions. His excuses were adroit. It was impossible to provide a daily schedule: in Peking Kendal had no fixed routine, going and coming at every hour.

Shuen rushed on into accusations. He was emphatic in his declarations that Kendal was a spy. Sun fully comprehended the motive for Shuen's assertions; having returned to Peking, Shuen was determined to remain. Nothing less than conviction would suit him. Sun felt almost sorry for the Englishman.

'Yes yes,' he said patiently. 'We have read your reports. They do not go further than what Hu reported when he heard the Englishwoman in Kendal's rooms. A letter we intercepted from her, sent from Hongkong, contained nothing. She said she was going to Singapore.'

'Ai, Singapore,' said Shuen in a significant tone.

'People do go there.'

'Yes yes, important.'

Sun laced his fingers over his stomach. 'Everything can be important. Last evening I went to an embassy reception. I saw a European being given a package and ordered an immediate investigation. A search of the European's rooms revealed that the package was half a pound of coffee. You must find more than coffee to prove Kendal guilty of espionage.'

Shuen broke into another spate of words. Kendal had changed his habits; he used his radio frequently; he went out less but often ate an evening meal in his room. And he got up earlier.

Sun listened carefully. He weighed what Shuen told him and contrasted it with his observations of Kendal in Shanghai, reports from Hu, comments by Mrs. Peng. Though he did not believe the Englishman to be a spy, it was wise not to take risks. The best spies spent months or years settling into their surroundings and getting themselves accepted. Kendal had made clever use of information given him by Mrs. Peng and the girl Hau in Shanghai, given to test his intelligence. He reached a decision.

'Continue for the present,' he instructed Shuen. 'Watch his visitors carefully.'

'Yes yes.'

'What about Tang? Have you remembered where you saw him?'

'It almost came back to me the other day.'

'His record is good.'

Shuen smirked. 'Every traitor seeks to establish a good record.'

'So I have learned,' said Sun heavily.

'When I met him he had another name and both arms. It will come back to me.'

After Shuen had gone Sun heaved himself wearily from his chair and went to the window, staring out at the great flat plain of T'ien-An Mên Square. Children were playing round the monument. He shook his great head; the names of those heroes would mean even less to them and to their children, printed words in history lessons, the mumbled recollections of old men drowsy in shadows, their courage, their strength, their splendid conviction and heart, burned out, waiting for the nothingness of death. The glorious years before comradeship died.

He narrowed his throbbing eyes to gaze at the bright grey sky. In places the clouds were broken, showing thin strips of blue softer than the ribbons Yi-hai used to tie her hair. They reminded him that spring was less than a month away. He had liked spring best, its silver sickle moon riding through sable darkness, a million stars hung like festive lamps, cool dawn winds sweet as hyacinths. Each winter now he thought of the approaching spring. But they passed without him seeing them, and suddenly scarlet and gold chrysanthemums in misty streets reminded that another summer had gone by in sweat and use-lessness.

He massaged his belly. What was the purpose if finally life had no meaning as the atheists said and the ancestors vanished like leaves? Why should a man strive, sacrifice happiness and health, for unborn generations to whom his humanity was less important than a wild dog? What did it all mean? Why sacrifice for right, if sacrifice, the gift of spirit, came from nowhere and meant nothing?

He sighed and watched the children leaping.

6

Tang spent his spare hours outside the hotel. He preferred to tramp through icy streets rather than stay in his room where

Shuen could find him. Shuen never stopped questioning him. He appeared at least once a day, outwardly affable, eyes probing, trying to find out. The lonely winter streets were safer.

Frequently Tang experienced a panicking terror. It urged him to flee. He only just overcame the impulse, sharpest at night, waking him from dreams of being tortured. There was nowhere he could go. No one would hide him. Absence would betray him. He had no money for the long journey south to try to reach Hongkong. If he stole money to go by train the police would be on his trail at once. He had no means of escape.

He trudged round the cold city through rain and snow, driven on by fear, reluctant to return to his room lest it was full of police waiting to take him to torture, secret trial, death. He dared not believe that Shuen would lose interest in him.

As days lengthened into weeks he became more familiar with the city than most people. It gave him something to think about. He came to know every *hutung*, every new building, people who went to the Workers' Club in the southwest, the Cultural Palace of Nationalities, other places of entertainment, even the new railway station where people collected to hear its marble clock chime; that was how he came to learn one other secret of hundreds shut in by winter. One night in January he went to the Shoudu Cinema to see the new colour film *Lin Tse-hsu*, a story of the British opium trade, and caught sight of the Englishman Kendal in the audience and not far off the girl who came into his lift sometimes, a girl whose scarred neck caused him to remember her. He thought no more about it. Then, one morning soon after the Englishman came back from Hankow, he saw them again, going round an exhibition at the Peking Centre. They were not together. She was guide to a party of Ceylonese; the Englishman was alone, some paces behind. Just as he recognized them the girl stepped back and the Englishman took two steps forward, and he saw their hands touch for an instant, then the Englishman went on. And that evening she came into his lift, her cheeks flushed, happiness shining in her eyes, excitement about her. She got out at the floor occupied by Chinese officials, thanking him in *pai-hua*; her voice had a slight American accent. He watched her walk away. Halfway down the corridor she broke into a run, as if to snatch back wasted time, hastening round the corner leading to stairs going to the floors above.

And two evenings later she got into the lift again. She was accompanied by Shao *hsiao chieh*, a plump pretty-faced girl who had a bubbling laugh. He detected a change in the scarred girl. Her manner implied she knew more than the light amusements of unattached young women.

By one means and another he discovered who she was. When she came into the lift he pretended not to recognize her. Usually she walked casually down the corridor, but sometimes her feet quarrelled with her mind, and then she ran as she did on the evening after the Englishman came back from Hankow.

Sometimes he lay smoking in his bed, thinking about her and the Englishman. Shuen would be pleased to learn that a Chinese girl from the country of the most bitterly hated enemy of the People's Republic was the friend of a British newspaper-man. He stared at the ceiling, thinking about them.

7

One late January afternoon Ilse walked stiffly into Clive's room. It was four o'clock. The blazing sunlit sky stung her eyes. Inside the door she stood rigidly erect, breathing rapidly, trying to hear through the pound of blood in her ears. Her initial relief at having got here gave place to weariness. She felt it rise in her trembling legs, threaten to sap her remaining energy. Faintness swept over her dazed mind. A spark of lucid purpose told her she dare not give in to weakness, not here.

Harshly she spoke his name, forcing herself to repeat it. There was no reply. He was not here. She had not even come to find him, wanting to hide in a place which gave her sanctuary. It gave her relief to be alone, entirely alone. She did not want him now. Him least of all. She dreaded the possibility of confusing him among the atrocious memories like raw wounds in her mind. She had to forget the last two hours. It must never happen again. Never again.

She stared blankly at the blazing window as memory crashed through her chaotic mind. She longed to scream. Suddenly she remembered where she was and turned the key in the lock. Another wave of weakness rose in her. She tumbled blindly through the bedroom and fell on the bathroom floor, dragging herself on, and was vilely sick, her whole body in revolt. She stayed on the floor, her face and hands burningly hot, her body shivering from cold. When she tried to get up another spasm of vomiting kept her on her knees.

At length she managed to get up. swaying unsteadily. Instinct told her to wash her face. Without being aware of what she did, she let the water run on until steam clouded the window. She put her hands into it, crying out at the scalding heat. She turned off the tap and ran cold water and washed her face. Then she got a bottle of antiseptic from the metal cabinet and gargled. Everything she did seemed unreal, dreamlike, not to be happening. She stumbled into the bedroom and sat down on a chair.

She willed herself to forget. She sat quiet staring at their bed. At first she longed to ignore it, then it began to calm her. She forced herself to remember how it gave her refuge, peace in her mind. And sleep. Sleep.

She sat staring at it, her eyes dull and vacant, heedless of the darkening copper sunlight, her body trembling uncontrollably.

Eleven

On the Thursday evening after Steven returned from Changteh he sat in his room compiling notes for an article on contemporary Chinese literature. Out of the radio poured an ardent hatred of America. He was engrossed in trying to evolve an outline of *The Hurricane*, the turgidly detailed Stalin Prize novel by Chou Li-po of land reform, and was unaware that Mei-ling had come until he heard the door shut. She wore a milky plastic slicker over her clothes. Without speaking she peeled it off impatiently and threw herself into his arms. For aching moments her cold lips twisted on his. At length she pulled her head free, burying her face in his shoulder.

'Steven.' Her muffled voice was shaken. 'Oh, my darling, those hateful empty days. I thought they'd never end.'

He kissed her hair. 'Here we are.'

'I can only stay a little while, but I had to see you.'

'All contributions gratefully received. Time for coffee?'

'Yes.'

Quietness returned to her while she sat curled up on the settee, holding her cup in both hands to warm her chilled fingers. Her fortitude reassured him. Against all the odds, she was actually more at ease now than during their first meetings, undaunted by insidious pressures which could have corrupted their peace together. Her eloquent eyes and contained face reminded him of women seen while on leave in the bomb-whistling darkness of wartime London. It showed the same bland disregard of personal danger, the unemotional face of endurance assumed to sustain others and self under a mask of ordinariness. Relieved by their reunion, she listened to a brief account of his excursion.

'Were you writing about it?' she asked.

'No, sketching out an article on novels written here.'

She raised her brows, smiling ironically.

'They're not worth your effort,' she said contemptuously. 'We produced the finest fairy stories, but less than a dozen outstanding novels. The Celestial Emperors were terrified of education in case it produced individuals opposed to their rule. The Party is equally afraid of novels about people of flesh and blood.'

'I don't see why that should be,' he commented.

'It's quite simple,' she said. 'Western literature is founded on the heroic concept that the individual is right to pursue personal fulfilment and to enjoy liberty based on abstract principles. Our rulers were always antagonistic to such beliefs. The Party has taken its attitude from the Celestial Emperors. Mao Tse-tung says art and literature must serve the people. Thousands of years ago Confucius taught that society must be harmonious, that people must conform to rules. Our literature has never escaped from servitude to our rulers.'

Steven nodded. He gathered from her direct manner, the total absence of indecision, that this was one of the subjects she had discussed with her father. He loved her schoolmarmly attitude. She was a creature of enchanting diversities.

'Darling, I still don't understand why the mandarins are opposed to realism,' he said. 'I would have thought that it suited their purpose.'

'So would I,' she agreed. 'But they refuse to countenance it, except in foreign novels which show the worst aspects of life in non-communist countries. They are required reading at the universities. The Party imports them to follow up Dickens and Jack London, Upton Sinclair, Theodore Dreiser, and other writers. The Party represents them as secret communists, not humanists.'

The discussion gave him another avenue of exploration in this acceptance world.

Soon afterwards she got ready to leave.

Behind the locked door he held her closely, his cheek resting on the curve of her neck. Her hair was still damp. Although they spared each other, their deferent caresses were torment. Each touch revived memory. 'Miss me, darling,' she pleaded miserably.

'You know damn well I do, my dearest, and it's hell.'

'That's good to remember,' she told him, mussed his hair, and went.

As he resumed work, the spate of hatred poured in effortless exhilaration from the radio.

That was the climate of their condition. Often they did not see each other for a week. He drew up an itinerary of daily calls by his new room-boy to avoid attention, and she planned her longer visits carefully. Twice he bumped into her in public to give them the slight alibi of recognition, but they failed to invent a satisfactory explanation for anyone who saw her leave his room.

By tacit consent they never spoke of the future. Nor did the past concern them; it was prudent not to entwine their previous lives too closely lest they betray themselves. They talked about books, music, topics tainted here by 'correct thinking'.

One evening they listened to a radio performance of Italian operatic music. Earlier, before they liberated each other from want, they had spent an hour searching the bedroom for a hidden microphone, crawling round on hands and knees, climbing on chairs to test the ceiling, tapping the legs of the bed, on account of her insistence that they ought to behave like an ordinary man and woman while they shared each other; she whispered that microphones were usually concealed in the bed-frames of suspected Party members to eavesdrop on what they said to their wives; but they had not found one. Now he stretched along the settee and she sat on cushions on the floor, her head resting on his side, an arm wound over his waist. He had turned out the lights to hide the sameness of their cell. Across the window a scatter of wan stars sanded the moonless sky. His fingers traced the curve of her cheek.

She broke their silence by asking casually: 'Would it frighten you if we went from being in love to loving?'

Her tone gave no indication of her thoughts.

'Here, you mean?'

'No, anywhere. This country, these people around us, don't come into it. No, I mean us, wherever we met.'

'You believe it might alarm you?'

'You understand me too well. Yes, I expect it would. I'd be frightened of committing myself to the finality of loving you, and terrified of wanting you to love me. I would want both, even if you slept with other women. I find I'm very primitive, horribly possessive. That is wrong. Possessive women disgust

me. They invent such degrading excuses to feed their insecurity
. . . I think the sadness of love would trouble me.'

'I don't see why it should be sad.'

'It is bound to be.' She pressed her lips to his shirt and drew them down over his ribs. 'Perhaps only for women.'

'What set you off on this? I'd like to hear about it.'

She laughed. 'Darling, I'm sorry. It's one of the things I've thought about since nineteen-fortynine.'

He rumpled her hair over her forehead. 'I'm sorry I took so long to get here.'

'You're laughing at me,' she said. 'You have a right to. I'm being abstruse. My thoughts are always confused when we've made love. It's been too sudden and overwhelming for me to be sensible yet. I don't want to be sensible.'

'Nineteen-fortynine,' he prompted.

'Yes. One of the mandarins, Chou Yeng, said "Love has retreated to a position of no importance; our new tasks are a thousand times more significant than love." While you were away I went to a discussion on right thinking about biological conduct. The speakers declared that love does not exist, mother love is a bourgeois concept, all such beliefs belong to a phase of capitalist society which has no place in the future, human nature is a theory without relation to fact. Then the chairman opened an exhibition of American and British advertisements. They showed coloured photographs of a man and a woman riding in an auto, in a plane, in railway coaches, buying a house, toothpaste, diamond rings, stockings, bath towels. The chairman said it proved that love was a capitalist invention.'

'And they passed a unanimous resolution condemning profit-making practices.'

'They said it was bestial, cynical, outrageous, nauseating.'

'I seem to have heard those words before,' he commented. 'So we cut out love, which leaves involuntary biological necessity. And it upset you.'

'I needed to see you badly.'

'But it led you to wonder if we're just being novel together.'

'I can't tell. I almost wish I hadn't been a virgin until I

became your mistress. If I had been experienced, I might be more intelligent about it.'

'It's a pity I didn't have the nous to realize what you said that evening or you'd still be one.'

'But that's absurd!' she protested in amazement. 'Virginity has no significance.' She hesitated, and went on in a puzzled voice: 'My confusion starts there. Darling Steven, don't laugh, but I'm glad you were the first to use me. I shall always be glad. It was the only thing I can give you.'

'You have given me more than anyone else. Let's forget it.'

'How can I?' she queried in distress. 'I want to give you so much. True peace. Laughter. Sunlight, the stars. Joy. The glances of people, so I can feel they are envious and will think "The Party is wrong, I have seen an ordinary woman brought to love by a man." But there are no new ways for me to show you my gratitude. Millions of forgotten women have given the same to other men, millions of unbegotten women will give men the same in their tomorrows. The me of us cannot be special for you.'

She was nearly crying, breath rasping in her throat.

'Be patient with me, dearest,' he told her. 'I'm not adept at expressing myself about these things, not yet. But to me you are unique . . . and never talk about gratitude.'

'Why not?' she demanded angrily. 'Without you I was nothing, fleshless, mindless, an animate female skeleton like a Tibetan *thanka* goddess. You have given me life. It hurts. My flesh and nerves, my fulfilment, are your creation. Sometimes, no, every day I'm afraid I shall die unless you remind me that your life needs me. That is being in love, my longing to serve you. It may be love too. I cannot tell. It has come too swiftly.'

Her hand kept opening and clenching on his side, mute evidence of unhappiness. For once darkness was his ally, hiding the anger in his eyes. Fury flared raw and bitter in him, rage at the merciless determination of Party mandarins to thrust intellectual confusion into the minds of intelligent people in this bamboo prison.

184

'Off-hand, I'd say you ought to steer clear of theoretical jam-sessions,' he commented and drew her up beside him.

They held each other in a lustless embrace.

'Don't let it alarm you.'

As if she had not heard, her shadowy face remained still and intent for some moments, her mind pursuing her own thoughts. Then she smiled, freed her hands to hold his face, and set her lips on his.

And on another occasion, while she sat in his arm, she asked: 'Are you sure you don't mind me being a Catholic?'

'Does it worry you?'

'I'm curious about your attitude. Everything about you is important to me. I think over what we say to each other. It helps the days when we are not together.'

'How can I pass an opinion on your faith?' he asked. 'Nothing the scientists have done can disprove it. What they've done in the past hundred years, though few seem to have realized it, is to increase the wonder of the miracles of God. The most amusing scientific squabble in Britain when I was last there was between astronomers over the origin of the universe. According to them, they knew all the answers. Theoretically, that is, though they were as vehement as if their theories had to be accepted as facts. They were as didactic as nineteenth century anthropologists. Most entertaining, provided one accepted their theories as theories. The weakness of scientists is that when they're in the heat of their careers they want everyone to accept as fact what is only statistical evidence to support their theories. Science is littered with discarded theories once accepted as facts.'

'Tell me your opinion about religion,' she ordered.

He kissed the palm of her hand. 'No, my darling. Your faith will give you far more comfort than my notions. I'll discuss the social effects of religions, endlessly, but not faith, no.'

'Do you believe in God?' she pressed.

'Of course. No one can disprove His existence on a plane outside our finite comprehension.'

Strangely, his logic caused her to weep a bit.

The Ming village swollen into an arrogant racialist Party capital debased their humanity but they defied it. Their defiance was accounted treason and demoralization; they ignored it. Quite often he thought she might well be a German woman and he a Jew in Nazi Berlin. That was how it felt. The atrocious microphone pried on them constantly.

Usually she came to see him without prearrangement, her appearances dependent on the changing winter schedule of her duties. Although he contrived to be in most evenings he could not warn her if unexpected calls summoned him to the Foreign Ministry building. They dared not write or telephone to each other. The only sign of her visits in his absence was her arrangement of top sheets of his typing paper, their secret code. And yet, despite every adverse circumstance, they found contentment together.

She gave him other reasons to forget the past. They endured early defeats of their passion, hastening to vent defiance of political and racial edicts through the neglected and inexpert substances of their bodies. The raw sting of failure did not alienate them. Imbalance ended in their quickening perception of each other's sensual needs. Then their union became a full deep rhythm, well-served by the continence which had led them to shun chance or sedative intercourse. 'There is no possibility of a man and a woman of different social backgrounds sharing common sentiments' declared Peking University students. They were utterly wrong. Even though either he or she searched the bedroom for another microphone on every night that she stayed, it did not spoil their pleasure in each other.

Within a short while love-making became part of the pattern of their shared lives. Though they restrained their ardour at brief meetings, they always made love on her longer visits. Too susceptive to be moderate, they used themselves fully and their enchantment was complete. Cautious routine offered them no joy and they forswore it. Her passionate submission gave their hours in this alien darkness an exultant pride which refuted the nonsense talked by the mandarins and their conditioned children. Once he asked if any religious scruples led her to regret having left behind their previous companionship. No, she said positively, and added that for the first time she understood the meaning of chastity.

And there they left it. Their need of each other in love-making certainly branded them as criminals in the view of the mandarins, and perhaps it made them sinners according to her faith, but they were not prideless. They accepted responsibility and sought each other without fear. They were alive in the eye of the storm.

2

As Steven read the daily sheaf of news-items harvested from the teletypewriter one evening, she hurried into the room. She was flushed and breathless from running up the stairs, her eyes sparkling, an air of excitement about her. She said: 'Darling, I can't stop. I told Pai-chen I had to post a letter. On Tuesday I'm having dinner at the Muslim restaurant with an East German movie delegation. Han and his wife will be there. Can you come? It'd be a wonderful chance for us to be introduced.'

'I'll be there. I'll try to bring Sheila Grant. We owe her for brandy and coffee.'

Her eyes sharpened. 'Golly, no! She's gorgeous and exotic and lonely. Don't you know someone ugly?'

He looked at her across the ten feet that separated them. 'You are very beautiful. I adore you. Even here I feel you against me.'

'Of course,' she said. 'I feel you too. It's shocking. And you're beautiful too and I don't want to go. Darling, I love you very much. Please find someone plain. I'll go crazy.'

3

Late next evening Steven and Clive had dinner in the Indian restaurant. There was hardly anyone present, a handful of womanless Asians catching up on required reading over their curries.

Clive said: 'Judging from instructions from home, people expect me to report riots after these food shortages here.'

'Rumours from Hongkong lead them to fancy trouble.'

'Might it happen? Harvests were far below target. Rice, wheat, and pig production are down on account of spring floods and summer drought last year. One Ministry official admitted to me without palaver that some regions have got famine. He sounded almost proud of it, like a self-confessed flagellant.'

'Famine didn't overthrow their rulers last century when a hundred million people died from starvation. Nowadays they've got a well-fed army to keep order.'

Clive massaged his stomach thoughtfully, belched happily, and said: 'Rice. Yes, you're right.'

As they went downstairs for a game of billiards in the lounge, he asked: 'How are you these days?'

'Pretty good. Why?'

'Sure?'

'Yes. Why?'

'Oh, nothing much. You seem edgy, on the jitter.'

'Being cooped up always irritates me,' said Steven.

'Ah, you think too much,' Clive told him. 'That's bad, real bad. You ought to get out, relax, have a good time. Mind you, I don't know where the hell you get it in this godforsaken dump, but you should. Look after yourself, son. No one else will.'

'There endeth the lesson?'

'I guess so.'

'Good.'

4

'Our sole desire is to serve the people,' said Han earnestly.

He had shown earnestness since they sat down to dine. His eyes radiated sincerity. It was he who invited Sheila Grant and Steven to join his party. His official guests were the usual film delegates seen in Peking; a solid young blonde actress, Hilde; two highly-strung and untidy cameramen, Curt and Gerhart; two phlegmatic, paunchy, spectacled directors, Franz and Wilhelm; a slinky black-haired actress, Elsa, whose heavy-lidded eyes and restless hands suggested drug addiction; and several party shepherds whose names had not registered with Steven. At Han's insistence, he sat between Sheila and Ilse Han. Ilse was remote, speaking only when spoken to, and then grudgingly. Farther off sat Mei-ling, lovely in her turquoise cheongsam. In moments when Steven and she did manage to exchange glances he saw quiet excitement in her face and relief at having accomplished her intention, and then she looked significantly at Sheila to indicate oldfashioned jealousy.

Han embarked on another of his Party homilies.

'You ladies and gentlemen whose joy it is to be cultural workers have read the works on true creative development written by our great and wise Chairman,' he said to Franz and Wilhelm. 'As our writers and all cultural workers agree, his own poems are of monumental genius. I am convinced that he would like to lay down his heavy burden and retire to the simple life of a poet-philosopher. But a million flowers of culture will blossom in our People's Republic because of his selfless devotion to duty.'

Franz took his cue faultlessly.

'Let us drink to your great Chairman.'

They had drunk toasts every few minutes for the last hour.

In the acclamation Sheila whispered to Steven that she thought the cult of the personality was officially tabu. She was by far the most picturesque member of the party. Silver brocade fringed her dazzling vermilion sari. The sleek precision of her intensely blue-black hair enhanced her lean features and the whites of her large eyes gleamed against her dark skin. She directed a demure sweetness exclusively at Steven to stave off the attention of both actors, patently oppressed by months of grim innocence in China. Their efforts to charm her got nowhere.

The food was delicious. Their appetites were stimulated by hors-d'œuvres of assorted cold chicken and pork spiced by sugar and ginger and a tart blend of oils. Then came duck, the one Peking feast which had outlived every change of government. No subtlety of culinary art was absent from duck served in nearly a dozen different forms: as a paté in a covering like wafer-thin 'spring cakes', in red peppers with a dash of pungent *hua-chiao* sauce, as slivers folded in tender slices of ham served with soy sauce and pickled onions, hidden in a delicate fish sauce, poached in oil flavoured by sugar and ginger, steamed on small pyramids of gluten rice, ducks' tongues in clear soup, spiced giblets in noodles, and finally as whole roast duck, the succulent meat a rich brown, carved in front of them by a woman chef. Between each course they drank toasts, to peace, to democracy, to the Chairman, to East Germany, to British workers, to world friendship, to the Indian masses, to documentary films, to cameramen, to film actors, to culture, to each other. Their drinks were the syrupy local grape wine, white rice wine, *pi-chiu* beer, hot yellow rice wine, and a deadly sorghum distillation *pai-chiu* which Steven and Sheila avoided. Mei-ling limited herself to formal white wine. Ilse and the German party drank everything. By the time they were served with pineapple both actors were well in their cups and Elsa gave an appearance of being in trance.

It took another half-hour to conclude additional toasts to peace and friendship. And when the party broke up Steven and Mei-ling had to content themselves by staring at each other out of blank urbane smiles.

At Steven's suggestion the car taking Sheila and himself

home went for a slow prowl round town to help clear their heads. They drove along streets awash in light from a brilliant three-quarter moon. At some points they passed gushes of jostling talkative hurrying men and women coming from cinemas and theatres to scramble onto late buses, their softly clicking voices whirled away by the blustery wind. High above one street-corner a gang of labourers were at work on a new office building, small antlike figures slipping across the square white eyes of floodlights slanted over skeleton steel ribs. Farther on a quartette of armed policemen bulky in greatcoats exchanged desultory comments. Close to the station another group of construction-workers clambered over another ugly functional new building.

They scarcely spoke until they reached the hotel and Sheila said: 'Come and have a drink in my apartment, Kendal. I'll make coffee. Brandy, coffee, me. What more can a man want? Apart from a million pounds?'

He smiled. 'Aren't you tired?'

'I'd've said so,' she replied in a return to her usual waspish tone. 'Besides, I need a bodyguard. If you will fling me at these starved heroes, you'll have to bar the door against them.'

'You won't have trouble from them.'

'Come and find out,' she challenged.

He laughed.

'You are slightly drunk,' she exclaimed pleasedly as if he had confirmed a theory. 'That's the very first time I've heard you laugh naturally. You ought to drink more often, let yourself unwind.'

As they went into her room she took off her overcoat and slung it carelessly over one of the chairs, told him to get comfortable, and, refusing an offer of assistance, pottered around collecting glasses, cups and saucers, brandy, and put them on the table, then went to plug the kettle into the wall-switch adaptor.

The telephone rang.

'You answer it,' she said peevishly. 'Let him imagine he's interrupting something madly exciting.'

When he laid down the receiver, she asked: 'Which one?'

'Gerhart.'

'That barrel of lard!'

Crouched down, her back to him, she did not see him smile. He heard her mutter exasperatedly over damage to the flex, a willowy girl with slender shoulders and small firm croupe in a vivid flamingo sari, cursing to herself like a Hooghly stevedore.

She was fortunate, he thought worriedly. Unfettered; an individual. 'Underneath all, individuals! I swear nothing is good to me now that ignores individuals!' And, by God, Walt Whitman had spoken for him too.

The thought spiralled in his mind. He hoped vexedly that she appreciated her good fortune. It was considerable. She had an unrestricted right to quit this land where the rank spreading weeds of conformity strangled individuals. If she wanted an affaire, worthwhile or worthless, she was free to indulge it openly. She could be fearless, indifferent, outspoken, defiant, demonstrative, reckless, complacent, and, above all, hopeful. She owned the right to spread her individuality through every hour, free of heart, of mind, of body. Million pounds or no, she could thumb her nose at officialdom; she could err and laugh it off. She could even curse faulty electric appliances without fear of accusations of disloyalty.

He stared at her curved figure, and looked away. Perhaps she was right about his being drunk. Or it might be his stinging recognition of her freedom from artificial strains and unhappiness.

He gazed at his hands.

'Shall I dash up for my home-repair kit?'

'Rude devil,' she snarled and gave a cry of astonished triumph. She stood up, dusted her sari like a schoolboy flicking grit off his knees, and picked up her coat. In an affable tone she mused: 'Where did I put the sugar? Oh yes, the bath. Have a drink while I freshen up.'

'I've had enough.'

'Nonsense! Their drinks have no kick. Besides, we must

celebrate getting away from Han. That man makes my flesh creep. We'll steer clear of him next time you take me out.'

She wandered elegantly into the bedroom trailing her coat. He poured out drinks and sampled his. It was excellent brandy. He felt its fire strengthen him. He finished it and poured another glass. The telephone rang. He answered it, finding more difficulty in getting rid of the caller. As he replaced the receiver she called out.

'Franz,' he told her and heard her blow her nose like a curse.

There was another call while they were having coffee. She stopped in the middle of a sentence, her eyes brightening dangerously, her lips drawn tight.

'I might be a convenient jam-pot. I wonder which one it is?'

'I'll lay you five to one it's Karl.'

'No, not him. He let me see that he thought I was much too old.'

'Oh?'

'Yes, one of them. It's either Curt or Wilhelm.'

'It could be one of their shepherds.'

'Even money in shillings it's Curt.'

He nodded.

'You're on.'

'Will you answer it?'

'Your turn.'

'No. They pay more attention to a man.'

'You,' he insisted.

She got up, glowering disgustedly, and slouched across the room.

They were wrong. At first she was vivacious, urbanely disclaiming compliments paid her, then her voice hardened, and died to flat formalities. Steven finished his coffee and put the cup on the floor. He saw her back go rigid. Finally she announced that she had to go out, and cut the connexion. Her shoulders squirmed. Abruptly she swung round, marched over, erect as a soldier on parade, and, speechless, sat down on his lap, shutting her eyes as she wound her arms round his neck. For long moments her lips twisted on his: her body remained stiff. She freed her head but kept her arms round him.

'You do that jolly well,' he said.

She studied his face, her eyelids partly lowered, an adequate hint of the right sort of quizzical smile on her lips. 'I like to do everything to the best of my ability. You could too.'

'Do you think so?' he parried.

'If you let some woman remind you that even you are, human.'

'A tall order for her.'

The points of her finger-nails dragged lightly across his neck. 'Oh, I don't know,' she said lazily.

'I wonder? Well. Who was it?'

She grimaced harshly. 'Elsa. Guess what she likes in addition to drink and drugs? Kendal, I'm probably cruel, but those like her make me feel dirty. Let's forget her. Are you always luke-warm?'

She let tension go from her, pleased to crumple against him while he eradicated heed of Elsa by a display of masculine fascination in her mouth. It did not take long. She stretched voluptuously and opened her eyes. 'Let's have another drink,' she said.

Thereafter they were left alone. She kept him entertained by stories of her experiences, always diverting, often scandalous. They shared an easy companionship, the wry humour of wanderers.

They really did talk the same language. And she did her utmost to help him unwind. Then she spoiled it by saying: 'I'm worried about you, Kendal.'

'You squander too much energy on other people.'

'Shut up,' she instructed equably. 'You're too much of an uncommitted idealist. I suppose it went like this—you've held aloof from personal attachments to search for an explanation of why you lived through the war. You want to justify your living. My father was the same. And there's probably a wrong woman in it too.'

'Whatever gave you such a notion?'

'Several things, including the poem you quoted about the years behind and ahead being a waste of breath.'

He reached for his drink. 'Did I quote that? Nice, isn't it?'

'Not the way you quoted it.'

'Let's leave me alone. I'm a dull subject.'

She ignored that. 'You must leave China,' she decided. 'You can't learn more here. You've seen how communism has given them a marvellous opportunity to hate the rest of us for new reasons. They are not inscrutable or impassive. Their greatest joy is to be instructed. They celebrate slavery with fireworks. It absolves them from personal responsibility. Go away, Kendal. Go and write something worthwhile. Or are you too idle?'

'Why don't you leave China?'

She smiled radiantly. 'If my application succeeds, I shall leave in April and go to Japan. I've had enough.'

It was one o'clock before she finished talking to him about what he should do. He managed to spend fifteen minutes telling her what to see in Tokyo and which places to visit outside the capital. As they bade each other goodnight, she kissed him fervently and said: 'Try to spare some time to see me. I shall be farther away there. Unless you come across to write a masterpiece.'

Twelve

WITHOUT prior notification by experts the hard winter relented. An invalid sun tottered weakly across the sky. The stiff rags of snow disappeared save from where they were sprinkled like lost handkerchiefs around the boles of trees. Prankish winds blustered and cavorted.

Steven delighted in an excuse to get out for walks. He saw the Pekingese welcoming this break in their long northern winter as if it were the Spring Festival itself. Housewives in padded blue coats did fitness exercises in side streets. Students resumed military training in public squares, charging their rifles against the fitful wind. At night small backyard furnaces cast their flickering orange glow over grimy men and women smelting pig-iron. The wives of ambassadors and consuls grumbled at their inability to get servants to give their buildings a thorough clean. On hoardings around town new posters blossomed in gaudy profusion, exhorting everyone to sustain the big leap forward through the new year. At diplomatic receptions to celebrate national days of uncommitted nations, Steven found official rooms gay with peonies, roses, lilies, and camellias, flown up from Canton, reported to be preparing for its largest annual flower bazaar.

Official news releases shouted renewed denunciation of American capitalism, British colonialism, Nationalist forces on Taiwan and daily criticism of those who did not hold to the tenets of basic communism. Several kept up their indirect accusations that the Kremlin was committing deviationism, the major heresy, the ultimate stigma.

Nowhere did he observe signs of extra human individuality. Such demonstrations were regarded as symptomatic of dangerous individualism seeking personal fulfilment regardless of nationalist ambitions. As if to underline the point one of the export propaganda magazines to reach him contained the character profile of a university girl student who was told by a Party secretary: *You cannot separate your private life from the Party struggle; personal happiness is safe only if it is based on collective well-being.* And the Party was arbiter of well-being and private life. The gentle sensitive nature had no lien on existence here; its intrinsic qualities were killed by this acid soil. The retreat into a stone shell of denial offered greater solace than constant interference by bigoted fanatics.

That withdrawal could not apply to the majority. Abstract principles were meaningless to those who interpreted life in terms of a satisfied belly, quiet loins and a roof against the darkness. Those who passed Steven on his next walk gave proof of what Sheila Grant said about celebrating slavery with fireworks. Their restless energy filled these sunlit windy streets, sloe-eyed volatile men who strode purposefully and women who bustled in pursuit of their preoccupations, complacent in obedience, acceptive of dictate, content to disregard individuality, fast in their Asian inheritance of resignation. They would do exactly what they were told in war and peace, blindly dutiful, rid of personal responsibility.

He stooped to retrieve a stray ball and tossed it back to a frog-faced boy who gave him a gap-toothed grin, and continued on his walk. Out of the late smoky sunshine the air struck chill.

2

Shortly before four o'clock the following Saturday afternoon Steven sat in his room reading official notes passed between Peking and Delhi. It was growing dark. The heavily clouded sky had the yellowish tinge of threatening snow. He had just decided to switch on the light when the door swung open and Mei-ling half-fell into the room. She righted herself, shut the door quickly, and ran across, almost dropping her shopping bag. Fear glinted in her eyes. She stumbled past the settee saying, 'Some men saw me, they're coming,' and shut herself in the bedroom. Their luck had run out.

He lit a cigarette. His hands were shaking. He felt a shiver of tension circle his loins and his heart pounded. He forced himself to scribble a marginal note on the report, affecting an outward display of unconcern. The bedroom was silent. It had been an absurd mistake for her to hide, an error due to panic, but nothing could be done about it. He set himself to find an explanation for her presence.

There was a knock on the door.

He steadied himself.

'Chin lai,' he said and his voice sounded harsh.

Clive ambled in. He was frowning, his long sallow face dim in the shadows.

'Busy, son?'

Steven tossed the report on the table. Men, she had told him; some men. He eased back on his chair, smiling at Clive.

'Open for business. Switch on the light, chum.'

Clive did so and said: 'Bless your heart.' His blinking eyes searched round the room. 'Sure it's convenient?'

'Of course. Get comfortable. What's on your mind?'

'I need help.'

'How much?'

'The rudery. Not money. Advice.'

He went over to the settee, sat down near the bedroom door. He had not shaved; a grey stubble made his jaw look dusty. His manner indicated that he was settling down for a long session.

Steven rubbed his cold hands together and waited. 'Advice on what?' he prompted.

'It's confidential.'

'Can you trust me?'

'The caution was formal,' Clive assured him. He took some folded typewritten sheets from an inside pocket of his jacket and threw them across. 'Can you read that for me now? I'd be grateful.'

Steven unfolded the sheets of flimsy. They were typewritten. The top one carried a Peking line undated. Its first sentence referred to rumours of continued Chinese imperialist repression in Tibet. The first paragraph suggested that Clive did not intend to avoid trouble. Steven ground out his partly smoked cigarette. He listened intently.

He did not have long to wait. As he started to read the second paragraph there was a quick light tapping on the door and Shuen entered without invitation. Clive got out his handkerchief, dropped it, and bent to pick it up. Shuen halted on the threshold, smiling ingratiatingly.

Steven ignored his inner agitation.

'What is it?'

Shuen bowed. 'I happened to be passing and thought you might require service.'

Steven turned to Clive. 'Shuen looks after me like a mother. If I let him have his way, I wouldn't lift a finger.'

'Jolly good,' said Clive and blew his nose carefully. 'Yes.'

Steven considered thoughtfully, forcing himself to indicate nerveless unconcern.

'No, I don't need anything. Is the service bell out of order?'

'No, sir.'

'I'll ring if I want your assistance.'

He smiled and turned his attention to the typescript in his hands. His nerves continued to flutter after the door shut. When he finished the article it required conscious endeavour to appear normal. He glanced up.

'Advice about what?'

'Ah now, several points,' said Clive. He got up to turn on the radio, waited until the available programme was coming through, and sat down again. 'Don't you love home comforts?'

'There must be some left,' said Steven shortly. 'What points?'

'Can I get it through without being slung out? I don't want to go yet. For several reasons.'

'You've seen how they act.'

'Hot today, cold tomorrow, roasting next week.'

'Yes.'

'Then it depends on their mood and how I write it.'

'Yes.'

''T'ain't what you say, it's the way what you say it, that's what gets results.'

'Yes.'

'Check. Now comes the liberty.'

'Yes?'

'You're cagey. Damned crafty, I'd say. You can see my words fresh. I've written it too often. What should I rephrase?'

'You want to file it.'

Clive scratched his chin. 'I think so,' he decided.

'You checked your sources.'

'Don't bark at me. Who can be sure of unofficial news here?'

'Are you reasonably confident that you haven't been fed anti-Party material in order to provide an incident?'

'None of the most detailed statements has been included.'

They went over it carefully. No one disturbed them. Half an

hour later Clive got slowly to his feet, saying he'd appreciate another discussion on it. He folded it back into his pocket. Then, talking about the frontier dispute which Peking had with Burma, he put his hand into another pocket and brought out a small red woollen slipper, one of those which Mei-ling wore here. Steven realized it must have fallen from her basket as she stumbled, and Clive had picked it up when he dropped his handkerchief. Clive talked on, measuring it in his hand, then gave it to him. Clive shook his head warningly.

'Will you be in for a bit?' he enquired casually. 'I might get an idea I'd like to mull over, if you've no objection.'

'I don't plan to go out.'

'Good. I'll give you a ring on the blower. Right now you can think over another idea lying in my attic. Why is Peking digging into Albania at the expense of Moscow? Why do the mandarins want a toehold in Europe?'

Alone Steven slumped on his chair fighting off an attack of reaction, spent and irresolute. It might not have ended yet: an even greater threat might present itself without forewarning. With an effort he stood up and went to the bedroom door, opened it slightly to say 'Stay there' and returned to his chair.

While he sat there the telephone rang. It was Clive.

'I forgot to thank you,' he heard Clive say. 'My manners are contemporary.'

'That's all right.'

'There was no sign of our friend Charley. I searched, but he'd scarpered. Give me a ring if he comes back. I'd like to see him.'

'Thanks,' said Steven in relief.

'You're welcome,' said Clive graciously and rang off.

Steven put down the receiver. He stared out at the darkening sky and saw a squeeze of whiteness like a sprinkle of soap flakes, floating down on the Forbidden City. He locked the outside door, picked up the slipper, and went into the bedroom. Mei-ling turned to him.

The change in her astounded him. She stood beside the wardrobe, her hands clasped in front of her. She had changed into a cheongam new to him, the dull crimson fabric stitched in gold thread, its collar up to her small ears. Her other clothes had vanished. She appeared wholly unperturbed, coolly composed, exactly as if nothing unusual had happened, eyes serene, cheeks slightly flushed, her hair carefully done, enhancing the flowerlike delicacy of her face. And she was able to smile. To smile.

And as they looked at each other her heart ached for this man whose woman she knew herself to be, who owned her mind and her body more completely than she had expected to give them to any man, who bound her to him by unchanging gentleness, whose image lightened their days of separation, and whose touch and smell and pulse when he used her were completion of herself. His face was grey, full of worry, drawn by anxiety, his eyes staring at unreality, not at her. She longed to run from him, to be spared her sorrow at his agitation. She smiled.

'I put on my dress in case you wanted me to meet your friend,' she said, lowering her hands to her sides. 'I did the embroidery myself. Do you like it?'

He clenched the slipper in his hand, took a step towards her and stopped. 'You look more beautiful than ever,' he said as if admitting something he hated to mention.

She refused to be put off. She turned her back to him.

'Does it fit? I think it's rather tight. There isn't a cheval glass in my room. People say women in love put on weight. Am I getting fat?'

'Fine fine, just right,' his voice said impatiently. 'You must go now. It isn't safe for you here. You mustn't come here again. They'll find out. That boy is suspicious.'

She faced him, assuming amazement. 'Darling, you mustn't be upset because I got frightened. I was only surprised to see them. I haven't met them until this afternoon.'

'You said they saw you.'

'Yes, they did. Is that my slipper? I dropped it.'

'Clive found it.'

'I like him.'

'Did you hear what I told you?' he demanded angrily.

'Yes,' she replied. 'Yes, my darling, I heard, and I'm sorry I upset you. But we mustn't let this get out of proportion. We've taken chances since the beginning. I'd completely forgotten we've given ourselves an excuse to be together. It takes a little while to get used to our having been introduced.'

'Listen to me,' he began.

'Darling, I misled you unintentionally,' she interrupted contritely. 'They didn't see me come in, though your friend must realize I was hiding while he was with you. I expect the room-boy mistook another woman in the corridor for me. We were about the same height. Darling, if we'd been married for years instead of my having been your mistress for weeks, we'd still take risks. We mustn't let small incidents get out of proportion.'

'You were scared.'

'Women always assume the worst,' she countered. 'Sitting here, I've become sensible. I'd completely forgotten we have been introduced. I'm sorry I behaved foolishly.'

He stared at her.

'You must decide if I am to leave you,' she said, careful to keep her voice submissive. 'I think it unnecessary, but I belong to you in loyalty. I will obey sooner than cause you sorrow.'

As they looked at each other, her instinct divined a change in him. It took her across every division that separated them, licensed her mouth and hands, her own longing kindled as she set herself to awaken his, refusing to permit separation, encouraging him by familiar caresses, gently brutal to prevent him from thinking, losing heed of her own fears, until they clung, renewed in enchantment, and then she enforced their return to the commonplace world, sensing how swiftly his mind might revert to anxiety, even while she held him in her arms. She forced her will on him, treating their alarm lightly, pretending it enhanced their day, her voice soft in derision. Her lying laughter strengthened him. Only then, smiling lazily, careful to keep his attention, careful to hold him in tender bondage, did she allow herself to weaken, quaking in misery, filled with unhappiness for them. None of her anxiety showed on her serene face.

Later, in the other room, Steven said: 'I'm normal again. Sorry I got in a flap.'

She leant forward to rest her face on his shoulder. More surely than words the tone of his voice assured her that he had regained self-control. It gave her a new experience in achievement. Every day in these unsought months the fact of him taught her some new lesson in living a woman's life, each acute, many raw, the majority of them tenuous perceptions, a loosing of intuition into dimensions of belonging hitherto denied her, its claim felt most clearly on their days apart. She prized his regained calm. It was her accomplishment. Surely no other man would permit her to exercise such sway over his moods? An ordinary man soon lost sight of the individual woman, relegated her to being a shadowy figure hovering in the background until he required her service to provide his comfort. Yet Steven risked much for her, dealt leniently with her spirit and mind. She kissed his hand and nipped one of his fingers in her teeth.

'Have another mooncake,' she said.

No one came to disturb them. While they watched a television film of life in a coalmining commune they supped off cold chicken, lychees, and coffee. When he heeded time it was near the moment for her to go.

They were sitting on the floor beside the settee. It varied the view of their cell. She was bent forward, forehead resting on her knees, hands clasped round her ankles. Out of the radio came a tinkle-pluck said to have originated in ancient Mongolia. He put his arm round her. Her head fell back on his shoulder, her eyes shut, lips smiling as if aware of his scrutiny. He smoothed a finger along her slanted eyebrows.

She sighed contentedly. 'I love you to make a fuss of me.'

He put a thumb and forefinger at the corners of her lips, squeezed them apart, and felt them hold his tongue as he kissed her.

'Time to go.'

Her eyes remained lidded. 'I'm coming back early tomorrow morning to spend the day with Pai-chen. I forgot to tell you.'

'You're a cheat.'

'You can beat me. Let's have a lovely bath and take books to bed. I would like that. I'll bath first to warm the bed for you.'

'You're a sly, crafty, secretive devil, my love.'

'Jolly good,' she said in passable mimicry of his voice, and shoved him aside to scramble up, exclaiming miserably that one of her legs had gone to sleep. Squeaking in anguish, she hobbled off to run water into the bath.

They read for an hour. As he finished he saw her watching him, her eyes strangely compassionate. Her feet prodded him out to turn off the light. The night outside was snowless, invisible under low cloud. He stumbled back to bed shivering. And there her changed mood was communicated through the first light exploratory touches of her hands. No trace of her earlier calculated incitements was evident. She was content to efface herself, sure of his ability to induce her response. And inevitably their peace held a new quiet sadness, shorn of their conflicting distress hours ago. She enfolded him in tenderness. There was no need for words. They could not solve anything, protest or question, her silence told him. Yet when they divided she curled close, averse to forgo whatever comfort they could share now and hold in memory. They went to sleep without exchanging a word.

Throughout the morning a wrinkled dirty sheet of cloud covered the city. Steven invented jobs to occupy his attention. While Shuen pottered around tidying the bedroom and bathroom he gave his typewriter a much needed overhaul. It was filthy. The letters were clogged with dried ribbon ink, the carriage suffered from hiccoughs which left spaces in the middle of words or jammed letters together, the roller deeply pitted from continual pounding. But it was a loyal old treasure, no worse for diets of Middle East dust lodged in its vitals. He let the dust remain, fearful of what might happen if he probed too deeply.

The task set his mind free. It occurred to him that those who kept their affections neatly shrouded in the winding sheets of convention would automatically condemn him for attributing undue significance to what their minds sneered at as infatuation. And on her side conformists would besmirch it as depravation, immorality, pollution. Yet those simple vilifications disregarded the two people they were. But where could it lead them? Was it doomed to end in precisely those memories which any normal man and woman could harvest without their essential nature being increased one iota? Was that to be their end? No more?

He used a pin to dig out an acne of dried type-ribbon ink.

Shuen trotted from the bedroom.

'Sir, I have finished,' he announced, beaming.

'Fast work.'

'I will change your sheets tomorrow. Will you be out?'

Steven glanced at his engagement list.

'From midday.'

'I will attend to this room in your absence.'

'Thank you.'

'It will be very nice for your return.'

'Yes.'

Shuen slipped through the doorway like a nimble shadow. Steven stared at the closed door, frowning, unable to drive out the anxieties trampling through his mind. Abruptly he got up to commence pacing round their cell, peace gone from him, plunged into black depression. He felt defeated.

At lunchtime, still sick at heart, he went upstairs hoping to find Clive or someone to talk to. There was no one. Only Butler, sullenly indifferent to a redhaired European woman doing her best to gain his interest. They did not see him.

Late in the evening she came back. He looked up from the book he was reading. She locked them in, fumbling in her haste, and ran across to throw herself into his arms, her lips straining on his. Whatever her doubts in their hours of separation, she was never neutral. The knowledge whipped him. Somehow he had to bring himself to stop it. He must spare her. She deserved far better than a furtive, transient relationship never free from corrosive secrecy. It could only harm her. He had been shamefully selfish for far too long. He had to heed the years ahead of her.

She hung onto him for support. Her eyes shone. 'Oh darling, it's been hell. You up here.'

'You down there.'

'I thought I'd go mad. People talked at me. I didn't hear half they said. It was so unimportant and stupid. I thought of you and what I ought to be doing here. I wanted to be here to wash and sweep and cook, be here for you to want me.'

He tousled her hair over her ears.

'I messed about doing odd jobs.'

'Have you had something to eat?'

'I fixed myself a dish just now.'

'True?'

'Cross my heart.'

She sighed. 'I ought to have got it for you. Let's have lots of coffee. How does black coffee taste if you put brandy into it? Have we got brandy?'

'About half a bottle.'

'Is that all? I'll have to let you flirt with Sheila so you can get another bottle.'

Her happiness to be back defeated him. The whole situation was absurd. Without knowledge of each other they had outgrown racial intolerance. They walked familiarly in the other's land. Religion set no barrier between them. They laughed at each other's national humour. They shared goodwill. They did not desire to suborn anyone. And yet everything which should have given them cause to rejoice was insufficient in this brutalizing century. The enormity of it drove from his mind all the kindlier phrases he had prepared to ensure their parting had compassion. It was monstrous.

On sudden impulse he jerked her face up, staring down at

her to fasten each detail of beauty in his memory. Love and bitterness and rage flooded through him. He wanted to brand his love and possession on her. Without her it was going to be hell, but the next time, the very next time, it must be done to spare her. She shut her eyes.

'Don't look at me like that,' she whispered miserably.

'You're the most beautiful, adorable woman I ever saw and I love you,' he told her.

'And I love you, my darling,' she said in a shaken voice, and trembled as he kissed her harshly, searching her mouth, his fingers digging into her shoulders.

She clung to him unsteadily, then raised her head and shook it, a radiant smile on her face. Then she took his hand to draw herself up. And later they shared a bath, sluiced each other, and towelled the other until their flesh glowed. And much later he glanced at his watch and saw it was half-past twelve.

'Are you tired?'

'Wideawake.'

'Me too.'

'When can you come again?'

'We'll be lucky this week,' she said. 'I'm to see Pai-chen on Tuesday, Wednesday, and Friday. Can you bear to see me so often?'

3

At that moment Tang the Mute stood in his lift watching the two Czech engineers walk tiredly into their fourth-floor rooms. There was no one else to come to this floor tonight. Everybody on the fifth floor had been in for the last hour. He should be free to go off duty soon. He did not welcome the prospect. Nowadays he was always fearful whenever he went to bed. Weeks had passed since he last slept soundly. The passing days brought no relief.

As he stepped back to close the lift doors, Shuen ran into sight round the distant corner. Tang recognized him instantly, saw his frantic gestures to keep the lift. He forced himself to wait, afraid lest he betray the alarm he always felt at the sight of Shuen.

Shuen ran swiftly up the corridor. His soft-soled shoes were noiseless on the thick carpet. As he drew nearer, Tang saw he was grinning jubilantly. There was a smirking joy in his eyes; his lips were drawn back from his long teeth. He stopped, swaying on his feet, his chest heaving. His face was stiff from cold.

'Come, I need help,' he ordered peremptorily.

Tang gazed at him blankly. 'I cannot leave my lift until I go off duty.'

Shuen glared.

'Do what I say. I will explain to the committee. *Kan k'uai!*'

Tang knew he must obey. He chained the lift doors open to prevent it from being taken. Irritably, his voice in a fever of impatience, Shuen kept urging him to hurry.

They ran down the corridor side by side.

'Why do you want help?' asked Tang.

Shuen could scarcely restrain his glee. Hu had been right, he said through chattering teeth; the British devil Kendal was undoubtedly a spy; there was a woman in his room, a Chinese, one of the accursed traitors.

'Are you sure?' asked Tang, and knew the woman Shuen meant.

'I am sure,' Shuen told him breathlessly. 'Yesterday she ran past me on the stairs. I followed her to the fifth floor and she had disappeared. The other Briton Dixon was with him. They must have hidden her from me. Today I saw the same woman downstairs with *hsiao chieh* Shao.' He drew a deep breath, and said there must be a big foreign spy ring in the hotel.

He was full of confidence, his manner authoritative, his voice emphatic.

Tang asked what they were going to do.

Shuen did not answer immediately. He took pleasure in describing how his guile and patience kept him outside the Briton's room until the radio was switched off. Then, standing on the fire-escape, he heard their voices in the bathroom but could not hear what they said because the window was closed. Now the window was open and they were talking in the bedroom. He said: 'You will help me stand on the fire-escape railing so I can get close to the window. I may climb in.'

Tang saw again the eyes of the scarred girl as she ran from his lift, her feet impatient to skip upon the clouds of destiny. 'Have you sent for someone to help us?' he asked.

'Not yet, fool,' snapped Shuen. 'Later I will have the police arrest them. They will persuade her to confess.'

He led them through the doorway onto the iron fire-escape opposite the staircase. Tang felt the chill air stab through his uniform. Over their heads a vast scatter of stars shone like raindrops hanging on huge dark trees. No lights showed in windows at the back of the hotel. On the ground spread a vague pallor of starlight.

Shuen scrambled hastily up the steps, his body bent almost double. And suddenly, without hesitation or misgiving, Tang knew what he must do to be rid of the awful danger of this panting, stumbling man. There was no other solution. It must be done. Instantly he drew level with Shuen on the left side, poised for an instant, his body braced in flight as he coiled his good right arm round Shuen's neck to drag him to a halt, tightening his hold inexorably to shut the other man's throat and prevent him from crying out. He hung on grimly, grasping his only chance to be free from danger. At first Shuen was unprepared, neither his body nor his mind expecting attack. It had happened too swiftly for him to think. Then he started to writhe. His body twisted and strained. His feet kicked out in the darkness, trying to entwine their legs, his fists flailing wildly. Tang hung onto Shuen. Spasms of muscular pain flickered up his arm to his shoulder as he increased pressure. He braced himself against the railing, his half-arm twitching uselessly. The realization of having committed himself beyond hope of freedom if he failed now lent him ferocious energy.

They swayed from side to side. Their soft-soled shoes slid awkwardly on the iron grille steps. Panic lent Shuen desperate strength, his whole body heaving and bucketing in great blind efforts to free himself from the grinding, choking pressure which shut his throat. One surge of energy nearly sent them toppling back down the steps. Their bodies arched, rising on their toes.

Tang felt the railing slide against his ribs. He thrust his back hard on it to steady himself. Through every instant he kept up his merciless pressure on Shuen's throat, until his arm throbbed and he feared his strength must snap. Then Shuen sagged weakly, legs buckling, hands clawing vainly at the darkness. Somehow Tang maintained his grasp. He held Shuen long after one part of his mind exulted in a conviction of triumph, of escape.

When he let his arm slacken the body under it began to collapse. He tightened his grasp again, his chest heaving, the night chill fastened on his forehead like a steel band. He let his body relax but continued to hold the other man upright. He realized that he was smiling in his drunken sensation of final release from fear. Slowly the need to devise a plan to dispose of the body rose uppermost in his thoughts.

He looked round, listening intently. No sound reached him. He peered down but saw no movement on the dim ground. It took all his remaining strength to haul the body up in his one arm, every grip uncertain, but at last it was done, and he was alone on the steps. No other noise followed the soft thud far below. He wasted no second, running breathlessly down the steps, a dark shadow hurrying through darkness, almost too impatient to pause on the final flight to be sure no one was about. Then he leapt down the last steps to kneel beside the body. His first spasm of fright came as he failed to lift it. He gritted his teeth, sweat running down his face. He kept imagining that he heard voices but knew it was fear chattering in his mind. Eventually he managed to hoist the limp figure. Stumbling and panting, he half-carried, half-dragged it across the black well and pitched it down under the fire-escape opposite. Then he ran silently back to climb the steps up to the doorway through which they had come out into the night.

Three minutes later he stepped into his lift. No one had

called him: the floor-call panel showed no light. He shut the gates closing himself in and leant against the wall of the lift until he regained his breath. Then he pressed the button.

As he waited on the ground floor for latecomers an attack of reaction threatened to unnerve him. He stared out at the deserted lobby convinced that he must have been mad to kill Shuen. Mad. Driven insane by what Shuen might remember. Had Shuen completely forgotten or decided it was not worth consideration? Had he already told the police? What would happen when the police started their investigation? A thousand panicking questions tormented him. He was terribly afraid of having left some clue behind him, some small sign which must bring the police straight to him.

Sick with anxiety, he saw the half-caste girl Grant storm into the lobby ahead of the other Briton Butler. She was talking angrily, her low voice flashing. The Englishman was sullen, his furious eyes darting about to see if people were listening. He walked unsteadily.

Tang quietened his face. As they came towards him, he heard the girl say: 'No, you can't come to my room. No, I don't want you to talk to me. You're despicable.'

'You bloody daft bitch,' said the Englishman.

Tang glanced at the clock above the empty reception desk. It was ten minutes past twelve.

4

When Steven awoke it was still dark. He put out his hand to search for her. After some moments his drowsy brain realized that she was not there. He sat up coughing and looked at his watch. It was nearly half-past five. Ahead of him the window was inky dark. He got out of bed whispering her name.

Every sign of her presence had gone. Her clothes, her enormous basket, her slippers, things they had locked into his suitcases for safety. His keys lay on his chair. Shivering in the pre-dawn chill, he wrapped a blanket round him and sat down on the bed. Then he found a torn sheet of notepaper which she had tucked under him. On it she had scribbled some words in Chinese, whether the actual language or his version of it he did not know: *Pu kan tang, pao hsin; man man tsou*—thank you, precious heart; take care. He read it again and wiped his nose on the blanket.

He had no further need of sleep. Holding the blanket round his naked body, he padded into the other room to find a cigarette. Coughing, his throat dry, he dressed and brushed his hair, and was drinking coffee as a wan dawn rose out of the Yellow Sea. While the sky yawned and stretched itself he settled down to work.

Tuesday gave him no sight of her. Through every hour the hotel was full of police investigating the death of his boy from falling off the other fire-escape. There were enough of them to repel a wartime parachute drop. Everyone likely to have seen the boy was questioned, including himself, but he answered them unhesitatingly and they took themselves off.

Wednesday passed. And Friday. A week crawled by. And he understood then what she had been thinking on those evenings which he too had decided must be the end, what prompted her glancing moods, the careful explanation of her days, binding knowledge of her to him, her secret setting off to walk out of his life through the bitter night, sparing them unhappy discussion.

One evening he sat staring at where she had liked to curl up during their conversations. It got him by the throat. He cringed under the onslaught of rage and loneliness and aching want. He went on looking at the emptiness till the room dissolved and he put his face in his hands.

The next evening Clive came to see him. They sat at the table for hours going over his article on Tibet, examining every sentence in order to find words which left its meaning unchanged but were calculated not to cause violent anger at the Ministry.

Thirteen

DIRECTLY Steven finished work his cell became unbearable. His errant mind peopled it with shadows, her voice echoing in his ears. Attempts to reconcile himself to what had so obviously been inevitable were unavailing. It was a defeat. Defeats were all right when you were young and could dip into seemingly inexhaustible barrels of self-sufficiency and hope. He was neither self-sufficient nor hopeful. This struck deeper, a denial of the right of two individuals of goodwill to settle their own affairs without interference from arrogant politicians. Their individuality had been debased by imposed fear, their freedom destroyed by others. Though they were only two people, unimportant in the vast unfolding pattern of events, it struck at the root of his principles. He could not envisage solutions of the larger issues unless individuals possessed the inalienable right to settle their private affairs free from duress.

One night he tried to liberate his memory by writing down what had happened to them. He worked through the night, his senses reinvaded and bludgeoned by her image in every guise, and read it over while dawn broke like surf on the wide empty beach of sky beyond the window.

It was an atrocious failure. Nothing in it reminded him of them. It was spiritless, lifeless, betrayal of his skill, a ramshackle structure without even the cement of their love to give it strength. He saw no sign of how their minds awakened need of each other long before their bodies joined. Yet those truths had brought them together. He had lived them. Exhausted and shamed, he struck the typewriter with his fists, and then laid his head on it. And that messed up the infernal machine.

Thereafter he rearranged his schedule. He spent most evenings out at places of entertainment. Quite often Sheila accompanied him. She seemed pleased to have his company and was always good fun, willing to share his mood, adding a positive contribution to their outings. He grew to understand her better, especially after one evening while he listened to her account of what happened to the British Army officer and Indian girl who defied the hostility of families and friends, and became her parents. Few had helped them. As she said, if they had possessed great wealth they would have found friends. Instead they were poor.

Suddenly it was spring, the reawakening of the green dragon. The Spring Festival provided a diversion. The first sign of this ancient festival was the appearance of New Year cards in the stores. Some were traditional, similar to those printed from woodblocks a thousand years ago. Others depicted scenes of contemporary significance, pictures of happy commune workers, allegorical figures led into resplendent dawns by the Chairman, cooing Chinese and Russian babies playing with their respective flags, highly idealized sketches crowded with fairy-tale figures. Then came displays of toys: cloth tigers, bamboo dragons, clay and porcelain figurines from Kiangsu and Kwangtung, dolls in regional costumes. And throughout lively days of celebration there were new films, new operas, street entertainments by various song-and-dance ensembles and diabolo players from factories and workshops, lanterns and flowers, and scarlet good luck scrolls inscribed with flowery greetings appeared on doorways. At night there were fireworks. Sheila accompanied Steven on his evening tours. She became more healthily cynical at every scene of festivity.

2

On the first Monday of March Steven sat at his typewriter in bright daffodil afternoon sunlight finishing an article on further Chinese attacks on Russian overtures for peaceful co-existence with America. Every day now Party speakers warmed up their attacks as Peking grew more convinced that Kremlin and White House intended to reach an agreement on arms without its consent. Every day the radio indulged vitriolic attacks on America or sang the praises of its mainland gun batteries shelling the Quemoys. It never mentioned food shortages and rumours of famine in distant provinces.

He glanced up as Clive came into the room. Clive wore his battered old hat at an angle; the collar of his storm-coat hung loose; his face was blank. He raised his hand.

'*Salaam alaikum.*'

'*Alaikum us salaam,*' said Steven. 'Sit down, give yourself a cigarette. I'll be with you in a jiffy.'

'No hurry, son.'

Clive extracted a cigarette from the open packet on the table. He lit it thoughtfully. On a stride he changed direction to switch on the radio, fiddling at its knobs until he discovered a programme of energetic tinkle-music. He sat down on the settee, scratching at a rough fingernail. As an afterthought he took off his hat and put it down beside him.

Steven yanked his piece out of the typewriter, tossed it aside, and turned.

'To what do I owe this high favour?'

'Goodbye,' said Clive simply and held out his hand. In the sunlight his face looked bonier than usual, its skin waxy pale. '*Auf weidersehn. Allah yesellineq. Tsai chien, tsai chien. Vaja con Dios. A rivederci.* Wish me luck as you wave.'

'No!'

'True, bless your heart. A bloke at our place has informed me that it was officially notified this morning that the Government of the People's Republic of China has declared Clive Launcelot Dixon, Briton, of no special address, to be *persona non grata* and will bung him on the Hongkong plane tomorrow. Furthermore, the aforesaid Government has notified the employers of the said Dixon that he is undesirable, a notorious disseminater of malicious falsehoods, and declared that the Peking bureau of his employers is closed henceforth. A reet happy attack of propaganda diarrhoea. In a couple of days I shall celebrate in Hongkong by going to see a couple of Western films of huntin', shootin', and dyin'.'

'Have you been to the Ministry?'

'Farewell posies will be exchanged at five o'clock.'

'That article!' exclaimed Steven. 'I've let you down. Honestly, I'd've sworn they would have rebutted it by other methods.'

'Don't get upset. I talked it over with a friend. I filed it, not you. And at present the Chinese are spoiling for a chance to fight anybody, just to show underdeveloped countries how strong they are.'

'Oh, God.'

'What is their phrase for saying nothing can be done?'

'I can't—*mei yu fa tzu-la*. Something like that.'

'Like a sneeze.'

'What did our people say?'

'What do our people ever say in dithers over members of the Fourth Estate? They are politely dim. Bothered. In trouble about their old school tie. A pat-pat here, a tug-tug there. Sorry, I forgot you sport one. Clever of you not to let it strangle you.'

Clive was wildly angry. His eyes matched the slash of his voice.

Steven shook his head. Another defeat. For him; not for Clive. Clive had trusted him to get round the difficulties.

'You did a ruddy good job,' Clive assured him. 'Better than I'd've done by myself. No, they're slinging me out for their reasons. Truth here is manufactured like ping-pong balls. No lousy trick barred, ladies an' gennelmen. Walk up and see the Chinese-conditioned laboratory mice!'

'Damn them!'

Clive reached forward to crush out his cigarette in the ashtray and lit another. 'Why did I file it?' he asked. 'Steven, I had to. That story has got to be kept alive or people will forget it under a mess of doorstep murders, snassy divorces, fat stock prices in the entertainment industry. They mean damn all, not even news. Tibet means more. Tibet is another march into the Rhineland. Why did this so-called People's Republic want to redominate that barren, poor, primitive country and build military roads and airfields? Protection my aunt Fanny. Old grab new style.'

Steven stood up abruptly. 'Let's have a drink.'

'No, I must see them sober,' Clive said, 'but I'm glad you reminded me.' He took a full half-bottle of brandy from one pocket, a partly tapped half-bottle of whisky from the other, and put them on the table, undid his macintosh and produced packets of cigarettes and stacked them alongside the bottles. There were over two hundred cigarettes of various British brands. 'For your birthday,' he said.

'What do I owe you?'

'Didn't I say a present?'

'We'll have a drink tonight. Sheila's having dinner with me. Why not come along? We'd like to have you.'

'We'd better leave it until we meet up again. As of now, I'm unclean. They might want to put you in quarantine. But I'd like a cup of *ch'a*.'

While they had it, Steven asked: 'Did you have an inkling that this would happen?'

Clive nodded. He helped himself to more sugar, stirred it into his cup like a ritualistic action, and lit another cigarette. Although his first rage had abated, it simmered below the surface. In some moments it shook his voice. And there was another emotion distinct from anger in his eyes. He took the cigarette from his lips.

'Yes. Two days ago, no three, my driver didn't turn up. Yesterday his wife sent me a note to say they've clapped him in gaol. No charge, just arrested. They probably blame him for not reporting who I met. She's just had another baby. Poor soul, she's either a widow now or as good as. Yesterday my usual waitress upstairs was carted off by the police. Like the one who got friendly with that fat Mexican, remember? She'll soon be in a colonial commune. Thorough. Just like the sweating Nazis.'

'Mmmm.'

Clive said: 'Damn them.'

'Where will you go?'

Clive scratched his neck thoughtfully. 'I favour America,' he said finally. 'Some folk there need to hear things they don't want to know. Too many American politicians who do take a benign interest in foreign affairs, meaning what concerns lesser mortals, whiz into other countries like beings from outer space. No common earthlings, they. They peer down their dollars at ordinary unAmerican people. The foreign policy they knit up for Asia would have been dandy fifty years ago. Alas, time marches on. They should get with it. This isn't nineteen-o-ten.'

'Are you chasing an Oscar as the most hated man of the year?'

'Hell, it's true. American politicians abroad have a fiendish aptitude for putting America in the wrong. I sweat in terror for America directly their flying politicians open their mouths. And so do locally based Americans. These characters whiz in smiling like starlets, deliver their maladroit platitudes, and whiz off to the next whistle-stop halt, eager to head for home. Old hat diplomacy. Unfortunately, America is held responsible for them. They're their own worst enemies. But I shall be able to criticize straight out and keep my neck intact. Lovely!'

'They'd accuse you of being anti-American.'

'Foolish. Once upon a time they were right to develop rapid loyalty in their immigrants by drumming into them ."our American way of life, our American heritage", etcetera. But they've fallen victim to it. It's like a contagious deafness. They lip-read everyone who says nice things as "a good friend of our America". Ergo, everyone who voices mild criticism is anti-American. Dotty. So they've just been led up the garden path by comrades in Cuba. Who works the trick next? Comrades in

Viet Nam, Laos, Thailand, Panama, Africa? Offhand, I'd say the Central Intelligence Agency should be renamed the Central unAmerican Mismanagement. It's cowboyish.'

'I once had a stand-upper with a New York taxi-driver outside a steakateria because he heard me say I dislike skyscrapers. He told me I was anti-American, a Communist Limey.'

'They'll have to do some agonizing reappraisal on their diplomatic stance. Unless they want to get real solitary. There ain't no two oceans up in the wild blue yonder. So they know it? Then why the hell doesn't it show in their diplomacy? The West generally is so uninterested in gaining the initiative you'd think we were still in the horse-and-buggy stage. When will its politicians come out of their comas?'

'You'll get turfed out,' Steven warned.

'Not to worry,' said Clive. 'Another country makes no odds. That reminds me. I hope you'll write a book about China. You've got pretty words . . . leastways, you could have if you cared more about people than about being a fuddy-duddy professor peeking at what the fishes left behind. Those around you are walking people. Let's not waste our last chance. Everywhere we're reporting the preliminaries to war. Leave professorial indifference to the intellectuals.'

'Are you saying I don't care about people?' asked Steven.

'You stare at specimens. Pity. You're more intelligent than I am, really bright. You're a better craftsman. You even write grammatically. Me—what is grammer? You've got a marvellous memory. Do you use these blessings? Not on your Nelly. You're a British intellectual, mummified in good intentions, taking a cool interest in this that and whatsit. I know it's a blush-making subject, but do you subscribe to an ideal? If so, do you expect not to fight? In this century? For God's sake, stop being the local representative of the apathetic society.'

At length Steven said: 'So that's how I strike you. What about "I'm-all-right-Jackism"?'

'An affectionate diminutive meaning greed in the apathetic society. I prefer Stevenson. "To travel hopefully is better than to arrive." '

'Then you write the blasted book.'

'Oh, I'll write one, full of my special syntax jobs et al. but you'd do it better,' said Clive. Suddenly his eyes blazed. 'Our only chance to solve the problems of this century is to make people more important than politics or science. That means more than squatting in an ivory tower. It means sweat. We can't leave it to politicos, priests, or scientists. They're mentally constipated with Isms. That's where we free newspapermen come in. However much we're criticized, we're the only ones who go in slugging for people. We don't try to turn them into walking theories. But we can't risk leaving it too late to say our piece for them. So don't you leave it too late either.'

Suddenly self-conscious, he broke off, smiled crookedly, and glanced at his watch. He stood up. 'Time to exchange formal farewells. Oh, I nearly forgot. Will you do something for me?'

'Of course,' said Steven vacantly.

Clive put a sealed and unaddressed envelope in front of him. 'I'd be grateful if you'd give this to Ilse at a convenient moment which will probably present itself,' he said in an unemotional voice. 'She won't be back from Shanghai until I've gone. Tell her——' He stopped. As they looked at each other, his thin hands gestured aimlessly and his smile was a litter of broken glass. 'Even me,' he said parenthetically. '——I had no chance to wait.'

'I will.'

'Bless your heart. Where's me titfer?'

They shook hands. Clive smiled. With his hat slanted on his head, old raincoat buckled close, he resembled the sort of foreign correspondent seen thirty years ago, older, the gilt rubbed off the dust of faraway places on his shoes, but still with a newspaperman's eyes, cynical of what was happening in the rat race.

'You didn't ask what this has to do with China,' he commented. 'Neither the Chinese nor the Russians are apathetic. They know exactly what they want. But in the West resolutions wobble like jelly.'

As the door shut, Steven sat down.

While he sat there his new boy Yan came in to tidy his rooms. The telephone rang; it was one of Mrs. Peng's assistants to announce that arrangements had been completed for him to entrain next morning for Sian to continue his series of articles; his guide, Mr. Lei, would arrive at the hotel in the next half-hour to discuss an itinerary. The information was like a blow in the face. It increased his consciousness of personal failure, of abasement.

3

Mr. Wang was an official of the Information Department. He was a short stout man whose balloon-shaped head rested on his shoulders without benefit of neck. Inside his tight dark Yat-sen tunic his fleshy arms tapered to slender hands. His pebble-lensed spectacles resembled a decoration. His shrill voice raved indignantly.

'Our Tibetan brothers welcomed the People's Liberation Army joyfully,' he shouted.

'I wasn't there,' said Clive.

'Are you calling me a liar?'

'I said I didn't witness their joyfulness.'

'They wept in relief at deliverance. Their only sorrow was that the Dalai Lama was abducted by capitalist conspirators.'

He carried on inexhaustibly. His three female assistants alternately glowered at Clive out of their slanted damson eyes or poised like cheer-leaders about to raise a huzza for their football team. They were pretty girls. Farther off, under an ornate chandelier, a narrow young man sat reading a foolscap typescript, the prepared statement being delivered by Mr. Wang. His lips moved soundlessly.

'The patience of the Tibetan people is exhausted,' Mr. Wang shouted virtuously. 'We have received thousands of protests from them demanding your expulsion. Your imputations are baseless. They demand our protection from you.'

'Why not let me or some other Western reporter tour

Tibet?' asked Clive. 'You say you've nothing to hide. Let me go there. If I'm wrong, I'll apologize publicly. Tell you what, let me tour Tibet and North Korea.'

But Mr. Wang was listening only to himself.

Clive sipped his ceremonial cup of tea. He speculated on the possibility of writing a play called *Green Tea and Rage*. While the tirade of Mr. Wang worked up to a crescendo he thought about Ilse, worried over Steven who was looking ill and lost. He felt guilty about his harshness, but the time to kick a man like Steven for his own good was when he was down.

He winked at one of the girls and saw her flush angrily.

4

Sheila had just finished dressing when Steven arrived to collect her for dinner. Seething with anger, he told her what had happened.

'We went over it thoroughly. It contained no item which didn't tie into their own admissions. They don't deny that resistance is still going on. Their own NCNA men say so at receptions. To deny everything is absolutely fatuous. How can they expect anyone to accept such fantastic contradictions?'

They had a miserable dinner. Steven was either dully uncommunicative or talked only about Clive. Usually she let herself show irritation at men who were too preoccupied to pay attention to her, but she listened to him sympathetically: he was too agitated to reason logically. She liked Clive Dixon but saw two reasons for their action, an assumption that he obtained his evidence from Tibetan students at the Institute of National Minorities and that they would arrange for others to meet him.

Directly they finished their meal she pleaded the excuse of a headache to get them back to her room. He did not protest. She gave him brandy and coffee, and put a long-playing record of Paraguayan guitar music on her gramophone. He sat frowningly absorbed in his troubles. She let him alone and went to loosen her hair and later sat down to do some needlework. Her glances at him told her nothing. When the record finished she put on one of an Argentinian symphony and refilled his glass.

Much later she laid aside a mended sari. He was still wrapped in thought. It was getting on for eleven o'clock. She was irritated by having no insight into how to lessen his despondency. Unsure, she poured out drinks and sat down on his lap.

He steadied her in his arm but did not speak. His hand touched her cheek as if she were a child. She settled against him to let his senses discover a more potent substance than childishness in her softness, and was almost asleep when he did. His vehemence sent a wild flame through her. Instinct told her he was kissing an available woman; not herself. To her astonishment she accepted the role, lenient to his worry. Abruptly his searching hands went slack.

Allowing him no opportunity for recrimination, she impelled him to kiss her mouth. Why am I always nurse to a man with problems, she asked herself while her lips clung to his.

Instinct led her on. Amazed at herself, she employed every subtle trick of embrace and caress to goad and entice him. People were bewildering, she thought. She did not understand them. Herself least of all. Under his touch a lovely languor crept over her. Once she remembered to protest but without interest. It was very enjoyable. She wished he was a millionaire too.

At length, murmuring in her throat, she freed her mouth reluctantly. It was a contrived pause. She stretched voluptuously without disturbing his hands, pleased and anticipating.

'Finish your drink,' she said lazily. 'It's late and I want you to see my Nine Dragon screen. You'll have to come into the other room.'

The reason for the police escort became apparent when they reached the airfield. There was an unofficial farewell party. Fear stabbed through Clive, daggered cold sickness into his stomach. He ought to have recognized the danger.

They were waiting silently, a small mob for this country, no more than three thousand, but his own. His mouth dried. Phlegmatic policemen stood in front of them. The flat heatless sunshine illuminated their banners: 'Down with Lying British Journalists', 'Clive Dixon—British Warmonger', 'Go Home, Scum', 'China Protests at British Liars—Dixon—Assassin of Truth'. His dread of mobs seared his mind as he saw their sullen self-righteous faces. It might be touch and go, he warned himself.

As they saw him led towards the plane, their silence ended. They shouted and yelled, waved their banners, brandished their fists. Tension shivered through him. His knees felt weak, likely to collapse under his weight. He was horribly convinced that he was going to faint. He walked blindly, counting each step.

The policemen who accompanied him, two on either side, were utterly expressionless, bland as commissionaires at an ideal home exhibition. He tried to ignore the howling mob, to feign casual disdain of their fury. His terror of mobs, their savagery witnessed around the world, prevented him from finding calm. Then some broke through the thin police cordon, charged across the field towards him screaming hysterically. Others followed. He thought it was all over for him, the yelling boys beside themselves with rage, their faces transformed into gaping masks of hatred. His defiance reasserted itself. He smiled widely, heedless of sweat running down his face, and gave them a sort of victory salute. And then hurrying policemen overtook the leading boys, and led them back to their whistling bawling shrieking friends.

They were still there, shaking their fists and bellowing, when the chocks were pulled away and the plane rolled forward. The other passengers avoided him as if he was virulently contagious. It was some time before he stopped quaking.

Fourteen

NORMALLY Steven responded to new surroundings. Their strangeness brought relief from unsolved problems which occupied his attention. Sian was no palliative. Though it was his first visit to the mother city of China, its sights and streets were untouched by novelty or the boon of excitement. He remained the prisoner of himself, unable to rid himself of responsibility for having given Clive bad advice. Their final conversation rankled in his mind. Those accusations of effete intellectualism were true. He admitted it. There was no escape from it for he had levelled similar accusations at himself on the afternoon he went to the Temple of Heaven, last autumn while Jane Crofton was in China.

So Sian in its fresh spring radiance, the sky above the mountains free from dust, new green foliage on young trees lining its recently laid concrete roads, failed to hearten him though he was kept busy in every hour by the indefatigable resourcefulness of Mr. Lei.

Mr. Lei was the brightest feature of a miserable excursion. He was a stocky jovial Cantonese of about thirtyfive. He laughed easily, wept easily, and never tired. He loved robust entertainment, particularly wrestlers, enthralled by heaving limbs, straining bodies, and copious sweat. He yelled frequent advice, telling one protagonist which part of the body to attack, and then shouted advice to the other combatant on how to avoid defeat. He worshipped jugglers, open-mouthed in anxiety while plates spun on bamboo wands and casually flipped cups fitted one on top of another until twenty of them were piled in a miniature tower of Pisa. At one exhibition of incredible precision, he admitted shyly to having longed to be a juggler since childhood. What a wonderful life! No man in his right sense could want more than to travel the endless roads of China from town to town, hear people gasp at his dexterity, laugh at his antics, be cheered up in their worry. He giggled.

'My wife is always threatening to leave me. I keep breaking our crocks. But our youngest chap has a great future. He can stand upright on the sole of one of my feet when I lie down and our eldest chap holds my leg up. And he, our youngest chap, is only two. By jove, what fun we have! When my wife is not looking.'

Mr. Lei left propaganda bombast to local guides and retreated into the background, his attention diverted to balancing a pile of coins on one elbow to see how many he was able to catch as he jerked his arm down. The tinkling crash of coins on concrete floors did much to humanize long recitals of production achievements in the big leap forward. Steven developed a profound liking for Mr. Lei.

Within days Steven's notebook began to fill up. Its pages contained a mixture of subjects ranging from the picturesque beauty of the Hua Ch'ing Ch'i mineral baths, lotus leaves spread over dark pools, sunlight shining on turquoise-tiled and crimson-pillared pavilions, to the mountain hide-out when Chiang Kai-shek was kidnapped in nineteen-thirtysix by the Young Marshal, and the room from which he escaped, aided by W. H. Donald, the Australian newspaperman; street scenes of workers' parades: a market scene of caged birds and goldfish in bowls, children eating *tang hulu*, sugared haws; long-limbed Mongolians playing football; a youth wearing a spray of white flowers like lilies of the valley on one ear; Russian officials peering from behind pink curtains in an ancient Daimler; files of men in dusty padded blue clothes stumbling under loads of rubble carried in buckets slung from their bamboo yokes; and everywhere, crawling, running, leaping, sloe-eyed children.

Other scenes were greyer. Steven went over two cotton factories, brightly coloured pennants fluttering in their worksheds, and toured their commune buildings, rows of dormitories set apart in categories of occupants. In one row lived single male workers who slept five to a room; in another were unmarried women, living up to seven a room; the third category was married workers, a family per room whatever its numbers. Summoned by bugles, they worked from forty-eight to sixty hours a week, attended educational classes for another twelve hours, and had fiftysix days off a year. But unlike their grandparents they lived in brick-walled homes, had electric light, dining-rooms which served dull but regular meals, and dumped their children in communal crèches. Posters lent colour to communal rooms.

Mr. Lei did not regain his cheerfulness until they went to a cinema that evening to see *Commissioner Lin Tse-hsu*, which told how Lin defeated British opium smugglers in 1839 and started the Opium War. He applauded Lin, hissed British villains, and persuaded Steven to share his melon seeds and candied fruit.

Later he said roguishly: 'You would not dare to show such a virtuous film in Britain, Mr. Kendal.'

'Most of our film villains are Britons or Americans.'

Mr. Lei blinked. 'By jove, I'm flabbergasted.'

'We say no man is perfect.'

'We must go to the tomb of Confucius,' decided Mr. Lei. 'As a philosopher, you will worship it. It's a People's Museum now, full of decent curios. The Empress's bed. Stone books. By jove, treasures.'

'I'd sooner see the pagoda erected in honour of Hsüantsang.'

'Gosh, you give me delicious gratifications!' exclaimed Mr. Lei and insisted they shook hands. 'You must not go back to Britain or they will stick your head on London Bridge for your Chinese sympathies.'

Steven smiled. The film had set an old question niggling afresh at the back of his mind: why did the Politbureau affect such outraged moral indignation about the immorality of opium smuggling by individuals a hundred years ago when

227

today it made more money from smuggling opium, heroin, and morphine, than all other countries combined? Communist China deliberately smuggled dope into Burma, Thailand, Viet Nam, Macao, Hongkong, the Philippines, and Japan, every week. It collected an estimated £8,000,000 on its dope annually. In Japan the profits were split, half going to finance the local Communist Party. It was a fascinating record of duplicity. He ought to do something about that too.

On a day of keen winds, the high empty sky polished by sunshine, pale blue shadows pooled among grey and biscuit-toned mountains, they went to both the Confucian museum and the fourteen-hundred years old pagoda fenced about by timid saplings.

At the pagoda Mr. Lei was reverential, affected by pride, emotion misting his sloe eyes. He kept swallowing noisily, saying he had a goldfish in his throat. Around them filed a conducted party of model workers, regional heroes and heroines distinguished by their industrial output or overtime records, and given two weeks' free holiday by the government. There were thin men, two white-haired grandmothers, hardy girls whose twin pigtails were tied in silk ribbons, and one hobbling ancient who wore the queue, one of the few Steven had seen. Their guide, a stocky woman, beef to the heels and plump jowls, shouted at them in a harsh metallic voice.

Steven wandered on by himself. It angered him that conditions in this land of 1984 had prevented him and Mei-ling from coming here together. They had discussed the monk Hsüan-tsang whose long lonely march across Asia in pursuit of his faith was an inspiration from its outset, his escape from troops sent by his emperor to prevent him from leaving, until his return fifteen years later, bringing over six hundred sacred Buddhist books, and under sentence of death for his disobedience, an epic of man's endurance amid the snows and heat of Asia thirteen hundred years ago.

Steven stopped, looking up at the pagoda. As Clive would say, it honoured a man who had travelled hopefully.

· · · · ·

On the last evening he sat in his brown and gilt hotel bed-room completing entries in his notebooks. He had enough material for a ten thousand word article. His entry on the commune alone was capable of expansion into a 'timeless wonder' piece for Sunday supplements: he could see sub-editors scratching out a banner head: What is happening inside the Chinese Communes? But there were holes. Every morning at third cock-crow he had heard bugles shrill in the nearest commune to summon day-shift workers to their stewed rice gruel and physical jerks: he had not endured it. And within an hour, every morning, he had watched blue-clad workers march behind bugles and drums to a new factory: he had not endured it. But he had dwelt in fear in one room week after week, learned how it could sap human resolve by insidious denial of dignity. Surely there were worthier methods than slavery to secure co-operation in hauling China out of its historic mess?

A rapping on the door brought him back to his surroundings. Mr. Lei hurried in, beaming. In one hand he carried a large bunch of hyacinths and in the other a new saucepan. He scurried across to switch on the radio. While it was coming up in volume they looked at each other. Then he trotted across and gave Steven the flowers.

'*Ai ya*, they entranced me so I bought them for you,' he announced on a spurt of laughter. 'This jolly old gadget is for my wife. She likes, she likes—utensils!'

'*Hsieh hsieh*,' said Steven, touched. 'You are extremely kind.'

'*Pu pu, mu yu shem-no*,' disclaimed Mr. Lei happily. He espied a slender glazed turquoise vase and fetched it, cartwheeled it into the air, caught it on the toe of his shoe, and tossed it up into his hand as he ambled off to fill it in the bathroom.

As he stepped back to admire their joint effort in flower arrangement, he said shyly: 'I know you think the absolute world of jugglers. I have arranged a happy evening for us at the circus. There will be a demonstration of *taijiquan*.'

He dearly loved professional exhibitions of *taijiquan*, shadow-boxing, he admitted gaily.

2

Peking was dull after the tonic gaiety of Mr. Lei. It was much lonelier now that Clive had gone. Even Sheila confessed to missing him, though they were never intimate. She was leaving for Japan earlier than she had expected, she told him. Her arrangements were almost complete.

'Make a fuss of me while you can,' she ordered.

He saw Mrs. Peng to discuss arrangements for future tours. She welcomed him graciously, agreeing to back his request for hard dates in advance for trips to Chungking, Kunming, Canton, and Shenyang. In an excess of affability, she suggested other places. Her friendliness put a sour taste in his mouth. He left her office under no delusion of their opinion of him. They rated him as a gulled do-gooder.

Late that afternoon while he was at work a knock on the door interrupted him. In response to his invitation Ilse Han came into the room. At first he did not recognize her. Her beauty had flown, her face like an accidental collection of unrelated features, her eyes dull. The changes in her shocked him. She sat down like an old, prideless woman. 'What has happened?' she asked in a flat voice. 'There is an African journalist in his room. We did not return till yesterday.'

He got out his wallet and unzipped it. 'I have a letter for you,' he said and took it across to her.

She tore it open. He leant a chair against the door, turned on the radio, and stood at the window. The farthest rim of sky showed a brassy dullness: a lilac mist crept into the streets below. He heard her whispering to herself and turned.

The letter lay on her lap. With it was a wad of folded paper money. Her hands fidgeted at the money as if she were playing with it. Her first words showed he had been wrong in assuming her to be prideless.

'He was all right?'

Steven reassured her. She nodded gently at the verbal message. Apathetic and preoccupied, she did not seem aware when he stopped speaking, her head continuing to nod. 'This money is for me to go away,' she said and gave a bitter laugh.

He let her alone to get over her shock. Soon afterwards she got up tiredly and went away without saying another word.

3

Every day Steven spent some hours preparing Sheila for what to expect on her arrival at Haneda airfield. Although the overall Japanese political situation had changed since he was there, his memory called up miscellaneous pointers which might help her. He told her what he had learned about SOHYO, the trade union movement, and bodies like the Japan-China Trade Promotion Association and the Japan-China Friendship Association; where to go on the Ginza and which districts, like Shinbashi, to avoid unless taken to them by male companions; where she might meet geishas in gorgeous kimonos and *shimada* hair-styles, and the *kaminari-zoku*, thunder-bird motor-cyclists; about Noh plays and *danchi* group settlements, Aso and Nikko parks, willow and plum-blossom in Hibiya, cherry-blossomed shrines under Fuji, the frequent earth tremors, and prepared her for social etiquette among traditional families who practised *shuyo*, and changes of food, the ginger and smoked duck sausages, salted thrush hearts and fried honey bees, the eternal tuna in soy sauce; and pronunciation of commonplace phrases. In other hours, free from filing material, he pursued another occupation which was taking up more time since his return from Sian.

On a Wednesday afternoon late in March he was at work on it as Sheila entered the room. She was leaving the next day. 'I'll be free in a jiffy,' he told her and went on copying from a book beside his typewriter. When he finished typing he yanked the paper from his machine. 'That'll show them,' he said savagely.

'What is it?' she asked.

'Turn on the radio,' he said and waited until its volume screened his voice. 'Listen. "The Soviet Government of China recognizes the right of self-determination of the national minorities in China, their right to complete separation from China and to the formation of an independent state for each national minority. All Mongolians, Tibetans, Miao, Yao, Koreans, and others living on the territory of China shall enjoy the full right to self-determination, i.e. they may either join the Union of Chinese Soviets or secede from it and form their own state as they may prefer." Guess what document stated that right to freedom? The nineteen-thirtyone *Constitution of the Kiangsi Soviet Republic*, whose chairman was one Mao Tse-tung.'

'No!' she exclaimed incredulously.

'But yes. And more. Here is one of a seventeen-point agreement drawn up in nineteen-fifty-one, two years after the People's Liberation Army marched in. Article Seven: "The policy of freedom of religious belief—and so on—shall be carried out. The religious beliefs, customs, and habits of the Tibetan people shall be respected and lama monasteries shall be respected. The central authorities will not effect a change in the income of the monasteries." ' He glanced at her. 'Damning?'

'Damning,' she agreed. 'Because of Clive Dixon?'

'Not really. Much too late, I'm doing what I've left undone. Men who dishonour one agreement will dishonour all. Their smaller neighbours have cause for alarm.'

She watched his grim face worriedly. His research struck her as a wasted effort. Supposing he did compile more evidence than Clive Dixon? He could not send it from here. When he left it might be too late. But there was no point in her saying anything.

She watched him fold the typed sheet into his wallet, and was pleased to see he looked much better than on the night when she had no insight to guide her. He represented a danger to her; she had come to enjoy their hours together. That defeated her.

'I've finished packing,' she said. 'I hope.'

They had cups of tea while she gave him details of her journey. She enforced attention by sitting on him to put herself between him and books beside his typewriter; from tomorrow he could attend to routine. She took bitter feminine pleasure from reminding him that it was their last day together, and enjoyed a sensation of imagining him missing her until she fell victim to her own inventive bright cruelty. One day she was bound to miss someone and be driven crazy by wondering if they missed her. This might be the time. You could never be sure. Tears sprang into her eyes. She sniffed unhappily.

'I wish you were coming,' she said. 'Don't let me be alone too long. There'll always be a place waiting for you.'

'I'll remember.'

They smiled at each other. With this appeal in her eyes she was rid of hardness. She brought her face up to his, and twined her arms over his shoulders. Her lips forwent their usual calculated provocation in order to express regret at losing his companionship.

An apologetic cough interrupted them. They saw Yan standing in the open doorway, smiling nervously, a small brush and dust-pan in one hand. She got off Steven's lap and stood up.

'Come to my place while I get ready for dinner,' she said acidly. 'No one will disturb us there.'

4

Sun listened patiently to what Yan Fu-ch'un reported. He had difficulty in breathing even in the oppressive heat of his office. Soong Shu-lan crouched on her chair, writing Yan's statement. Sun was relieved to hear it. It was wrong-thinking to have a personal liking for an Englishman, for any *man-tze*, but he had respected Kendal since their conversation in the Long Bar in Shanghai. It pleased him to learn that it was obviously the half-caste girl who Hu and Shuen had believed was the secret visitor to Kendal's room. He saw no reason why she or the Englishman should tell others of their liaison.

As Yan finished, Sun said: 'You need not spend so much effort on watching him in future. I want you to bring full reports of a new African resident and an Egyptian who has been there for the last two weeks . . .'

5

Three days later Steven had an early evening meal at a Szechwan-style restaurant and walked home under a cloud of stars.

The Hsinshih lobby was full of irate strangers, North Africans, slumbrous-eyed men and women talking in the tongues of Morocco and Algeria, expostulating, arguing, scowling amid their luggage, infuriated by some mix-up over their hotel reservations. Their unabashed temperament added a touch of novelty. Around them hovered Chinese officials, retreated into the meek arrogance which earned their ancestors a reputation for inscrutability.

Steven saw a hint of it on the face of Tang the lift-man. He greeted Steven politely. The wintry smile on his lips was like a melodramatic flourish. It did not lessen his appearance of unhealthiness. Loquacity was not in his nature, yet in recent weeks he had taken to talking during their rides. On one journey he had asked to be reminded of the words of hymns he claimed to have learned while a boy attending an American Baptist mission school. Tonight he voiced indignation at the group of North Africans, a theatrical troup whose argument arose from protests at being divided from members who were staying at the Hsinchiao.

Steven wandered down the corridor to his room thinking that Tang provided another proof that in China events were in the saddle and rode mankind. According to the official view, twenty percent of the population disagreed with the government. Others put dissients at around thirty percent. Tang was obviously among them yet fearful of conversing frankly, one of those whom the Politbureau suffered in its belief of their youthful memories being silenced ultimately by death.

He went into his room and switched on the light. Everything was orderly, formal, and neat. Its impersonality struck at him. He took off his overcoat, lit a cigarette, coughed, and went to the cupboard to get the brandy. He collected a glass and took them over to the table, poured out a drink and sat down. He disregarded a temptation to work. Tonight was an ideal opportunity to decide how to apply for a transfer.

He finished his drink and gave himself another. Nothing kept him here in this monolithic society. He was sick of it, sick in spirit and mind, in dire need of air unpolluted by the rank stench of dictatorship. It might suit people like Butler, but despite Clive's stricture he did not count himself one of them. No, by God, he was not spiritless, not a do-gooder to be fobbed off with pleasantries. He had a sour memory of Mrs. Peng's affability.

He foresaw objections in London to his leaving here. A newspaperman needed certain mental aptitudes and adaptabilities to endure China. It would drive most free newspapermen up the wall. He shook his head. There was absolutely no help for it. He had to get out.

He stubbed out his cigarette and went over to switch on the English newscast to Hongkong. He had to go, he told himself as he crouched at the radio to fidget the wave-length on beam. As he straightened up a chill in the room told him that Yan had left the bedroom window open as usual. Thinking over what to tell London, he went into the other room, switched on the light and closed the window, and suddenly his heart seemed to stop beating. It was not a delusion; blinking in the light, Mei-ling sat on the bed, terribly nervous, tense in the duffel coat and slacks, her feet turned in at the toes. In the open neck of the coat he saw a small gold crucifix on a thin chain round her neck. What he saw in her eyes of loneliness, indecision, weariness, and more, mirrored his own feelings in these last weeks. As they looked at each other she tried to smile, but instead her face went stiff trying to contain her emotion and abruptly the tears brimmed over and ran unchecked down her cheeks. The radio howled its megaphonic hatred of America.

Turning, he went back to adjust the volume and then locked the door. A sensation of unreality clouded his mind as he walked back into the bedroom. And then it took some while to overcome their distress, words clumsy in their mouths, overcome by a loosing of the loneliness since they last held each other. It took even longer to regain heed of the hostile reality which surrounded them. But eventually she released herself, tried to stop crying as she slumped against him. He took off her jacket and shoes, persuaded her to lie down, and went into the other room to get her a drink and make coffee. The task brought some sanity back to him. While she drank the coffee he massaged her cold feet.

Afterwards she insisted on getting up and going into the other room. They sat on the settee, keeping their voices below the hate-mush on the radio. No sound of people reached them from the corridor. She told him how Clive had emplaned, her voice agitated, her hands shaking. He read a confession of shame as she told him how she was one of nearly three thousand students and junior civil servants given two hours off to parade in an organized demonstration which shrieked hatred at Clive. Horror thinned her face.

'He was terribly frightened.'

'Mobs frighten him and me,' said Steven. 'The lowest form of mental immaturity. No true adult ever joins them, only old children. I ought to have been there.'

'Thank God, you weren't!' she exclaimed, trembling in his arm. 'They arranged for you to be out of Peking.' She kissed him fiercely. 'I would have died if it had been you.'

He squeezed her trembling hand, smoothing his thumb over her knuckles. Time changed the tune. Six months ago he would have tried to accept the demonstration by telling himself how these people were an organized fear, forced to do whatever they were told rather than attract official suspicion to their wrong-thinking. Now he was no longer prepared to exonerate. Tolerance had to end somewhere short of suicide.

'You took a dreadful risk to come here,' he said.

'You once told me fear is a natural condition. And I cannot have pride in love. I had to come, dearest, I had to.'

They talked of easier things. When his inner disquiet sought expression she stopped him. 'Not tonight, darling,' she whispered. 'Tonight I want your arms round me. That will be strange.'

Next evening they heard drum-rolls of thunder sweeping towards Peking from the Gobi. Reports told of severe storms raging over distant gorges of the Yangtzekiang though southern rivers were said to have fallen below seasonal levels on account of prolonged dry weather. They sat in darkness to watch the approaching storm.

He stroked her arm, and summoned resolve. 'We'd better talk.'

'Please no.'

'Yes.'

Eventually she gave in.

'Very well. But, darling, you must do something first. I will not let myself harm you or your work.'

'What has that to do with it?'

'Be patient,' she pleaded. 'Your work is essential. We must add our protest. We, you and I, must not be voiceless. Though I'm proud of my people and eager for them to be rid of poverty ——'

'And so am I.'

'I know, of course I know—I hate what's happening here. This isn't China. It's a country ruled by tribal politics based in the last resort on fear.'

She spoke mechanically. Flashes of lightning showed him her blank face, the restlessness of her hands.

'Go on,' he prompted

'I've tried to relate the larger situation to us, us to it. We are only individuals. But every human issue depends on life as individuals experience it. These conditions were forced on you and me . . . I am not a traitor, only another fleeting heretic, protesting against this orthodoxy. It frightens me what this China will do to the rest of the world if its present attitude is unchanged. That is why your work is important.'

He laughed but said nothing.

'Oh yes, it is. It will do more than I can. You mustn't doubt me. If we'd met in human circumstances, I would live with you, do woman's work for you gladly, and try to keep you. But I cannot have holds over you. Whatever happens, one day you will leave me . . . and if we are found out they will deport you. I will be your mistress if you want me, but before you decide you must go to bed with another woman often enough to find out if it is only a woman you want.'

'Is that all?'

'It is sensible. You must. I cannot help myself if you want me. But you must do it for your own sake.'

A great flash of lightning seemed to burn whitely inside the room for some moments. It outlined her stiffly erect figure sitting on the settee, her head lowered, motionless. The crash of thunder deafened them.

In the muttering silence, he asked: 'Are you afraid of living?'

'Why should I be? People who fear death are afraid to live. We must use what is inevitable.'

'Sure?'

'Of course. What are you thinking?'

He rubbed his hands along his thighs.

'I'm taking decisions.'

'You will do what I say?'

'Oh, that. It's unnecessary. I've been through it, my dearest. I found out in your absence. It was charming, delightful, uncomplicated. And empty. I want you. I intend to have you. It wasn't you. That's all there is to it.'

For long minutes she said nothing. Lightning showed she had raised her head, her eyes looking at him, her lips slightly parted. Her fingers clawed at her skirt. Then in a calm voice she asked:

238

'What were you deciding?'

He let another tumult of thunder blow away. 'It may be tricky, but we're getting out. Together.'

'It's impossible!'

'Nothing is impossible.'

'You wouldn't have a chance.'

'No?'

At first he feared that she intended to indulge in useless arguments about being sensible, get lost in the maze of grey practicalities which cheated others. Instead she lapsed into worried silence. Long after she was asleep, holding his hand between her breasts, he lay awake hunting for a plan. He felt better than he had for years. He had spent too long being a member of the apathetic society. Now the years of indifference lay behind him. And, by God, he felt infinitely better.

Fifteen

Han was furious. As he walked back from the Ministry building on T'ien-An Mên Square, the bright late March noon sunlight warm on his neck, he could scarcely contain his anger.

He wanted to vent his fury by some means which would not risk Party censure. Alarm added to his wrath; a Party member who fell into disgrace was so friendless that he had no chance to reinstate himself. Ai, he had witnessed it, often, because he obeyed the General Line and had to revile men who had shown him friendship. Several were high officials whose defection was delay in supporting campaigns inaugurated by the Politbureau; the Three Antis campaign, the Four Aids campaign, the new Three Red Banners campaign. Two Politbureau members had been executed, and he knew several who were in gaol. But their crimes were real, their punishment justified. He had done nothing. Nothing! He had never failed in his duty.

He scowled at children who ran into him. It was unjust. The Party had no member more loyal. He had proved it by devoted work which entitled him to one of the high respected offices. Was it a sin to want authority over men to ensure his own part in accomplishing the destiny of China to rule Asia and more than Asia? Whatever had persuaded him to allow his lust for Ilse to threaten his destiny? He had been obsessed. Ai, no good came from a man lowering himself to marry a European woman even if her skin was like snow and her hair shone like sunlight. Why did they not warn him of his peril in letting her seduce him? Why did he have to overhear those men, high-placed important officials whom he believed had admired his work, talking about him and Ilse in the Ministry lavatory, saying that the position he had worked hard to get must go to Hsu because he was not married to a white-skinned foreign devil? Why had no one told him? Ai, unjust! Foolish too. Hsu was an idiot, brainless, stammering, weak. Hsu was frightened of his own shadow, ran to a dozen people for guidance, unwilling to accept responsibility. Unlike Hsu, he always accepted responsibility readily. It was his destiny. He had always been conscious of destiny beckoning to him, leading him to high office, perhaps the highest in the land. And the *man-tze* fascination of her writhing white body had cheated him, doomed him to cheat his destiny. He swallowed nervously.

Why had he been so blind? He saw years of endless defeat stretching ahead of him, barren and brutal. And solely because of a woman who crawled out of the European cesspool to lay at his proud feet, luring him with her strangeness. These women delighted in chances to entice innocent men uncorrupted by their European lasciviousness. She was responsible. Ai, he hated her. Every night he realized that in the darkness all women were meaningless. She had chosen him for her victim, corrupted him to gratify her desires. She had ruined him. Him, a young loyal Party member whose career had once been unblemished.

Engrossed in his thoughts, he blundered into Kendal in the hotel lobby. He apologized profusely, smiling friendlily at the barbarian, hating him. The Englishman carried a suitcase.

'You must just be back from Chungking,' he said to Kendal as they walked to the lift. 'I hope everybody gave you a nice time.'

'Four days isn't long enough.'

He found Ilse lying down in the bedroom. Although awake, she was doing nothing, staring vacantly at the ceiling, the skirt of her dressing-gown fallen off her strong beautiful white legs. It enraged him to see her European idleness, her slothful body doing nothing to honour his sacrifice for her while his country-women laboured joyfully in factories or fields since their liberation from domesticity. Her eyes were defiant. He fetched the bamboo cane from the other room and went to discipline her, locking them in.

2

At the same moment Steven let himself into his room. Its cell-impersonality did not affect him. He felt more buoyant than he had for years.

After lunch upstairs he returned to his room to go through his correspondence and two hours later went down to find his car already waiting. Yen, his usual driver, was at the wheel. They drove west along Chang-an Chieh, turned north past Beihai Park, and west again through the Hsi Chih *mên*. On the journey to the Summer Palace he read his notebook entries on Chungking, the city seldom mentioned by the mandarins on account of it being the Nationalist wartime capital. Yen, usually full of *kwantchee* questions, was revealingly incurious, his tongue flapping a mere formalistic routine probe.

Few people enjoyed the Summer Palace gardens on ordinary days. Steven idled around, increasingly afraid that they were going to miss each other, a malice of fate added to dogma to keep them part. Just as he began to despair he saw her in a group of grey-suited Africans being photographed beside the bronze lion. Although she saw him, she gave no sign of recognition. So they went for the walk planned on the eve of his departure, she in front, surrounded by delegates, and he behind, alone. It was a gruesome homecoming to be separated by the political frenzy of others, and they ran a risk to have a defiant reunion here. But he saw her, knew she was safe. He detoured to avoid attention, regaining sight of her slender figure near ornamental trees. A quantity of flowers were coming into bloom, violet and white lilacs, Chinese 'yellow bells', crisp ivory and white jade magnolias; fragile blossom showed pink on the flowering plum and new green lotus leaves spread on ponds; sunlight flashed on the lake. They shared the spring beauty, and once they looked at each other. She stood beside pink apricot blossom under the pines, sunlight on her face, her eyes haunted by loneliness. He turned away heavy-hearted. They couldn't have gone on like this. It was unendurable.

That evening he dined upstairs and read a translation of a novel about the Korean War bogged down in propaganda; there was a new big leap forward into foreign literary markets with books.

When he returned to his room he took the precaution of humming a tune. His premonition proved correct; she appeared in the other doorway, waiting until he raised a drone in the radio, and then ran to him, eyes glassy, the tiny crucifix shining, her lips unsteady on his. He kept his arms round her as she freed her head.

'I had to come,' she said tightly.

He held her roughly. 'Thank God you did.'

'We must never do it again. I couldn't bear it. I felt insane.'

'Never,' he said, and she wound her arms round his shoulders, her eyes closing as he dug his fingers into her hair, her voice whispering: 'My darling, my darling.' There was wildness in them as they kissed and clung together.

When they were calm again she gave him news; she was to be guide for Australian trade unionists in Canton the first week in May. 'Will it help? The husband of Fourth Aunt may hide us. Everyone will be busy with rallies to support the Japanese political strikes.'

He thought for a moment. 'Let me get angles on it.'

She nodded. 'I'll make coffee.' Then she asked hesitantly: 'Did you find out with Sheila Grant?'

He pinched her ear, kissed her eyes, and said nothing.

The hours passed quickly. He brought her up to date on Chungking, the city of steps worn smooth by centuries of sweating coolies staggering under loads which reached it on the mud-thick Yangtse, recounted his talks with men and women who recalled the urgent *ching-chi* alarms heralding *ching-paos*, Japanese air-raids, in weeks of terror when thousands of people perished in their bombed and blazing streets. In the middle of relating one incident he stopped abruptly.

'Tell me,' she said.

'I'm getting an idea, a shot in the dark, but it's worth trying.'

'Can I help?'

'I'd like more coffee.'

He read through his material on Chungking and marked favourable items. Forgetful of tiredness, his mind in pursuit of an idea, he began to write. After a while her arm circled his shoulders, her cheek touched his, and she went off to have a bath.

The finished piece pleased him. Mainland Chinese who read his praise for how people in Chungking withstood their war-time experiences and his obvious approval of their work in rebuilding their city had cause to feel kindly disposed to him. Though it was nowhere stated, it implied that his viewpoint might be shifting. He glanced across the room. She sat on the settee watching him, the sleeves of his dressing-gown rolled back from her fragile wrists. He looked at his watch, exclaimed, and shook his head reprovingly.

'You should be asleep.'

'Can I read it?'

He tossed it over to her.

As she finished going through it, she said: 'You're impressed by what they've done.'

'I hoped you'd say so. Now. They get after foreign news-papermen, Clive, Butler, all of us, not because their own are incompetent, they're not, but we have angles on our markets and we've got names in those markets. They ease regulations for those likely to cooperate. I've ignored their blandishments. This should persuade them I'm changing, so they may—may— let me go to Canton at my convenience. I can cook up a reason for the dates. Tomorrow I'll do another piece on similar lines. Mrs. Peng will be told about them within hours. Then I'll flatter her. Charm can work wonders. Even my brand. This straw may prove stronger than elaborate plans.'

She listened frowningly. 'Must you lower your standards?'

'Needs must when the Party drives.'

'Are you sure?' she asked hesitantly.

'For the last time, let's get this straight. What I told you about getting us out of here was final for me. Why? Because, my darling, I intend to have you and where we can live like civilized human beings responsible for their actions, and because everything comes alive where you are involved and because even words taste differently in my mind on account of you. Those things didn't happen during your absence. It didn't happen some months ago over a European woman who might have been prepared to be my mistress or something if I left here alone. She was lonely. You and I weren't lonely. We had accepted being alone. I like to believe our need is fundamental, main stream. Darling, I intend to have you if you are to be had.'

Her eyes answered him.

He raised his hands. 'Well then.'

Long after she had gone to sleep he lay awake writing another piece in his head. At length her restfulness drew his attention to her, and then his confidence faltered. She curled peacefully beside him, vulnerable beyond his power to spare her if he failed. He gazed at her quiet face. Light from the risen moon showed the long scar curving down into shadow beside the rise of her breast. Doubt darkened his thoughts. Was it right to persuade her to run the risks? Both of them were so hellishly identifiable. Full of despair, he watched her peacefulness. Surely he ought to be able to get a revolver from somewhere? An old Japanese memento? Two bullets for emergencies?

3

His articles and endeavours to charm Mrs. Peng were successful. Four days later she herself telephoned to announce agreement for him to go to Canton before the full summer heat. He knew their consideration was not entirely disinterested: rumours told of parched land, lower streams running dry, millions of hectares of cultivated land affected by a lengthy dry spell affecting every area except Sinkiang and Tibet in the far west. They would not want foreign newspapermen prowling round later if a bad year caused famine; it took months to decide the Party line on how to announce natural calamities. It suited their purpose to accommodate him now. Who cat, who mouse, he thought as Mrs. Peng hung up.

He looked at the sunlit sky. Excitement swept through him. He fought down an impulse to build castles in the air, reminding himself that the most beautiful reality was always a dream. Nonetheless, he had difficulty in concentrating on a study of the constantly revised maps of Chinese frontiers with countries which Peking intended to suborn and blackmail into becoming states of the Republic.

4

Han spent most of April away from Peking, his mercifully infrequent appearances restricted to days getting out reports on his journeys. While at home he attended evening functions likely to be honoured by the presence of high-ranking Party officials, anxious for them to see him.

He and Ilse quarrelled frequently over her refusal to accompany him. Though she had told him in Leipzig of her lack of interest in politics, he evidently interpreted it as a convenient fiction and mistook her for a political Cinderella hungry to enjoy the excitement of Party rallies. Their most violent quarrels occurred after they got back from visiting his family in Shanghai. She discovered an insidious pleasure in goading him until he lost control of himself, reduced to a ridiculous creature who raved like a lunatic about his masculine authority while his conduct stripped him of every claim on it. Her pleasure soon ended. There was no lasting satisfaction to be gained from reducing him to an arrogant screaming braggart who burst into tears of self-pity over her betrayal of his sacrifices for her.

She lost interest. He revenged himself for her disdain by inventing new abasements to remind them that she was his property, without right to expect him to heed her pleas to be left alone. Nothing she did or did not do lessened his appetite for her. Driven into unfeelingness, she waited for his hunger to be satiated by the pleasure he took from treating her like one of the whores he picked up in Hongkong and Singapore. She began to think it was an incipient madness in him, an uncontrollable lust to believe himself superior through possessing a white-skinned woman, as Adolf Hitler had rejoiced in his mastery of Jews in Central Europe; the madness of racial supremacy had to begin somewhere. She wondered if a Jewish woman had ever refused her body to Hitler.

Han spent an unexpected evening at home, swallowing angrily and biting his nails in chagrin at being instructed to deputize for a minor official on an unimportant mission instead of leading a delegation to another place. It was her fault, he kept saying, and later his pleasure with her gained new inventive expression. When he flew off next morning she dragged herself from their bed to make another search for her passport.

She did not find it.

On the third day she realized he must have destroyed it, not hidden it as she once told Clive.

She could not imagine another explanation for its disappearance. Every day she hunted for it, praying to find it, hoping it contained a clause to set her free from this land where personal freedom was dead and no man owned more substance than his shadow. She ransacked each room, searching corners she had searched while Clive was here. She did not find it, not even a trace of her origin and birth in another country.

Frenzy took possession of her. She had to find it. The consequences of failure assumed monstrous dimensions in her mind, the years ahead reaching back to soil her. It must be somewhere, she told herself chaotically, crying hysterically as she searched.

On the fourth evening she forced herself to put on a dress which had once suited her and spent an hour at her mirror trying to restore attraction, even youth, to the dull face staring at her from the glass, and then set out wearily in search of a man who might lessen her loathing of her body.

The restaurant upstairs was full of men. Most of them were Europeans and alone. She sat down at a vacant table conscious of several of them studying her in the expressionless manner of European men speculating about an unknown woman who caught their interest. They were so easily fooled, she thought. None of them could detect the extent of a woman's guile. Only the undimmed yellow flame of her hair owed nothing to artifice and they blindly disregarded a possibility of her having had experiences to which they could add nothing. There was her peril, she told herself as she had once told Clive in a sudden desire to confess her weakness and draw strength from him. She dreaded the loss of the hard old German morality which she had been surprised to find in herself. In her position it would be easier to give in to her owner. Yet how could she become one of those women whom she had heard gloating in pride of their degradation at the whim of men, boasting as if sexual excesses exalted their flesh? Her pride had found their admissions repellent.

She affected disinterest in these men, in no haste to decide which to encourage. And then one spoke in German. His voice was like Clive's, casual and thoughtful. She turned involuntarily, hoping he had come back to her. After then it was no use. She saw what was ahead of her through the years. She went downstairs alone.

From then on it was worse. The incident loosed two floods of thoughts which she had dammed, of her home, of Clive. They drove her frantic with grief and dread.

For three days she stayed in the flat, longing to leave, terrified of the total admission of defeat when she returned. She could not stop crying. Only exhaustion lessened her distress. Every hour pushed her nearer to Han's return for the May Day parade. When she did finally control herself she could not tell if her listlessness meant an end to torment or only of one emotional storm.

The days flew past like clouds. She cleaned the rooms in readiness for his return. When she finished they gleamed in tribute to hausfrau pride learned from her mother. Late in the final afternoon she looked round dully at their alien appearance, felt them close on her like a vice. And suddenly her mind was lucid. She acted calmly. Without haste she gave each room a final dust, and then went into the bathroom, picked up her hand-mirror, and smashed it against the wall. She stooped to pick up the largest sliver and knelt down, leaning over the bath. A distant medley of street sounds came to her through the small open window. The apricot sunlight was warm and cheerful. 'Mercy,' she pleaded and bared her wrists.

5

John Butler picked moodily at a dish of bêche-de-mer and pork. He did not want lunch. He felt only half awake. He had hardly slept for the past week, worried by finding his name printed on four articles in Havana and Montevideo editions of *China Awakes* and *China Pictorial*. Underneath each a line in Spanish read: 'John Butler, the distinguished British author, is on an extended tour of China.' By now those articles were inside British embassies in South America and must have sparked off diplomatic curiosity; Whitehall knew he had stayed here three times longer than ordinary tourists, and its agents were probably going round pubs and restaurants in Kensington and Chelsea which he used in earlier days. The hell with them and their dotty little oldfashioned methods. Chinese security arrangements made British methods look bloody childish.

His frown deepened. Fou Ting-kai had assured him the by-lines were a mistake. Was it true? He wouldn't have seen them at all if Maria hadn't given him her copies of *China Awakes*.

And he had other worries. They refused to let him send out money he earned here. That was a shock. No one had told him of currency restrictions against aliens. Did they expect him to pay his creditors by shipping out bales of silk and tea?

He glanced up, startled. 'Oh, you, Kendal.'

'It's rather crowded. May I join you?'

'Sit down. They're arriving in droves for May Day. What happens?'

Kendal looked horribly confident. Fit too. Butler nodded at what Kendal told him and an idea occurred to him. 'Were you surprised about the Han woman?' he asked. 'She was looking an old bag the last time I saw her.'

'I'm only just in from Nanking. What about her?'

Butler related what his room-boy had told him. For an instant he saw shocked sorrow in Kendal's eyes, then it faded and the older man asked matter-of-fact questions. Typical, by Jesus!

They stood up as Maria Errázuriz joined them. She was lovely to look at, a typical Chilian girl with her soft oval face, peach-like complexion and dark eyes, and flamboyant grace. She was also hot-tempered, dull witted, and he thought her a deathly bore.

Later in the afternoon, Butler went back to worrying about those blasted by-lines. Yet why should he? People soon forgot. And here he had no troubles. He had money, more of it to come, and they treated him decently. He wasn't committed to supporting the General Line of the Party. Hell, there were screaming injustices at home, and back there it was every man for himself. Why should he worry?

Sixteen

NORTHERN CHINESE said their most morose fellow-country-men were the Cantonese. You never saw the Cantonese smile, they declared; men and women trudged through life as if carrying a thousand rotten melons no one wanted to buy; Cantonese wives had a reputation for being scolds. Others swore they had seen Cantonese convulsed by delirious merriment, their faces like iron masks of joy. On one point everybody was in complete agreement. The Cantonese were unlike other Chinese.

In Steven's opinion the cause of the Cantonese being taciturn was the Pearl River.

Standing at the window of his room in the Ichung Hotel, high above the river, he knew that he too would be reticent if he lived near its thousands of decrepit sampans jammed together like matchboxes, the vast town of hopelessness inhabited by the sixty thousand 'People of the Egg', where people were born and died in squalor, and from which the corpses of hundreds of unwanted babies had drifted off among garbage and excrement. Outside Canton the Pearl gave glimpses of beauty, pensive children using hopeful string to fish, heraldic cormorants, old men in 'fragrant cloud linen', black oiled-silk gowns, lazing on its banks, but here it was a gigantic slum, life reduced to its nadir. He did not understand why Peking let these people remain derelict; in Canton Dr. Sun Yat-sen had launched campaigns and Mao Tse-tung organized his peasant movement. Its revolutionary past had not aided the hapless sampan people.

His guide, Mr. Hung, was a Cantonese.

Mr. Hung was about thirty. He was tall and bony. He wore an expression of ineffable sadness, and hardly spoke. When words were essential, his English had a marked Cockney accent; Steven learned that Mr. Hung had learned it at a mission school run by two maiden sisters from the East End.

When they saw a Russian car in the huge House of Sino-Soviet Friendship, Mr. Hung said disgustedly: 'Gracious me, wotta flivver.'

He implied disdain of exhibitions, museums, and of Chunan University for children sent by *hua-chiao* parents in Singapore, Calcutta, Hongkong, Cholon, Latin America, Canada, wherever overseas Chinese were domiciled. The only historic sites to interest him were the tomb of Huanghuakang, Yellow Flower Hill, to seventytwo members of Sun Yat-sen's Revolutionary League slain in an abortive attempt to seize Canton fifty years ago, and a house on Yuehhua Road which was the League's headquarters. He paid no attention to people, the men in black oiled-silk, blue-clad coolies dogtrotting under their laden *t'iao* shoulder-poles, women in similar attires or wearing floral blouses or *shans*; even a rebellious use of black market cosmetics by younger women did not capture his eye. Two things gave him extreme pleasure. He munched shrimps all day long. And he loved the countryside, its sights of people in palm hats wading barelegged through sun-flashing *padis*, lethargic buffaloes attended by snowball egrets—'old mates' he said weepily—squealing piglets, networks of canals. He gazed at them in sorrowful joy.

The silences of Mr. Hung suited Steven. For three long hot days he sought to ignore his mounting tension. He wrote notes mechanically, uncertain if she intended to keep their rendez-vous on the fourth night. At their final meeting she begged him to trust her, swore she was bound to him and nothing else had meaning, but she was a vessel filled with woman's truths and the prospect of flight accompanied by a foreign devil across two hundred miles of this hostile land was guaranteed to daunt the most indomitable spirit. On such a journey he would be her greatest menace, instantly recognizable, tattle for every perceptive child. If she did not appear he did not have to scratch the surface of compassion to understand her dilemma. And if fortitude did desert her, then his own actions were clear. These last months had changed him. He need spend only a few days in Peking clearing up and go, safely, unchallenged. The barriers were against them, not against him. That idiocy represented sanity to the rulers of the bamboo prison.

And on the fourth morning Mr. Hung greeted him at breakfast with an item of news which set fear and despondency flickering coldly in his stomach. 'Did you hear last night's news, Mr. Kendal?'

'I was too tired to bother.'

'Mad.'

'Oh?'

'Yes.'

'What was it?'

Mr. Hung gazed sadly at his dish of shrimps and rice. 'Russian announcement. Shot down American spy plane. Over Russia.'

The brilliant May sunshine seemed to go black.

'Is it official?'

'Full details.' Mr. Hung shook his head. 'Wotta hullabaloo. American planes over China every month. From Formosa. Our Government says so.'

Hope died in Steven. Sitting full in the hot sunlight, he went cold. It was ended. They hadn't even got started. The spy mania of mainland China, the neurotic excesses employed as a useful method for sharpening patriotic fervour, meant that for months now there would be a spy-hunt; every security measure would be tightened; from the Ministry of Public Security word had already gone to each province to search for spies and traitors; within hours, if not already, reports would be going in from 'Small Group' housewives of strangers seen lurking mysteriously; and nowhere more energetically than on the coastal fringe, particularly in this province of Kwangtung on whose coast were Hongkong and Macao. He cringed.

'What price their summit conference for peace now?' asked Mr. Hung. 'Dear me, wotta farce.'

'Mmmm.'

Before they set off Steven managed to hear a Hongkong news bulletin on his bedroom radio. Its details of the Russian announcement of the American spy plane, and first American reactions, were far worse than he anticipated. His last hope vanished.

The day was hot and airless. By mid-afternoon Steven had developed a splitting headache. People mouthed statistics at him, expounded routine dialectical theories, delivered propaganda sermons. It came as a relief to discover himself being driven back to the hotel but it brought no elation, no hope, only consciousness of defeat and his lack of energy.

As they neared the hotel, Mr. Hung said: 'I hope you'll excuse me this evening, Mr. Kendal. I'm fair tuckered out. I need a good old laze to get me strength back.'

'I need a rest myself.'

'Can you eat alone? I may give meself forty winks.'

'You go ahead.'

'Ta ever so,' said Mr. Hung as they got out of the car. He wrinkled his nose in disgust at smells coming from the Pearl. 'Wotta pong.'

The hotel was like an oven. Although the window of Steven's room was wide open it served no purpose except to admit more heat. The fans gave no relief.

He acted methodically. No one disturbed him. For some while he soaked out fatigue in his bath, a dreamlike incongruity blanking his mind, and then he had a brisk towel and lit a cigarette as he wandered round aimlessly, his restlessness increased by news coming from the radio. Mainland bulletins did not mince words. They raged at attempts by 'vile American imperialist beasts' to build spy networks in the Republic in vain efforts to revive the situation of forty years ago 'when foreign devils ruled China and demons were rampant'. Each newsreader raved through lists of alleged violations of Chinese airspace by American military aircraft from Formosa. Later bulletins were caught up in fiery denunciations of plots by white men to dominate Asia, dragging heels in the cold dust of the nineteenth century.

The hours dragged by. He kept looking at his watch, surprised by how slowly they went. At times he believed his watch must have gone wrong. Then, half an hour earlier than he had intended, he put on his darker suit and went up to the restaurant for dinner. The absence of Mr. Hung helped to steady him. There were less than a dozen people scattered around the restaurant, mainly Western businessmen reading glossy trade brochures.

Down in his room again an unreal calm descended on him. He made sure he had his passport, an ornamental knife bought last year, the only weapon at his disposal, and money. Then he rumpled his bed and pillows to give them a superficial appearance of having been used; it ought to allay suspicion until Mr. Hung became curious about his absence in the morning, or until he returned in lonely defeat.

Directly it was dark he set off from the hotel, walking along less frequented streets by a roundabout direction, avoiding people wherever possible, heart in mouth as he approached the House of Sino-Soviet Friendship, and there she was, waiting, and turned immediately she saw him, setting their pace ahead of him through a warren of streets where clogs gave warning of unseen people round them in the darkness. Her pace did not falter. It gave no hint of what she would say. Once or twice he imagined a pad of footsteps close behind. It was imagination, tension, fear.

Gradually the dark roads took on a countrified atmosphere. The weak pallor of heat-hazed stars provided no true illumination. Several cars passed, heading in either direction. A city-bound bus droned towards them, headlights chopping the night, its belly casting a sliding yellow glow over the dirt road. He stopped, turning his back. As the bus howled on, he set off at a quicker pace. A mile farther on she let him overtake her on a lonely stretch of road, waiting in darkness under a large loquat tree.

There had not been nearby voices for two or three miles. The night held no nearing whine of a car. The harshness in her voice telling him to hold her was unfamiliar, and she trembled against him, momentarily bereft of words or animus. He knew then that even if she purposed to accompany him the effort, the strain involved, might prove too great despite her spiritual integrity. The leaves of the loquat tree gave off a faint scent of pomegranates. And while she leant on him the night suddenly held the vicious bark of gunfire. She shook violently.

'An air-raid.'

'Wait a moment.' He listened, watching shells explode in the sky. 'No, no plane . . . propaganda,' he decided.

The gunfire boomed menacingly, shells bursting under distant stars. Another bus came towards them on its last journey into the city. He shielded her from its headlights. A curl of petrol-laden air licked over them. He continued to hold her and listened to the gunfire, and asked what they were to do, and she told him of changes to their plans.

The news from Russia had been broadcast just before she went to see her relations, and sitting in the bus she had decided to tell them he was a Swedish businessman. They were not anti-British or pro-communist; they were Catholics, but they were Chinese. Her hands clenched his arms. And there was another alteration, she confessed. Fua-tuan, their youngest son, a boy of nineteen, was coming too, and would be their guide; he had planned his escape for a whole year.

He concealed his dislike of this news. 'What will Mr. Hung do in the morning?' he asked. She said that the procedure was to notify the local police and then telephone the Information Department in Peking, which would then notify the Party Department for Social Affairs, the Ministry for Public Security, and the Ministry would communicate with the police. Another burst of gunfire overlaid her voice. He estimated it would be between seven and eight when Mr. Hung took action.

He tilted her face up in his hands. Its shadowy stillness was placid. 'Have I told you how beautiful you are,' he said suddenly, and smoothed his thumbs down her cheeks.

'Please please, always think so.'

The gunfire led his thoughts back to other hostile nights. She put her hand in his as they walked forward.

He cursed silently at it being like this for her in summer, the season of the scarlet bird.

2

Among those who heard the guns was a man riding a bicycle. Although muffled by distance, their bark lent Mr. Hung new energy. He had forgone too much to be cheated now. Sweat ran down his face and thighs as he increased speed on the stolen bicycle, pedalling furiously along the road to Kowkong and a sampan in Hikkai, the beckoning dream of freedom beyond the small hot gateway of Macao.

3

Sun listened intently to the voice on the telephone. Down here in the room of ears under the Hsinshih it was cooler than outside in the Saturday afternoon sunshine. He saw other men watching him covertly, biting their nails. The man who had searched the Englishman's room came in; his face wore an expression of disgust. Yan followed him sheepishly.

Sun was annoyed by having been duped by a smooth-tongued *man-tze*. He was regretful too, his heart heavy, for he had thought this Englishman had spoken on that night in the Long Bar like a man seeking truth. A man could not tell what deceptions lurked behind their inscrutable faces. He interrupted the voice on the telephone.

'Was there no report of the theft of other bicycles? Yes yes, I heard you, only one. Yes yes, no report was sent yesterday on account of Hung having spoken of their early departure and Intourist helping to arrange a mass protest demonstration over the American spy plane . . . yes yes, there are big demonstrations. What what? Yes, I will fly down later today. Over-praise over-praise. Goodbye goodbye,' he said and laid down the telephone.

He stared at his knees, thinking. Then he started to massage his belly and raised his heavy eyes towards the man who had just reappeared. The man shook his head.

'He left everything except his binoculars.'

'Everything?'

'We've checked it against the quarterly lists sent by Hu and Shuen.'

'Did he leave evidence of his criminal association?'

'No.'

Sun lowered his eyes. That deepened his perplexity. According to Han he had met her recently, and Shuen merely said he intended to prove an association though Shuen was in a mood to prove dogs had wings. He turned his eyes to the blank-faced lift-man, who repeated that he had never seen them together and she only visited Miss Shao. There was a ring of truth in Tang's voice.

Sun turned his eyes to Ying, his chief assistant. 'Take the Shaos for questioning and search their rooms,' he ordered. 'Put them in separate cells in the political prison and leave them for fortyeight hours.' He did not expect to prove more than laxity of social conduct. It would have the Shao family split and sent to farm communes for work and corrective right-thinking.

After some minutes he heaved himself up, and went back to his office. There was nothing new to add to the girl's refusal to attend freed Catholic churches and her independent attitude to literature; she was a rebel. Old letters intercepted from her family in America revealed nothing. He glanced up as Soong Shu-lan crept in, carrying a suitcase brought from his home.

On the flight down to Canton in a noisy old Russian plane, his perplexity over the stolen bicycle increased. It did not fit in. There were two possible explanations. One was that they were involved in espionage though no record existed of Hung having met the Englishman, and none had sought to obtain secret information. The other was that they had become refugees, Hung alone, the others together, two who did not play safe by choosing their own kind, ready to shake their fists at whatever heaven was revered, trample orders into straw, tear bare-handed through man-made jungles of convention, to have each other. Mad mad. Splendid! Ai, he was sentimental, but did a man forget his own flowering? Ai, he hoped the fragile blossom was theirs, but could not preserve its beauty for them. The state he had helped to create depended on regulations.

He pinched his nostrils to force air into his ears to clear them of pressure. His thoughts reverted to himself. The doctors who examined him last week said he might live for a year. So long?

4

It was Tuesday morning. Less than an hour ago a dawn like a swift vibrant arpeggio on a harp had risen above the bleak humps of the Kai Lung Mountains, pulsing across a naked sky until it flooded the land, a sheeted yellow radiance outside the mouth of the cave in which they were hiding. She wore the black blouse and loose trousers of peasant women in this area, the crucifix on her breast. Her face gave no sign of fatigue.

For three nights they had walked. During daylight they rested in hiding-places chosen by Fua-tuan for his flight. The first two nights had been tricky. They were forced to go slowly round marshland from Shekung to Waiyeung though much of it was dry from lack of spring rains swelling the rivers, their journey irked by knowledge that Lo Wo bridge and the barbed wire frontier to Hongkong was only fifty miles to the south. But they had ignored temptations to go faster and had avoided villages where disturbed dogs barked fretfully at passing footsteps and men came from their homes into the silvery gossamer moonlight to relieve their bladders.

Inner tensions kept part of their minds conscious even in sleep. Their legs no longer ached.

Fua-tuan seldom rested. Whenever Steven looked at him in their hideouts he was awake, bird-bright eyes alert, listening to his dearest toy, a small Japanese transistor radio smuggled in from Hongkong. He was a stocky cheerful youth and relished every second of their adventure. They had no communication when she was asleep. As interpreter she employed a quaint mixture of European phrases and invented jargon which she called Swedish. Nevertheless, from it Steven learned that Fua-tuan, a botanical student, had somehow obtained information of small guerrilla resistance groups, the Shensi 'Army for Justice', the Fukien 'Revolutionary Army', Yunnan 'Anti-Communist Corps', the 'General Staff' outside Chungking, Muslim groups in Uighur and Sinkiang, 'Mimeng' in Tibet; he had described the abortive risings in Honan two years ago. Fua-tuan hoped to get to Singapore on money left for him at a Hongkong bank by an uncle.

As the sun climbed on the third morning, Fua-tuan announced his intention to go to the nearest village to get food. Anxious at his casual manner, she pleaded with him to avoid taking risks. He grinned assurance at them and went off.

Standing back from the entrance, Steven saw a brace of francolin and cuckoos flying under the next hillcrest. He turned and looked down at where she lay, her head on his jacket. He squatted on his heels and took her hand. She smiled, her eyes full of fondness, and thanked him for trusting Fua-tuan. He ignored her needless gratitude, relieved to see no strain in her face.

'How do you manage to get comfy?' he asked.

She kissed his hand and laid it on her neck. 'We did not have to come,' she reminded him.

They searched each other's eyes. Her lips parted as if to speak. No words came. She reached up to him.

Afterwards they were quiet, slack and fortified by having set a seal on one reason for being here. She sighed.

'It will be good to talk again. Without a radio. We will talk?'

'We have still to get to know each other.'

'Yes, it has been only the beginning.'

Soon after noon Fua-tuan plunged into the cave and flung himself full-length on the ground, wriggling towards them, panting that he had seen police nearby. They waited uneasily. None relaxed until the late afternoon sky glowed a deep velvety blue.

Seventeen

IT WAS Friday, six days since their walk began. They were farther on, but in foothills of the Kai Lung Mountains to avoid military convoys patrolling the main coastal road. And now they were over a hundred miles from their goal. For two days and nights they had hidden in a small airless cave overlooking a village less than three miles off. According to Fua-tuan it was Laokoi, home of upwards of a thousand people, end of a cul-de-sac from Kungping. Only in darkness did they dare go out for a breath of fresh air on account of a risk of being seen by villagers, unusually active in their streets, bustling in and out of their mud-walled cottages to cluster in groups which often talked for an hour. Steven assumed they were discussing news of demonstrations against America for its spy plane flight.

In every hour they heard a distant drone of lorries and military trucks shuttling back and forth along the main road, presumably an increased vigilance inspired by propaganda or lest there should be parachute drops by Nationalist agents from Taiwan. The radio left no doubt of a spy mania having taken hold of Peking; they kept it on to hear if it gave mention of themselves, but heard instead of Nationalist agents, sabotage plots, details of executions in recent years. And late on the third day, after it became obvious that they must stay hidden for another day, Fua-tuan went off over the hill to get food and refill their flasks, slipping out in the shrill evening light.

Steven lay on his stomach watching the village through his binoculars. Something was going on down there. For an hour more and more people had assembled on waste ground at one end of its main street. He saw other figures in blue work-clothes, bobbed-haired women, twin-pigtailed girls in loose floral blouses, walking towards the village along grass-bordered paths. One child, a girl in a red patterned blouse and dark trousers, was accompanied by two energetic geese. And a boy in a faded blue shirt and khaki shorts brought a mule. Steven lowered his glasses to rest his eyes.

When he took another look a meeting was in progress. Nothing in his experiences could account for its quietness, and there were no red banners bearing slogans. He saw speaker after speaker climb on a chair and deliver an impassioned harangue, but the audience kept quiet, wrapt in thought. It was still going on as night deepened canted lilac hill shadows to purple and indigo, darkness hissing over the broken crests of mountains in the east. Flares were lit in Laokoi, tinily flickering orange-red feathers of flame which reminded him of makeshift wartime flare paths seen from a distance. As he watched. she came alongside him, but they did not speak immediately If anyone had asked him why his newspaperman's instinct detected something peculiar about the meeting, he could not have justified it; but he felt it in his bones. Had a *kanpou* come from a neighbouring town to organize search parties on hunts for spies?

'Quite frankly, I haven't the foggiest idea,' he admitted in reply to her question.

'Is it an instruction class?'

'Well . . .'

'Tell me.'

'Most speakers appear to be local people. And they are making speeches.'

While she used the binoculars he remained tense, his accumulated impatiences jangling, alarmed at a prospect of having to waste even more precious days up here. Or was that his own irritability taking hold? Small annoyances, particularly delays, had always aggravated him worse than larger setbacks. She handed back the glasses.

'Yes, strange,' she agreed levelly. 'Let's have an orange. We've two apiece until Fua-tuan gets back.'

As they sat eating them on the open hillside under a cloud of stars, watching the firefly glimmer of flares below, the warm air scented by wildflowers which had the sweet smell of mignonette, he asked if Fua-tuan had said when he would get back.

'Not till after midnight.'

'He's a nice boy.'

'Thank goodness he's not a political or racial fanatic. It's terribly hard for those who've grown up behind these gigantic walls of propaganda not to accept what they've had drummed into them about the world outside. They've no criterion. And every one of us has streaks of bigotry and arrogance. . . .'

They talked desultorily. Down in Laokoi the flares burned steadily. He saw that the meeting had gone on for over three hours. Its implications niggled in his mind. She collected their orange-peel into her handkerchief to throw away at some place where it would not attract attention, and raised her head and sighed.

'I'm glad we're alone. The first time in three days. This is how I expected it would be. Us. Alone. The rest is so unreal. Am I silly?'

Her quiet voice contrived an atmosphere of their being remote and exclusive owners of those wheeling stars and this air smelling of dust and flowers and dust again; by some means she lent the hour inevitability.

'I feel rather unreal myself,' he said.

'That's because you're not working. . . . Steven.'

'Mmmm?'

'Do you mind if I admit I'm frightened?'

He took her hand. 'What of?'

After a pause she said: 'The world outside. Oh, I thought I'd succeeded in closing my mind against what happens here. Forgive me. Some of their propaganda has crept in. Words, sentences, right-thinking. Is it crueller out there since I last saw it? Shall I see hatred or contempt in people's eyes and know they're thinking "There's a Chink woman who used her sex to entice a weak fool to get her out"? Shall I? Will the fact of me harm you? Has love made me selfish as well as absurd by longing to be every woman so you will never leave me? You'll say I ought to have thought about this months ago. I did . . . I did. But I wanted you and when you wanted me back I thought it would be simple away from here . . . free . . . settling in good faith whatever divided us. Now, I'm frightened, complicated. I'm terrified of gossiping people with malice a cancer on their tongues. They're everywhere, a disease of humanity. Steven, beloved Steven, I won't let them harm you through me. You will be free to leave me. There won't be a scene or recriminations,' she promised and laid her forehead on her knees.

Some flares had gone out. He saw two vanish behind cottages. Others remained in a close ring, broken by dark shapes moving across them. One jigged slowly up a hillside.

'Steven?' she said in a small voice.

'Oh, finished?'

'Did you hear me?'

'I don't plan to live with such people.'

'You heard my promise?'

'Ah. Tell me, do you want to go to America?'

There was a pause, and then she said: 'Not yet. They wouldn't let me in. You'll want to go to England.'

'Want, yes,' he said. 'You've seen it, a very green island graced by low skies and friendly people who've got no real racial prejudices. But not yet. Last time I went home the prevailing mood didn't suit me. It was trivial, too worshipful of the devalued pound sterling and entertainment notorieties. And the manners were pretty bad. So, not yet. I like to keep my patriotism intact.'

More people were leaving. Those who had come from farther off were going in groups. Some had torches; through the binoculars he saw flutters of milky light delicate as moth-wings dancing erratically along formless paths across fields and over higher hills.

He lowered the glasses. The fault, dear Brutus, might lie in himself. As she said, he was not working, and his brain was like a buzz-saw. Yet it was peculiar.

'Don't fret,' he said. 'We'll find some place, come hell and high water, and have a private life. Does the prospect of a private life bore you? It's oldfashioned.'

'Is it bad for your work?'

'It's good for me. I've never licked up enough enthusiasm for a contemporary ambition. Other people can get ahead, climb the golden rungs, set the world on fire. Consumer-nostalgia doesn't afflict me. Gadgets won't warm the shroud. You must make do on my earnings.'

'It isn't because of me?'

'No, I've always been unfashionable about ambition.'

'You will write?'

'Try and stop me. And this first. You must help me.'

He scrambled up and helped her to rise, and her lips were smooth and firm on his for a moment.

'How easily you can rid me of fear. Only you have given me freedom. It is right for me to belong to you.'

'That is because you let me rid you of it. Never fear, we'll avoid those people. You'll soon get adjusted. Me too.'

'You are my bridge between death and life.'

'Now you are being silly.'

'No, I never never said anything more true. You shall never regret letting us love each other.'

They walked pace for pace towards the cave, their arms round each other. As they neared it, she laughed quietly. 'Did you realize we were deciding what we should do and haven't got there yet?'

'It hadn't entirely escaped me.'

'Isn't it glorious?'

She was asleep when Fua-tuan got back at one o'clock. He brought oranges, water, Hainan bananas, cherries, and a cooked duck.

2

Sun gasped for breath beside his hotel window, watching another sunrise over Canton. It was going to be hot again.

What day? He could not remember. His head ached. Every day he felt worse, exhausted by this heat, his lungs starved of air, his body heavy as a sack of rice. Saturday?

Wearily he finished dressing and drove down to police head-quarters. When he got there sweat was trickling down his groin, wet patches spreading under his armpits. There was news for him. He struggled for breath as they told him of a bicycle found in Hikkai, a fishing village. He nodded, cautious in front of these educated young men, whipping his mind to listen to them. Ai, it was worthless. What did it matter if an ignorant fellow like Hung did escape? He could not harm the republic, an unimportant man without information. And if Kendal had taken off a woman who wanted to be his, as Yi-hai had chosen to give herself to a Swatow labourer once upon a time, why did it matter? Whatever Kendal wrote, if he escaped, could be denied. They wanted opportunities to call foreigners liars; it was important to their propaganda to shout until people could not tell paper tigers from real ones. He sucked breath into his mouth.

'Indigestion,' he apologized. 'You are too hospitable to visitors. Are there other developments?'

Shih frowned impatiently. He was young and swarthy, diligent in performing his duties, a local man keen to prove his ability. 'There is trouble in Laokoi village. It may be due to spies. I thought we would drive out to see if villagers can tell us of strangers they have seen recently.'

Sun wiped his sweaty jowls. 'You are right,' he said heavily, dreading a long day in this heat. It did not seem important now.

3

Since midday something had been going on in the village. Steven had heard the whine of the first old Russian truck coming up the road. It was full of armed soldiers. Others had followed it, a convoy of travel-grimed lorries full of khaki-clad men and automatic rifles, young men, the skin of their faces glowing, laughing and joking as the trucks stopped and they jumped down.

The other trucks had begun to appear soon afterwards. Steven had lost count of them. There were at least twenty, probably more, out of sight now behind the houses. And each of them had brought a load of people, men and women and children, two hundred, possibly more, people who wandered around like a party which had expected to find a fairground in full swing but discovered it closed. They went for short walks. An even larger number of empty trucks had followed them, and was drawn up in three lines through the village. Last to come was an official car. Out of it had got two men in Yat-sen tunics, one short and agile, the other physically huge and slow on his feet.

Now it was early afternoon. Steven and Fua-tuan lay on their stomachs just inside the cave and shared the binoculars. Between them was the radio. Fua-tuan had tuned it into a programme giving eye-witness accounts of recent mass rallies against American imperialism and containing lengthy excerpts from speeches. They kept it low, voices whispering against imperialism and war-chariots of aggression and an upsurge of oppressed Asian people. Every speech referred to the spy plane; at one point a studio announcer read a poem which began 'While the world celebrated a glorious May Day the Soviet Union shot down a dark plane which proved false the façade of peace . . .' and ended 'U-2 planes blacken the fair soil of Japan; China's millions will not tolerate their evil plan!'

Fua-Tuan passed over the glasses. Steven diverted his attention from lamblike clouds frisking over a radiant heat-paled sky, wiped sweat from his neck, and propped himself up on his elbows.

To his eyes there was no change of tempo down in Laikoi. People strolled aimlessly, gazing around. Thin-legged children leapt in pursuit of chickens whose wings beat flustery protest. One difference registered on his mind. In big cities everything was done to increase fraternization between civilians and the

People's Liberation Army, the élite and favoured. Various publications singled out the happy relationship. These wandering civilians paid these soldiers scrupulous respect by ignoring their presence. No one spoke to groups of soldiers lounging idly on plots of grassland at either end of Laokoi; their rifles were stacked neatly like Italian bean-poles. He eased over as Mei came alongside him. Whatever were they doing, he wondered worriedly.

'What's happening?'

'I can't fathom it,' he said and gave her the glasses.

He assumed they were preparing a large-scale search. For whom? Nationalist spies on a drop? Themselves? Why should it be themselves?

The radio murmured: 'This rally of six hundred thousand Canton workers demands that United States imperialists get out of Japan, south Korea, and China's Taiwan!' Applause purred like mush.

In mid-afternoon a change came over Laokoi, a change full of ominous significance. Soldiers arranged a row of chairs on the waste ground and shepherded civilians into a hollow square in front of them. Others carried spades a short distance on and took off their jackets and commenced to dig.

'Oh God no,' whispered Steven to himself.

'What is it?' she asked.

'A people's trial.'

'No!'

They spoke English, regardless of Fua-tuan. Through the glasses Steven saw a group of officers come into sight, followed by a crowd of villagers. With the officers were the two men who had arrived by car; the large man stumbled wearily as if he felt the heat. Steven ignored pleas to be given the glasses, kept them trained on the lumbering heavy man. He was half-convinced that it was Sun. But what could he be doing down here?

Suddenly Fua-tuan hissed. Steven paid no attention, trying to get the advancing group into focus, and then heard 'her startled exclamation. As he lowered the binoculars he caught

267

sight of a man's legs at the entrance of the cave. For a moment he gazed at them blindly, his thoughts centred on the gathering crowd below, then his brain grew clear in an awful conviction of disaster. There were two of them, not one, black upon the flashing tender sky. He tried to think coherently, determined they should not take her, sliding his hand down to the knife in his pocket. He gathered his strength and wits. A shiver went round his loins.

'The People's Government of China solemnly declares its unyielding support for the sacred cause of liberating the oppressed peoples of Asia,' whispered the radio.

He lifted his head, narrowing his eyes against the sky glare. Yes, two. The second one was a woman, a round-faced girl in a blue and white blouse and blue trousers, stolid and healthy, two pink plastic slides in her bobbed hair, a baby slung on her back. The man was young, wiry, his face covered in dust.

Men reveal consternation more openly than women. This one looked about to faint, staring at Steven as if he did not believe his reason, his narrow lips agitated. 'Tell them to come in,' said Steven, and shuddered. 'Quickly.'

From questions put by Fua-tuan it came out that their name was Lin. They lived in Laokoi. They had climbed the hill during the night because Yok-ching, the wife, overheard two villagers under *kwantchee* discussing events planned for today, but they told no one else lest they were security spies. No man could trust his own family, Lin told them.

Steven lay still, watching and listening to what she told him.

According to Lin, Laokoi was a rebel village. Its people took pride in being independent like their ancestors. They had never formed a commune. They were left alone, thinking their home too unimportant for anyone to disturb them. Then *kanpous* had come. At the Spring Festival they drove up in big cars bringing dancers, high-spirited students from Canton who sang patriotic songs: and photographers. There was feasting. Then the *kanpous* held a meeting to persuade villagers to sign a voluntary petition asking for Laokoi to set up as a commune and told them they must select a delegation which would carry it to Party and government offices in Canton. After a heated discussion, the villagers took an open vote which overwhelmingly rejected the setting up of a commune.

Last week other *kanpous* came, said Lin. They told villagers they must leave their homes: Laokoi must die. People were stunned, disbelieving their ears. Why why, they asked, what have we done? A *kanpou* told them that because of drought and other natural calamities hundreds of thousands of men and women were being taken from towns in Heilungkiang, Hunan, Anhwei, and other places, many others, and from backward villages like Laokoi, and being sent to save farm communes by digging canals, reservoirs, field terraces, cut open mountains and divert rivers. Half a million people would leave their homes for large farm communes this summer, the *kanpous* said.

Amazed, people in Laokoi asked where they were going. No one knew, only that they were to leave today. Mrs. Liang, who had spent her life in Laokoi and had eleven children, asked if they were going together. No one knew. The *kanpous* thought not. At once there was uproar; women wept, tears streaming down their faces, crying out about their families and friends here and in other hill villages; men shouted fiercely; youths sprang to their feet and made speeches; elders shook their fists. The important *kanpou* said everyone must be ready to go today, and each person could take one bundle of personal belongings. And yesterday leading citizens and elders of Laokoi, surrounded by their families and life-long friends, vowed their defiance and pledged not to be sent from their homes.

The radio murmured: 'China will wage its unflinching war against American imperialism to drive the hated Yankees and their British and French lackeys out of Asia, Africa, and Latin America.'

Lin declared passionately that he and his wife were making for Hongkong, but spent the night on the hill in case the *kanpous* relented and did not carry out their threat.

'Peoples of the world, unite,' whispered the radio.

Down in Laokoi there was new activity. A file of men and women was led in front of the seated officers. There were about forty of them. Each had a long strip of white cloth pinned on the front of their blouses. Armed soldiers prodded them into a line. The imported audience was shouting and singing, and then its mouths shut as a man was shoved forward, forced to kneel and bow his head. A soldier addressed the officers. Among them the large man like Sun sat like a collapsed sack, head fallen forward on a cushion of fleshy jowls. Steven gave her the glasses.

'Tell me what's going on.'

She raised herself, supporting her body on her elbows. 'The soldier is reading out the crimes the man is accused of committing,' she told him tonelessly. 'Then people will testify against him. There will be no witnesses for the defence. Their names and major crime are written on the labels.' She handed him the glasses.

Fua-tuan came down alongside Steven, demanding he should be given the glasses. When Steven got them again the accused was a kneeling woman and the accuser a small boy, not more than seven or eight years old, probably her son or nephew. Then a thin man took the place of the child, waving his arms vehemently. At the end there was a rhythmic opening and shutting of mouths in the audience and it dawned on Steven that the people were shouting 'Sha! Sha! Kill! Kill!' A bent elder who could scarcely hobble was the next accused, and then a strongly built young woman in a pink blouse, her pigtail reaching her solid hips as she knelt.

It went on for some while. As the sun sank lower Steven caught sight of the officers' faces; all young, one thin, tight-lipped, proud as Lucifer, another fleshy and utterly expression-less, a third blank and bored, another eyeing the crowd, all arrogant and fearless and merciless, untouched by humour, the faces of men who would have felt at home in Imperial Rome, wherever power was worshipped. The audience raved. People ran forward to spit on the accused without restraint by conscience. Steven wished he had a camera with a super Long Tom to record this scene. It sickened him yet he had to watch.

Then a fire started. Another woman crouched on her knees,

a diminutive figure in a faded blue blouse, hair fallen over her ears, thin body swaying. As she cowered, a pillar of oily black smoke rose from a distant cottage, mushrooming into the tender sky between two bleak hills warm in apricot sunshine. Another cloud of smoke sagged up. There was a howl of motors, and lorries full of people clutching bundles drove off, jolting over ruts and stones.

'Oh, my God,' said Steven. He saw the Lins lying beyond Fua-tuan. The girl cried noisily, thick under-lip hanging slack, her face contorted.

'Why do human beings do such things?' asked a hopeless voice beside him, and she too was crying.

More cottages were burning. Some were isolated, their smoke rising behind poplars and shrubs. More loaded trucks set off down the dirt road. The crowd applauded frenziedly, like crazed children, unconcerned to draw distinctions amongst the condemned, unrelenting in its joyful obedience, dwarfing its own humanity. Another house belched fire. Lin shouted hoarsely and shook his fists in rage, crying out that it belonged to his First Uncle. And then the condemned, those who had spoken at last night's meeting, were led to the fresh communal grave and made to kneel on its verge. Armed troops lined up behind them.

All of them heard the volley which rang out. This was how an estimated six million people died in China in recent years, victims of the frightened, raving conformists. The crowd clapped and cheered, besotted by joy at the terrible death of these people in sight of their homes, its pleasure the ultimate degradation. None abstained or forbore. They cheered wildly until soil began to mantle fallen bodies, and then they turned back into the burning village. There was no sign of the military tribunal which had guided the mob. Parties of soldiers chased strayed chickens and ducks through wreathing smoke.

At length, nauseated, Steven lowered the glasses. 'I don't know,' he answered. '*Yan to, meng ping*—many men, life cheap. Truer now. Absolute power, absolute corruption.' He fought down a sensation of sickness rising in his throat.

271

Thereafter an unreal tranquillity brooded over the scene. Laokoi burned steadily. Its mouldering walls stood after its roofs had collapsed and sent sparks flying into the pale sky. Loaded lorries drove off. More soldiers fanned out to search fields, but stayed close to the cottages. They carried back geese and pigs and ducks. The imported audience drove off, completely silent now, its inhuman duty done, like bunches of dolls.

Later on Lin asked Fua-tuan if his name was Hung Tien-pei. Steven turned at the name and asked why he used it. Lin told them how police had searched their home last week, hunting for a man named Hung who had disappeared from Canton. Steven shook his head, unsure.

It was a beautiful tropical evening, warm and fragrant and placid. For several moments the entire wide sky flushed a vivid turquoise green, a single star glittering whitely in its waste. Over in one corner stretched a delicate veil of smoke.

In the darkness that followed she rested her head on Steven's shoulder, then pressed her face against his neck, crying as if her heart was breaking.

Eighteen

IT WAS the evening of the eleventh day. They rested on another hillside in flaring copper sunlight. They were worn, bodies weary, nerves frayed, and they were hungry. For two days they had existed on oranges. Their water had almost gone. Fua-tuan had made two expeditions to refill their flasks but returned from his second trip without a drop: the drought had imposed rationing which meant he would have revealed that he had companions with him if he approached anyone directly.

For four nights since leaving Laokoi they had crept through foothills, driven back time and again by motorized army units patrolling against the possibility of Nationalist invasion, a frequent warning on the radio. Steven reckoned that Nationalist airfields were not much more than three hundred flight miles away across the Straits. Mainland planes were seldom out of the sky.

He glanced at the others. Most of them dozed uneasily, never quite at rest. Since Laokoi Fua-tuan had lost his boundless enthusiasm and retreated into a fierce silence. A slight movement under Mei's eyelids suggested she was awake, listening for motor traffic on the road below. Lin slept soundest, holding his baby son. Only Yok-ching was wide awake. Her docile endurance astonished him. She walked uncomplainingly for hours, her baby on her back; she seldom slept yet gave no sign of weariness. And she had hidden reserves of strength. This morning he had awakened from a dream of evil chaos, sweating miserably, and opened his eyes and saw Yok-ching. She was lying still, holding her husband's head on her, one milk heavy breast bare for him to draw nourishment from it in the manner of peasant women in times of famine.

Now she stared at him through the frothing twilight, her eyes blank, nether lip slack, waiting for his instructions.

For some extraordinary reason, they expected him to get them out. It beat him. With Fua-tuan as pathfinder they would travel faster without him. He lacked essential requirements for leadership here.

He waited until daylight was a smoking crimson bar broken by black hills, and then awoke the others, infusing a note of determination into his voice as he spoke to Fua-tuan. They had stopped the pretence of him being a Swede.

'We're going to get across that road tonight.'

2

Two nights later as they walked round a hill in sight of the sea Steven stumbled among stones, lost balance, and sprawled headlong. The toe of his right foot caught in soil, wrenching his foot. He lay winded and heard Fua-tuan speak anxiously.

'I'm all right.'

'Steven, what's the matter?'

'Nothing,' he told her, and they helped him up. He took two unsure steps, and stopped. 'Mmmm.'

'What is it?'

'I'll have to hang on for a bit. I twisted my ankle.'

It was more than his ankle. The sole of his shoe flapped, half torn off. So he took off both shoes, tied their laces, slung them round his neck. Then he got up.

They were two hours late in reaching their destination, a cave above a small *wan* somewhere between Hunghai and Shenchuan Bays. At once Fua-tuan went off in search of food. While the Lins went inside to sleep, Steven and Mei sat watching the grey sea cloud up blue-green under a fragile rose-shot golden sky. The sun came out of the South China Sea dripping fire onto its placid surface. It was a glorious sight: the shore of this land of 1984. The radio whispered of American plots. He rasped fingernails down his bearded jaw and inspected his shoe to see if anything could be done. Nothing could.

3

Every day and night planes flew low overhead. To judge from their activity, a Nationalist-American invasion was imminent. Fua-tuan and Lin brought back news of increased army patrols. Whatever its motive, Peking was unquestionably employing the American plane episode to test its coastal defences. It contrasted oddly with hopeful predictions of a successful West-Russian summit conference given in newscasts from Hongkong radio.

Steven put scant reliance on assurances by Fua-tuan of hearing no mention of descriptions issued by security departments of wanted fugitives. Villagers were unlikely to volunteer such information to strangers. This section of coast, the pirate coast of earlier days whose centre at Bias Bay had gained world-wide notoriety, had a reputation for tight-lipped secrecy.

He longed to be able to find out what was happening instead of being cooped up in a small cave where heat lingered long after the sun had ceased to shine straight into it, but even if his physical self had not betrayed him instantly he could not have understood the dialect of these fishermen.

Inactivity aggravated him unutterably. How the two women managed to endure it, accept every discomfort, he could not tell. The memory of Laokoi was never absent from his thoughts.

He tried to hide his distaste for their meals of rice and raw fish, usually puffer, thrown out as valueless. One day they had bits of octopus and unsalted toadfish, both regarded locally as delicacies. Nowadays, Fua-tuan told him, the once profitable catches of bream, golden thread, cuttlefish, and garoupa, were transported to Canton under supervision by petty *kanpous*, and catches had to be larger for the fishermen to maintain their previous standard of life.

Day followed monotonous day in sullen implacable heat, noise of planes, and frustration. The cave heat must have been bad for Yok-ching's baby but it slept without a whimper. By the fourth night, after day-long heat burning up from the sea, when even Mei began to show signs of strain, he thought they were doomed.

As Fua-tuan was out most of the next day in search of a friend whom he expected would help them, they spent hours sitting near the cave entrance. They seldom spoke. The heat gave him a splitting headache. Though her manner did not forfeit the tenderness linking them since they left Canton, her responses to his infrequent comments were slower. Late in the afternoon they held each other for a moment, smelled each other's sweat and dirt and tiredness, and her lips were dry and hot, but she begged him not to worry; she was merely drugged by heat and stiff from lying on the ground.

'I wouldn't rather be anywhere else without you, darling,' she said.

Another Republican plane droned over the surface of the

sea. She rested her hot face on his bare chest, then kissed his ribs, and went to see if Yok-ching needed help.

Daylight expired in a violent paroxysm of colour; the sea horizon merged into the sky in a mauve-grey offshore mist.

Fua-tuan had promised faithfully to return at eight. There was still no sight of him at half-past nine.

At eleven they sat outside in the moonlight listening to the slow rhythmic motion of the sea, though up here it sounded stronger in their fancy than in their ears, and watched light speckle the water. He talked to relax their communicated strain, telling her how this shimmering radiance reminded him of a night on New Guinea when he saw millions of white moths perform their death dance above the Sepik River, an annual event which transformed the river into a white veil as they fell exhausted and drowned, and then described ceremonies down in Bechwanaland. It filled in their waiting.

'How did you come to be in China?'

'I can only tell you the mundane details which brought me here. No man can account for why his life takes its course. His finite intellect traces its path, not its purpose.'

'If you only have ideas, as you once told me, why are you sure there is a purpose?'

'Simple. We can turn to our account almost everything which surrounds us. Perhaps everything. Why should it be there for us to use yet we ourselves be void of purpose? Why were we, mankind alone, given the intelligence to utilize it? Why were we alone given the knowledge of our birth and death? There is a reason for everything around us, otherwise we could not turn it to our account, so why should we be without a reason for existence? No, it is only our recent cleverness in science which has restricted our vision to material things that has caused us to lose sight of spiritual truths. We live in the turmoil of a scientific age which is like a heat-haze hiding the stars from our sight.'

'You make atheists sound like the last survival of the animal mind.'

'In a sense, they are. They're obsessed by material things,

276

by provable facts and concrete objects. They say nothing else exists, but they cannot prove that. Who can prove the non-existence of a thing? It may merely be outside the scope of our finite comprehension in a particular age. Matter is the alphabet of our life here. Spirit is the language the alphabet should enable us to speak. At Laokoi we saw what happens when men deny spirit, the true language.'

'You must write about that.'

After a pause he said: 'I wish I could do it properly.'

'You can.'

'Oh no. I have ideas, too many of them, but I don't know the best way to put them together.'

'You will do it better than anyone.'

'I doubt it. But we must get started. We daren't waste time. Unless the West is careful, China is the world's tomorrow. It will influence the underdeveloped countries more than Russia . . . you know, Clive is right. This must get to people. Not intellectuals. They're an effete, treacherous little mob. They'll conform to save their necks. Fortunately, their wasp whine is too insignificant to influence the issues. In the age the West can only serve humanity by having the larger heart, the wider vision, faith in the new beliefs of freedom and justice for every man without interference by rulers whether their label be emperor or party chairman—the label is meaningless if use of power is basically tyrannical. We've set ourselves a tricky problem. This is only the beginning.'

'You will do it better than anyone,' she repeated staunchly.

'At any rate, we'll have a stab at it. And you, my love, are responsible for my intending to make the effort. I feel infinitely better. I've dragged around too many overloaded dustbins . . . Lord, I could do with a shave.'

'I'm glad we got out into the air and sunlight and this glorious moonlight,' she said pleasedly. 'Isn't it a change?'

At midnight soft footsteps padded towards them. It was Lin, returning from a long trudge to get rice gruel for his baby. His face was peaky from fatigue and nerves. He told them he had not seen Fua-tuan since noon, and stumbled into the cave.

They sat on, gone silent under an oppressive weight of dread and doubts, each questioning his non-appearance, dissecting his grim offhandedness since they left the murdered village. And eventually tiredness overtook her. She lay down holding his hand and went to sleep. Not even the purr of a police launch searching the darkened shores awoke her. As it disappeared behind a headland he saw her eyelids were quiet, a pulse flickering in her neck under the thin gold chain, her breast scarcely moving.

So he watched the moon slide over the wheeling darkness, and at four o'clock a weary but jubilant Fua-tuan climbed up to them. If all went well, they would go on board the night after next though they must be ready for difficulty in getting past the police and 'Small Group' members in the village. There was going to be a crush; four other men were going, two from Laokoi, young brothers, sons of one of the executed men. They had seen him die.

Peeling an orange in his dirty hands, he looked at Steven through the pre-dawn dark. 'I told them you were a Yugoslav,' he said, giggling.

Each of the intervening hours seemed interminable, somnambulic in an unsparing heat which fastened unreality on their stupefied minds, even tension a dreamlike meaninglessness. At her plea they spent the next night outside in a concealed corner where they were alone on the soil of China, and for a while she could not restrain her distress, not at their going but at their having to go from this land in order to live like human beings, and in one moment she repeated: 'You are my bridge.'

And directly darkness came again they set off, warily, preys of hope and misgiving, their descent slowed to avoid an error which might betray them to someone under kwantchee out for a walk in this moonless quietness.

Along the last few miles they heard occasional voices around them, more numerous down near the shore. There they crept through shadows alive with menace in their imagination if no more, hearts in their mouth, every footstep a separate peril on this unfamiliar ground. And she held his hand tightly, sweat from her palm a guide to her thoughts. But after an enforced halt they came to the shore, then a boat materialized from the night, and they waded out to it through the shining warm surf and were taken round the next *kiao*, a headland like a bitten thumb, to a fishing junk whose high butterfly-wing yellow straw sails covered the southern stars.

It was a good thing they had been warned of a crush. They descended into a sweltering tiny hole normally in use as a galley, lengthened to accommodate people but scarcely more than hip-high from floor to deck level. Its heat stank of fish and incense burned to propitiate sea gods to give safety and a good catch. They lay on old straw mats, another load of 'coiled serpents', refugees for Hongkong. By comparison, the crew's cramped cubbyholes forrard of the mainmast were luxurious. Within moments an unseen man vomited furiously, retching hollowly for some while after his stomach had emptied itself. Then a woman member of the crew burned more incense, and the junk moved off. As they sailed towards Bias Bay a plane circled slowly overhead. Heat soon caused more sickness. Two men were unable to stop vomiting.

Towards dawn it became worse. Smells of food were added to soured heat as two trousered women came down to prepare the breakfast mess of rice, fish, and vegetables in a bucket and brewed tea. The sun did not help. Not at all.

Nineteen

Nothing is impossible. Fragrant Harbour had developed a social conscience. Since the British came to its ignored hump over a century ago it had become one form of lighthouse whose gleam illuminated a few minds across the frontier; Dr. Sun Yat-sen, the true father of the Chinese Revolution, speaking in its University forty years ago, said 'I began to wonder how it was that foreigners, that Englishmen, could do such things as they had done, for example with the barren rock of Hongkong within seventy or eighty years, while in four thousand years China had no place like Hongkong' and other Chinese shared his desire to provide material wellbeing for their unprivileged, hungry, illiterate fellow-countrymen, the millions whose existence was disregarded by the self-obsessed Manchu court. And the British administration now showed no sign of slackening the programme of social development begun after the Christmas Day fire in Shek Kip Mei tenements seven years ago which made sixty thousand refugees homeless and nudged it into action to lessen their plight.

So maybe the light glowed warmer and more steadily than hitherto. Certainly it did for the refugees whose exigencies though harsh in the extreme did receive heed by the outside world though it should have done more for them by unloading its stores of unsaleable surplus foodstuffs. Even the wealthiest taipans of Hongkong could not alone satisfy the hunger and human problems of two million refugees crowded into four hundred square miles, less than a quarter of that area capable of development for farming or building. So Steven said often in the first fortyeight hours following their creeping ashore at night near Big Wave Bay like a band of criminals, alarmed by recent escape from a Hongkong police launch tracking down sea-borne refugees. And then Lin and his wife and baby went off to find space in a squatter camp in hills of the New Territories, close to the communist frontier, and the other men vanished, and Fua-tuan went to arrange to go to Singapore, and they were alone, but unquestioned, incredulous, the last weeks darker on their minds.

They had trouble in finding a hotel. Those they tried were full of American tourists off two sleek luxury prowl liners, and their bedraggled appearance told against them. Evading attention of official eyes, they discovered a Chinese place in Kowloon, a dump, too shabby to entice large bank balances. Their room was small and hot and dirty. And that was how they felt, plus thankfulness and relief. Their surroundings were un-important.

Through every hour Chinese whores in rooms on either side shrieked merrily at jocular admiration expressed by sailors scooped up from a congested doorway downstairs. In the small hours of the first night they were awakened by a sudden uproar; a bull voice roared drunken accusations of theft, a woman screamed, other women cried out sleepily, crockery smashed, and then silence ached. Neither squealing girls nor their admirers bothered them. They were content to remain unseen while they unwound to reorientate their minds and relax their bodies. For two days they went out solely for meals. Then Kowloon boiled frighteningly around them, human chaos spilling between dazzlingly lit yellow and scarlet shop fronts. From one meal they went back to find a blaring radio installed in their room. It was atrocious. Steven disconnected it.

'All right?' he asked.

'I never want to hear one again.'

Somehow the incident marked an end, a fact she com-mented on later. That night there was another violent quarrel. He woke up in startlement, raising his head from her shoulder, but her arms held him and she said the squabble had been going on for some while. So they went to sleep again, and awoke to find a flamingo red dawn.

Then they got up, yawning, and were dressed when their room-boy brought their breakfast, and immediately afterwards they set off in the morning rush by ferry to the island. Although they were only twenty-odd miles from the barbed-wire Bamboo Curtain there was no sign of its nearness reflected among the crowds. Around them the harbour was full of cargo junks, launches, yachts, tugs, a fleet of sampans plying from merchant-men to shore and back, more sampans round a steel grey destroyer and an aircraft carrier. At the terminal Steven was momentarily lost so they stopped a taxi passing the row of green-topped rickshas, and started off to buy clothes and he resumed identity at a bank and via his passport. His announce-ment at lunch of their plans precipitated an argument which went on all afternoon. Stubborn as a mule, she kept declaring her refusal to bind him to her, explaining his need to be free and describing the disadvantages of having a woman among his luggage. Coming out of a chemist's shop, he undid her shiny new handbag and slipped a roll of notes into it and wagged a cellophane-wrapped sponge at her.

'What is the money for?' she asked.

'It ought to last three or four months. Go. Now.'

'Steven . . .'

He gave her no chance. 'You prefer to be alone.'

'You know perfectly well what I mean,' she retorted indignantly.

'If you want a ticket from here to anywhere, tell me.'

They walked the length of the Praya without speaking, and at dinner her attitude was distinctly cool. She refused a drink. Later on he found the notes lying ostentatiously on his new suit. She disregarded his presence. Judging from the motion of the rickety floor, someone in the adjoining room was rehearsing a tap-dance to their booming radio. He set himself out to wheedle her into a better humour.

And early the following morning they shifted into a hotel on the island, and for the next four days they were swamped by the noisy exuberant vitality of Hongkong, drawn into the life of a city blossomed on a rock where the twain had met in greater mutuality of evolving purpose than in other places, or so it seemed to them. They were seldom alone in this world of taipans richer than Croesus, enchanting slim-bodied grand-daughters of the 'liberty girls' who were China's first 'modern' women, black-clad coolies squatting on street-corners to play mahjongg, European women missionaries, fluty-voiced Want-chai tarts, old opium addicts, American tourists, Chinese businessmen in sharkskin suits, Hakka women in fringed lamp-shade hats, communist and Nationalist spies, Sikh bank guards, refugees, refugees, refugees; the distinctive smell of musk and ginger was never far from them.

They found it wonderful to idle and exclaim and wake to a morning paean from a golden oriole and watch the evening flutter of mynahs, to stand and stare at porcelain, whole roast pig, silk embroidered by refugee Cantonese craftsmen, shop windows offering medicinal concoctions of centipedes, snakes, and lizard intestines. One day they took Fua-tuan to lunch, and later Steven stopped him from talking about his plans for half an hour while they called on an old priest, and then Fua-tuan hurried off to dream of his impending wealth. Back in their room they found a more amiable cable from London than Steven had expected and one from Clive which read: 'Good for you stop any news for me stop will join you Sunday en route for Tokio.'

'Where is he?' she asked.

'Vientiane. He doesn't know. We'll have to tell him.'

'Oh dear.'

'Bad.' He shook his head. Suddenly his eyes focused on her in appraisal. 'Lilac is a ridiculous colour on most women but you were obviously intended to wear it.'

'You're trying to get round me by flattery.'

'Not by flattery now. Let's go up the Peak and smell the sky. I have a thing about the sky at present.'

They stayed up there for hours, high above the mansions of taipans and settlement blocks of migrants, fintailed American cars and crowded green trams, and loitered in the warm air until nearly sundown when the curving black shores were spangled with millions of gold and scarlet and white lights, and from among piled clouds the vast majesty of the sky flushed the harbour water purple and crimson around *tongkangs* and junks and battleships. As they watched she raised a protest, complaining that he ought to have let her help to select the ring, and shook her hand to show how easily it slid down her finger, looking at him in mingled shyness and astonishment. He sighed in exasperation, telling her to think herself lucky to have got a manacle at all considering her lengthy argument against having one. There weren't many men who would be so patient, he told her.

For some reason she started to cry. 'I am lucky,' she said miserably.

'I'm glad you enjoy it.'

She smiled through her tears, pleased by his happiness and new lightness of heart, and then wept more bitterly, clinging to him in a paroxysm of pride and humility and relief. He held her until she got over her distress and freed herself.

'Let's go and eat,' she said. 'I'm hungry.'

'Nothing like good clean fresh air.'

At the hotel they found another cable from London. He was not out of favour despite all. They too had evidently realized that it was hopeless to get candid news out of China, agreed to give him three months' vacation for which he had asked, and offered him their Beirut bureau. The holiday would give him a chance to write. At dinner they discussed the plan already in his mind, and spent a couple of hours working it out by method and material. He wrote it down. At the end he glanced up and said they would have to do something about her passport in the morning and he would arrange for them to leave directly they had seen Clive.

'You will write it,' she urged. 'You mustn't let anything stop you. Nothing.'

'Obviously I won't get a moment's peace until I do, so for what it'll be worth, yes,' he said. Then his smile faded. 'Yes, we'll add our contribution. None can be complete or final, and it's newspapermen who have to do it. There's no one else. The results of letting what they are doing in Peking pass without continuous comment is too dreadful to contemplate. The way they keep redrawing their maps is one sign of their intention to turn Asia into colonies. The money they extort from overseas Chinese is another proof. They won't stop in Asia. Despite every setback, they're preparing for bigger adventures. Once they've got machines they'll dominate Russia and stride out across the Pacific.'

'It frightens me to think how much you must put into it.'

'You'll have to help. I don't know the minds of the people. I've never been able to talk freely to them.'

'No one can. They never talk openly. It isn't safe, even in front of their own families. I don't know what they think.

You've seen how it is for the people. They were always poverty-ridden and illiterate. Even the slightest improvement, however simple by Western standards, is wonderful to them. They do not have free minds. They'll do whatever the Party orders.'

'As you said, they've no criterion.'

She wandered round the room frowning, hands clasped in front of her. The simple lilac cheongsam looked remarkably elegant on her slender body. Her eyes were clear, strain and fatigue gone from her lovely face. And now she had forgotten about the scar, did nothing to hide it. And they were free, able to breathe. He watched her with love and pride, oddly moved.

At length she said: 'Why does America keep Peking out of United Nations? There's no valid justification. Strategically America is putting the free world at a disadvantage, implying it's beyond the ability of Western statesmen to take the initiative. She keeps on putting Peking in the right and herself in the wrong. Peking could dominate seven other countries unless America risked a world war. At United Nations Peking would have to justify her aggression. She couldn't walk out in front of those new independent African states. America may have to pay a bitter price for losing diplomatic initiative in Asia and other countries may easily lose their freedom.'

'Freedom. A beautiful word. Swaraj. Merdeka. Uhuru. In every language. A man without freedom to disagree without fear of death is a creature without dignity, a serf dominated by fear.'

She sat down, her brows drawn together as she looked at him. 'Only three months,' she said worriedly.

'Never mind. I wish I could wear a lilac dress and be beautiful and talk commonsense.'

'You'd look silly,' she said absently. 'I remember how willingly village boys went to fight in Korea and the jubilation at finally overrunning Tibet. Everyone was a crusader fighting for a sacred cause. The army has the most efficient organization in the country. It could take control in a week.'

'And fifty years ago an American professor wrote "One who goes up and down among these teeming proletarians realizes that the last traces of the military spirit evaporated long ago. The folk appear to possess neither the combative impulses nor the energy of will of the West Europeans." '

After a pause she said: 'Thank goodness you've got such a wonderful memory. You've so much to do.'

'We,' he corrected gently. 'We. Now, as you're a respectable woman tonight, *nei-jen*, or whatever it is, and as neither of us has to hurry off, have a drink with me. I'll see you get home.'

At first she demurred, but finally gave in, and discussed how best to get free from people, revealing a grasp on practical problems which led him to express relief. She smiled.

'Stupid, I can take care of that. And I'll try to help when you come back from writing.'

'Just be around. Thank God, you're resilient. Incidentally, in case I haven't said it before, I don't expect you to share my views. You can plant and grow your own.'

'I agree with you about this. The humanity of all peoples surpasses the politics of one race.'

'We'll use that.'

'It's been said before.'

'It can't be said too often in this benighted age.'

'Where shall we go now?'

'India?'

'Wherever you say,' she said. 'It would be cheaper if we went by sea. I was looking at the advertisements for the Indian ships. We must begin to be practical about money. You could work in the cabin.'

'That's an idea.'

They took another brace of brandies up to their room, drinking them while they watched reflections of ship lights stir on black water. Her silence prompted him to ask if she had another idea, and she said no, they had talked enough for one night. And then, encompassed, an unescapable pain in their joy, they celebrated themselves and their journey.

When dawn came it searched an empty sky. They idled over breakfast, reluctant to lose the sensation of owning a slice of time, and later he bathed and dressed and went off to arrange for their departure. She got up lazily, lay in her bath for a while, and then put on the lilac dress to please him, glad to be alone to decide if she should tell him now of her suspicion that they had begot another life, a belief come to her on their walk and her reason for wanting him to go free, or to wait until she was positive instead of sure.

It was not easy to decide. He carried much in his mind, yet she did not want to disturb him suddenly when he was at work. It would be a denial of her love for him if she could not guide and spare him in their joint life. And still undecided she answered a knock on the door and saw two European police officers who asked her to identify herself. She was nervous lest they had come because of her illegal entry, and then the nightmare began, for he was dead they said, shot down on a noisy street by Chinese who used silenced revolvers from a car which got away. At first she was sure they were lying for it was unbelievable, his life warm and vital in her mind and body; then she looked at their eyes. 'What have I done?' she asked in anguish and kept asking herself, over and over, while they took her to see it was true.

Night followed.

And day in golden sunlight, when every other corner echoed with life. And night and day and night again for women to sigh easily, some of them, it being their nature to conjure sighs like tinsel and velvet stitched on their design of quest: hollow night. And day.

Stunned hours, desolate, wrenched apart in moments like gaping wounds. None more brutal than when the mind groped back from drugged sleep to find wakefulness a void.

The question turning over and over through light and darkness.

2

Hongkong never rests. And amid its rush of life, of struggle, some individual human rites must be attended with despatch.

The flat official voices speaking through them, tongues in search of kindness, fell away like dissolving shadows. They could not lessen repentance or ease contrition. Yet they brought purpose.

This was no time to waste on idleness or dreams, not yet. That would be betrayal. Life imposed obligations, and remorse must be honoured. What was achieved should never be disgraced by defeat at the hands of a primitive mentality, no better than the oldfashioned *tongs* who had sent their hatchetmen. There was the scribbled plan to guide, memories to gather to renew purpose, and Clive would help when he came. There must be courage, always, and defiance, to challenge endlessly whatever life brought. Through them love and remorse could be honoured. Destiny was never lonely, only solitary under its bright garland of memories.